JUDGE
DREDD

DREDDLOCKED

Stephen Marley

Virgin

First published in 1993 by

Virgin Publishing Ltd
332 Ladbroke Grove
London
W10 5AH

Text copyright © Stephen Marley 1993
Cover picture by Arthur Ranson
Judge Dredd and all associated characters and settings ©
EGMONT H. PETERSEN FOND,
GUTENBERGHUS. Licensed by Copyright Promotions
Ltd.

Typeset by CentraCet, Cambridge

Printed and bound by
Cox & Wyman, Reading, Berks.

ISBN 0 352 32875 4

'There's nothing worse than a bent Judge'
Judge Dredd

'There's nothing worse than a straight Judge'
Mister Cairo

DEDICATIONS

For Anita and Anna, in praise of voodoo and English country villages. And side-dedications to Paul, who's probably wandering the boulevards and back-alleys of Europe by now; and also Gerald (sorry – I *refuse* to call you Gez) who's disappeared somewhere to the north.

ACKNOWLEDGEMENTS

Many thanks to Jane Judd, my agent, for getting the ball rolling; Peter Darvill-Evans and Rebecca Levene at Virgin Publishing for all the much-appreciated effort; and Steve MacManus at *Judge Dredd The Megazine* for the helpful pointers. Dave Stone and David Bishop for the phone conversations. Desmond and Sonja for faith, hope and charity. And particular thanks to Rob for the Crawling Chair.

PROLOGUE

October 31, 2085

He started out the way he meant to go on.

Born with both eyes open.

Born in a brothel at midnight on Hallowe'en . . .

. . . Slam bang in the middle of a crossfire of bullets at the height of a Judge raid.

He was pumped from the womb in tempo with the bullets his mother pumped into the black-uniformed lawmen.

The first sound he heard was the thunder of gunshots in the exchange of fire between Judges and hookers. The first voice that greeted his birth was a loud bellow:

'I AM THE LAW!'

Then a Judge's bullet exploded his mother's head to the four quarters of the sleep-eezie room. Slapdash spatters of blood and brain tissue sprayed red action paintings onto the glossy pink walls.

A reflex finger action from the dead woman loosed off a terminal round from the machine-pistol in her hand. Triggered by the spasm, another infant began to part company with her headless body.

Within minutes, the mother's twin offspring were scooped from the floor into makeshift carry-cots.

A Judge with 'Dredd' inscribed on his badge cast a brief look at the second child. His one-word statement decided the infant's fate: '*Mutant*.'

The two children were taken their different ways.

The twins weren't to meet face to face.

Not until thirty years later . . .

1

CHAPTER ONE

October 29, 2115

One of the six men in black suits and black bow-ties looked almost human.

The men hadn't stepped in through the door, or blasted through the thirty-second storey window of Lorelei and Lucia's habhold in Happy House. Their mode of entry to the young women's habhold was – impossible. And so hush-quiet. Not a word spoken.

The six intruders stood in a ring and smiled at the two young women they encircled. Quick as sleek eels when slipping into the sleep-eezie habhold, the men were now motionless as freeze-frames, silent as deep space.

The men in black suits were the stuff that dreams are made of.

Some dreams are nightmares.

Hallowe'en had come two days early.

Lorelei glanced at Lucia trembling at her side. Lucia's face was a white mask of terror, her wide mouth trying to force out a scream lodged in a constricted throat.

Lorelei's gaze slid back to the circle of smiling faces. One of the men – a man that looked almost human – slowly unfolded his clenched hands. In the dim blue luminescence of the room she glimpsed steely flickers at the ends of his fingers.

One moment he was uncurling his glittering hands. The next he took a long stride towards her, arms reaching out.

All she saw of the finger-razors were streaks of light.

When a spray of hot red hit the glowing blue wall she didn't have time to identify it as the liquid life that throbbed in her veins.

3

She wondered why she could only see with one eye all of a sudden.

Lorelei felt a second mouth slash open in her throat. She lifted her right hand to touch the lips of this new mouth.

And discovered her right hand wasn't there any more. She saw only a stump spouting like a hose-pipe.

That's when she thought she heard Lucia screaming.

The clairvoyant slammed back into her chair as though a sledge-hammer had smashed her midriff.

Madame Dragora struggled to subdue the bedlam that had broken loose in her head . . .

a windmill of whirling razors . . . smiling faces, one of them almost human . . . crazy red patterns on a blue wall . . . dark grey raincoat . . .

The scrambled pictures whirlpooled in her skull.

Finally her eyesight cleared and the shadowy corners of her roomy habhold swam into focus. She listened to her pulse for a while as it eased down the fear scale.

She heaved a deep breath and peered down at the spread of Tarot cards on the twentieth-century antique table. Steadying her dithery fingers, adorned with a score of silver talismanic rings, she studied the four cards she had displaced in the fit of psychic invasion. The four formed a neat row. Significant coincidence. Synchronicity in full flow.

Her vision travelled along the four Tarot images: the Fool – the Priestess – the Chariot – the World.

Madame Dragora spared the Priestess the briefest of smiles. 'Mandra,' she said softly. 'Mandra the Anti-Judge.'

The smile died as her eyes settled on the picture of the World. It was the only inverted card of the four. The World turned upside down.

The clairvoyant threw a look at the night city outside the plexiglass window. The real world, hard as grit.

'Once upon a time there was a Judge called Mandra,'

she whispered. 'She tried to turn the world upside down. Now the world's going to turn Mandra inside out.'

Her gaze flicked back to the Tarot, and settled on the Chariot. The longer she looked, the more the image of an armoured knight in a wide-wheeled chariot seemed to bend and shift.

The chariot abruptly re-formed into the turbo-powered Lawmaster motor bike, metal steed of the Judges.

And astride it sat Judge Dredd, blackest of knights.

On impulse, she grabbed the hilt of a ritual *obeah* dagger, lifted it high, and plunged the sharp point into the image of Dredd.

The blade bit deep.

So did her sharp tone:

'I'll drag your world down to hell, Dredd. Join the devil's party.'

The door didn't give way until the tenth kick.

By then Lucia's screams had stopped shrilling from the audio-coms of Happy House.

Dillinger pistol already drawn from a pocket of his dark grey trench-coat pocket, he rolled forward into the room the instant the door crashed open. He landed in a low crouch, gun arm extended, Dillinger sweeping the dimly lit interior.

Nothing. No one.

Exotic Fruit habhold, the most plush and lush of the thirty sleep-eezies that made up Happy House, seemed to be empty of the two most popular girls in the eezie-squeezie joint.

Seemed to be empty . . .

But the door had been locked on the inside. The women hadn't left. And whoever had put the fear of hell into Lucia had not left either.

With the practised stealth of a veteran private eye, keeping low, staying under cover, he darted from arm-chair to sofa, sofa to magneto-table. No sign of Lorelei or Lucia.

His narrowed eyes moved to the open door of the

bedroom. He slid round the door-frame, Dillinger in unwavering grip, brain on red alert.

The bedroom was empty except for the customary vibro-bed and pleasure unit.

That left only the kitchen.

Twenty seconds later he emerged from the kitchen, a puzzled frown creasing his forehead. From the time Lucia's distinctive Luxorian wail first sounded over the audio-com to the moment he broke into the room, barely half a minute had elapsed. The main door was the only entrance or exit. Where had Lucia and Lorelei gone?

A swift scan of the fixed-frame window showed it was intact. Nobody had come in or out that way.

Perplexed, he rubbed his unshaven chin. Blinked the last vestige of sleep from his eyes. Maybe when his mind cleared he would figure this out. He'd been in bed when Lucia's cries sliced through his dreams. As always, he slept fully dressed, trench-coat and all. Before he was sure he was awake he'd been up and running.

He took a deep breath. His mind was clear now. Take stock. Assess the situation.

Exotic Fruit habhold had lost its exotic residents. In Happy House, exotic meant alien. Alien girls for male clients with otherworldly tastes, five hundred creds an hour. Pimps and bent Judges were always trying to muscle in on the Sisters of Gramercy who ran the place. Abducting two prize aliens was as good a way as any of undermining Happy House. Lucia Lux was a silver-skinned Luxorian, top of the demand list. Lorelei Whinwindrel was an Algolian, second on the list. Prime targets.

That still left him with the mystery of how the two had been spirited away.

He stopped by the vid-screen. The sound was off, but the screen displayed an old 2-D flik: *Escape from New York*. The scene switched from a close-up of Kurt Russell to one of Lee Van Cleef.

Both men's features were sprinkled with dark droplets.

He lowered his Dillinger a fraction. 'Hi-Glo White,' he spoke aloud.

At the vocal command, the room switched the wall luminescence from subdued blue to a bright white illumination. Every curve and contour hardened into clarity.

His gaze roved the carpet.

He didn't remember the carpet being red.

That was when his hindbrain sense of smell finally contacted his forebrain.

He realised he'd been inhaling the scent since he kicked the door wide. That unique, coppery scent. Red carpet. Red scent.

Like the crimson spots on the vid-screen.

His stare travelled further along the wall. Splashes of colour. All the same hue.

Lorelei's blood. The Algolian woman was near-human in physiology. Her veins pumped the same colour fluid as humans. Lucia's blood was light silver.

Pocketing the Dillinger in one of the twenty pockets of his long raincoat, he walked slowly to the far end of the wall.

Bits and pieces of Lorelei, none larger than a handful, littered the far corner. They resembled scattered fossils. When Algolian flesh was severed from the body, it petrified in seconds.

Surveying the pitiful remains, he recalled the living, breathing Lorelei. Big eyes and a soul to match.

Grief was a tight fist in his chest. It squeezed his heart dry.

Above the relics, red smears criss-crossed the wall in inverted letters, spelling out an upside-down message in alien blood:

WHAT TURNS AND TURNS AGAIN? ONE LITTLE PIGLET DEAD. IN SIX HOURS THE OTHER PIGLET GETS THE CHOP. SIX HOURS TO FIND HER. HAPPY HUNTING.

A card had been fixed under the message. Nailed to the wall by a petrified Algolian finger. A Tarot card of the World, inverted, like the message in blood.

Wincing, he wrenched Lorelei's severed finger from the

7

wall. The Tarot card dropped into his hand, still inverted. The World turned upside down.

The Sisters of Gramercy had hired him as a bodyguard. He'd failed them.

'Lorelei – ' he said hoarsely, struggling to keep sorrow from swamping him. 'Lorelei – '

He'd failed a friend.

Backing away from Lorelei's relics, he stumbled to the centre of the room. Floundering in remorse, anger, confusion, his gaze swung wildly about his surroundings. Someone or something had accomplished a series of hideous impossibilities in this place. Sliced Lorelei to chunks in seconds. Written an inverted blood message in seconds. Rammed a severed finger into a solid wall. Whisked Lucia into thin air.

Without thinking, he slipped the Tarot card into a raincoat pocket. His fingers touched a battered playing card: the Queen of Hearts.

'Mandra,' the private eye muttered instinctively, then transferred the Tarot card to another pocket.

His wandering stare alighted on a skimpy black dress laid out nice and neat over the back of an armchair.

One of Lucia's favourite dresses. It had been his present to her on her sixteenth birthday a few weeks ago. He bit his lip at the memory.

Six hours to find her.

On the silent vid-screen, Kurt Russell was being injected with timed micro-detonation capsules to ensure compliance in locating the President marooned in the prison island of Manhattan.

The private detective wouldn't need micro-bomb implants or any other tek spur to make him search for Lucia. He had all the motivation he needed in the crimson writing on the wall, the greying relics on the floor, and the little-girl-lost black dress.

'Six hours,' he exhaled sharply. 'Six – '

Escape from New York was suddenly blanked out from the screen by a priority news-flash from the Justice Department.

The face that appeared on screen, helmeted and visored as it was, sparked instant recognition – and an old hate.

'*Dredd* . . .'

He needed to hit out at something, and the man he hated most was right there to satisfy the need.

Raising the Dillinger, he took a bead between the visored eyes. Squeezed the trigger.

Flame and thunder blasted from the muzzle.

And blasted a hole bang in the middle of the visor.

Cracks zigzagged from the scorched hole in the vid-screen, shattering the Judge's image. Dredd wore a crooked scowl.

The private eye pocketed the Dillinger.

'Regards from Mister Cairo.'

Then he swung out the door, his mind already descending to the midnight streets.

CHAPTER TWO

A helmet and a mouth.

The mouth was a smile turned upside down: an inverted crescent as fixed as though a scimitar had carved a perpetual scowl into the flesh.

Above the downturned mouth, the face was hidden by the dark visor of a glinting black helmet bordered in blood red.

No one had ever glimpsed the face under the Judge helmet. There was a rumour that its wearer hadn't seen his own features in a decade – that there were no mirrors in his habhold. Staring up at the helmet and mouth that filled the two-metre vid-screen, the crew of the airborne h-wagon, jolted by the latest order from that scowl of a mouth, were glad they were spared the features of a man capable of announcing so sharp a judgement sentence in so flat a tone.

A general news-flash had already been relayed to the civilian population. The order he had just delivered was for Judge ears only.

In the dark cabin of the h-wagon, the four-person crew was dwarfed by the grim-lipped image on the vid-screen. Although the Judge was some three hundred metres outside the hovering airwagon, his overwhelming presence permeated its bullet-proof walls. His stony voice, like teeth crunching gravel, still resonated in the confines of the h-wagon.

Captain Weller, as dumbstruck as his crew by the order from that mouth magnified to a metre on the screen, fleetingly entertained the fantasy that the helmet *was* the Judge's face.

A man with no face.

Dredd.

The name was made for the man.

Or the man was made for the name.

'The Helmet of War,' Weller whispered, scanning the helmeted image on the vid-screen.

War . . . The captain winced. A verbal slip. He had meant to say 'Helmet of Law.'

But perhaps he was right the first time.

The Helmet of War. The Helmet of Mars.

Glancing at the monitors which strobed Judge Dredd's latest command in blood-glow characters, Weller coded the audio unit for vid-sync music. Soon the first movement of Holst's *Planets* suite commenced. Music for the Man. The movement dedicated to Mars, Bringer of War.

As the first bars growled in the cabin, the second pilot was already swerving the box-shaped aircraft away from its hovering position a kilometre above Mega-City One. One kilometre high, level with Judge Dredd.

Weller glanced once more at Dredd's order spelt out in red on the monitors. He could hardly believe what he was seeing, even now:

EX-PSI JUDGE MANDRA NAMED PUBLIC ENEMY NUMBER ONE. CRIME: INFORMATION SABOTAGE. SENTENCE: LOBOTOMY AND TWENTY YEARS' SERVITUDE ON TITAN. LOCATE AND ARREST WITH MAXIMUM CAUTION AND MAXIMUM FORCE.

Mandra – Public Enemy Number One?

Mandra had thrown in her badge a few months ago, but she was well remembered in Justice Central. She wasn't long out of her rookie years when she earned a chestful of commendations in the battle against the Dark Judges during Necropolis. Just as fast, she was carpeted by an equal number of reprimands for repeated insubordination. She excelled herself again in the mayhem of Judgement Day; and then nearly landed herself a spell in the iso-cubes for condemning the Chief Judge's nuking of half the world's mega-cities as history's worst crime of genocide.

Three months ago Mandra gave Chief Judge McGruder the finger and threw her Psi-badge in the Chief Judge's face. Only her exemplary record of service in the field saved her from a long stint in the cubes for that final act of defiance.

Half the men on the force, Weller included, had rued the day Mandra had quitted Justice Central. Mandra – young, curvy, coffee-skinned Mandra – a sultry temptation for uncounted scores of male Judges to stray from the Justice Department's strict code of celibacy.

Look-but-don't-touch Judge Mandra. Mandra with the voodoo eyes and black magic smile.

There had always been stories about her. Forbidden sexual affairs. Bizarre occult practices. Stories . . .

But Mandra – Public Enemy Number One?

Weller gave a small shake of the head. It was hard to take in.

And as for the sentence, they didn't come any worse. A lifetime as a cyborg-adapted zombie on an airless satellite of Saturn.

As the h-wagon sped on its seek-and-arrest mission into the western sectors of the night city, Weller kept the main camera trained on the Judge, the magnification modulated so that several seconds passed before Dredd was visible at full length.

Judge Dredd stood legs astride and arms akimbo, a muscular figure in tight black synthi-leather with jutting, golden shoulder-pads, one of which thrust a moulded eagle's head from the Judge's right shoulder. The green-gauntleted fists rested on his hips, knuckles pressing on the eagle-fronted utility belt crammed with everything from a med-pak to stumm grenades. In one of his plas-teen-reinforced green boots was tucked the essential weapon of all Judges – the bulky Lawgiver handgun, complete with seven types of ammo.

On his left breast, at the end of a weighty chain, hung the badge that said Dredd.

Never was a badge more superfluous. Hidden beneath all the armour and paraphernalia of Law, that powerful physique proclaimed the name Dredd in every line and contour.

The music of Mars was building to a pounding climax in the cabin as the Judge's receding figure shrank to a speck inside the right eye of a red-bordered visor. As the h-wagon increased its speed to five hundred kph, Dredd finally blinked out of sight as the visored black helmet of a metal Judge filled the screen. Soon the gargantuan shoulders and upper torso of the kilometre-high Judgement Day Colossus emerged against the stars, its chunky golden shoulder-pads gleaming in the radiance of numerous arc-lights.

The Mars movement thundered its crescendo as the illuminated giant Judge came into full view, bestriding the bay, its right fist held aloft like an upraised hammer poised to strike. Scores of other foursquare h-wagons and sleek Gunbirds were circling around or streaking from the colossus, intent on a single mission, a single arrest.

Weller's gaze flicked to the monitors:

EX-PSI JUDGE MANDRA NAMED PUBLIC ENEMY NUMBER ONE.

His eyes returned to the Judgement Day Statue, a prodigious feat of engineering completed ten weeks ago in memory of the fifty per cent of the world's population wiped out in the nuclear holocaust of Judgement Day. The Justice Department had named it the *Dies Irae* – Day of Wrath. A pun on the Latin name had soon made the rounds: *Deus Irae* – God of Wrath. The nickname fitted the colossus snug and tight as the black uniform of justice.

Deus Irae – a plasteen icon of Grud, god of the twenty-second century, Judge of the living and the dead. To many, Judges and citizens alike, the Judgement Colossus was Grud made visible. Far from being a memorial to the dead, it was a warning to the living: the eyes of Justice are upon you.

Inside the Judgement Colossus was a small world. A world of uniformed servants of the Law fulfilling their duties in two hundred observation chambers linked by a network of passages and elevators. And in the dome of its helmet, a brain – the new computer: Omnipotens.

'You haven't got a prayer, Mandra,' Weller observed under his breath. 'Not a prayer in hell.'

The h-wagon accelerated and the bay came into full sweep. The Judgement Colossus, feet planted on massive pylons embedded in the bay, reared from the sea to more than twice the height of the nearby Statue of Judgement. The older Judge statue stood, fists resting on hips, and stared the new plasteen giant right in the eagle belt-buckle across a kilometre of oily water.

Behind the Colossus stretched the black sludge of the polluted Atlantic, the dark waters barely reflecting the gibbous moon. In front of its visored gaze sprawled the bulging towers of Mega-City One, home of four hundred million citizens and as many forms of madness.

Weller cast a glance at the Statue of Judgement. As the Colossus dwarfed the older statue, so the Statue of Judgement lorded it over a female icon.

At the booted feet of the Statue of Judgement, the pale Statue of Liberty raised the arm stump that had once lofted a torch.

Old Liberty was the tiniest of girls under the towering might of the Colossus and the Statue of Judgement. A shrunken image. A forgotten ideal.

Weller's gaze ascended the colossus once more. The long-dead Judge Fargo, Father of Justice, had provided the model for the effigy in the bay. And Dredd was Fargo's sole surviving clone, the living replica of the revered founder of Judge rule.

To Weller's mind, the Judgement Colossus personified not Fargo, but Grud and Dredd. God and man, standing between black sea and manic city.

Over that city Judgement cast a long shadow.

Mister Cairo slipped like a phantom through the dense shadow of Rat's Alley.

In his dark eyes, for those who cared to look, were the stories of the streets.

Stories of starved girls with bodies for hire and respected gangsters with entire citi-blocks for sale; petty thieves with the faces of saints; street-corner preachers bought and sold for thirty pieces of silver; druggies who had glimpsed a chemical god and OD'd on a lethal fix of divinity; con-men sporting manicured nails and clever-devil tongues in shady gaming halls and smoke-easies.

In Mister Cairo's gaze lurked all the stories of the streets, also known as Tales from the Pits. The Pits was the gutter-level name for Ground Level, the maze of streets that wound about the feet of the rearing citi-blocks, some of which surpassed a height of five kilo-metres. In the city's middle and upper reaches it was all glitz, ultratek, frantic bustle. Down in the Pits it was murk and muck and stealth and the silence of a quick knife.

Most of the stories of the streets were short, concluded by the small black circle of a gun muzzle, terminal as a full stop.

Mister Cairo stalked those streets of short stories in a dark grey trench-coat half as old as his twenty-nine years of life. He never took off that trench-coat except in the bathroom and, on rare occasions, the bedroom. Although young for a private eye, he had ten thousand streets-worth of experience in his wary stare to rival a grizzled veteran of the Big City's low-life.

Tonight he'd need every moment of that experience if he was to find Lucia in the next few hours.

The message in Lorelei's blood stained the darkness behind his eyes:

WHAT TURNS AND TURNS AGAIN? ONE LITTLE PIGLET DEAD. IN SIX HOURS THE OTHER PIGLET GETS THE CHOP. SIX HOURS TO FIND HER. HAPPY HUNTING.

Lorelei – chopped up like old meat on the block . . .

You never got used to the violence of the Big City, not if you lived in the thick of it. But you learned to adapt. Managed to get by without blowing your wits and ending up in a psycho-cube. You needed mental equilibrium to survive, and he'd just about regained it in the last hour.

Almost an hour had passed since he'd taken the upside-down World card of the Tarot and slipped it in his trench-coat pocket before quitting the butchery of the Exotic Fruits habhold. Minute by minute, he'd come to some kind of terms with what he had encountered there. The saddest thing was that he'd seen a lot worse in his time.

An image of the World, inverted. What did it mean? *What turns and turns again?* The World? What of it? His forefinger brushed the plastic surface of the card.

He had the World in his pocket, and wished he hadn't.

Just five hours to go before Lucia became one more story brought to a premature end.

Keeping to the shadows, he turned the corner of Rat's Alley and paced down Ascension Avenue, hands thrust deep in his raincoat pockets, collar turned up against the chill of an autumn-fall midnight. Around him stretched the vast warren of the Mumbles, one of the most dangerous districts in the Pits.

Even the Judges went two-by-two in the Mumbles' meaner-than-mean streets. That was why Mister Cairo lived there.

'Judge' was the second worse swear-word in Cairo's vocabulary.

'Dredd' was the worst.

The next time I meet you, Dredd, I'll blast your head off and kick it up to the Great Judge in the sky.

An h-wagon hummed high overhead. The third in as many minutes.

Something must have shaken the Judge world down to its oversized boots tonight. That thought didn't break his heart.

Cairo didn't glance up at the hover-ship. His gaze rarely ascended to the shimmering heights of the Big City; his viewpoint was essentially street-level, sometimes sewer-level. As far as the private eye was concerned, the Pits didn't stink as much as the ultratek heights.

The hum of the h-wagon faded and his shoulders

relaxed. Then he realised that his taut, nervous hand had bent the Tarot card in one of his left pockets. The packet of illegal drugs in a right-hand pocket was close to splitting from his sweat-slick grasp.

'Dredd,' he swore, loosening his grip. 'The helmet-heads are getting to me.'

Skirting the rats and garbage of Ascension Avenue, Cairo reached the main entrance of Ricardo Montalban II Block, the first port of call on his search for Lucia. On the verge of extracting his miniature circuit panel of skeleton-codes, he was stricken with a sense of foreboding. Maybe this was not such a good idea. He had pumped information out of Max Normal plenty of times in the past. No problems. No come-back from Judge Dredd. But tonight felt different. Tonight *was* different. Something big had to be going down for Dredd to broadcast a news-flash.

Another h-wagon hummed in the night sky, accompanied by the shriek of a sleek Gunbird. This time Cairo looked upwards, concerned that the stepped-up airborne surveillance might interfere with his search.

The overhead view was enough to spin the steadiest head. It was worse than peering up from the floor of a Martian canyon.

Mega-City One, built partly on the plascrete that formed a lid on the ruins of New York, was a dour and dizzy sight.

The Big City didn't so much rise into the sky as *bulge* into it. The cone-shaped citi-blocks, uniformly dark blue in this sector, had an organic, bulbous appearance. Pot-bellied cones with folds of metallic blue flab.

On the middle levels was the Cobweb: slender walkways reaching like flights of fancy between gargantuan cones. A little lower, but still five hundred to a thousand metres above ground level, stretched the Tangle – the suspended labyrinth of megways, zoomways and slipways, laden with incessant traffic, most of it going nowhere from nowhere. The h-wagon and Gunbird were weaving above

17

the Tangle, two shimmering fireflies amongst the curious mix of gloom and glitz that was the Big City.

'Top of the world, Ma!' he smiled thinly, misquoting James Cagney's farewell line from the old 2-D flik *White Heat* as his thoughts roved back fifteen years to a girl with night eyes and good-night lips. The once-famous Cagney misquote was Cairo's farewell to her.

He hadn't seen her since that farewell, but he still carried her goodbye gift.

His fingers brushed one of the cards in a right-hand pocket.

The Queen of Hearts.

Then the bleak present intruded. The two Judge ships thrummed above the Tangle, busy conducting aerial sweeps of the Pits. Two out of a hundred flying reminders of Justice Hall's omnipresent scrutiny.

Also, the night had a thousand Eyes: surveillance Eye cameras on every street, monitored from Justice Hall.

But it was the city's summits – free of cloud tonight – that commanded attention. The swollen peaks of the towers reminded Cairo of squat helmets: it was easy to imagine the glowing windows as multiple eyes glaring down at you. For an instant he saw the blocks as obese giants with hunched shoulders and helmeted heads. Bulging Judges gazing down on the earth.

A memory from youth roared at him like a hyper-express train bulleting from a black tunnel:

A helmet and a mouth.

A bellowing mouth. The blazing muzzle of a Lawgiver.

A mouth like an open mantrap, bellowing, 'I AM THE LAW!'

Bright red blood on a black-and-white movie . . .

Cairo blinked and shook free of that old, old memory. It was always there, demanding continuous replay, like a vid-loop. Sometimes he went along with the repeats, viewing the rerun of that night in the Casablanca, taking in every detail, over and over.

But not tonight. He had five hours left to search. Five short hours.

The two Justice airships had sped out of sight and sound. He gratefully dipped his gaze back to the Pits. The vast presence of the cone blocks still pressed down on him, pinned him with their million window-eyes, but the after-image would recede in a while. Just so long as he kept his mind on the streets.

And on the job.

There were risks in dealing with Max Normal, risks involving Judge Dredd, but Cairo was willing to take his chances.

However, as he turned back to the plex-screened entrance to Ricardo Montalban II Block, flanked by two roving Eyes transmitting their observations back to Justice Central, the misgivings sprang back with redoubled force.

Max Normal was inside this block.

And Max Normal was Judge Dredd's stoolie.

Cairo might be walking straight into a trap.

Well – it was walk right in or leave Lucia to her fate. The second option amounted to an untidy heap of sleepless nights stretching to the Last Goodnight.

So it was walk right in.

'What turns and turns again?' he murmured. The World? Fortune's Wheel?

Five hours to go . . .

Madame Dragora sat inside a Hi-Glo-painted pentacle with a candle flickering at each tip of the five-pointed star.

Uneasy shadows, her sole company, hopped like nervy phantoms from the prance of candlelight on the walls of her spacious room.

Eyes closed, the clairvoyant's silver-ringed fingers extracted five cards from the Tarot pack and spread them out on the polished oak of her twentieth-century antique table.

She opened her eyes and studied the five-card display.

The Devil. The Fool. The Chariot. The Tower. Death.

All five were drawn from the major arcana of the Tarot. Symbols of power.

She peered at the Devil. The horned goat on the picture

leered back. She struggled to see *through* the printed picture, but nothing was revealed. The Devil kept his secret hidden.

Her attention glided to the Fool, the only unnumbered card in the major arcana, showing a jester-like figure stepping off a cliff. He was the symbol of wise folly, reckless innocence. He also represented one about to start on a journey, a search.

For an instant, she saw a man within or beyond the card, one of many visions in the bedlam of her brain an hour past. It was a man in a long grey coat in a dark street, but the glimpse was too brief to pin down.

Her gaze shifted to the dagger-pierced Chariot, in the figure of a heavily armoured knight driving a large-wheeled chariot, the closed visor hiding his face.

Like last time, the picture virtually came alive.

The chariot became a monster motor bike. The Law-master, plasteen stallion of the Judges. The Beast of the Streets. And the armoured knight was transformed into the grim image of Dredd, astride his hurtling metal steed.

Then the Fool reappeared at the corner of her eye. He wore a dark grey trench-coat, and hid in the shadows as he searched the streets. She sensed a link between the raincoated searcher and the ominous shape of Dredd. The link converged at the Tower –

Her glance darted at the cards displaying the Tower and Death.

– the Tower – the Tower leads to Death.

The Fool and the Chariot's paths would cross, and they would reach the Tower that meant Death.

And the Devil had a role to play, as yet unknown.

Madame Dragora ran shaky fingers over her face. 'I don't understand. I still don't understand.'

She leaned on the back of an old wooden chair and listened to the sputter of the pentacle's candles as her gaze skimmed over the five outspread cards: Devil, Fool, Chariot, Tower, Death; then alighted on the stack of the Tarot deck.

Without thinking, she drew a card from the centre of

20

the pile and dropped it on the table. It landed in an inverted position.

It was the World, the final card of the major arcana. It lay upside down on the waxed oak.

The World inverted.

The World turned upside down

CHAPTER THREE

The *Dies Irae*, the Judgement Day Colossus, slowly turned its huge head like a god surveying its domains, towering above the Statue of Judgement as the older effigy dwarfed the Statue of Liberty.

In the vast circle of the jointed neck, a complex magnetic ring of opposing forces powered the head's rotation, positive and negative poles delicately balanced to supply support and direction at the touch of a finger on a plastiplex acti-pad.

Judge Dredd's was the finger on the glowing acti-pad.

The Statue of Judgement and the Statue of Liberty gradually wheeled to the right as the visored eyes of the Colossus Judge turned its stare due west on the city.

At a signal from the Chief Judge, Dredd lifted his gauntleted finger, and the Colossus's head came to a halt. The head glared over its left shoulder across the bulging blocks of Mega-City One.

Chief Judge McGruder, technically a woman but undergoing chromosomal changes that had taken her more than half-way to manhood, seated herself in an eagle-crested chair and studied the Mega-City skyline with hooded eyes. One hand scratched her steel-grey beard while the other scratched her eagle's beak of a nose. 'You're a big, big city,' McGruder muttered. 'But you ain't big enough to hide her.'

She was out there somewhere. The traitor. The turncoat.

Mandra.

It proved the time-honoured adage of the Special

Judicial Squad: never trust a Psi. They think too much. She should have remembered that axiom from her old SJS days. She should've cubed the bitch when Mandra flung her badge over the Chief Judge's desk. It had banged McGruder right on the nose. Gruddamn it – Mandra made even Anderson look like a team player.

The so-called Voodoo Judge had been a trouble-maker since her cadet days in the Academy of Law. But who would have dreamed she was capable of attacking Justice Central in so spectacular a fashion?

At midnight, ninety minutes ago, Mandra had dealt a blow to the rule of Law. However, McGruder consoled herself, it was just a body blow. The head was unaffected.

McGruder's lean lips twitched into something resembling a smile as she scratched the grey hairs on her protruding chin. Ah – Mandra thought she was so clever. Truth was, she hadn't a gruddamn clue.

Judgement rule was drilled core-deep into the plascrete and corporate soul of Mega-City One.

Mandra had not only taken on Justice Hall. She had challenged the city's god.

Out there, in those blocks that sprawled hundreds of kilometres in every direction, there were over eleven thousand religions. The most prevalent was Judgement worship. Its god was Grud, Lord of Law, Judge of the living and the dead. The god first promoted eighty years past by Chief Judge Fargo, revered Father of Justice. In Mega-City One, Grud had no recognised temples, priesthood, theology or sacred image. He didn't need them. For a temple, Grud had the monumental magnificence of the Hall of Justice, headquarters of the Judges. For a priesthood, the celibate caste of all-powerful Judges. For theology, the Law. For a sacred image –

McGruder chuckled inwardly.

It was never stated openly, not even in the Council of Five, the supreme Judges that guarded and guided Justice, but everyone knew the score. The people needed a god. A god they could see. A god on high. When the people looked up, what looked down on them?

The Statue of Judgement, unveiled sixteen years ago. And the choice of site was no accident: right beside the Statue of Liberty, diminishing that maudlin relic to the relative size of a little girl.

And now, with the completion of the Judgement Colossus, Liberty was shrunken to a kiddie's doll.

She was also outnumbered, two to one.

Liberty was dead.

Judgement ruled.

The mega-city gazed into its sky, and saw Judgement looming over it. And in the Judgement Day Colossus, arm upraised and fist clenched in a hammer blow, the citizens saw the fearsome image of Grud more surely than they ever perceived it in the Statue of Judgement.

God is Judge.

From there, the next step was short:

Judge is God.

And when people thought Judge, they thought Dredd.

'Mandra never realised what she was up against,' chuckled the Chief Judge, swinging the eagle chair round to face Joe Dredd. 'She never stood a chance.' The chuckle faded. 'But she hurt us. A hornet's sting hurts. I want her alive, Joe. Alive and kicking. I want her to pay. And pay. And pay.'

The downturned crescent of Dredd's mouth barely moved with his gravelly voice. 'I'll bring her in alive. I want to know why – why she did it.' The inflexion should have changed after the pause, but the tone still resembled crunched grit.

Judge Hershey, who had been hanging in the background, pensively fingering the ends of her black, shoulder-length hair, abruptly left her split ends alone and stabbed a glance at Dredd. 'We *know* why. Judgement Day started Mandra on the downward slide. You proposed the nuking of half the world's population, and the Chief Judges went along with it. History's worst act of genocide.'

'It was a *necessary* act,' McGruder cut in, jabbing a bony finger at Hershey, who for once was looking all of her thirty-two years. 'In half the meg-cits the walking dead outnumbered the living. It was a matter of days before the last of the living were infected and joined the zombies. If we hadn't nuked all those meg-cits we'd have been overrun by Sabbat's undead armies. Gruddam it – we lost millions of our own citizens from zombie infection.'

Hershey was uncowed. 'Just after you wiped out half the world, Dredd and Alpha destroyed Sabbat, and the undead hordes dropped – dead. On the spot. Everywhere. Half the world was sacrificed for nothing.'

Judge Dredd stood beside McGruder and folded his brawny arms. The Chief Judge caught the essential odour of Dredd – dried sweat and spent ammo. She inhaled with approval.

'Judgement Day was the right decision at the time,' Dredd declared. 'That's why I proposed mass nuking. It was a judgement call.'

McGruder jutted her bearded chin at Hershey. 'You gettin' Anderson's Disease? Gettin' *doubts*, Hershey?'

A sideways slash of the hand. 'No way, Chief Judge. The Law is the Law. And the Law's my life.'

'Yeah, I know it,' McGruder grinned, leaning back into the plush recess of the eagle chair. 'Just kiddin', Hershey. Don't take it personal. In fact – ' A root-knuckled finger wagged between her two subordinates. 'I want the two of you to hunt Mandra as a team. Hunt her down, my tireless hounds. And drag her in *alive*.'

'I wouldn't have it any other way,' Dredd responded.

'Same for me,' nodded Hershey.

McGruder sighed contentedly. 'Mandra has as much chance as a celluloid cat in hell pursued by asbestos dogs.' She shut her eyes for a moment, then swung the eagle chair round to confront a tall, slim man descending on a slide-ramp into the eighty-metre Visor Chamber.

Judge Sejanus, rising star of the Special Judicial Squad.

Dredd stiffened at the arrival of the SJS officer. The two men were the same age and the same height. They had little else in common.

25

Everything about the SJS man implied calm command. His compactly muscled physique moved with fluent authority. The receding grey hair added an extra touch of refinement to the gaunt features. It had been Hershey who first spotted his resemblance to Patrick Stewart as Captain Picard in the old *Star Trek: the Next Generation* vids. A few called him Captain Picard behind his back. None risked it to his face.

Neither head nor deputy head of the SJS, he had more effective power than either. Since Judgement Day his proven skills and formidable intellect had unofficially instated him as McGruder's right-hand man in all security matters. A month after the skies rained thermonuclear warheads he had proposed combining a back-up computer to MAC and Barney in case of sabotage and, he suggested, why not place it inside a giant statue to commemorate the dead of Judgement Day? It would be an impressive memorial. And it would also remind the citizens who was in charge. Unlike the Statue of Judgement, the Judgement Day Colossus was a statue with a brain in its head: the supercomputer Omnipotens.

McGruder leaned forwards in the eagle chair as Sejanus approached. 'Want your chair back, Colossus Chief?' she grinned, using his newly created title.

He waved a graceful hand. 'The honour of your visit is mine alone, Chief Judge.' His voice, like his manner, was calm and fluent. 'Why not take up permanent residence? The Deus Irae has better defences than Justice Central. And everything in the Deus Irae is state of the art.'

'*Deus* Irae?' broke in Hershey. '*God* of Wrath! I thought the whole point of this plastisteel giant was to serve as a reminder of the *Day* of Wrath.'

'Just an in-joke for those who work here.' His smile was folded silk. 'A Latin pun.'

Hershey twisted her lip. 'Sounds to me like you're *celebrating* Judgement Day.'

McGruder wagged a knobbled finger. 'Enough of that, Hershey. Sejanus knows exactly what he's doing. The Colossus is a memorial, sure. But it's also an icon of the

God of Judgement. *And* it's a fort, bristling with weaponry. To top it all, it's got a brain in its head. What would we have done without Omnipotens when Mandra blew hell out of MAC and Barney a while ago? Omnipotens kicked in just two minutes after the other computers blanked out. I'd say that Sejanus showed considerable foresight, wouldn't you?'

Hershey reacted with a shrug that showed precisely what she thought of Sejanus and his creation.

Sejanus ignored her and turned his full attention to the Chief Judge. 'Have you reconsidered my suggestion that Mandra be executed on sight? It's clear she's been hiding the full extent of her Psi powers for years. Who knows what havoc she might wreak in the minds of arresting Judges? The safest course would be an instant kill whether she's armed or not.'

'Have you read Judge Fargo, or did you sleep through the Academy of Law?' Dredd exploded, neck thrust forward, chin jutting out. 'You never shoot an unarmed perp without a warning. Never!'

The Colossus Chief arched an eyebrow. 'Never say never. And don't point your chin at me.'

'Enough!' McGruder cut in. 'We need Mandra alive for interrogation. The only place she's gonna be shot is in the legs. Got it?'

Sejanus inclined his head. 'Whatever you say, Chief Judge.' He glanced across at Dredd. 'Would you care to make another broadcast from here before you go? How about a general warning to all perps?'

Dredd folded brawny arms. 'Once was enough.'

'Come on, Joe,' McGruder urged. 'We can't match all this transmission power back at Justice Central. Omnipotens can break into every vid-channel in the city. 'We'll transmit a vid of the Judgement Colossus to go with your voice.'

Dredd's lip curled a centimetre. 'Not one of your better ideas, Chief Judge.'

'Not one of my *worst* ideas, either,' she said pointedly, lips pursed between her beak of a nose and jab of a chin

27

and looking even more like the Wicked Witch of the West than usual.

Time stretched close to snapping point as Dredd stood in grim silence. Then his head nodded a centimetre or two. 'One last time.'

McGruder broke into a toothy grin as she stood up from the eagle chair. 'That's all I ask, Joe. Make the cits tremble. Show 'em who's boss. After all, You Are The Law!'

Dredd sat in the vacated eagle chair and entered the codes for a ninety degree to-and-fro sweep of Mega-City One, then cued Omnipotens for transmission on all channels.

As the Colossus head began its soundless back-and-forth sweep, Hershey glanced up at the domed ceiling. 'Any prospect of taking a peek at what's up there? I don't mean now. Next month, perhaps.'

Sejanus responded with an apologetic shrug. 'Omnipotens is sealed in at the moment. I'll arrange access on your next visit, if you wish.'

Hershey lowered her gaze. 'Omnipotens – the Almighty. Sort of scary, if you think about it.'

'It's only a computer.' Sejanus smiled sleekly.

'Omnipotens Deus,' Hershey muttered under her breath as she mused on the vast prodigy above the ceiling, the scientific miracle that crammed the upper dome of the gigantic head.

Omnipotens Deus – Almighty God.

With a grimace, she glanced at Joe Dredd as he touched two acti-pads simultaneously.

Red lasers lanced from the eyes of the Colossus, twin ruby spears that pierced the night, swerving slowly to and fro, probing each corner and crevice. Vid relayed that awesome image to every home in Mega-City One.

This Colossus Judge had eyes of fire.

Judge Dredd pressed for audio, and gave the Colossus a voice. The voice of Dredd. It blared out from every vid-screen in the city.

'THE EYES OF JUDGEMENT ARE UPON YOU!

YOU WHO TREMBLE ARE THE GUILTY! YOU WILL BE PUNISHED! THE LAW WILL FIND YOU! I – AM – THE – LAW!'

McGruder gave the thumbs up. 'Nice one, Dredd.'

Five hours to go . . .

And Max Normal was his only viable informant. Lucia's chances appeared slimmer by the moment.

Mister Cairo faced the entrance to Ricardo Montalban II Block, then stepped up to the access panel.

At that moment Dredd's voice issued from a number of giant street-vids and rumbled about the curved flanks of the buildings.

'THE EYES OF JUDGEMENT ARE UPON YOU!'

'Oh, here we go again,' groaned Cairo.

'YOU WHO TREMBLE ARE THE GUILTY!'

'Yeah, yeah, yeah.'

'YOU WILL BE PUNISHED!'

'Put a sock in it.'

'THE LAW WILL FIND YOU!'

'Suck a bomb.'

'I – AM – THE – LAW!'

Cairo lifted an eyebrow. 'Why does he keep *saying* that?'

The barrage stopped. Silence reigned. It was one of the briefest Justice broadcasts in Cairo's memory. Short and sour.

'Well, back to work,' he sighed, flicking a glance over Ricardo Montalban II Block.

Max Normal had recently shifted residence from the sixtieth floor to the ninety-sixth, fondly imagining his hide-out was a secret between himself and Dredd. Truth was, his refuge was a secret shared by everybody all over the block.

Max Normal – Dredd's most favoured stoolie.

Both Normal and Dredd seemed to believe their relationship was confidential. Fat chance. It was one of the worst-kept secrets in the Big City. Normal had a loose

29

tongue when he got drunk. And he was drunk a lot of the time.

It was fear of Judge Dredd, not secrecy, that kept Normal from being torn apart by all the relatives and friends of the people he had ratted on for the sake of a fat cred-balance.

Normal was one of those rare men who achieved the anatomical tour-de-force of sitting firmly on the fence while keeping both ears simultaneously planted on both sides of the ground. He listened, watched, gathered information, then traded it. If Cairo struck lucky, Normal would have word of Lucia.

With practised ease the private eye fooled the block-access computer, using a sequence of skeleton-codes, and was inside and speeding up Elevator One in less than a minute. He got out at the ninety-sixth floor, jumped into the wheeled bubble of a whizaway, and drove the five hundred metres to the door of Habhold C157.

'Message from Judge Dredd for Max Normal,' he addressed the door Eye a few seconds after buzzing for admittance.

'What?' Oh Grud – I ain't – I don't – Who the drokk are ya?' crackled Normal's scared, slurred tones from the Eye's audio unit.

Cairo spread his palms to the spy-vid. 'Your location and special relationship with Dredd are A-classified. The fact I'm here *proves* Dredd sent me. But if you want to play little piggy in your little home here's one big, bad wolf who's got better things to do than huff and puff. I'll go and tell Dredd you refused to accept his urgent message.'

'Why didn't duh Judge contact me by vid-com?'

'Vid-coms can be intercepted.'

A brief hesitation. 'I'll check with Ole Stoney Face on the drokkin' vid-unit,' Normal muttered.

'He's busy.' Cairo hadn't expected Normal to open up readily. He prepared himself to deliver a hypnotic command he'd implanted in the stoolie years ago: a hypnotic access command – 'Ali Baba's Camel' – the equivalent of 'open sesame'.

But he was stopped by Normal's boozy voice as the door whirred open. 'Yeah, Judge Chin-Face would be busy-lizzie with this gruddam perp Mandra fritz-blitz. Get your tippy-toes in here, fella. Hope you gotta drinkie-winkie with ya. Feel drokkin' dry and hung up high, ya know?'

Cairo stepped into the habhold, masking his emotion at the man's mention of Mandra. The sound of her name put Lucia to the margin of his thoughts, just for the moment. What had Mandra got herself into this time? He tried not to dwell on the subject as he studied his surroundings. No sign of an Eye lens. Normal hated having Eyes in his habhold, and Dredd liked to keep him sweet. Just as well there were no Eyes, considering the stunt Cairo was about to pull.

The luminous grey walls enclosed nothing of note except for an expensive Meg-2000 vid-unit, a shuggy table complete with an array of cues, and scores of empty bottles scattered across the floor. Normal crouched over the multi-pocketed shuggy table, cue poised, and executed a showy ricochet shot that propelled the ball over the bumpy surface into one of the central pockets. Not bad for a man on the morgue side of fifty. He tossed the cue into a magnetic holder and swung round.

'Kinda neat shot, yeah? A hot pot. Deserves a warm tot before ya pass on Dreddy's word and head yer ways, don't ya think?'

Max Normal, from the crown of his bowler hat to the hem of his pin-striped trousers, aped the Brit gent. But the nasal Pits accent and Meg-Cit slang didn't fit the outfit. It only underlined the sleaze.

'I see you've grown your moustache back,' Cairo remarked. 'Or has a worm died on your top lip?'

'Grud-crud the drokkin' moustache!' Normal snorted. 'Stoney give zip-lip. No-namey give head-dip. Maxie want slip-sip. Maxie want hip-trip.'

'Uh-huh. Tell me – do you come with sub-titles?'

31

'I want a drinkie, man! Ya got one?'

'No.'

'Ah, Grud!' He stomped towards Cairo. 'Drokk it. And drokk you, mother-drokker.'

Cairo tilted an eyebrow. 'I'll make a deal. If you don't say "Grud" or "drokk", then I won't say Pantocrator or fu — .'

'Ya what?' the other cut in.

'Forget it. About Mandra – ' He preserved an impassive mask. It wasn't easy. ' – I'd keep the news to yourself, if I were you. That's if you know the real truth, of course. Justice Central might have fed you the cover story . . .'

Normal wasn't drunk enough to swallow the bait. His stare narrowed.

'Ya tryin' to pump me, pal? Wanna know what I know about cutie-ass Mandra? Who are yah, man? Maybe Normy makes a li'l call to Dreddy, huh?'

Cairo decided he'd wasted too much time already. He needed to release the shuggy-playing soak from the memory-block he carried in his head. He spoke the hypnotic release words:

'Casablanca Falcon Airways.'

The memory block lifted. The man's mouth fell open. Limbs trembled. '*You . . . Mister Cairo*. Oh Grud. Ya name's *trouble*, man. T-R-O-U-B-L-E. Oh, drokk. I remember ya.'

'And you'll forget me again when I leave. Like all the other times.'

'Gruddit – ' The stoolie's mouth tightened. 'Yer one o' dem Psi freaks like Mandra, ain't ya? Get into a guy's head. Make him see things. Yah walk in here wearin' a blue suit an' lookin' like a sawn-off, fair-haired cit wid a alco-gut. An' now – '

'Now I've grown inches, lost weight, changed hair colour, and gained a scruffy trench-coat.' Cairo's lips bent in a crooked smile. 'Take a good look. You won't recall a single detail.'

'Gruddam Psi freak – hate Psi, man. Psi's weirdie-feardie.'

'I call my gift "the Wild". You call it what you like.'

A sly look stole into Normal's expression. 'Weeell, Mister Grud-Almighty Cairo. Maybe I won' be so forgetful dis time. Not if I *concentrate*. Take it all in. Yeah.' He studied the private eye, filing each impression. 'Six foot – could be an inch less. Build on da slender side, but wide shoulders. Black, kinda spiky hair dat needs cuttin'. Face kinda narrow. Needs a shave. Sorta good lookin' – kind the ladies go for. Age – I'd say twenty-seven, twenty-eight – '

'Twenty-nine.' Cairo drew his Dillinger. 'You can stop counting. Your time's up. Unless you start singing.'

Normal acted the wide-eyed innocent at sight of Cairo's gun. 'As in one o' my celebrated song-and-dance routines?'

'As in canary. Dredd's canary.'

'And if I don't?'

'You sleep the Big Sleep.'

A gulp travelled down the shuggy player's creased throat. 'Yah *kiddin*'? Yah touch me – Dredd'll *kill* yah.'

Cairo, expressionless, aimed the Dillinger at Normal's heart. 'Screw Dredd. I've killed three Judges so far. You'll be my first civilian – in cold blood, that is.'

The shakes were really making a twitch-dance of Normal's muscles now. 'Hey, man – why'd yah wanna kill me? What harm have I ever done?'

'What harm?' Cold anger frosted the flat, low-pitched tone. 'You're Dredd's stoolie. That's enough harm to get you killed.'

Normal flung up his hands. 'I'll talk!' he screeched, approaching falsetto. 'In duh name o' Grud – I'll talk!'

The Dillinger lowered a fraction. So did Cairo's voice. 'Not in Grud's name. Choose another.'

'Hey – I mean – what's wrong with Grud?'

'Because Grud equals Crud in my book.'

'Okay. Okay. Whatever ya say. I swear by – by my shuggy cue action.'

'I'll buy that. Tell me about Mandra. Remember – if you lie, I'll know.'

'Right, right. Mandra's wanted alive by Justice Central. Guess yah heard about Dreddy's broadcast 'bout that an hour ago. No? Report on sight – yah know the kind o' thing. Broadcast didn't give the reason. But I hear stuff – yah know? She left some kinda Psi time bomb in MAC and Barney, a sorta computer virus. It went off round midnight. Wiped out half duh files. Duh Council of Five named her Public Enemy Number One, at Dreddy's elbow nudge.'

Lines furrowed Cairo's brow. 'The MAC and Barney computers are electronic. Electronics aren't susceptible to Psi attack.'

'Dat's what I said when Dreddy called through. I got zip-lip. Nada.'

Cairo fought to keep his slip-sliding wits on even keel. 'Any idea what sentence Mandra will get?'

'Sentence already decided. Lobotomy and twenty years o' hard labour on Titan.'

Cairo's blood congealed. *Mandra. They're going to cut her brain. Make her a zombie. Seal her nose and mouth. Replace her soft skin with plasteen. Cram her full of pneumatic machinery. A witless cyborg slaving on an airless satellite of Saturn.*

Mandra . . .

Normal viewed Cairo with a shrewd eye. 'Yah know Mandra, *personally*?'

Cairo thought of a card in his pocket. The Queen of Hearts.

Voodoo eyes . . .

The flash of beauty was expunged by the *prip-prip* of the vid-com. A message flashed on the blue screen. DEREK RED CALLING – ANSWER IN AUDIO-VISUAL IF SECURE.

'Dredd,' Cairo swore. 'Don't even dream of answering that, Normal. If you've got a remote in your pocket, you're dead if you touch it. Derek Red – I can imagine who that is.'

CHAPTER FOUR

'Creep's not answerin',' Dredd snapped, after waiting more than thirty seconds for a reply.

He lifted his gaze from the Lawmaster's vid-com and settled back in the seat of the gargantuan motor bike, gauntleted hands gripping the sturdy handlebars. The soft hum of an h-wagon's magno-engines resonated through the Justice bike as the hover-ship took him and Hershey down to Pagliacci Plaza, jump-off point for the duo's Mandra hunt.

Hershey sat alongside, dressed in the same Street Judge uniform as Dredd, and astride her own Lawmaster, facing the drop wall and raring to go. Another twenty seconds or so and she and Dredd would hit the Pits at 500-plus kph on the mighty, weapon-wielding Lawmasters, known amongst the cits as Beasts of the Streets.

'Born to be wild,' she murmured in anticipation, rubbing her firm thighs tight to the metal steed's flanks. Then she glanced at Dredd, noting that slight extra downtwist at the right corner of his mouth, the nearest he ever got to displaying rage, loathing, frustration, contempt or downright hate. She often wondered if Joe Dredd's mannerisms were identical to those of the revered Chief Judge Fargo, Father of Justice. If so, the Chief Judge must have been one mean father.

Joe Dredd, along with Rico, the brother he killed, was a clone of Fargo. The sole surviving clone. Dredd was the twenty-second century replica of the twenty-first century Father of Justice, founder and forger of Judge rule. The nearest thing this side of mayhem.

'Creep should answer,' Dredd growled, glancing at the altimeter read-out on the pilot's panel:

SIXTEEN SECONDS TO JUMP-OFF

Hershey kept a straight face. Joe Dredd had made a call to a man name of 'Studs Ramrod'. She knew that Studs Ramrod was one more pseudonym of Max Normal, Joe's canary. Half the Justice force knew who Max Normal sang to. But she didn't push the point. No one pushed the point with Dredd. Not even Hershey, his nominal superior.

'He's probably taking a leak,' she said. 'Try later.'

Dredd pressed for repeat call.

Hershey shrugged and studied her own Lawmaster vidcom. It was the third rerun of an alarm from Tek Division. The last scenes of a serious slip-up at Tek Cine-Lab were played out on the vid.

Tek Division's Project Lazarus, coded Double-A secret, had gone wildly haywire. She watched the replay of a group of Tek-1 operatives sitting in front of what an untrained eye would have mistaken for a twentieth-century style cinema screen. The screen was in fact a hyperplasma field, and the monochrome movie it showed was just one step away from solid reality. One step away – until now.

A line sliced her brow as the rerun reached the point where a character in the movie jumped clean off the screen and shot his way out of the cine-lab. The Teks stampeded. Panic stations.

Pursing her lips, she clicked off the vid. The Project Lazarus accident – coded 'JC 1' – had happened a minute after midnight. Midnight was the time Mandra psyched out the MAC and Barney computers. It took two minutes for Omnipotens to kick in and assume control on all networks. The JC 1 incident had occurred inside that two-minute gap. Had to be a connection. It wasn't much of a lead to Mandra, but it was all they had, unless the concentrated minds of Psi Division pierced Mandra's blocking defences or Dredd's super-canary had a song to sing about a coffee-skinned girl with voodoo eyes.

36

She threw a look at the altimeter:

SIX SECONDS TO JUMP-OFF

Her back muscles rippled with excitement as her hands took a firm grip of the handlebars. She loved jump-offs.

Dredd broke off the call to 'Studs Ramrod' with a fierce thump of the hand.

'Ricardo Montalban II Block,' he snarled.

THREE SECONDS TO JUMP-OFF

He was Hershey's nominal subordinate, so she felt obliged to make a token stand. 'No. We trace JC 1 and see where it leads.'

'RICARDO MONTALBAN II BLOCK!' he thundered.

ONE SECOND TO JUMP-OFF

'Okay,' she shrugged, 'Montalban it is.'

The drop wall fell away and an alternation in the magnetic field of the h-wagon's floor propelled the two Lawmaster riders out into the open night and a drop of thirty metres to Pagliacci Plaza.

The surge of turbo boosters rocketed the bikes forty metres across the plaza.

The bikes' 500 cm Firerock tyres hit the ground in unison at an impact speed of 420 kph.

A crowd of cits scattered in panic at the descent of the monstrous Lawmasters, leaving Dredd and Hershey a clear path as the Judges accelerated to 550 kph in two seconds, streaking along the megway that snaked north to Ricardo Montalban II Block.

The call from 'Derek Red' finally blinked out on the vid-com.

Mister Cairo didn't expect Dredd to rush round on the strength of an unanswered call, but he didn't want to take too many chances until he found Lucia.

Get the information fast.

He subjected the shuggy-player to a penetrating stare. 'What else can you tell me about Mandra?'

'Nothin'. Dat's it, pal.'

'Have the Helmets any idea where she is?'

'None. Dat's why da h-wagons and Gunbirds are blowing up a storm. All out lookin' for li'l Miss Mandra. Major woman-hunt, man.'

He wanted to press Normal further, but he let it go. Mandra was a woman of infinite resource. She could keep one step ahead of Justice Hall – for a few days at least.

Lucia, however, had less than five hours left.

One task at a time.

Leaving the Queen of Hearts in his pocket, he pulled out the other card and held it up. 'It's a Tarot card, Golden Dawn pack,' he said. 'It shows the World, twenty-first symbol of the major arcana. Lucia Lux was abducted from Happy House an hour ago. Whoever took Lucia fixed this card upside-down on her wall. I need information. Fast.'

Normal made a sour face. 'I don't know nothin' 'bout Tarot, fella.'

Cairo raised the pistol level with the man's breast-pocket. 'You know something about something.'

'Yeah – well, dis Lucia Lux, she's an alien, right? Second generation Luxorian.'

'You know her?'

'Heard of her. An eezie-squeezie. New meat on da block.'

New meat on the block. Cairo suppressed a scowl at the expression. Lucia was young – and fresh to the game. New meat, in Pits lingo.

Normal winked a bloodshot eye. 'One o' your girls, eh? Gone AWOL?'

'No girl's one of *my* girls,' Cairo snapped. 'The Sisters sometimes hire me to protect them from pimps or Judges who want to bleed them dry, lock them up, or bury them. Someone's taken Lucia. It's my job to get her back safe. It's that simple.'

Another sly wink. 'Yeah, well – what yah don't condemn, you condone. Know what I mean?'

'The girls choose their living. I don't condemn or condone. I don't judge.'

Instantly furious at himself for wasting valuable breath

38

on Max Normal, Cairo didn't blow any more time on recounting how he'd tried to persuade Lucia out of the business. He wasn't obliged to explain his life to Dredd's stoolie. He pushed the business end of the Dillinger into the man's waistcoated chest. 'Spill the beans about Lucia, or learn about your internal anatomy the hard way.'

The bootlace moustache glistened with hot sweat. 'Yeah, I hear yah man. Keep it cool, okay? Straight from duh fridge. Okay? Okay?'

'Get on with it.'

'Well – I dunno much, I swear by Gru – by my cue action. All I know is Lucia has an older sister. Much older. Meat past its prime. Name of Lucinda. Works the streets from Aliens Corner – yah know, the nearest Squid Row. Providence on Ascension. She's gotta be wise to somethin'. Dat's it, man. All I know. I swear it. I swear . . .'

'I hear you.'

The shock of hearing Mandra's inhuman sentence had thrown Cairo off course. He had frittered away precious time on the Judge's stoolie. He launched straight into the hypno-code that would block all recollection of Mister Cairo from Max Normal's brain:

'I am the best worst man in the worst best world.'

As he delivered the code, he visualised himself as a bug-eyed, crop-scalped mesomorph by the name of Head Banger.

And that was who Normal saw in Cairo's place when the trance took effect. The notorious Head Banger, terror of handsome men.

Checking that Normal wasn't tracking his movements, the private eye picked off a shuggy ball from a magneto-board near the shuggy table and bounced it in his hand as he advanced on the older man.

He needed the stoolie to stay put while he got clear. Normal no longer knew that Cairo was in his habhold, but he believed Head Banger was there, and when the visitor left he would be on the vid-com to Dredd and the block would be swarming with Judges before the elevator hit ground floor. Cairo had a scheme to keep Max Normal well and truly put.

'Head B-Banger,' Normal stuttered, glazed stare fixed on Cairo.

Head Banger was an exceptionally ugly psychopath who specialised in exploding the heads of good-looking men, on the grounds that the fewer the handsome men, the less ugly he would appear in comparison.

Small wonder the shuggy-player was standing scared.

Max Normal's mouth gaped wide in fear. 'Head Ban—'

Cairo plugged Normal's squeal with a shuggy ball rammed into the mouth.

'Looks like a shuggy ball,' he said, aware that the stoolie's mind would translate his words into Head Banger's guttural slang. 'But it's one of my special head bangers. A motion-activated, self-disarming bomb. It's primed to detonate if you move as much as a centimetre in any direction, vertical or lateral. After one thousand seconds it self-disarms, and you're safe. Until then, stand still. *Stand absolutely still*.'

The stoolie stood as still as stark fear allowed while the private eye let himself out of the habhold.

His last sight of Max Normal displayed a shivering figure swimming in perspiration, spine ramrod-straight and shoulders back like a Judge on sentinel duty, a harmless shuggy ball making a horrified O of his mouth.

Cairo had counted up to three hundred before he was clear of the block's main entrance. Under the strobing illumination of a streetlamp on the fritz, he entered a podule activation code on All-Purpose – the 'wristwatch with a thousand functions' as the ad described it on Channel 99.

He had parked his podule, named Sam, nearby on the corner of Rat's Alley and Eliot Street. The activation code would bring the hover-bubble to him in five seconds or so. Squid Row on Providence and Ascension was five kilometres' distance. He needed speed more than stealth. Lucia's life was ticking away its countdown.

Max Normal would be conducting his own silent count-down up on the ninety-sixth floor. Seven hundred seconds to go. By the time the stoolie reached zero – and then added at least a hundred, for safety's sake – Cairo would have contacted Lucia's sister and be ready to roll.

Sam the Podule, a bead-shaped mini-hover with a bubble casing of plastiplex, whisked out of Rat's Alley and opened its lid. He vaulted in, instructed the hover-pod to head for Providence and Ascension, and leaned back in Sam's single seat as the vehicle sped close to 200 kph, at its pre-programmed height of two metres. The ETA display on Sam's compact console showed ninety-eight seconds of travelling time to Squid Row.

Enough time for a song.

Despite the urgency of his search for Lucia, Cairo had Mandra on his mind.

Mandra – erect shock of hair like optical fibres. Skin like coffee with a dash of cream. Body curves that would have made the Venus de Milo bitch in envy. Mandra . . .

It was a long fifteen-year gap back to the place they'd met, the place they'd said goodbye. Fifteen years since the psycho-cubes.

Fifteen years since they'd shared a song.

Cairo turned his moody stare to the speeding monotony of Ascension Avenue, seeing another place, another time.

'Play it again, Sam,' he quietly instructed the podule.

'Oh no, sir,' Sam protested. 'You don't want to hear "As Time Goes By".'

'Play it, Sam.'

'But you know what it does to you.'

'Play it.'

The opening bars of the song filled the pod with the notes of a gentle piano.

'Sing it, Sam.'

'But sir – '

'Sing it.'

41

Sam recommenced the opening bars, then sang in a wistful, husky tone:

'You must remember this,
A kiss is just a kiss,
A Psi is just a Psi . . .'

Cairo let the pain happen as the song went through him. He had loved several handfuls of women in his life. But he'd been in love with only one.

As Squid Row hurtled into sight and the song concluded, he took out a creased, battered playing card and twitched a smile at its red queen.

Memory dealt an underhand trick. It dealt him that final farewell in the psycho-cubes, sharp and cruel . . .

Alarms beeping and flashing all over the place as he makes his escape. He runs slam-bang into Mandra in her Psi-Cadet uniform. 'Where you going, Jo?' As always, she shortens his name to Jo. He does the same right back and calls Mandra 'Ma', just for the hell of it. He flicks his head, indicating the roof. 'Top of the world, Ma!' She puts a card in his hand. 'Something old. I bought it for you. Hope it brings you luck.' He glances at the Queen of Hearts. 'Remember me,' Mandra says, then waves him on. He starts running again. Looks back just once at her sad smile . . .

'We'll always have the psycho-cubes,' he murmured to the Queen of Hearts as the podule whispered to a halt.

'Here's looking at you, kid,' he said to the queen.

Then he slipped the Queen of Hearts back in his pocket and descended from the podule, thoughts focused on Lucia. Memory Lane was closed to traffic for the next five hours.

'Stay here, Sam, nice and close,' he instructed, observing a dozen eezie-squeezies parading their wares on the street corner and two pimps skulking in the shadows. 'Electro-repelo field on eighty.' He caught sight of a juve gang joyriding an Armageddon Tank at the far end of Providence Street. 'No – make that a hundred. Max security.'

'You got it, Mister Cairo,' Sam responded, shutting its

lid as the private eye homed in on a girl in a black synthi-leather jacket and white tutu.

Lucinda Lux, had to be. Like her sister, she glowed in the dark.

Lucinda wasn't typical of the ladies of the various Squid Rows in the city. Her appearance was almost human. High City guys came down here for the exotic, the otherworldly. There wasn't a lot of call for near-human humanoids. The High-Towners who frequented Squid Row were in it for the slime and bug-eyes and pseudopods.

He eyed a Hi-Glo scrawl someone had sprayed on a wall: TEASE MY TENTACLE. That just about summed it up.

Cairo strolled towards Lucinda, kicking rotting garbage and the occasional rat out the way. Squid Row was one of the Big City's unofficial dumps. It had a strong smell, and it wasn't roses.

Dream gum ballooned out of the girl's mouth as he drew near. At the instant it popped he caught sight of a Hi-Glo scrawl on the wall she leaned on, within kicking distance of her crossed legs:

ANARCHOPOLIS

He'd seen the name Anarchopolis Hi-Glo'd on walls plenty of times. Some said it was a city. Others believed it a fable for the hopeless and helpless. Anarchopolis was the great myth of the Pits; a formless rumour of the streets. It represented a kind of Low City hope. A hope without a face. For Cairo, it was simply another story.

Anarchopolis was just the writing on the wall.

But up until this moment, the writing had always been the right way up. The scrawl beside Lucinda was upside down.

What turns and turns again?

His Psi gift – the Wild – prickled the nape of his neck with the haziest of premonitions. Before he could pin it down, the future stopped breathing down his upturned collar, and he was left with the crud and rats and general low-life of Squid Row.

43

Keep the future on hold. He had enough problems dealing with the past and the present.

About five hundred seconds of countdown was left to Max Normal, shuggy ball stuck in his moustached mouth. Not too long after he reached žero he would be on the vid-com to Dredd, and Dredd would be on his way.

Five kilometres from Ricardo Montalban II Block was too close for comfort. He wanted to be ten blocks away by the time the stoolie made a call to Chin Face.

'Lucinda?' he said to the eezie-squeezie, trying to ignore the ominous rumble of the approaching Armageddon Tank and the hollering of its joyriding juves.

She blew another pink dream gum bubble, popped it. Hallucinodreams bubbled out.

'What took ya so long, Cairo?' she said in the characteristic Luxorian twang. 'Dah man said dah writin's on dah wall. Dat's what dah man said.'

Cairo's gaze slid back to the scrawl:
ANARCHOPOLIS

Max Normal had counted down to five hundred and six when his nostrils started to tickle.

Four hundred and ninety seconds to go and he wanted to sneeze.

Badly.

A sneeze. A bang. Goodnight Maxie.

He silently prayed to Grud that his trembling limbs wouldn't shake the head banger into explosive action, that his treacherous nose wouldn't blow the Last Trumpet.

Please, Almighty Grud, don't let me sneeze. I'll be a good boy if yah keep me from sneezin'. Real good boy. Honest.

Mind over matter, with Grud's help – that was the key.

He wouldn't sneeze.

He wouldn't –

'AHHHH-CHOOOO!'

The shuggy ball shot out of his mouth. He reeled back in mortal terror.

I'm dead I'm dead I'm dead

The ball bounced harmlessly, hit the door, rolled to a halt.

I'm dead I'm dead I'm dead

The ball lay nice and quiet on the floor.

I'm dead I'm dead I'm dead

The ball stayed where it was while he backed away.

I'm – I'm not dead

Head Banger never planted dud bombs. Never.

But there was a first time for everything.

Normal sprinted into his bedroom, screeching for his Hab-droid. 'Mug! Get dat ball by duh door and fling it out duh window! Fast, Mug, fast!'

A droid composed entirely of numerous flexisteel arms and legs scrabbled from under the bed and scuttered into the front room. 'On it, man.'

Normal listened to the whine of the window opening. Then released a big breath of relief as Mug called out. 'On its way down, man.'

When his pulse rate stopped doing the hundred-metre dash, Normal made his groggy way to the vid-com. Head Banger was gonna pay for the Grud-Almighty scare he gave poor ol' Maxie.

Dredd would make him pay.

'Studs Ramrod to Derek Red.'

Judge Dredd's image flashed on the screen. The speeding background showed he was on his Lawmaster. 'Where the Grud you been, creep? I've been calling.'

'H-Head Bang-banger shoved a bomb in muh mouth,' Max stammered. 'It was a dud. Coulda *killed* ol' Maxie, Judge. He can'ta gone far. Get him for me, huh? Huh?'

'Head Banger shoved a banger in your mouth?'

'Too right, man.'

'No way. Head Banger's in the cubes. Hulligan collared him couple o' days ago.'

'But – he was here. Right here.'

'I'll check with the Eye.'

Normal broke out in a sweat. An Eye – oh Grud. It

was understood that no spy-cameras be installed in his habhold. With an Eye in your hab, Judges saw – *things*.

'Hey! You plant an Eye in my hab? Hey, man, yah promised. I hate Eyes. Yah – yah didn't see what I was doin' with Voluptia, did yah? I was drunk, man. Anywäy, it was all her idea – '

'Shut it, Studs!' Dredd growled. 'I'm accessing your Eye record. Last ten minutes cover it?'

'Er – access it from fifteen minutes ago.'

There was a fifteen-second silence as Dredd reviewed the Eye's replay.

Then a microscopic tremor twitched the right corner of the Judge's tight lips as he called in:

'Priority call to Omnipotens. Transmitting SRZXX101211/ PZ999T/ XX7/ 362PP/ VYT 85521/ WQEB/ 595XL Eye record. Ident intruder in grey raincoat.'

It was a matter of seconds before a canine growl vibrated between Dredd's clenched teeth:

'*Mister Cairo.*'

CHAPTER FIVE

The writing's on the wall.

A cryptic message, passed on by Lucinda, by a man as yet unnamed.

Cairo's eyes strayed back to the upside-down scrawl that spelt out ANARCHOPOLIS.

'Anarchopolis – is that the message?'

'He didn't say,' Lucinda twanged in an alien tone.

'Who was he?'

'Toots Ritzy. Snappy dresser. Works duh shuggy halls.' He nodded. 'One of Big Boy's boys.'

Did she know about her sister's abduction? If she did she was putting on a hell of a cool act. Something about this whole business was beginning to smell of a set-up. Cryptic messages ready and waiting for him on street corners. And Big Boy, one of the slipperiest crooks in the Mumbles, was behind it somehow. Big Boy had several scores to settle with Cairo. And Big Boy specialised in set-ups. Lucia might be a lure for Cairo to walk into a trap.

Come into my parlour . . .

He surveyed the sprawl of Hi-Glo scrawls on the wall, seeking an alternative hint to the upside-down Anarchopolis.

A couple of the luminous scrawls caught his eye:

NECESSITY – WHO NEEDS IT?

The other scrawl was aimed at Dredd, using one of the Pit-names for the Judge:

THE MAN WITH NO FACE – GOOD, BAD, OR UGLY? TWO OUT OF THREE CAN'T BE GOOD.

He recognised the style. He should. It was his own, sometime back when he was nine or ten and didn't know any better.

The majority of the remaining scrawls were variants on the 'Judge Death for Chief Judge' theme.

Lucinda shifted from the wall and sashayed towards him, hips rolling more than the dream-gun in her mouth. He'd spotted her as a Luxorian at first glance. Hard to miss. Luxorians were silver from the erect swirl of their hair to the nails of their seven toes. And they glowed faintly in the dark. When roused by rage or lust, they blazed like silver suns.

On the area of the wall the Luxorian had vacated, a Hi-Glo scrawl was revealed:

OOO – BABY . . . YOU LIGHT UP MY LIFE.

Figured.

'Hey, good-lookin',' she twanged like an out-of-tune harp. 'Wanna get cookin'?'

The rumble of the nearing Armageddon Tank and the overhead thrum of an h-wagon distracted him from the jaded eezie-squeezie patter. The joyriding juves were an open invitation for the Judges to descend like the wrath of Grud.

'Come on, baby – light my fire . . .' the girl cooed. She leaned up close and peered at him, her squint acute. Luxorians had terrible vision in any but the brightest light. 'Yeeaah, you're a real looker, Mister Cairo. Glad to meet yah. The word was you died on a case in Brit-Cit. The Case of the Crawling Chair.'

'The case got solved. A lot of people died, but I wasn't one of them,' he answered quickly. 'Tell me – any idea where Big Boy is tonight? I've got urgent business with him.'

Sparks abruptly flew from the ends of her rigid hair, the Luxorian equivalent of a frown. 'Ain't I good enough for yah?'

'You're a doll, but Time's a winged chariot and my podule conks out at 400 k's.'

The sparks began to fizz out. 'Sis always said you wuz a real regular guy for anyone in a jam. Sis in trouble again?'

He would tell her the good news or bad when it was all over. Till then, he couldn't deal straight with Lucinda. He felt like a louse.

'Life is film noir,' he murmured.

'Huh?' she frowned. 'What's film noir when it's at home?'

'Oh – just a canful of downbeat movies they made back in the 1940s. Painted a black view of life. No clear line between right and wrong. Everything and everyone gets screwed up.'

'Includin' sis? Hey – she in real bad trouble?'

'Just need to talk to her, that's all. She might be with Big Boy. Any idea where he is?'

She was in the middle of shaking her head, sending diaphanous silver hair every which way, when the meaning of the message hit him.

He thumped his forehead. 'God – I'm an idiot! It's obvious.'

'What is?'

'The writing on the wall. An inverted Tarot card of the World. The writing on the wall's the Ultra-Glo sign of a diner. The Upside-Down World Turned Downside-Up Diner. One of Big Boy's crooked joints. The World turned upside down – I should have guessed it right off.'

'Well – ' she shrugged. 'So long as you get there it don't matter how long it takes.'

'It matters,' he murmured, preparing to head for the Upside-Down World Turned Downside-Up Diner. 'Er – you all right for money?'

She angled her lipless mouth. 'Well, times have been hard since Judgement Day . . .'

'I can imagine. Times can't be easy when half your customers been eaten by cannibal zombies.'

He passed over a twenty bill and lifted a hand in

farewell. 'Take care of yourself. You'd best get off the street before the joyriders arrive.'

The noise of the advancing tank had risen to the level of a Cursed Earth thunderstorm.

'Hey,' she said. 'Tell me – why do they call you Mister Cairo?'

His lips bent half-way to a wistful smile. 'It's a long story.'

He'd started to head for Sam when all hell decided to break loose.

The Armageddon Tank rounded the corner, draped in members of the Crab Gang from Guy N Smith Block, and swivelling its swivel guns to great effect. The Crabs were probably the most stupid gang in the city, no mean feat with such hot competition. That made them all the more dangerous.

They proved their stupidity by launching a mini-Schnitzel missile at the h-wagon above. The wagon easily vaporised the missile and replied in more than kind.

A laser-directed Ragnarok Raver streaked from the hover-ship like a nuclear cat on heat.

The world somehow got mixed up with the centre of the sun.

Cairo found himself somewhere in the air as the Ragnarok Raver took the tank and the gang to several kinds of hell.

A fireball ascended into heaven.

He was spared the din of explosion. The first sound-wave had deafened him.

Operating on instinct he rolled up before hitting the ground and kept on rolling, his survival-psyched hindbrain directing him towards the partial protection of a doorway.

Scorching metal and bloody chunks of Crab members threatened to give him a red-hot shower.

Cairo's legs made a decision on their own and pushed him upright.

Hands pulling him into the doorway . . .

Bleary vision focusing, he distinguished Lucinda's

fraught features peering up close. His hearing staged a partial come-back.

'Yukah?' she asked.

'What?'

'YOU OKAY?' she shouted.

'Terrific.' He squinted past the raging column of fire and smoke. Even as he looked, the flames died under the deluge of riot foam sprayed from the h-wagon. 'Where's Sam?' he mumbled, barely catching his own words through the wailing banshees that had got into his ears. 'We've got to get out of here.'

'If you're all right, I'm going right now,' Lucinda shouted, and took to her heels.

'No – ' he warned, but she was already at full pelt.

A searchlight from the hover-ship caught her cold. The blinding light transformed her into a fleeing black silhouette.

Cairo shut his eyes and willed Lucinda to stop running. There was nothing else he could do for her.

If you ran from the Judges, you died. First rule of life and death in the Big City, written in corpse-cold blood.

A challenge boomed from above: 'Stop and surrender or you're charcoal, creep!'

'Stand still,' Mister Cairo urged in a low whisper, willing Lucinda to halt. 'Don't give the bastards an excuse.'

As the last syllable left his lips he heard the blast of a gun and the *whump* of a bullet striking home. The runner was launched ten metres by the impact and landed face first in a heap of garbage on the far side of Ascension Avenue.

The h-wagon circled overhead for a brief space, dousing the last embers of the tank's fires, then sped up into the night, leaving the Pits to their customary shadows. The airship Judges would already be contacting a meat-wagon to scoop up the bodies.

Meat. That was what the lawmen had made of Lucinda.

One more reason to hate Justice Hall.

The hum of the h-wagon had died away by the time

Cairo made his way to the body in the garbage, still glancing round for sight of Sam. It wasn't until he was almost on top of Lucinda that he realised she was still alive.

Her head and limbs did a jerky dance as she hauled herself up and swayed round to face him. Shock had made a rictus mask of her features.

Blood bubbled from her mouth as she opened it in a plea: 'Help me . . .'

The voice was tiny as a child's.

The hurt in it went right through him.

So did a lance of fear.

The red life in his veins raced with alarm. The h-wagon's sophisticated on-board computer would have registered a failed kill. And there was no exit wound in her chest. The bullet was engineered to lodge inside the torso.

That meant only one thing – they had hit her with Hi-Ex Delay, a bullet timed to explode between five and fifty seconds after strike, the ultimate deterrent to scavenging pickpockets. Anyone within a couple of metres of a detonating HED bullet was strictly past tense. Ten metres distance and you had a fifty-fifty chance of getting home on your own legs.

'Cairo . . .' Lucinda stumbled up close, arms outspread for a little compassion. Someone to hold. Her glazed eyes echoed the plea in her voice. 'Cairo . . . Help me . . .'

Cairo's natural instincts led him one pace towards her before his brain told him to run like hell. She was a walking time-bomb, and he had fifteen seconds at most before she detonated.

A cold, rational section of his cortex started the lethal countdown:

Fifteen – fourteen –

All of a sudden the girl's arms were around him. Hugging him tight. Desperation made a steel vice of her embrace. 'Help me, Cairo – *please* . . .'

– thirteen – twelve –

Part of him wanted to hug her right back, assure her

everything was fine. The other part screamed at him to break free of the deadly grip. To reject her was criminal: to comfort was suicidal.

Life is film noir.

Large, scared eyes looked up at him through floods of tears as her lips spilled a dribble of red. 'Please . . . help me . . .'

– eleven – ten –

He tasted every flavour of guilt as he pushed her shoulders away and twisted against the locking arms.

But she held on. The girl's need for someone – anyone – was stronger than his survival instinct.

– nine – eight –

His struggles became frenzied as he fought to swing free of her tenacious clutch. Whirling to and fro in a grotesque parody of a waltz – one-two-three, one-two-three – man and girl swirled across the street with the female leading in a dance of death.

– seven – six – five –

Lucinda's anguished face, full of hurt at his rejection, peered up at him and mouthed her entreaty: 'Please help me – Mister Cairo . . .'

– four –

Heart tearing in two with remorse, Cairo slammed his elbows down on her shoulders, biting blood from his lip at the shrill squeak of dislocating bones.

– three –

Bringing his knee up hard into the pit of her stomach, he sent up a prayer to an old legend in the sky as her screech of agony ripped through him. *God forgive me – if there is a God.*

– two –

Doubled-up and flung back by his stomach blow, the girl staggered away, dislocated arms flapping at her sides.

– one –

The look of accusation in her eyes made him feel damned at heart as he spun round and sprinted over the slime and litter of the street.

– zero –

His racing feet devoured some ten metres.

Zero.

About twenty paces covered.

Moving down a gear to a less frantic pace, Cairo glanced over his shoulder.

Zero – it had to be.

But the girl was still intact, and by some miracle of will was weaving a groggy path in his direction.

He skidded to a halt, appalled at the thought that he had hurt the girl for no reason. God – if the bullet had not been HED after all . . . The taste of guilt was vinegar on his tongue.

The more seconds passed as she hobbled up to him, mumbling words he couldn't catch, the more sure he was that he'd made an unforgivable mistake.

She must have been hit by a standard bullet. Must have.

There was no way of making it up to her, but he had to try. Carry her off the street and into hiding and phone the nearest underworld doctor before the Med-Judges arrived and patched her up for captivity.

Cairo stepped forward when she was within fifteen metres, his tongue trying to frame words that came within a few light-years of expressing his remorse.

'I'm – sorry,' he heard her mumble. 'HED – didn't realise at first why you – you didn't want to touch. Sorry.'

She took an unsteady step back. 'Said it now – said I'm sorry. Turn away – flash'll blind you. Keep – distance. We need you alive – Mister Cairo. You're on our side. The – shadow people's side. Stay away. Stay alive.'

He shook his head and strode towards her. 'We'll both stay alive. That's a promise.' If it *was* an HED slug in her chest, then the timer was faulty. Even with his minimal first-aid skills he could extract the bullet in a couple of minutes.

Lucinda was going to make it. She wasn't going to be the latest name on the long obituary list he carried around in his head.

Lucinda attempted to totter away from his approach. 'Stay – alive.'

Cairo forced a smile on his lips. 'This could be the beginning of a beautiful friendshi—'

The blast of a detonating body hurled him clean off his feet.

Lucinda became red bits and pieces flying from the white-hot heart of an explosion.

Blinded by the flash, deafened by the detonation, he sailed through the air in a spinning arc.

In his shattered wits he thought he heard James Cagney misquote a line from an old movie – 'Top of the world, Ma!'

Then Cairo and the hard ground met with a terminal thud.

He was still dead to the world when Dredd roared up to Squid Row on his mighty Lawmaster.

A smooth hand planted the Tarot card of the World, twenty-first of the major arcana, on the polished oak of an antique table from the twentieth century.

The card was inverted, depicting the World upside down.

Another card was placed at its side: Judgement, twentieth card of the Tarot's major arcana. It portrayed an angel blowing a trumpet as the earth opened its graves.

The same two cards again. They came so often these days.

Madame Dragora, musing on the symbols of cartomancy, fleetingly scanned the Hi-Glo pentacle that surrounded her in Apartment Diodati, then glanced at the head of the Judgement Colossus, clearly visible from her window on the five hundred and ninety-third floor of Mary Shelley Block.

She was hardly aware of her low whisper: 'Let the Judges of the Earth be judged.'

'Ooo . . . Madame Dragora, whatever do you see?' gasped Mrs Merriman, plump face purpling as she clutched an anxious hand to an ample bosom.

The young clairvoyant turned back to her client who sat on the other side of the table, and adopted a reassuring smile. 'Nothing that concerns you, Mrs Merriman. Let's complete the circle of ten and then see what we'll see, shall we?' She already knew her client's future – fifteen to twenty years of hypochondriac existence, in which the death of her budgerigar acquired the dimensions of Shakespearian tragedy. All read instantly in the woman's eyes at first meeting, but Mrs Merriman wanted the Tarot to tell her fortune, and the customer was always right. Especially a new-found customer who paid as well as Mrs Merriman.

Madame Dragora's occult practice was only a couple of months old. She couldn't afford to lose a single client from her sparse clientele.

One by one, Madame Dragora took eight cards from the deck.

Card by card, a chill premonition branched in her veins.

There were seventy-eight cards in the Tarot pack, and only twenty-two belonged to the major arcana. But all of the ten randomly chosen images were from the major arcana.

The circular display said nothing about Mrs Merriman.

It said a great deal about the world.

The clairvoyant shut her eyes and leaned back in her chair. In the murk behind her eyelids she saw the gaunt figure of top-hatted, frock-coated Baron Samedi, voodoo Lord of Cemeteries. He supplied no answers tonight.

Madame Dragora exhaled heavily. 'It's no good, Mrs Merriman. The – the vibrations aren't right tonight. Come back tomorrow – the cards will speak clearly then.'

After some persuasion, concluded with an offer of two free readings, Mrs Merriman departed in a huff and the clairvoyant was left with the cards and her speculations.

The Fool, the unnumbered card of the major arcana, commanded her attention. Despite appearances the Fool, according to the Tarot, was no fool. He symbolised wisdom in apparent folly. He also signified one about to set out on a spiritual journey; a seeker.

In the playing cards that evolved from the Tarot, he was the joker in the pack.

The wild card.

The moment she had laid eyes on the Fool, the card seemed to burst wide open. Inside it she'd glimpsed the face of a blind man in a dark grey trench-coat flying through the air from a fiery eruption. The face stamped itself on her brain. The resemblance to a boy she had known fifteen years ago was unmistakable. His parting words echoed in memory:

'*Top of the world, Ma!*'

'Joel,' she breathed gently.

Her gaze shifted to the card right of the Fool.

The Chariot. Behind the picture of the chariot and its knightly armoured driver, symbol of force, she discerned a more contemporary icon. As if the plastic had become semi-opaque, a grubby window on the world, she saw a Lawmaster, plastisteel steed of Judge Dredd.

The next card was the Hanged Man, suspended upside down by his heels from a tree, and grinning as though he hadn't a care in the world.

Then came the Magician, whom she intuitively linked with the Hanged Man.

After the Magician – the card displaying the intertwined bodies of the Lovers.

The Lovers. A love restricted to looks and words, long ago in the psycho-cubes. The man in the grey raincoat. It *was* him.

'Joel.'

Her eyes travelled along the three remaining cards.

The Devil.

The Tower Struck by Lightning.

Death.

Death shot a few hints at her. None were sharp. All went astray.

Red writing on the wall . . . 'Anarchopo– . . . Top of the world . . . The world blows its top . . .'

She bit her lip and the welter of visions receded. Slowly, she shook her head. She had pushed her Psi faculty too far. Laid herself wide open. Dangerous. They were searching for her, out there in the mega-city. Her Psi defences, even in concert with the pentacle, could not block them out permanently.

Psi Division, working with the entire might of Justice Hall, were sweeping the city for a Psi adept. A Psi adept by the name of Mandra.

Mandra, who now practised as a clairvoyant under the pseudonym of Madame Dragora.

Mandra swept the cards from the table.

To hell with the Tarot. It gave tantalising glimpses of the future, but no more than glimpses. And there were many possible futures.

She had little hope that she would survive in any of them.

After a lifetime serving the Law, she had finally taken the plunge. Mandra had turned against the system she'd served. Once a Judge, she was now the Anti-Judge.

Her moody gaze roved the books scattered on the bare floor around the table. 'Something old, before Big Brother,' she remarked wryly, sighting a 1948 first edition of Orwell's banned novel, *1984*.

Her glance darted out the window to the head of the Colossus Judge. She found herself quoting from the last line of *1984*: 'He loved Big Brother'. The line of her mouth hardened. 'But I never will.'

Brooding, she stroked the neck of her suit of black *sleather*, an ultra-fine, ultra-tight form of synthi-leather.

Finally her full, wide mouth curved a little. Whatever the Judges did, they could never make her love Big Brother.

She'd die first.

Inside an upper molar she had implanted a trace of *hypma*, stolen from Tek Division's Project Lazarus. Tek had kept the invention of hyperplasma, abbreviated to hypma, secret for decades. Small wonder. The strange energy/matter that composed hypma supplied a link between mind and matter. She had used her Psi powers to attune the hypma implant to her mind, and encoded the implant with a destruct command, triggered when she spoke a sequence of words.

When the words were uttered, her brain would be transformed into a hypma-activated bomb. Not a large explosion. Just sufficient to blow her head off.

All she had to do if arrested was speak those trigger-words; an old rhyme:

Here comes a candle to light you to bed.
Here comes a chopper to chop off your head.

She would blow her mind and go out with a bang.

Mandra stood up from the chair and stretched, the contours of her curvy physique on full display under the skin-tight black sleather suit.

She swayed her tall, graceful body to and fro as she murmured:

'I'll judge the Judges. And I'll carry a torch for Liberty.'

At length she sank and squatted on the floor, finger weaving over the cover of a copy of Mary Shelley's Frankenstein.

Gradually, her mind roved into the near past.

'Cassandra,' she breathed softly, recalling her friend Judge Anderson, two years Mandra's senior, who had finally turned against Justice Central following an upsurge of Christianity among the citizens. After more than three years of indecision Cassandra Anderson had decided whose side she was on. Her reward was virtual exile on Mars.

'Cassandra – you shouldn't have waited so long to act. And you shouldn't have acted alone. Together we'd have shaken the pillars of Justice Hall. But you wouldn't have gone that far, would you? I'd have killed that lunatic man-bitch McGruder. You wouldn't.'

But then, Cassandra wasn't the daughter of a *mambo*, a voodoo priestess. Mandra was a true *mambo*'s daughter, despite her mixed parentage. White father. Black mother. Mandra didn't give a damn about her father. She was her mother's girl. Mambo mother. Mambo daughter.

Mandra followed the religion of *Obeah*, known to outsiders as voodoo.

The pentacle and Tarot cards were Mandra's sole concession to the magic born in medieval Europe. The rest of her candlelit apartment was a veritable *hounfort* – known to the uninitiated as a voodoo temple, and an *Obeah* sanctum to those wise in the ways of the old Caribbean.

Mandra's *hounfort* was crammed with *Obeah* images, from the *veve* symbols sprayed on the walls to the *poteau-miton* column, entwined by two life-size snakes, at the centre of the main room. Plaster effigies of *Obeah* gods stood on a candle-crowded altar: Papa Legba, Mama Erzulie, Damballah Ouedo – and Baron Samedi, Lord of Death.

Baron Samedi. She had taken the King of Death as her patron god three months ago, after she uncovered the truth about her mother. And her father. Now she fought in Baron Samedi's name against the Judges of the earth.

Three months ago . . . the truth about her father . . .

She forced the grim recollection aside and her thoughts ranged back further. Deep into the past . . .

Fifteen years. The psycho-cubes. Joel. She often wondered if he survived after escaping the cubes. That song he used to sing . . .

She crooned the lyrics quietly to herself:

'You must remember this,
A kiss is just a kiss,
A Psi is just a Psi . . .'

An audio-com *prip-pripped* at her from a far corner of the room, but she ignored it. No more clients for Madame Dragora. Too risky. Maybe it was time to change identity again.

For no reason she could fathom, the *prip-pripping* reminded her of a recurrent dream. A dream of a black falcon.

prip-prip

A black falcon battling a golden eagle in the sky.

The stuff that dreams are made of.

prip-prip

In the dream, which she forgot almost completely on waking, the falcon was linked with a rumour, a fable of the deep, dark streets. The myth of Anarchopolis.

prip-prip

Musing on the black falcon, she was reminded of a poem Joel had taught her way back in the cubes:

'Turning and turning in the widening gyre
The falcon cannot hear the falconer;
Things fall apart; the centre cannot hold;
Mere anarchy is loosed upon the world . . .'

prip-prip

Joel . . .

'Top of the world, Ma!'

prip-prip

'Hell!' she snorted, springing up and scooting to the audio-com. 'Have to step outside the pentacle just because someone won't stop prip-pripping. Probably want Madame Dragora to tell them if there's any danger of another energy blackout during their favourite Oz soap.'

prip –

She jabbed the ON button and adopted a mystical tone. 'Madame Dragora – Mistress of Mysteries. I'm not in at the moment, but if you'd care to leave a message – '

'Drop the Dragora act, will ya?' a nasal tone retorted. 'I got the cops on my tail, but I'm smart, see? I figure you for a classy dame stuck in the same hole as me. Public Enemy. Get it? Let me in, toots, and we'll give those no-good dirty-rotten cops the run-around. Whadya hear, whadya say?'

She couldn't say anything for a time. She was literally speechless.

Mandra recognised the voice on the audio-com.

It couldn't be the man she thought it was. Impossible. But the impossible had been known to happen from time to time.

'Come on up,' she finally managed to blurt out, pressing the admittance button.

As the elevator started to hum on its long upward journey, Mandra retreated from the door, still struggling with a mixture of dread and astonishment.

Imagination ran riot. She imagined that the elevator cage was rising from an urban Hades, an UnderBlock –

an underground mirror-image of the building she stood in.

The man she'd heard on the audio-com must surely come from Hades.

After all, he had been dead a hundred and forty years.

His memory still lived in the movies he'd starred in: black and white movies from the 1930s and 1940s which ensured his status as the supreme cinematic gangster. He had immortalised the line – *'you dirty rat . . .'* But the man himself was as dead as the twentieth century.

Had Baron Samedi, Lord of Cemeteries, sent him to her?

Still watching the door as the cage mounted to her floor, Mandra sat on the floor.

And awaited the arrival of James Cagney.

CHAPTER SIX

'You let him go!' Judge Dredd bawled into his Lawmaster vid-com.

The captain of the h-wagon quailed on the screen.

'I – I didn't know he was a perp,' Captain Lorenz spluttered. 'Anyway, the Eyes showed his podule just scooped him up and whisked him off. There was so much going on . . .'

'You let Mister Cairo go!' bellowed Dredd, sending echoes flying all over Squid Row.

'Calm down, Joe,' Hershey mumbled.

'We got your arrest order after he left,' Lorenz protested. 'And I reported the sighting straight back to you. How was I supposed to – '

'You're doin' six months' rad-pit duty, creep!' Dredd thundered. 'Keep you nice and warm. Now get off my gruddam screen!'

The screen went blank.

Hershey leaned back in the seat of her Lawmaster. 'Now, perhaps, we can get back to the business in hand. Mandra.' A slight smile brushed her lips. 'The voodoo devil-woman.'

'I want Mister Cairo. He's doin' *time*! He's doin' *twenty*!'

'Mandra first. Cairo second.'

'You watched the Eye replay. Cairo's a Class A maverick Psi runnin' loose and wild! I want that mother-drokker rottin' in the cubes!'

Hershey whistled between her teeth. 'Now listen, Joe. I don't want to pull rank, but Mandra – '

The exchange was terminated by a priority flash on the vid-coms. McGruder grinned from the screens. 'Gotta trace on JC 1. Region of Mary Shelley Block. Could be our lead to Mandra. Want you inside if Mandra's located in the block. Want her *alive*, right?'

'Right,' nodded Hershey as McGruder cut the connection. She turned to Dredd. 'Mandra. Talk of the devil. Any more arguments?'

His scowl was more pronounced than ever, if that were possible. 'What exactly is JC 1?'

'James Cagney.'

'Never heard of him.'

'James Cagney as Tom Powers in a 1931 2-D gangster flik, to be precise. A flik called *The Public Enemy*. Tek were using the flik in a Project Lazarus experiment with hypma – you know, hyperplasma – when Mandra blitzed MAC and Barney. Somehow Cagney escaped from the screen and shot his way out of Justice Hall.'

'Public Enemy,' Dredd said slowly. 'Like Mandra.'

'Yeah – and you know how coincidence and Psi go together.'

Dredd gunned his Lawmaster into action and swerved the bike round. It's forty kays to Mary Shelley Block,' he shouted. 'What're we waiting for?'

Dredd's Lawmaster roared up a storm as it streaked south.

Hershey followed with a silent curse.

Cairo was dead to the world.

But he was making his way back like Lazarus.

At first he received mere impressions. A translucent dome overhead. Streaks of light. A low vibration.

Then he swam up to a hazy level of awareness, bleary eyes roving his surroundings.

Sam.

He was inside Sam.

What had happened?

Then he remembered. He remembered it all. From

64

Lorelei's blood on the wall to Lucinda's blood in the gutter.

Lucinda Lux.

The HED bullet.

The dance of death that played a sorry tune on the heart-strings.

Lucinda. Another story cut short. So many short stories. He'd never get used to it.

He eased up in the seat, wincing at the pain in muscle and joint, and was greeted by Sam's solicitous tones.

'Ah – I see you're up and stirring, sir. I took the opportunity of applying vibro-med while you were out. Several contusions and extensive bruising but no vital damage. I also expunged the abundant blood stains from your raincoat without disturbing the grime which you feel supplies a certain authenticity to your appearance.'

The blood stains. Lucinda's blood.

'Thanks Sam. You're a poem. I thought you'd bought the whole can of beans back there.'

'Strategic withdrawal, sir. Hopped straight back in at the earliest opportunity and operated an emergency scoop.'

'You certainly scooped me right out the gutter.' Cairo rubbed his throbbing head. 'How long was I out?'

'Four minutes and fifty-three seconds.'

'Good going. You brought me round in record time.' He peered through the plastiplex dome, but couldn't distinguish anything through the shimmer of the cloaking field Sam had switched on to hide the vehicle from prying eyes. 'Where are we?'

'Just cruising, sir.'

'Then head straight for the Maze.'

'The Maze!' exclaimed Sam. 'That high-rise, low-down part of town big on trouble and small on pity?'

'Stow the badinage, Sam. I'm not in the mood. The Upside-Down World Turned Downside-Up Diner's in the Maze, and that's where we're going.'

'As you wish, sir. ETA in approximately thirty-four minutes.'

'Only approximately? Are you less than omniscient?'

'You know what the Maze is like. Even I can get lost in there.'

Cairo knew the Maze all too well. The Futurist architect Lloyd Mazny had designed what was intended as a shining example of modernist urban complexes. Complex was the word. Many of the people who moved into its seven hundred and fifty-nine high-rises starved to death searching for a way out of its Gordian knot of looped zoomways, slipways and pedways. The Maze quickly fell into dilapidation and vice. And the architect moved to another planet.

After six wrong turnings on the MC Escher spiral roundabout Sam swerved north-nor'-east from Tagliatelle Tangle to Moebius Strip and the Upside-Down World Turned Downside-Up Diner hoved into sight.

'Stop here, Sam. I'll walk the rest. Go hover somewhere, but keep the cloaking device on.'

Cairo's joints protested as he slid from the podule and felt the hard pedway under his bruised feet. Two hundred metres' walk. He should have parked nearer.

Making his painful way to the diner, he reminded himself of how two of his heroes, Philip Marlowe and Sam Spade, would have reacted to contusions and bruising. Got on with the job, that was how. He ignored the pain and lengthened his stride.

He threw a glance at the block overlooking the diner. Gropius Block. It was constructed in the slab form of the Terminal Brutalist School. Just to look at its expanses of jagged plascrete was enough to make your fillings drop out. There must be around a hundred thousand habholds in Gropius Block. The way life went in the Big City that meant ten thousand hells, twenty thousand purgatories, seventy thousand limbos, and not a heaven to be found.

He tensed as a Gunbird streaked overhead, his packet of illegal drugs burning a hole in his pocket.

When the Gunbird was out of sight and sound he

expelled a soft breath and walked the last twenty metres to the diner.

That's when someone turned the rain on.

Probably the androgynous Chief Judge: 'Hermaphrodite' McGruder.

The Chief Judge frequently countermanded the collective weather votes of the city's four hundred million citizens and turned on the cloud sprinklers. There was less crime in rainy weather. There had been a lot of rain in the crime-ridden months since Judgement Day. The downpours tasted of toxic crud, the flavour of the twenty-second century.

The weather, which should have been left to its own good sense, was Mega-City One's sole concession to democracy. All the world's mega-cities tampered with the weather, resulting in floods, hurricanes and more holes than ozone in the ozone layer.

The rain would be sluicing away all that blood on Squid Row.

Some century you got here.

Flicking a furtive glance at the lenses of the street Eyes, he walked into the Upside-Down World Turned Downside-Up Diner, glad of the snub comfort of the Dillinger inside his raincoat.

The diner was a vegetarian joint, a hang-out for drop-outs and New Space Agers. He didn't have a problem with that. Everyone had their story.

The interior decor was fashionable Hi-Tack. The swirling colours made a lot of noise. He tried not to have a problem with it.

Ignoring the curious stares, he made straight for the toilets. Third cubicle on the right, if he remembered correctly.

Once inside, he faced the wall above the toilet and pulled out the drug packet from his pocket. He had brought it in case he had to do a tour of the smoke-easies in search of Lucia. If he was lucky, he wouldn't have to look any further.

He held up the packet of two-year-stretch drugs in one

hand, and a one-year-stretch lighter in the other. He had bought a pack of Camel cigarettes from an underworld tobacco manufacturer specialising in twentieth-century brands. The tobacco merchants had done a roaring trade since the start of smoking prohibition in the early twenty-first century. Lighting up was only permitted under the giant dome of Mega-City One's Smokatorium, which was a fat lot of use unless you lived next door to the thing. Outside the sanctioned smoking dome, putting lighter to cigarette was a criminal act. Sales went up thirty percent the moment tobacco acquired the glamour of criminality.

That was the beginning of the smoke-easies.

A vid-screen materialised like magic on the toilet wall. The ugly mug of a mesomorph Smoke Enforcer glared from the screen.

'How's the family?' Cairo asked.

'Ask my great-great-great grandmother,' snarled the goon.

'Nobody's that great.'

Passwords exchanged, the vid-screen turned back into a wall and the toilet turned into an elevator, going down.

He stepped round the toilet bowl when the back wall slid up, revealing a world of blue smoke and smudged outlines of tables and patrons. His eyes smarted from the dense clouds as he wove a path to what he remembered as the location of the stage.

He had remembered right. Waving the smoke from his eyes, he stumbled onto a stage-side table and sank into a tobacco-coloured Hug-U chair.

A comedian, name of Denny Leery, was holding the stage. He was number three on the Judges' smoking-criminal list. His ambition was to be number one. Cairo smiled as Leery, smoking through his ears as well as his mouth, rounded off his patter:

'. . . and I'm gonna be smoking when I'm *dead*, man. Ain't no way they're gonna haul my body off to Resyk. You know what comes out when Resyk's finished churning up your guts and bones? *Food*, man. And I ain't just talking dog-meat. I'm talking munce-burgers and all that

68

crud they serve in street-diners. I'm talking Soylent Green
– you hear what I'm saying? Resyk? No way. When I'm
dead I'm gonna be *incinerated*, okay? Incinerated with a
mouthful of cigarettes. And when they fire that coffin it'll
be the Big Light Up. And when they bring my remains in
a jar all my friends'll smoke my ashes. And I'll ascend in
a cloud of smoke and drift round this cruddy Judge world,
gettin' into non-smokers' lungs. When I'm the nicotine
ghost and can't smoke any more then people will be
smokin' *me*, okay?' He grinned a broad grin. 'Be seeing
you – but don't hold your breath.'

As he left for the wings to a burst of applause and
hacking coughs, Leery lifted a hand to Cairo. 'Heard you
were in Brit-Cit, friend.'

'I was,' Cairo replied. 'In Rita Tushingham Block.
Investigating the Case of the Crawling Chair. Case solved,
I came back.'

'Should've stayed there,' Leery said as he disappeared
into the wings. 'You can smoke all over the place in Brit.'

Following Leery's exit, a black lady sashayed on stage.
She had an ocean of a stomach and a string of fat pearls
reaching down to her South Pacific. He recognised her as
Beulah, Queen of the Dark Night of Soul. The *chanteuse*
launched into a post-neo-blues golden-oldie from the
twenty-first century: *My Dead Dog Done Did Me Wrong*:

'Well I woke up this morning –
Found I wasn't in bed.
Well I woke up this morning –
Found I wasn't in bed.
I wasn't in the bedroom.
I was on the roof instead . . .'

It wasn't the stuff pipe-dreams were made of, but her
clogged bassoon of a voice more than made up for the
lyrics. Beulah had a big heart inside her roomy chest, and
she was pouring it all out. He liked her. She looked like
she had a story to tell.

He turned round to observe the customers, but he
could see hardly any through the choking haze. His chest
thought his body was in the fiery pit. God – he hated

visiting smoke-easies, even if it was one more way of giving Justice Hall the finger.

A girl wearing nothing but spike-heeled shoes and an attitude slid down beside him. 'Welcome to Downside-Up smoke-easy. I'm Candy Umpty,' she drawled. 'I smoke – and I'm easy.'

Sure. Right. One out of every dozen eezie-squeezies called herself Candy Umpty, reversing the brand-name of Umpty Candy, a candy whose taste was reputedly so exquisite that it was psychologically addictive and highly illegal. He had tried some of the sugary, sickly stuff once. It tasted like a line from *Love Story*.

'Candy Umpty,' he nodded. 'Right. Call me Ishmael.'

He noticed the yellow stains of nicotine between the girl's forefinger and middle finger. Tobacco junkie. High tar. Probably on more than thirty a day. Poor kid. Didn't get the breaks. He could read her story through the frost of thick make-up. Scoring Umpty Candy at school before she was six. Running with a juve gang by the age of twelve. Parents' eyeballs glued to a vid-screen sixteen hours a day. She broke loose at fourteen or fifteen, looking for freedom. Ended up in the Maze, a burnt-out case in a smoke-easy.

Catching the glare of the Smoke Enforcer, he ripped open the pack of Camels and thrust a cigarette between his lips. To sit in a smoke-easy for more than two minutes without lighting up was asking for trouble.

In the outside world smoking was illegal. Here it was compulsory.

Break that underworld law and you got dragged off to a flame chair and torched to a crisp.

As he searched his pockets for his illegal lighter Candy leaned up close and lit the cigarette for him.

Peering through the swirling smoke, she said, 'Hey, ain't you Mister Cairo?'

'The same.'

'Heard you were in Euro-Cit. On the Case of the Rampant Rhine-maidens.'

'I was. I came back.'

'Whydya call yourself Ishmael?'

'It's a line from Moby Dick.'

She averted her profile. 'I don' like dirty stories.' Then she laughed. 'Thass a joke. Like it?'

'I always have.'

'Wanna score some Downside-Up smokes?' she invited, pressing the pop-up display on the laminate table and indicating the choice. 'We got 'em all – Jolly Jack Rough Tar, Lungbuster Leary's, Cough Up, Lounge Lizard Smooth . . .'

'What I want is to see Big Boy. Is he here?'

Candy sulked and jabbed a blood-red finger-nail to the right of the stage. 'Private office. Howdya know he'd be here? Big Boy's got hunnerds o' joints.'

'I'm psychic,' he smiled as he dropped a tenner bill on the table and blundered through the churning fog, hands doing a blind man's bluff routine as he apologised for the toes he trod on.

Beulah had finished her song.

'Any requests?' she husked in a voice like a million stub-ends.

'Yeah,' he called out. '*Smoke Gets In Your Eyes*.'

The soulful refrain dogged him to a door marked PRIVATE, which led to a slightly misty corridor and a door marked STRICTLY PRIVATE. He walked right in without knocking. Big Boy never did quite know how to handle bravado.

The man himself was plumped in a large chair behind a huge table covered in cream cakes. Big Boy was not fat enough to rival a sumo. But he tried. The middle-aged gangster still dressed as a Brit schoolboy from the early twentieth century, from his little cap to his short grey trousers. The badge said Eton High. Big Boy had class. At least that's what he told everyone. Everyone who could follow his ghastly pseudo-Brit lingo, that is.

'Cripes, Cairo,' the gangster snorted, pointing at a NO SMOKING sign. 'Can't yah gruddam-well read, yah bounder?'

Big Boy didn't smoke. He just made a living out of it. The same went for the heavy drugs.

Cairo flicked the cigarette into a suck-tube. 'Sorry. I'll write out a hundred lines in prep.'

Big Boy's eyebrows shot up. 'Dat some kinda joshing, yah rotter? I ain't stonking well dyin' o' chortling, Mistuh Cairo.'

'Really? You're killing me.'

'Any more o' yer lip and I'll get my chums to boogie-woogie on yah bones.'

Give the gangster half a chance and he would carry on like this come dawn. Cairo didn't have the time. 'You left a message for me. The messenger's dead, if you're interested.'

'I'm not.'

'Choke on a cream cake, Big Boy. I'll keep it simple so your brain won't overheat. Lucia Lux gets snatched from Happy House by persons unknown, by means unknown. Lorelei is sliced into chunks in seconds and her blood's used as ink for writing on the wall. The intruders leave an inverted Tarot card of the World. The World turned upside down. You sent Toots Ritzy with a message to Lucinda Lux, expecting me to contact her. And here you are under the Upside-Down World etcetera Diner. All the signs point to you. Weird thing is, you must have put those signs there yourself. You giving me the run-around?'

Big Boy stroked his blubbery lip. 'Some big honcho could be, old bean. Run-around as in round and round.'

Cairo tilted an eyebrow. 'As in "What turns and turns again"?'

'Just so.' Bulbous lips stretched wide. A cream cake went the way of all pastry. 'I'm a messenger too. Well-paid messenger. Hearken to duh message, ol' sausage – "What goes around, comes around. Turning and turning . . ."'

Whether it was a logical progression from Big Boy's sawn-off sentence, or the Wild in him supplying a Psi insight, Mister Cairo saw clearly where all this was leading.

'I hear you, Big Boy. What comes around – the Second Coming. Yeats wrote a poem by that name. It started – "Turning and turning in the widening gyre/The falcon cannot hear the falconer".'

Another cream cake was engulfed. 'Duh man said you'd catch on fast.'

'What man?'

'Duh *Man*. Piano Smile. If you guessed right I was to tell ya where to find Lucia Lux. Casablanca.'

At the mention of Casablanca, Cairo mentally recited the next two lines of the *Second Coming*.

Things fall apart; the centre cannot hold;
Mere anarchy is loosed upon the world . . .

Those lines took him back fifteen years to an underground smoke-easy cinema called the Casablanca. The 2-D monochrome movie – *The Maltese Falcon*.

Fifteen years ago . . .

Judge Dredd blasted into the smoke-easy cinema on his Beast of the Streets.

'I AM THE LAW!'

That was when the Wild in Cairo first burst loose.

And he remembered.

Everything.

That was when bright blood splashed the black and white movie.

And the movie screen came alive.

Then a youth called the Preacher declaimed the first four lines of the *Second Coming* before he disappeared.

And the *way* he disappeared . . .

When the cinematic phantasmagoria was all over, Dredd hauled Cairo off to the juve-cubes.

He had entered the Casablanca that night as a boy called Joel.

He left as Mister Cairo.

'You in some kinda rum dream world, Mistuh Cairo? Gotta last message from the Man. Wanna hear it?'

Cairo tried to shake loose of the past, but Bogart's

73

voice pursued him, repeating the last line from *The Maltese Falcon*, the Shakespearian misquote that summed up the black-painted falcon statuette:

'*The stuff that dreams are made of.*'

He silenced the inner voice. 'Go ahead. The sooner we're finished, the sooner I'm out of here.'

Big Boy downed another cream cake, then took out two Tarot cards from the pocket of his short trousers and placed them on the table. One was the World, right way up. The other was the Wheel of Fortune.

Lips pursed, the gangster concentrated on the cards. 'Now lemme see – I was told to move duh cards as I repeated duh words – duh *exact* words.' A stubby finger rotated the Wheel of Fortune, then swivelled the World to an inverted position. 'The world turns – ' he intoned. Another swivel of the World card back to right way up. ' – and turns again. The underworld becomes the overworld.'

The instant he completed the chant, Big Boy froze, mouth agape.

And one of the cream cakes started talking in a throaty baritone:

'A little under four hours to find Miss Lucia Lux, Mister Cairo. Mister Big Boy, however, has a little less than three minutes before he breathes his last. Tough world.'

Cairo recognised the rough-edged voice of Piano Smile in the articulate pastry. Must be a micro-com embedded in the cream cake.

Big joke.

Piano Smile was Big Boy's Overboss. One of the Big Three. The word in the Pits was that Big Boy had been short-changing Piano Smile on the drug-take. Whatever – Big Boy was heading for the Big Goodnight.

The door at Cairo's back slammed open and a rush of dark air almost threw him off his feet.

'The last message contained a fancy code that made stiff spaghetti of Big Boy's central nervous system and also activated a – smoke signal,' the pastry informed as a cloudy tentacle of tobacco smoke swept into the room from the corridor leading to the smoke-easy.

The churning cigarette smoke poured into Big Boy's gaping mouth. And poured. And poured.

'I thought of finishing him off by a surfeit of cream cakes,' Piano Smile went on. 'But a death like that, it lacks – kinda – style. Big Boy's inhaling his smoke-easy clean as a baby's lung. Sweet, huh? I'll see you in what they used to call a Dream Palace. You know which one, Cairo. Ciao.'

The smoke had mounted to a tar-tanged wind that shook the NO SMOKING sign. It stormed down the corridor and whooshed into the gangster's wide open mouth. Down into his hitherto smoke-free lungs.

The broad chest started to swell.

Lungs fit to burst.

Mister Cairo didn't stay to watch. Hand cupped over mouth and nose, he bent his head and ploughed into the smoky gale, squinting his eyes as he beat a path into the smoke-easy.

The smoking den was visible from wall to wall for the first time in years. The cowering customers blinked in the unaccustomed light as the last wisps of blue smoke fled down the passage to the STRICTLY PRIVATE room.

The messy *schlup* of a squelchy explosion sounded from the room at the end of the passage. Big Boy had been smoked to death.

As Mister Cairo quitted the smoke-free smoke-easy, Beulah, oblivious to all but her song, was throbbing out the concluding lyrics of *Smoke Gets in Your Eyes*.

The private eye had neither eyes nor ears for the singer. His thoughts were on the Casablanca, and the stuff that dreams are made of.

Some dreams are called nightmares.

CHAPTER SEVEN

The Lawmasters streaked at 550 kph along the megway into Sector 42, location of Mary Shelley Block.

Civilian traffic swerved out of their path, frequently crashing in the panic to stay clear of the dreaded Beasts of the Streets.

Dredd kept ahead of Hershey all the way.

'*As usual*,' she reflected wryly.

A glance at the bike's vid read-out showed ETA in five minutes and twenty seconds.

The JC 1 trace had just been confirmed. James Cagney was in Mary Shelley Block. Tek Division gave an eighty-eight per cent chance that Cagney would be drawn to Mandra. Something to do with the nature of hypma. And with Project Lazarus. She didn't like the smell of Tek's ultra-security project, but what the hell. Hershey obeyed orders, even when they stank.

McGruder wanted to make an example of the renegade. But Hershey was determined to bring Mandra in alive for her own reasons. Like Joe Dredd, she wanted to discover why the ex-Judge had sabotaged the computers.

Looking ahead at the speeding figure of Joe Dredd, she wondered what he thought of the mission. Had Mandra's one-woman rebellion reminded him of Cassandra Anderson's earlier revolt? Was he thinking of Cassandra now, on this Mandra hunt? Dredd and Cassandra had shared so many battles in the past. They were the two who had defeated the Judge Child mutant and Judge Death. If anyone had come close to Dredd, it was Cassandra. What would show if he took off his helmet and revealed that permanently hidden face? Anger at Cassandra's rule-bending and Mandra's law-breaking? Confusion?

Grief?

Perhaps that was why he kept his face locked away from the world's sight. His features might give away what his voice never betrayed.

One thing was sure. Dredd would not flinch from carrying out the Law. When the Judge caught up with Mandra – and he would – she was as good as on the Med slab with a laser making mush of her brain.

Another h-wagon swished overhead, bound for Mary Shelley Block.

Hershey fixed her eyes on Judge Dredd's broad back.

'We're coming for you, Mandra,' she whispered to the racing wind. 'And we're bringin' you back. Alive and kicking.'

Hershey would do it. Sure she would. But she wasn't obliged to feel good about it.

She might have asked Grud for forgiveness. But the God of Judgement and Retribution was not acquainted with the word.

No forgiveness. No mercy. No pity.

She glanced at the ETA readout.

'You've got five minutes, Mandra.'

An apprehensive Mandra sat crossed-legged on the floor as the elevator clicked to a halt outside.

Just moments remaining before the elevator door slid open and James Cagney walked through the door to her room. James Cagney, king of the celluloid gangsters. Cinematic Public Enemy Number One.

She shook her head. No – it wasn't happening. Couldn't be.

The door whispered open and James Cagney walked in.

Yeah – it was happening.

In imagination, she could hear him say that immortal line: '*You dirty rat.*'

James Cagney was straight from a black-and-white

movie. From snap-brimmed hat to leather shoe, he was a solid silver screen character in black and white and all the shades of grey.

Everything about the glowing monochrome gangster was essential Cagney, almost to the point of caricature. Legs planted wide in a cocky stance, he jerked back his shoulders and twitched his dangling hands as if ready to land a punch or reach for a gun.

He was drenched, as though standing in an invisible downpour, silvery rain from nowhere streaming down his fedora and double-breasted suit. But where the raindrops hit the floor, they vanished. Just one more curiosity to add to the list.

One more puzzle she couldn't solve.

Then it clicked. He was the living image of Cagney playing Tom Powers in a climactic scene from *The Public Enemy*, the episode where he advanced through a rainstorm to avenge his partner's death.

The man in front of her had emerged from a rainy movie scene and brought the rain with him.

Cagney's mouth split into an impish grin. 'Hey, toots, you're one swell-looking dish. That black suit you're wearing – didya pull it on or *spray* it on? Another time, another place, we could play a hot tune. But the cops are heading this way, see? We gotta get outa the joint.'

She rose slowly to her feet. Now she viewed him at eye-level, he was not as short as he came across on the movies; barely an inch below her own five-feet-nine. 'James Cagney – I still don't believe it.'

He brushed a knuckle over his chin. 'Well – it's kinda complicated, babe. I'm Tom Powers, Public Enemy. But I'm no dumb bozo. I know I'm Cagney, too. Some sorta hypma creation encoded with virtual memories and a personality matrix an' all that twenty-second-century baloney, but let's stow all that. We ain't got the time for no Tek-talk. You got an old ouija board, doll?'

'Er – I've got one, yeah. About twenty years old,' she mumbled.

'Aw – that ain't old. Ouija boards are like classy wine,

they need heaps o' time to soak in all the right kinda hocus-pocus.'

'The table's late twentieth century. Any use?'

He gave a uniquely Cagney shrug that jerked his muscles from shoulders to fingers, then dropped into a chair. He didn't sit or sink or descend, he *dropped*. 'Hell, it'll have to do. Put your hands on the table. Like mine. See? And think of Peter Lorre.'

None of what was occurring made any sense, which was as good a reason as any to go along with it and ask questions later. 'Any particular Peter Lorre movie? *M*? *The Maltese Falcon*? *The Mask of Dimitrios*? *Casablanca*?'

'*The Beast with Five Fingers*,' he snapped. 'Get with it, doll. We got one minute, tops, before the goon squad hits the joint. Now concentrate – Peter's real sharp with the mystic moonshine, like all this voodoo-hoodoo you got here. He'll give us the low-down on who's pulling a stunt on us.'

Mandra concentrated, visualising the middle-aged Peter Lorre of *The Beast with Five Fingers*. The bugging eyes peering owlishly from wire-framed spectacles. The idiosyncratic Middle European accent.

Cagney's hands, still streaming with rain, suddenly distilled a silvery radiance to the polished oak. 'Hyperplasma extrusion,' he confided out the corner of his mouth. 'Got a little to spare.'

A circular patch of table shimmered. The wood trembled like rippled water.

And from the silvery pool rose Peter Lorre's head, wire-framed spectacles and all. The ascent stopped at the neck.

He bent a shy, hesitant smile at Mandra. His voice was equally shy and hesitant, underscored with a mournful tone:

'It eez a pleasure to meeet you, Meez Maahhndra.'

'Never mind about the broad, Pete,' Cagney complained. 'Whadya know about this Anarchopolis set-up? Is it on the level?'

Peter Lorre only had bug-eyes for Mandra. 'I haf

admired you from afar, oh yeez. You are well named, oh yeez. Your future eez spelled owt in your full naame – Maahhndragorrra. Maahhndragorrra – the maahndrake root. Are you fameeliar with the Elizabeeethan poet John Donne?'

She nodded, way ahead of him. ' "Go, and catch a falling star/Get with child a mandrake root/Tell me, where all past years are/Or who clove the Devil's foot".' A frown sliced her brow. 'But my name's Mandra, plain and simple. It's not short for Mandragora. I wasn't named after the mandrake root.'

'Ah, but you were. By your mother. She was a *mambo*, and she named you after the maahndrake. The root of the weeetches. Small doses of maahhndragora breeng euphorrria. Laarge doses – maadness and deeaath . . .'

'Hey – guy,' cut in Cagney. 'Save the botanical lesson. Tell me about the Anarch – he a stand-up guy or what?'

Lorre carried on, oblivious to the gangster.

'You are the poison een the Body Judiciary, Meez Maahhndra. Eet's all in a naame . . .'

Mandra's scalp prickled. Her fate was spelled out in her name. She was Mandragora, the Witch Root.

'Gimme a break, will ya?' groaned Cagney. 'Tell me somethin', ya mug!'

But Lorre was already sinking back into a rapidly shrinking silver pool.

'Top of the world, Ma . . .' intoned the fading voice of Lorre.

Cagney twitched a begrudging smile. 'Pretty neat line. Ma – short for Mandra. Wish I'd come out with it.'

'You weeell, Cagney, you weeell,' Lorre faintly echoed as he sank out of sight. The pool dwindled to nothing.

'Ah – ya mug,' the gangster complained, but with an affectionate undertone. 'Didn't give with the goods on Anarchopolis. Now we'll have to sniff out a Crack with the cops hot on our trail.'

He sprang up and whisked out a pair of .38 revolvers from his pockets. 'Get your tush movin', Ma. This joint's gettin' hotter than the electric chair.'

His sense of urgency was enough to convince her. 'Give me just twenty seconds.'

'I'm counting.'

It took her twenty-two seconds, but Cagney didn't grumble. Instead he whistled appreciatively at the mid-thigh length flared-top purple boots and purple gun belt, packed with Gotterdammerung ammo.

'You look like mortal sin on censored legs, babe. Let's go take on this no-good dirty-rotten cop world!'

'You know something, Cagney?' she said as she stepped into the elevator and pressed for ground floor.

'What's that, toots?' He swayed with the rapid descent of the express elevator.

'I like you.'

'Hey – gimme a break, will ya, Ma? I gotta reputation to live down to.' Despite the retort there was an extra touch of cockiness to the characteristic Cagney shoulder-roll.

He studied her shrewdly as the floors sped by. 'You got hypma in ya somewhere. I can tell. Hypma had a lot to do with bringing us together.'

Mandra didn't have time to probe him on the mysterious hyperplasma link, so simply nodded. 'A tiny hypma particle in my tooth, encoded to blow my head off with a spoken trigger code.'

As the ground floor and possible threat came near, the activation code circled round in her head like murderers dancing in a ring:

Here comes a candle to light you to bed.

Here comes a chopper to chop off your head . . .

'Never let them take you alive, huh?' Cagney said approvingly. 'You're a real class act, honey.'

The thirtieth floor whizzed past. Fifteen seconds and they would hit ground floor. Half a minute from now they would be out of the block. After that –

'Have you got a hide-out somewhere?' she asked.

'Well – kinda. I reckon there's a Crack somewhere near.'

'Not sure I understand.'

'A Crack to take us down below.'

'To where?'

'Anarchopolis.'

Mandra digested the news. Anarchopolis. The street myth. The slum fable.

What did Cagney know? Come to that, who *was* this black-and-white apparition streaming with rain from nowhere?

'You're not the original James Cagney, the Brooklyn actor born in 1904,' she said. 'And you're more than a solid-state hologram. Just what are you?'

He gave an 'I'm just a wicked little boy' smile and paused before answering. His tone, for the first time, was quiet and enigmatic:

'I'm the Public's Dream from the Dream Palaces. The Public Enemy they hate to love.'

The elevator shushed to a stop.

A panel displayed GR UND EVEL in dithery characters.

'Let's go, kid,' Cagney winked, stepping out into the huge foyer with Mandra at his heels.

The elevator cage exploded, flinging them flat on the floor.

Coughing and spluttering, they were back on their feet and peering through the billowing smoke pouring from the black, blistered mouth of the elevator.

'Grenade,' Mandra gasped. 'A *Judge's* grenade.'

Dredd's bellow seemed to part the curtains of billowing smoke, revealing the black uniforms of Judges ranged around the hall.

'We got you cold, creeps! Surrender or try crawlin' out without arms 'n' legs!'

There were dozens of the bastards, each with a Lawgiver trained on their quarry. Dozens.

The clearing smoke unveiled each detail of Judge Dredd's grim figure, black as death. Dredd's Lawgiver was aimed straight at her legs. The slightest pressure on the trigger would blow her limbs clean away.

She was done for.

End of the line.

Dredd's downturned mouth twisted into a snarl.

'Don't expect any slop about old time's sake from me, Mandra. The only difference between you and stomm on the floor is that I'm gonna *tread* on you.'

Mandra's head sank.

Judgement had tracked her down, and that was the end of it.

She hadn't a prayer.

A helmet and a bellowing mouth.

That image from way back hit Mister Cairo smack in the eyes and teeth as he slipped out of Sam and stood under the five-hundred-storey cone of Ozymandias Block. The block looked like it suffered from carbuncles.

It was a fitting centre-piece for the district known as Big Joke, birthplace of more gangsters than anywhere else in the city.

Mister Cairo was one of those born in Big Joke.

'You appear somewhat forlorn and palely loitering, sir,' observed Sam.

Sam was doing his best to raise Cairo's spirits, but this was not the time or the place.

This was the entrance to the underworld where it had begun, all that time past. Fifteen years ago, that mayhem night in the cinema.

The night he became Mister Cairo.

The path to that underworld was bad enough. It was populated with bad memories – and perhaps more than memories. If the circuitous front entrance wasn't thronged with Eyes he would have chosen the long way round instead. But he couldn't risk attracting Justice attention. Keep your head low.

'Find somewhere to hide yourself, Sam,' he said. 'Stay on fastcall. I might need you in a hurry.'

'May I point out that you stole me from the gentleman you're about to meet? If he's aware that you're the thief it may not go well with you, to put it mildly.'

'Don't worry, Sam. Piano Smile hasn't a clue it was me. Go on, hover off.'

Sam whispered away and left Cairo confronting the subterranean car park under Ozymandias Block.

This was the old haunt of the UnderJudges, aka the Egyptians. They were the silent terror of the district. Gangs were a familiar affliction of the Big City, especially in Big Joke. Marauding bands of psychopaths were the equivalent of flu to Big Joke's inhabitants. Just a part of life's little trials.

But the UnderJudges were special. The UnderJudges belonged to that hinterland between the everyday world of guns and knives and that hushed, night world of the supernatural, be it ever so dark. No one knew where they came from. Not a soul dared find out.

People just – disappeared, from time to time.

It was fear of those stealthy night walkers that kept the eyes of Justice from the Casablanca. In those days, this back entrance was the only access to the illegal cinema, and fear came in handy. More handy than any number of secret passages and passwords.

Cairo recalled how as a juve he had often walked what seemed the longest of walks through the underground park to the Casablanca, jumping at every flicker of a shadow. Each time he'd thought – *it's the Egyptians . . . it's the Egyptians . . .*

The longer he stared into the UnderBlock dark, the more the dark seemed to stare back.

He reached into an inner pocket and touched the metallic comfort of the one-off Dillinger pistol. The Dillinger was in a class of its own, custom-made by Arbuckle, the subversive toilet janitor, a man in a class of his own. The sights and balance of the weapon were perfected by Blue Angel, the gun-toting hooker. Just one of many gifts from the couple who had been Cairo's surrogate parents. With seventeen different modes, each packed with ammo and gadgets ranging from standard to balloon bullets and hyperblast, the Dillinger made the Lawgiver look like a pea-shooter. There were more powerful machine-pistols in the Big City – the Gotterdammerung, the Overkill – but none more versatile.

The Dillinger should make short work of childhood fears.

Besides, his trench-coat was a virtual armoury. It held thirty pockets, most of them secret, containing everything from a Lawmaster By-pass disk for stealing Judges' bikes to a Biased Bomb for getting out of very serious trouble.

It was not a raw youth called Joel who was returning to the Casablanca.

It was Mister Cairo, heavily armed and downright dangerous.

If he met the Egyptians, they wouldn't stand a chance.

'Keep telling yourself that,' he whispered, 'and you might start believing it.'

He began walking, and heard the acoustics throw his footfalls back at him as he dipped under the park entrance. He counted sixty steps, then veered left. A hint of orange light dawned, the start of the passage to Grav-Chute 6 and a straight drop to the maintenance level. From there, he could trace the tortuous path through magneto-coil mazes to the secret door leading down to the Casablanca.

The Casablanca. Almost fifteen years ago . . .

A helmet and a mouth.

A mouth like an open mantrap.

A crack of command snaps out of the ring of teeth.

'I AM THE LAW!'

He shook off the stark memory. He had to keep his brain on red alert in the coming hour. Piano Smile was waiting for him down in the Dream Palace, and the Overboss never went anywhere without a small zoo of bodyguards with muscles growing out of their brains.

But it was the choice of rendezvous that troubled Cairo most. Why this disused cinema, of all the places in the Big City? The Overboss was making a point. A sharp point. Sharp as a razor.

Piano Smile . . .

He could picture that sonofabitch Overboss waiting

down there in a Palace of Dreams. Could see him shove a Havana between those rows of teeth with each alternate ivory extracted. Could hear the chuckle as the gangster smiled his black-white-black-white keyboard smile, like a grinning piano smoking a cigar.

'I'm coming, Piano Smile.'

Approaching the orange glow of the passage entrance, he experienced the onset of fear, despite packing the Dillinger and a trench-coat full of armaments.

The terrors of childhood returned in full force.

It's the Egyptians . . . it's the Egyptians . . .

He could go back. Run. Take the long way round, Eyes or no Eyes.

The reluctance was so fleeting he didn't even break step in mid-stride as he entered the door.

If this damned mystery trail he followed was something more than a game played by Piano Smile, then Lucia had to be down there. In the Casablanca. He wouldn't leave her in that place a second longer than he had to.

You're a private eye. Do the job. Don't count the cost.

The overhead lamps at the far end of the long corridor were out, leaving half the passage in darkness. Nothing much had changed in Big Joke district. Mechanical breakdowns were a way of life.

He passed a plethora of scrawls, painted in Hi-Glo-treated blood. Only one was worth a second glance:

MAKE MEGA-CITY ONE A HAPPIER PLACE – KILL YOURSELF

Several paces more and the Hi-Glo blood messages came to an end. That was because fresh scrawls had been sand-blasted into the plascrete.

Sand-blasting messages on walls was a speciality of the Egyptian UnderJudges.

His feet slowed as he read the jagged scrawls, and the prospect of the dark at the end of the corridor almost drew him to a halt. A pack of horrors could easily secrete itself in that murk.

The writing on the wall told him more than he wanted to know about the UnderJudges:

TO THE CURSED WHOSE CRIMES ARE FEW . . .
WE WILL BITE OUT THE TONGUE FROM YOUR MOUTH
WE WILL SCOURGE YOU WITH THE SANDS OF SET
WE WILL STING YOU WITH THE SNAP OF THE SCORPION
WE WILL DELIVER YOUR BONES TO THE JAWS OF THE
   DEVOURER
   TO THE BLESSED WHOSE CRIMES ARE NUMEROUS . . .
WE WILL DRAW OUT THE MOISTURE OF YOUR BREATH
WE WILL BLEED YOU WHITE AS THE MOON
WE WILL FILL YOU FULL WITH BLACK BLOOD
WE WILL ENFOLD YOU IN ANCIENT WRAPPINGS
AND YOU WILL WALK WITH US IN THE CITY OF NIGHT

The creed was the converse face of the Judges' Law.
The Egyptians punished the innocent and rewarded the
guilty. Weighing punishment and reward, Cairo couldn't
decide which was worse.

Underneath the sand-blasted outline of a sphinx was a
solitary juve scrawl in Hi-Glo:

THE SFINKS STINKS, DUDE

That was Mega-City One's educational system for you.

He pulled out the Dillinger and warily eyed the dark
ahead. Legend had it that a bullet could not kill an
UnderJudge. He hoped he wouldn't have to put that to
the test.

Vision becoming accustomed to the murk, he advanced
a step, gun aimed level from a straight arm.

A few stealthy steps further and he realised that there
were no Egyptians waiting for him.

The shadows ahead were clear of enemies.

That was because they had crept up behind him.

A soft hiss like a breath on dry papyrus made him spin
round.

The illuminated stretch of passage was filling up with
helmet-crowned UnderJudges. They were rustling out of
a flexing fold in the ground that sure as hell wasn't there
before.

Looked like Hallowe'en had come two days early.

In all his boyhood years he had not once caught sight

of the Egyptians. Why tonight? he wanted to yell. What's so bloody special about tonight?

Like a Hallowe'en reunion of ancient Egyptian rulers, the mummy-wrapped, Pharaoh-helmeted UnderJudges shuffled down the corridor, the crook and flail of kingship in left and right hands of crossed arms.

Incongruously, they bore massive twin cylinders on their backs with tubing connected to the crooks. When he noticed the nozzles in the crooks' curled nub-ends it struck him what the cylinders contained, and struck him hard. The shambling mummies had sand-cylinders slung over their shoulders. The crooks were sand-blasters, with ample force to rip his flesh to scarlet ribbons.

We will scourge you with the sands of Set.

The flails fizzed and crackled like static, and he knew, he just knew, their sting was lethal.

We will sting you with the snap of the scorpion.

They were advancing slowly, just like mummies in the movies.

The thought made him smile. Slow, lumbering mummies. The old cliché. He could *crawl* faster than they could walk. He turned round to head for the grav-chute door.

Oh great.

A score of UnderJudges stood between him and the door. And more were rising from a fresh, fleshy aperture in the floor.

He was surrounded by the terrors of his childhood. The stalkers with white skin and black blood.

The nearest UnderJudge, marked out from the rest by the Eye of Ra painted on his visor, raised the whitest of white hands.

His voice was like starched paper rubbed on rough concrete. 'I, Osiris, accuse you of the Five Great Omissions, Mister Cairo.'

Cairo's eyes narrowed. They knew his name. Someone had told them his name.

Piano Smile.

The Overboss had put a word in their ears.

Another damn set-up.

His mind raced as Osiris went through the charges:

'You have not stolen from the poor, Mister Cairo,' accused Osiris, decayed molars on full display, eyes hidden under the visored Pharaoh helmet. 'You have not committed murder for gain. You have not betrayed your friends. You have not slandered the blameless. You have not purloined the cakes of the gods.'

Purloined the cakes of the gods? Cairo let that one skip.

He levelled his Dillinger at Osiris's visor. 'I don't want to shoot, but I will if I have to. After all, you *are* Judges – of a kind.'

There were thirty standard slugs in his Dillinger. Enough to drop more than half of the UnderJudges. He tried not to think of the legend that bullets had no effect on them.

'He stands accused out of his own mouth,' Osiris declared. 'He admits a reluctance to kill. Let the punishment begin with the severing of his tongue.'

They lumbered straight at him, and they lumbered *fast*, arms outstretched and mouths agape.

Taken by surprise, he only got off six shots before they were on him. The shots didn't seem to do much good. The mummies just leaked a little black ink.

Weight of numbers bore him to the floor, pinioned his arms.

'I will bite off your tongue,' whispered the dry crackle of Osiris.

'Get fuhgged,' he spluttered, cheeks puffing as parchment fingers crammed his mouth.

Two hands thrust between his teeth. One yanked down as the other pulled up, wrenching his jaws apart.

Osiris's visored face filled his swimming vision. The barbed-tooth oval of Osiris's mouth held Cairo's gaze. He wasn't even distracted by the pliers heading for his tongue.

'*I will bite off your* . . .'

Cairo slammed down his teeth on the ten brittle fingers.

Two fingerless hands sprang back to a chorus of wails. He spat a mouthful of fingers straight in Osiris's face. One landed in the Egyptian's mouth and lay there curled, as if inviting him in.

CHAPTER EIGHT

The entire foyer of Mary Shelley Block was walled with sculptures: moulded plasteen images that told the gothic tale of Frankenstein.

The black shape of Dredd stood close to one wall, framed by a sculpture of the Creature rising from a bubbling vat.

'I haven't a prayer,' Mandra whispered under her breath, eyeing the death-end of Dredd's Lawgiver.

'Prayin's for Confession, doll, and Father O'Brian ain't around.' The words spat like a pistol volley from the corner of Cagney's contemptuous twist of a mouth. Finger and thumb snapped the brim of his hat. Shoulders performed a forward roll. Arms poised, hands dangling, he squared up to Dredd.

'You dirty rat – ' Cagney sneered, ' – talking tough to a dame with a fancy heater in your mitt and a squad of bullet-heads at your back. Real hard guy, huh? Try me on for size, yah dumb cop.'

'I'm outsize trouble for you, *runt*,' growled Dredd. In the millisecond that his Lawgiver shifted fractionally from Mandra to Cagney a pair of revolvers appeared in the gangster's hands.

Mandra didn't have time to blink at the sudden apparition of the guns. One instant Cagney's hands were empty. The next they were full and firing.

Judge Dredd took a slug in the chest that rocked him on his heels. A second bullet, on the tail of the first, blasted the Lawgiver from the Judge's grip. An involuntary burst of hi-ex bullets slammed into the moulded ceiling, dislodging a chunk of masonry.

Hershey's weapon spun into the air as her gun-arm took a hit. Her Lawgiver could not have completed two spins when three other Judges were blown off their feet by three shots so rapid they merged into a single thunder-clap from the greased magic on lightning-wheels that was James Cagney.

Mandra was no slouch on the draw, and her brain had signalled her hand to reach for the firepower of her Gotterdammerung machine-pistol as Dredd reached the 't' of '*runt*', but Cagney had loosed off six slugs and her fingers were still inches from the rifle in what by any normal standards would be counted the fastest of draws.

He was still blasting away at the Judges when she whisked the Gotterdammerung free of its magno-holster and hit the deck, firing off a round as she dropped.

Be with me, Baron Samedi, Lord of the Dead.

She sent two Judges to Baron Samedi in a thousand flying pieces before her chest thumped the floor.

Cagney's pumping revolver unleashed a continuous volley of thunder and death. Judges dropped like unstrung marionettes, cords of life severed in a hail of revolver shots.

Mandra finally realised that Cagney had caught some of the bullets. He bled the dark grey blood of the silver screen from a dozen wounds. And didn't bat an eyelid.

'You'll never take me alive, coppers,' he snarled, downing another couple of lawmen. 'You'll never take me *dead* either. You can't kill the stuff that dreams are made of.'

A hubbub from the foyer entrance betrayed the arrival of more Helmets. A dozen Blitzen grenades were lobbed in to cover their advance. Not the cleverest manoeuvre she had ever witnessed.

Hershey grabbed her Lawgiver with her left hand and the wounded Dredd stretched for his gun as twelve Blitzen explosions knocked them flat.

Mandra sailed backwards to land with a thud on her

back, instantly rolling sideways to avoid a plunging effigy of Baron Victor Frankenstein blown loose from the plasteen ceiling. Frankenstein made a fair dent in the floor.

Coughing and spluttering, she sprang to her feet, barely able to distinguish Cagney through the smoke, flame and general chaos. The gangster was still blasting Judges to Grud from his apparently inexhaustible .38 revolvers.

Cagney could take care of himself. But he could not take care of her – not with all these bombs and bullets flying about. She had to take care of herself.

She glanced up at the damaged ceiling. More than ninety per cent of the ceiling-sculptures were intact, despite the hi-ex and Blitzen grenades. A score of scenes from Frankenstein were virtually unaffected by the mayhem beneath.

But the moulded ceiling hadn't taken a faceful of her micro-missile yet. Her Gotterdammerung was side-loaded with two *Fenris* missiles, each no longer than a finger.

The Fenris was named after the world-wolf of Norse mythology. It lived up to its name.

One should be enough to bring the house down.

She pressed the machine-pistol for Fenris mode. Then shut her eyes tight as a pull on the trigger launched one of the missiles straight at the ceiling above Dredd and Hershey's heads. The recoil slammed Mandra to the floor.

When the Fenris impacted it was as if the eye of the sun had blinked in the foyer. And then dropped its wrath on the heads of those below.

The ceiling came down and joined the floor.

A deluge of Frankensteins and Creatures descended.

Dredd, Lawgiver back in gauntleted hand, its muzzle swinging towards Mandra, was directly underneath one of the falling sculptures. A plunging effigy of the Creature.

The plasteen Frankenstein's monster plummeted upside down.

The monster's head met the dome of Dredd's helmet. The helmet cracked like an eggshell.

Dredd toppled like a felled ox.

93

Smoke and confusion reigned supreme. Mandra, who had narrowly missed being squashed flat by both Frankenstein and his Creature, crawled over the debris in search of Hershey.

Somewhere, in the swirling folds of grey smoke and dust, Cagney was still firing.

After a brief, blind search, her questing fingers found Hershey's dust-plastered face. She was alive – probably just stunned. Mandra was glad of that. Hershey was okay – as Judges went. They had been friends once. Although Hershey wouldn't thank her for what she was about to do.

'Whyda hear, whadya say?' said a voice in her ear. She hadn't heard Cagney's approach.

'Find something to stow my gear in, will you?' she asked, extracting a small spray-cylinder from her belt. Directing the nozzle to and fro, she sprayed it over her sleather suit. The ultra-fine skin dissolved on contact. In ten seconds all she was wearing was boots and belt.

'You were right,' she said, meeting Cagney's impish smile head-on. 'I did spray this suit on. It sprays right off, too. Now go and find a bag or something for my gear before the Devil's cavalry arrives, will you?'

'You got it, toots,' he winked, disappearing into the roiling murk.

'And make it fast,' she muttered, unbuckling the belt and kicking off the boots. Pulling a multi-shade spray from the belt, she sprayed *veve* symbols on her body, alternating the colour with a slight shift in pressure on the nozzle. As bright symbols of Papa Legba, Baron Samedi, Mama Erzulie and Damballah Ouedo snaked over her skin, she attuned her mind to the myth-pool of *Obeah*, the way of voodoo.

Naked, she swayed from side to side, head lolling, deep in a trance, The Voodoo Girl from finger-nail to toe-nail.

She chanted low and slow:

'Papa Legba, guardian of the gate, open that I may salute the *loa* and beg their aid. Turn the key, Papa Legba.'

She felt the gate opening. Sensed the *loa*, the spirits of the old Caribbean, walk barefoot down the ancient mountain trails in their top hats and tattered frock-coats.

Then, in a long moment out of time, they whispered in her ears and worked their magic.

She emerged from the trance with a shudder.

Then choked as Hershey's powerful fingers closed on her windpipe.

As the pressure tightened, she saw black stars dancing.

Then the strangle-hold pulled her down into a black hole.

She thought she heard a faint voice from a distant place:

'*You ain't got a prayer.*'

The severed finger inside the UnderJudge's mouth seemed to beckon Cairo to follow it within.

Cairo had no intention of accepting the invitation.

The other nine fingers he had bitten off spilled over his shoulders, their stump-handed owners screeching. Black blood spouted from the mutilated knuckles.

But a crush of Egyptian UnderJudges still held him down, sand-blasting crooks and electric flails in their grip.

Where was his bloody gun? Must have dropped it when the Egyptians descended on him. It hadn't proved much of a weapon against the UnderJudges, but he would have welcomed the metallic comfort of the Dillinger in his hand.

If he could just get one arm free . . .

No chance. He was pinned down like a stapled butterfly.

The UnderJudge named Osiris leaned down, inches from Cairo's face, displaying rotten, jagged molars and exhaling a sour-milk breath as the white lips parted wide:

'*I will bite off your tongue.*'

The crook of a sand-blaster fell across Cairo's cheek, released by one of the death-white hands that was minus its fingers.

A sand-blaster, pointing left – with its nozzle-trigger close to his mouth.

He couldn't move his arms or legs.

But he could move his head.

Use his teeth.

He craned his neck forward, clamped his teeth on the nozzle, pulled his lower jaw back.

And flipped the sand-blaster's trigger.

The nozzle released a pressurised Sahara.

The streak of concentrated sandstorm played yellow hell with the Egyptians to his left. The roar of the gale couldn't blot out the thin, high-pitched shrieks. He felt the multiple grip on his left side tear free.

Osiris bellowed in wrath, and sank his splintered teeth into Cairo's mouth.

But not quite fast enough to outrace his victim's freed hand. Cairo flipped the trigger off, rammed the nozzle between the oval of sharp teeth before they touched flesh.

Then flipped the trigger on again.

Osiris got a mouthful of his own desert desserts.

The force of it blew the back of his skull off as it propelled him to the ceiling.

Cairo directed the thunderous jet to the right. Smiled as the white-skinned, black-blooded freaks hit the walls.

A lash of his legs and he was back on his feet. Spotting the Dillinger within grabbing distance he scooped it up while continuing to spray the Egyptians with their own yellow medicine.

Yanking the sand-blaster's twin cylinders off its former possessor's shoulders, he spun round, saw the passage to the grav-chute was clear, and sprinted for its promise of escape.

Just fifteen or so paces and he'd be free.

He had hardly covered ten when a hammer-blow to his spine knocked him flat.

He lay, winded, for a long moment, scrambled wits quickly unscrambling.

He'd been hit by a sand-blaster. One of many. At a

ten-metre distance. Any closer and he'd be wearing a hole in his back.

That thought launched him upwards and onwards, with a swift glance over his shoulder.

A score of UnderJudges were aiming those deadly nozzles at him as they thumped down the corridor.

We will scourge you with the sands of Set

He hurtled forwards in a low dive, hair flattened by the sudden wind of sand jets howling over his head.

In the second he plunged into the dark rectangle of the grav-chute, his heart turned to lead and plummeted.

There was no red light showing ON beside the grav-chute door. As happened often, the power was off.

No power.

As he fell head-first into the shaft he tasted raw panic at the prospect of two hundred metres of empty space stretching below.

No power.

No anti-gravity in the grav-chute.

Just lots of gravity, all the way down to a hard floor.

Grav-chute? It was a gruddam grave-chute.

He plunged upside down, gathering speed, and tried to think of a quick prayer before dying.

CHAPTER NINE

The main entrance to Mary Shelley Block was jam-packed with Judges.

Judges perched on Lawmasters. Judges pouring from parked h-wagons. Judges in patrol wagons rumbling into position, gun turrets fixed on the grenade-blasted aperture that had once been a plex-screened set of sliding doors.

Inside every helmet pulsed the same question:

What's happened to Dredd and Hershey in there?

Flame and smoke gouted from the building's broken mouth, but no sign of a black uniform, not a single one. Nor was there the merest glimpse of the woman variously known as Mad Mandra, Judge Mental, or the Anti-Judge.

Blue, red and yellow lights from wagons and Lawmasters strobed manically as Judge Baden stood in his Pat-Wagon and yelled his final warning into the meg-com, 'Come out with your hands up! We've got you surrounded!'

He stiffened as a black-and-white apparition burst out the door, firing in all directions as it ran. 'You'll never take me alive, coppers!'

The figure raced through a hail of bullets as though they were a spring shower.

'What in Grud's name is *that*?' gasped Baden as the escapee mowed a bloody path through the ranks of the Law, leaped into an h-wagon and emptied his gun into the crew before Baden could rally his thoughts. The stolen h-wagon had taken off by the time he regained his wits. He was on the verge of ordering it shot down when a Lawmaster erupted from the fiery mouth of the doorway and screeched to a halt alongside his armoured patrol vehicle.

'Judge Hershey!' he exclaimed at sight of her badge.

'I'll take Gunbird 2,' she shouted hoarsely, coughing from smoke inhalation despite the gas-mask pulled down from her helmet. 'Leave Cagney to me. Now get riot foam on that doorway, and stumm gas once you're inside. Dredd and a few others are still alive in there – just. *No more drokking grenades*, got it? Mandra's alive too. She tried to work some voodoo spell on me but I throttled her senseless. Give her plenty of gas when you bring her in – keep her in dreamland, okay?' She gunned her bike towards Gunbird 2, leaving a last reminder via vid-com. '*Remember to bring Mandra in alive.*'

Her orders were relayed around the squads as riot foam killed the flames and stumm gas was pumped into the interior. Hershey's Gunbird was a vanishing firefly in the night sky when Baden led his gas-masked squads on a sweep of the foyer. Calaghan, a veteran of the streets, and his fresh-faced rookie, Wincher, dogged the leader's steps.

'There she is,' Baden said grimly. 'Beside Dredd.' He switched off the vid-com. His followers did likewise. 'Keep close, you two,' he muttered over his shoulder. 'Keep me well hidden.'

Shielded by Calaghan and Wincher, he stood over the prone figure of Mandra.

'Well, lookie here,' Wincher sniggered. 'Now we know. Mandra's got white underwear to go with her choc skin. Hey – let's pull 'em off. Channel 99's outside. Let's give the cits a show to remember.'

'There's not many who'll get turned on by a headless corpse, kid,' Baden said, aiming his Lawgiver right between Mandra's eyes. 'Dead on sight, as promised.'

'*Alive*,' growled a throaty voice. 'And kicking.'

The three men froze as Dredd reared up, blood seeping from his cracked helmet and dribbling over his nose and mouth.

Baden hesitated for a moment, then swung the

Lawgiver at Dredd, finger squeezing the trigger. Calaghan and Wincher copied his actions a fraction of a second later.

Baden got off the first round.

But Dredd had hurled himself to one side, firing as he went. Baden's bullet sliced Dredd's shoulder. Dredd's bullet drilled a hole in Baden's heart.

Before the leader hit the ground, Calaghan and Wincher spun on their heels, a bullet in each brain.

Dredd staggered back to his feet as the officers of the Law ran across the broken statuary of Frankensteins and Creatures. They milled round, glancing in confusion from Dredd to the dead Judges, from the dead Judges back to Dredd.

He slapped a med-pack on his chest wound, a small hole well to the right. Some flesh missing, a little mess. Nothing serious.

They didn't expect an explanation. They didn't get one.

'Get Mandra to Justice Central,' he snapped, spitting blood from his mouth. 'And give her plenty of gas. Keep her well under.'

'That's what Hershey ordered, sir,' Judge Calthrop said.

'Where is Hershey?' Dredd asked him.

'In Gunbird 2, pursuing that JC 1 trace – whatever it is.'

Swaying slightly, Dredd walked over to his Lawmaster and addressed its vid-com. 'Gunbird 2 link-up . . .'

His command was answered by Omnipotens: 'Gunbird 2 is failing to reply. Electronic failure unlikely, but unable to establish contact. Stand by for further instructions.'

'Calthrop,' Dredd rumbled. 'Did you get a good look at Hershey?'

'Good enough,' Calthrop shrugged. 'Her badge was clearly visible.'

'Her badge?' Dredd snorted. 'What about her face?'

'Well – her lower face was in shadow. Most of the light was overhead. The visor shadows the – '

'She was wearing a helmet?'

'Yeah – sure.'

The corner of Dredd's mouth twitched a millimetre. 'Hershey wasn't wearing a helmet when she came in.'

He glanced at the strapped-in figure of Mandra as the hover-stretcher slipped into a med-wagon. 'Voodoo girl,' he murmured. 'What happened to that sleather suit she had on? Where are her boots and gun-belt? Voodoo girl . . .'

His right fist clenched. The growl that escaped his clenched teeth was rabid. 'Hershey's not the one in that Gunbird. And Mandra's not the one in that wagon.'

Mandra's full lips curved in a smile as she crossed her feet shod in Hershey's boots, and scanned the skies for hostile craft as she flew west towards the Cursed Earth.

Hershey's uniform was a half-size too large for Mandra, but the fit was close enough. As for the helmet – she flung it to a curved corner of the Gunbird's cockpit. Stuff the helmet. It still had Winstanley's dandruff in it.

'We sure fooled 'em, eh, toots?' Cagney grinned, sitting at her side. She had just hauled him in with a tractor beam from the h-wagon and he was beginning to make himself feel at home.

'Yeah,' she grinned back. 'We fooled 'em.'

Cagney was entitled to include himself in the deception. It was he who stepped in before Hershey strangled her senseless. She had heard his voice, on the edge of her consciousness: '*You ain't got a prayer.*'

The warning was directed at Hershey. So was his kick to the head.

Hershey had lapsed into oblivion as Mandra came fully round, rubbing her bruised throat. She had recommended the *Obeah* ritual immediately, casting a mirror spell of illusion on her former friend. Spell concluded, Hershey reflected Mandra's image. Fair exchange. She had lent Hershey her appearance, and then borrowed Hershey's uniform.

The illusion would wear off within an hour. An hour provided plenty of time to make plans. War plans.

No more hiding under assumed names. No more stalking the city at night. From now on it was total war.

'Pass my boots and belt, will you?' she said.

'Here they are, babe, clean as a whistle.'

'What's so clean about a whistle?'

She pulled off the green Judge boots and undid the Justice utility belt. Then, with a sigh of satisfaction, she eased on the thigh-length purple boots and snapped the purple gun-belt round her slim waist. Patting the Gotterdammerung pistol fondly, she murmured:

'This machine kills Judges.'

'You're still wearing a copper's uniform,' Cagney pointed out. A mischievous smile lit up his face. 'Kinda miss that sleather suit.'

Mandra peered down at her outfit. 'It's only the badge that needs altering.'

She extracted a small laser-cutter from her belt, wrenched off the badge, and set to work. First she smoothed out the middle surface, erasing Hershey's name. Then she inscribed a new name:

ANTI-JUDGE
MANDRA GORA

'Peter Lorre said my full name was Mandragora,' she mused. 'He knew something I didn't. Perhaps some day soon I'll find out what it is.'

'Sooner than you think, toots.'

She shot the mysterious gangster a sharp glance. 'What do you mean?'

'There are a lot of answers – if you look under the surface. *Deep* under the surface.'

'Come on, Cagney, what are you keeping under your hat?'

He tilted his head, snapped down the brim of his hat. 'Ever heard of Anarchopolis?'

'That's just a legend. Or nothing but another name for the Undercity.' A hesitation. 'Isn't it?'

'Aw, the Undercity's nothin' but a walk in the park. Central Park, if you wanna get smart about it. You want a war, you get an army, see? An army from under the underworld. Anarchopolis on hell-wheels.'

'Just how big is Anarchopolis?'

'It don't have no size. It just sorta goes on and on.'

'That's crazy!' she snorted.

'You said it, doll. Crazier than hell. That's Anarchopolis for ya. Crazy. Hell. Like the boss who runs the joint. The Underboss.'

She frowned dubiously. 'How come you know all this?'

He smiled enigmatically. 'Because I'm the stuff that dreams are made of. Like Anarchopolis.'

She shook her head. 'Sounds more like a nightmare.'

He flicked the brim of his hat. 'You're learnin', babe. You're learnin'.'

Mandra was about to deliver a barbed response when the vid-screen, which she had turned off after boarding the Gunbird, came alive all on its own.

Dredd's cracked helmet and scowling mouth filled the screen. 'System override, Mandra,' he announced. 'We can do that these days.'

'You don't sound too surprised,' she grimaced. 'I reckoned on another half-hour before you saw through the reflection spell.'

'I saw through it in my own way. We're bringing you in – by remote. You're automatically sealed in. And you'll find your controls won't respond. See you in ten minutes.'

Mandra jabbed at the controls as the Gunbird banked east, against her instructions. She tried every trick she knew on the ship's computer, but a vastly more powerful computer was in control of the craft. Omnipotens.

The Gunbird lost altitude as it flew east. Omnipotens was reeling her in. And dragging her down.

Down to Dredd and Judgement.

CHAPTER TEN

A quick prayer before dying?

There wasn't one short enough.

Cairo plummeted head-first down the two-hundred-metre shaft of the inoperative grav-chute.

A long way down, but a quick way down. Too quick for a prayer.

But there was time for regrets. Regret that he had failed to save Lucia. Regret that he would never see Mandra again. And regret that he had not blown Dredd's head off with a well-aimed bullet.

Eyes shut, he gripped the Dillinger snug in his hand.

Tightened his grasp on the sand-blaster's nozzle.

His eyes sprang open.

The sand-blaster . . .

Action: reaction.

Continuous recoil . . .

The action was one with the thought. Finger flipping the sand-blaster's trigger, he pointed the nozzle down the shaft.

Sand roared from the tube and ripped into the chute's floor.

The immediate recoil damn near dislocated his shoulder, swaying him to and fro as he struggled to maintain equilibrium.

But it didn't do much to break his fall. Insufficient pressure.

Would the pressure increase if he pulled the trigger back further?

About a hundred metres to go . . .

He pulled the trigger to its full extent.

The sandstorm roar quadrupled in the narrow shaft.

A savage jolt ran up his arm, playing hell with his shoulder and neck muscles. The compression of the abrupt deceleration squeezed his spine. He had the devil's own time preventing his body from rolling in any and every direction.

He wasn't complaining.

The concrete square at the bottom of the shaft was not charging up at him any more. It was coming up fast, but not fast enough to kill.

He hoped.

Maybe he'd survive, after all.

Then a torrent of sand screamed by his head.

Glance swerving upwards, he saw an UnderJudge at the top of the grav-chute, blasting yellow death down on Cairo.

Doggedly keeping a firm grip on his sand-blaster with one hand, he aimed the Dillinger at the Egyptian.

Still dropping at a scary speed, he pumped bullets up at the mummy-bound figure.

'Die, you bobbin-bound bastard,' he gritted between his teeth.

A slug hit home. Right in the Egyptian's visor. He reeled for an instant, then toppled into the shaft.

Cairo glanced back down.

The recoil of sand from the floor blinded him.

On pure instinct, he dropped both weapons and forward-rolled, bracing his legs for impact.

Not a split second too soon.

His feet met the floor the instant he completed the turn. The shock ran from the soles of his feet to the crown of his head.

Aching in every joint, he lurched upright, eyes shut from the swirl of sand. Fishing around, he located the sand-blaster and Dillinger.

Then he heard the terminal *splack* of flesh and bone on concrete. The Egyptian had landed.

Guiding himself by touch, he traced his way into the

maintenance basement. He halted, rubbed his eyes free of the burning sand grains, and then looked around. A sigh of relief escaped his lips. His eyes still smarted, but his vision was intact.

In front of him, rank on rank, stretched half a kilometre of towering magneto-coils, chief source of power to the block overhead. A pity they weren't up to sustaining the grav-chute.

On reflection, he thought, wincing from head-to-toe pain as he headed for the distant door to the lowest level, perhaps it was better this way. The UnderJudges couldn't follow him.

A faint smile flickered his lips as he passed a door marked FLUSHWAYS MEN'S CONVENIENCES. Fond memories of Arbuckle, the subversive toilet janitor, welled up for a brief spell. Overweight, erudite Arbuckle, the one-man university – and his gun-toting partner, Blue Angel, hooker by trade, Judge-killer by inclination. He had run into them a few days after escaping the psycho-cubes. They adopted him on the spot.

Arbuckle had taught him everything he knew – about the old American Republic, about all the past. Especially the twentieth century – the last century of freedom. And Blue Angel – the almost over-the-hill hooker – she had taught him the secrets of survival on the streets, how to shoot straight and, more importantly, *who* to shoot at.

Both dead now. Dead, but not forgotten by Mister Cairo.

His smile, thin as it was, faded as he stared at the door that led down to the Casablanca.

Piano Smile was waiting down there.

Cairo's grip squeezed the butt of the Dillinger.

'I'm ready for you, Piano Smile.'

He wasn't ready for what appeared from behind the ranks of magneto-coils.

UnderJudges. Hundreds of Pharaoh-helmeted Under-Judges, sand-blasting crooks, electric flails and all. They blocked the path to the door. And they were coming in from the sides, too. A closing arc of Egyptians on shuffling, whispery feet.

Some of them were levelling the nozzles of sand-blasters in his direction.

'Oh *no*,' he groaned, glance darting that way and this for escape. His eyes fixed on the Men's conveniences.

Nowhere else to run.

Assuming he wasn't cut down by a sand fusillade before he took three paces, that was.

He forgot about his strained muscles in the sprint to the toilets. He zigzagged as he ran, presenting a more difficult target to the sand-blasters.

A funnelled sandstorm whipped inches past his ear, temporarily throwing him off balance. A yellow jet raked the ground to his left. Another exploded the concrete to his right.

Lucky, lucky, lucky.

He slammed into the toilet door, swung it wide and dived in, kicking the door shut as he fell to the gleaming tiles. Springing up the moment he hit the floor, he snapped the lock shut. Breathing hoarsely, he backed towards the pristine cubicles.

The door was plasteen. But that wouldn't hold the Egyptians for long, with those sand-blasters of theirs. It was the only access door to the Flushways Men's Conveniences. The only door in.

The only door out.

Its smooth grey expanse trembled at the first onslaught of the sandy gale.

He checked his Dillinger. Bad news. Three standard rounds left. He had counted on at least ten. As for the sand-blaster, there couldn't be much ammo left in the cylinders, no matter how compressed the sand grains.

The door was shaking fit to burst. The plasteen split in the middle with a loud crack like a rifle shot.

Still backing away, he aimed the blaster's nozzle at the shuddering door.

With a slight pressure on the trigger, he tested the weapon.

No response.

He squeezed the trigger tighter. Nothing.

Pulled it back all the way.

A few grains shot out to embed themselves in the door. After that, no more. Empty. He'd used up the full store in the grav-chute. He dropped the weapon with a clatter on the tiles.

'That's all I need – '

The door exploded inwards, launching jagged lumps of plasteen into the toilets.

The UnderJudges lurched in, sand-blasts ripping floor and walls.

Cairo hurled himself sideways into the third cubicle, banging his head on the toilet bowl as he whacked the door shut with his foot.

The cubicle door should keep the Egyptians out for all of ten seconds, if he was lucky.

He sprang up and frantically scanned the Flushways cubicle console. The console, marked 1 to 9, contained four touch-pads for different types of flush, three for bidet conversion, one for the miniature vid-screen on the door, and one to give you a nice feeling when you sat on the seat.

Only three people knew of another way to use the console, and two of those were dead.

Thanks, Arbuckle, Blue Angel.

Cairo wasn't sure if he had chosen the right cubicle. It had been years since he'd visited this convenience. And the code was different for each convenience. He wasn't even sure of the correct code for this console.

Was it press 1, 4 and 8 simultaneously for access, or 1, 4 and 9? If he entered the wrong access code, the computer would ignore any further entries.

He pressed 1, 4 and 8.

A short, faint buzz assured him he'd chosen right.

He still had an eighteen-digit sequence to enter. A lot of that would be guesswork. Any second now an Egyptian would blast open the door, and then his insides, in swift succession.

Cairo's fingers flew over the touch-pads. He had entered fifteen of the eighteen digits when the door erupted at his back, revealing a nozzle-wielding UnderJudge.

Ducking the sand-blast, he whirled round, firing his last three rounds at the Egyptian while his other hand completed the Flushway code.

The three slugs formed a neat row in the visor. The Pharaoh-helmeted mummy fell back on its heels.

And half a dozen UnderJudges took its place, weapons of sandstorm trained on Cairo.

'Goodbye, Mister Cairo,' husked the dry voice of one of the Egyptians as he squeezed the trigger of his sand-blaster.

'So long, suckers,' Cairo said as he jumped into the bowl and flushed himself down the toilet.

CHAPTER ELEVEN

'Now what?' Mandra muttered to herself, glowering at the ominous bulk of the Grand Hall of Justice as it reared up in the east.

Gunbird 2, helpless in the grip of the Omnipotens override, hurtled straight for the cold heart of Judgement in Mega-City One. That man-bitch McGruder would be waiting for her inside the plascrete tower of Justice Hall. And so would a Med Squad, laser ready to lobotomise her brain.

Ahead of Gunbird 2, some two kilometres away, was another Gunbird, speeding east on an identical course. She knew, she just knew, that Dredd was in it.

'*Now what?*'

Cagney gave a quick shrug. 'We ain't doin' time in the slammer, honey, that's for sure. We go down with heaters blazing.'

'Heaters?'

'Guns.'

'Oh – right. That may have been the style in 1931, but this is the twenty-second century. They'll fill the cabin with stumm gas before we reach Justice Hall. We'll land as sleeping babes.'

But, she reflected darkly, I'll recite an old rhyme before I go under. A rhyme to detonate the hypma in my tooth.

Here comes a candle to light you to bed . . .

Go out with a head bang. That was the way.

The screen read-out showed ETA at Justice Hall in forty seconds. Maybe she should start the death-rhyme now.

'Ain't there some kinda escape capsule in this thing?' Cagney asked.

'Can't activate it. System override. Omnipotens is calling the shots. There's nothing – '

A sudden downward lurch whipped the words from her mouth and left her stomach somewhere in the stratosphere.

'Jeez!' exclaimed Cagney as the craft plunged headlong into the mega-city. 'Looks like they're rubbin' us out the fast way, doll.'

A block roof hurtled up at them.

The read-out displayed ETA eleven seconds to the roof of Hindenberg Block at a contact speed of 800 kph.

The rate of descent squeezed the air from Mandra's lungs.

Omnipotens had decided a swift fate for the Public Enemy Number One.

'Bye, Cagney,' she hissed between her teeth.

'Bye, toots.'

Enthroned in the hovering eagle chair, lips pressed tight, the strain of waiting tautened his facial muscles. Then the tension drained from his gaunt features.

A slow smile curved his mouth. A cold light glinted in his blue eyes.

'She's gone,' Sejanus announced to the Hierarchy of Five in the Sanctum. 'Departed in a blaze of glory from the top of Hindenberg Block.'

The five SJS officers, dangling in zero gravity, opened their eyes and echoed the Colossus Chief's smile.

In the small oval of the Sanctum there was a profound sense of satisfaction. A job well done.

Mandra was dead.

Sejanus pressed a button on the eagle chair. It descended gently to the level of the curved floor of the anti-grav chamber. He surveyed his secret room with quiet approval. His sanctum. His seat of power.

The Sanctum, seven metres in span between sloping

walls, was the secret chamber in the head of the Judgement Colossus. A chamber with direct access to the brain.

It had been Sejanus's idea to shape the chamber's interior to resemble the inside of an egg. From this small egg would hatch a new world:

The world of Absolute Law.

With Sejanus as Absolute Judge.

His lieutenants would be the Hierarchy of Five, the five fingers of the hammer-fist of Justice, poised to strike when the day of reckoning came. The Day of Wrath: *Dies Irae*.

He had chosen his elite of five with painstaking care. Three had been inducted from Psi Division to the Special Judicial Squad. Two were SJS officers with advanced Psi capacities. They formed the upper echelon of a secret organisation he'd been covertly establishing for years. Its full membership exceeded a hundred Judges, each placed in a strategic position for Sejanus's impending coup of Justice Central.

Mandra had been the sole threat to his planned coup. She had known too much. If brought in alive, she might have talked. That danger was cancelled in an air-crash inferno.

Five minds had combined to bring down the Gunbird. Five minds working through Omnipotens, but untraceable to the supercomputer. There would be no record of the signal to nose-dive transmitted from the Hierarchy of Five to the aircraft. Electronic sensors were unable to register a Psi signal, and if a member of Psi Division picked it up they would have no hope of locating its origin.

Dredd's urgent request to override Gunbird 2's controls had provided the Colossus Chief with a heaven-sent opportunity. Sejanus had sent mixed signals to the aircraft. The electronic command had guided the craft to Justice Central. But a Psi-hypma command had nose-dived the Gunbird to destruction.

Neither Dredd nor McGruder nor Hershey had an inkling of the power at the heart of Omnipotens.

There was a secret at the core of Omnipotens' brain. Sejanus's prized secret. His ultimate weapon.

Under the thick mantle of Omnipotens' electronic circuitry there was a sphere ten metres in diameter. The sphere was a giant ball of hypma. Fluctuating constantly between pure energy and matter, hypma formed a bridge between thought and machine. It linked mind to matter, attuning the human brain to the electronic shell of the supercomputer.

The hypma core of Omnipotens was a sentient sphere of elaborately constructed Psi-patterns. It was a living mind, encoded by Sejanus. The veritable image of his psyche.

He called it the Arcanum.

Here, in the ovoid Sanctum, was the sole access to the Arcanum. The entire outer surface of Omnipotens was shielded with lead, impervious to Psi-waves. Entirely shielded but for two small exit points in the Colossus Judge's eyes, their five-centimetre lead shields opened only for Psi-transmission; and just one, ultra-secret access point –

Sejanus glanced at the life-size hologram of a human brain on one of the curved walls. It marked the location of a thirteen-centimetre circular hole in the lead under the plasteen veneer. A tunnel to the centre of the Colossus's brain. Nowhere but in the hidden Sanctum could the Arcanum be accessed. And no one but Sejanus and his conspirators were aware of the existence of either Sanctum or Arcanum.

The Colossus Chief was supreme master of the brain that controlled Mega-City One. Thanks, in part, to Chief Judge McGruder. McGruder's increasingly frequent bouts of insanity and her ingrained bias in favour of the SJS had made Sejanus's rise to power as effortless as riding up a grav-chute.

Now Mandra was out the way, the final step to Sejanus's total dictatorship was short and sweet.

Just two words.

'Dies Irae,' he declared to the expectant Hierarchy of Five.

They grinned at the order to commence the coup, then shut their eyes as they attuned collective minds to the Arcanum core of Omnipotens. The mental labour of his elite would soon bear fruit.

In less than twenty-four hours the brain of the Colossus Judge would be fully independent and fully operational.

He was about to give Mega-City One an omnipotent god. A god with the mind of Sejanus.

A god whom everyone would worship and obey, whether they liked it or not.

'Deus Irae,' he murmured softly. 'God of Wrath.'

He touched an acti-pad on his eagle chair. A section of wall shimmered momentarily, then seemed to resume solidity.

At a press of an arm-rest button, Sejanus propelled his chair through the hologram of a seemingly solid wall. The wall reverted to plasteen as he emerged into the ramp spiralling down to the Visor area.

He sighed with contentment.

Thirty years of meticulous planning was reaching fruition.

As the eagle chair whispered in a spiral glide down the ramp, he tasted sweet success on his tongue. Luxuriated in its exhilarating flavour.

Then he remembered the dream. And the taste of success went stale.

The recurrent dream . . .

A black falcon battling with a golden eagle high in the sky . . .

He thrust back the unsettling recollection as the eagle chair flew into the wide expanse of the Visor.

Whenever he recalled that dream, he was instantly reminded of a line of Shakespeare, from the mouth of Hamlet. His thin lips stirred as he recited:

'"I could be bounded in a nutshell, and count myself a king of infinite space, were it not that I have bad dreams".'

But tonight was not a night to brood on ambiguous dreams. He straightened his shoulders, brought the eagle chair to a sighing halt in front of the wide vista of the Visor and regained his former contentment as he leaned on the head-rest and surveyed the bay.

The Statue of Liberty, tiny from this height, raised the arm stump that had once carried a torch. He gave vent to a low chuckle as he visualised the raised fist of the Judgement Colossus.

Liberty was not quite dead in Mega-City One. In every block, a hard core of Democrats still sowed dissension.

That would soon stop.

Come tomorrow night, Mega-City One would have a deathless dictator. Grud – the Omnipotens Deus. Grud – the Almighty God.

He would be a stern Judge.

Just like his creator.

Musing on the power and the glory, Sejanus activated a vid-screen and punched in the codes for the hover-eye above Hindenberg Block. The screen came alive with disaster.

Huge flames still gouted from the splatter of aircraft wreckage on the block's devastated roof. A read-out informed him that much of the top five floors were squashed flat. Death total estimated at twelve thousand minimum.

'Goodbye, Mandra.'

He experienced a small twinge of remorse.

Viewing the scene of destruction, he couldn't suppress a tiny pang of regret at Mandra's death.

It didn't spoil his sense of victory – the feeling of sorrow was much too muted for that.

But – yes, he admitted it – he felt the faintest touch of sadness over the girl's demise.

He permitted himself a brief moment of wistful reflection over the death of Mandra.

After all, she was his daughter.

CHAPTER TWELVE

Plummeting towards the roof of Hindenberg Block.

The Gunbird failing to respond to the flicker-play of her fingers on its console.

Seven seconds to impact.

Mandra stared Death right in his bared teeth.

That was when the ultra-priority EJECT sign flashed on, responding to the escape-or-die situation by cancelling the override on the escape pod.

'*Yes!*' Mandra exulted, recalling that in extreme emergencies the escape capsule operated independently of the main on-board computer, or any external control.

But there were only four seconds to impact . . .

The cockpit closed in around Mandra and Cagney, curved roof and curved floor locking tight, forming a capsule.

Two seconds to impact.

The escape capsule disengaged from the hull.

The Gunbird crashed in a thunderous eruption of blinding flame.

But the escape pod was free and intact. It arced away from the block roof, skimming its rim by a few metres.

Mandra painfully gritted her teeth at the sudden deceleration and abrupt change in trajectory.

As the pod plunged down the three-kilometre canyon between Hindenberg and Bader Blocks, the deceleration gradually eased.

'Close call, huh, toots?' Cagney smiled.

That was when it finally dawned on her that she was

not going to die. The happy realisation bubbled up inside her and broke out in wild, free laughter.

Close call. Right.

Over and again she relived the experience of liberation. She relived that glad moment now, as she raced over the grime and rats of Ground Level, the open shell of the escape capsule already out of sight in the coagulated shadows.

Close call.

Struggling to keep up with the remorseless pace of the black-and-white gangster, she swept the darkness on either side with the muzzle of her Gotterdammerung, alert to trouble.

No threat showed its ugly face.

There was nothing on this lowest of levels that its denizens called the Pits but muck, rodents, the occasional sprawled alcohead, and dark, dark, and more dark.

She welcomed the dark like a black velvet coat. It was a perfect fit.

There were Eyes in the Pits, of course. There were Eyes everywhere in Mega-City One. Eyes that saw in the dark. Pits people were always taking pot-shots at them. But each Eye was programmed to transmit only events on a par with medium to large-scale riots back to Justice Central. A couple of running figures were unlikely to attract notice.

But come the dawn . . .

Cagney gradually slowed his speeding legs from sprint to marathon pace. She drew alongside.

'This slow enough for ya, honey?' he grinned crookedly.

'Just about,' she panted. Did the gangster have any weaknesses at all? Even the multiple bullet wounds he had received had healed up. 'What are you *made* of, Cagney?'

'Hell and hyperplasma, babe. Hell and hyperplasma.'

They ran in silence for the next two hours, Mandra darting frequent looks at the intermittent Eyes or periodic firefly glint of an h-wagon high overhead.

She almost slammed into Cagney's back as he pulled to an abrupt stop.

Instinctively, she crouched and circled low, machine-pistol levelled.

'Lighten up, doll,' he drawled, flicking the brim of his hat. 'You know where we are?'

'Sector 44, and not far enough past Justice Hall,' she grunted, holstering the gun. 'Let's keep heading west.'

He shook his head. 'So you don't know where we are. Aw, hell, I guess it was all a long time ago.' His gaze lowered to the sloppy grime of the ground. She thought she caught an echo of nostalgia in his tone. 'We're standing on top of New Jersey. Another hour of running and we'll be right over Manhattan. Good old New York. The Big Apple.'

'It's just the Undercity,' she shrugged, although she couldn't resist a downward look. She wasn't quite sure of the thickness of the plascrete lid that covered the Undercity. Was it a hundred metres? Two hundred? A kilometre?

Whatever its depth, it suddenly struck her that the lid was a brittle shell, with all the gargantuan citi-blocks weighing down on it. One fissure in that lid – a single split – and Sector 44 would tumble down into a titanic hole in the ground.

Mandra's head spun with vertigo of what lay deep under her feet. Like most people in Mega-City One, she considered the Pits as Ground Level. But although she was in the Pits, she wasn't standing on the ground. She was standing on a floor.

And her floor was someone else's ceiling.

She hoped there weren't too many cracks in it.

Best forget that thought.

'Come on, toots,' Cagney called out, his rain-streaming luminous figure up and running again. 'I wanna hit the isle of Manhattan before sunup.'

'And then what?' she muttered to herself, keeping pace with the gangster from 1931. 'The Undercity?'

Best forget that thought too, she decided.

Mandra knew it was her imagination, but the ground she sped over seemed to shake each time her boots thumped the ground.

Someone else's ceiling . . .

'White underwear – now we know,' someone chuckled in a recess of the h-wagon.

'That man on report,' Dredd said without taking his eyes from the vid-screen. A fresh helmet covered the swift med-aid applied to his head. If he was in pain he wasn't showing it – as usual.

Hershey gave a nonchalant lift of her shoulders. 'The colour of my underwear isn't a state secret, Joe.'

His scowling mouth twisted a centimetre. 'It drokkin' well ought to be.'

'Oh, forget it, Joe,' she exhaled heavily. 'I'm back in uniform, badge and all. No harm done. Drop it, okay? I've got more important things on my mind.' Her expression hardened as she slung a leg over the saddle of her Lawmaster, poised for jump-off on sight of Mandra. 'Like why three Judges tried to kill me.'

'They thought they were aiming at Mandra,' he rumbled. 'But – point taken. Someone wants Mandra dead on sight. Someone high up. I know who's top of my list.'

Hershey kept her voice low, out of earshot of the h-wagon's crew. 'McGruder's new right-hand man. Our exalted Colossus Chief. He's wanted Mandra dead on sight from the beginning. Why?'

'Because the dead don't talk. That's the usual reason. Something tells me Sejanus won't be jumping for joy at Mandra's escape from the crash.'

'Extra-Judicial Killing,' she snorted. 'Typical SJS. Them and their Gruddam death's head insignia. I had my fill of their Death Squads a year ago. They ran wild while McGruder sat back idle. She's never forgotten she was SJS once. Those drokking death's-head earrings of hers – '

'You forgetting she was SJS before she took the Long

Walk in the Cursed Earth?' Dredd cut in sharply. 'The Long Walk changes you.'

'It didn't change you much, did it? Sure, you needed a face-lift, but you were still the same old shoot-'em-up, blast-'em-high Joe Dredd we all know and indulge. All the Long Walk did for McGruder was raise her testosterone levels.'

'You're pushin' it, Hershey,' he warned, turning briefly from the vid-screen. 'Way over the edge.'

She arched an eyebrow. 'So report me. Then McGruder'll make sure I never make Chief Judge. That'll raise a cheer in the SJS ranks.'

'With Sejanus cheering the loudest. Don't play into his hands by bad-mouthing the Chief Judge.'

'Who needs a Chief Judge when we've got a Colossus Chief? He's in charge of the most powerful computer in the world. And the weaponry in that Judgement Day Colossus – it could wipe out the mega-city ten times over. Face it, Joe. The real power's slipped into Sejanus's hands by default.'

Dredd had returned to his study of the vid. 'First we find Mandra. Make her talk. Then maybe we'll learn something about Sejanus.'

She glanced over Dredd's shoulder to the action on the screen. It had just switched from Mister Cairo in Normal's hab to a silent Hover Eye replay of Cairo's encounter with an eezie-squeezie on Squid Row. She gave a small shake of the head. 'How many more times are you going to replay those scenes?'

He watched in silence for several seconds, then transferred the vid to street surveillance. 'That was the last time. I think I've found a couple of connections.'

'Oh?'

'Mister Cairo kept pumping Normal about Mandra. Like he cared about the woman. The kind of care that's personal. And on Squid Row, he paid a lot of attention to that upside-down scrawl of Anarchopolis. An inverted scrawl, like that World Tarot card he quizzed Normal about. Cairo – Mandra – Anarchopolis. There's a connection. I'm sure of it.'

Hershey stroked a forefinger across her chin. 'I remember Anderson once suggested that Anarchopolis might be more than a street fable. But what's that got to do with Cairo and Mandra?'

His lips tightened to a thin line. 'We'll have to ask Omnipotens.'

'Oh, *great*.'

'No choice, Hershey. Omnipotens is the only game in town.'

He jabbed out a code that transmitted the Cairo vids to Omnipotens, along with an urgent request for an in-depth investigation of Mister Cairo with special reference to Mandra and Anarchopolis.

Transmission concluded, he resumed his street surveillance.

And spotted them almost immediately.

They were running along the base of Barker Block.

Mandra and that Cagney perp.

He had them cold.

'Weller!' he thundered, vaulting onto his Lawmaster. 'Jump-off descent! Fast!'

Captain Weller initiated rapid descent the instant the command was delivered.

As the craft dropped into virtual free-fall, Weller scanned the read-outs. 'Laser cannon primed. Nine h-wagons converging on target. Total of thirty-eight Lawmasters.'

Dredd took a firm grip of the handlebars.

'We've got 'em cold,' he growled.

Still alive.

His daughter was still alive.

How much did it take to kill the drokking bitch?

Sejanus sat with his elbow propped on the eagle chair's arm-rest, moody head resting on clenched fist as he gazed blankly into the night beyond the vast visor of the Colossus.

He had overlooked the priority of escape activation in life-threatening emergencies. Rescue from death cancelled out the most imperative of overrides.

Even so, she'd had more than her fair share of luck to escape in time. The Devil's own luck.

He had been mulling over his options for hours. Omnipotens would not be primed until tomorrow night. In the interim, he was vulnerable. And Mandra had just been sighted. Dredd would bring her in alive and kicking – just a figure of speech: he would probably shoot her legs off. But then Mandra might well shoot her mouth off. She didn't know all of Sejanus's plans, but she knew enough to wreck them.

And Dredd's request for in-depth info on Mandra, Mister Cairo and Anarchopolis had added an element of intrigue to the whole messy business.

Omnipotens had come up with a speedy verdict on Anarchopolis. It was spelt out in green on one of the monitors:

ANARCHOPOLIS HAS NO EMPIRICAL EXISTENCE. IT IS A FABLE POPULAR AMONGST THE DISAFFECTED ELEMENTS OF MEGA–CITY ONE. ANY RELATION MANDRA AND MISTER CAIRO MIGHT HAVE TO ANARCHOPOLIS MUST BE PURELY SYMBOLIC.

So Anarchopolis was merely a story. He could discount it.

Mandra's full biography was very familiar to him. It would remain a secret between himself and Omnipotens. He would ensure the computer transmitted only the standard, official account.

Mister Cairo, however – there was an unfamiliar name. According to the Justice files, Cairo was born in Brit-Cit in 2086, and moved with his parents to Mega-City One at the age of nine. Educational performance – average. Held down a few nondescript jobs between long periods of unemployment. Took up private investigation at the age of twenty-two. Strictly small-time stuff. Average case results.

And not a single conviction for overstepping the Law.

Mister Ordinary. Mister Law-Abiding

Sejanus eyed the Cairo read-out with increasing suspicion.

Not one conviction.

Too ordinary. Too law-abiding.

The man was a private eye, after all. It was virtually impossible to be one of the few private eyes in Mega-City One without treading on the Judges' boots. Judges and private investigators were natural enemies.

Besides, the Eye replay from Normal's habhold strongly suggested that Cairo was personally acquainted with Mandra. And any friend of Mandra's . . .

'File on Mister Cairo unacceptable,' he addressed Omnipotens on a private channel. 'Discount all current info. Re-investigate Cairo, using SRZXX101211/ PZ999T/ XX7/ 362PP/ VYT85521/ WQEB/ 595XL Eye record.'

He leaned back and awaited the results. Most of Omnipotens' files were inherited from MAC and Barney. The older computers were vulnerable to exceptionally clever hackers but Omnipotens was immune to assault, as Mandra had discovered. The tiny hypma cores he had covertly implanted in MAC and Barney had laid them open to Mandra's Psi-attack. But Omnipotens' lead shield had thwarted her attempt to sabotage the supercomputer.

Just as he had planned.

His daughter had disabled the rival computers for him, in the false belief that she was wrecking his grand design. Perhaps his not-so-beloved daughter realised by now that she had helped to fulfil that design. Omnipotens was in total control.

But if she talked . . .

A message from Omnipotens flashed on the screen:

MULTIPLE MISMATCHES ON MISTER CAIRO FILE. 98.365% LIKELIHOOD OF HACKER ACTIVITY. SUGGEST CURRENT FILE INVALID. RECONSTRUCTING FILE. ESTIMATED COMPLETION OF RECONSTRUCTION TWENTY MINUTES AND FORTY SECONDS.

Sejanus tapped his fingers as he counted away the minutes. Omnipotens was well-named. It was capable of accurately reconstructing a citizen's life from what a lesser computer would regard as near-zero data.

And the Colossus Chief was eager to learn Cairo's true history.

Sejanus's formidable Psi gifts, studiously cloaked and underplayed throughout his career, told him Mister Cairo might prove the wild card in the power game.

The Joker in the pack.

At last, Cairo's real biography was revealed on the private vid-screen.

His eyes were wide shocks before he had taken in more than a couple of lines of the long account.

He could scarcely believe what he was reading.

'*Grud*,' he breathed hoarsely. '*You*. It's *you*.'

His gauntleted hand compressed into a fist. 'I know you, Mister Cairo.'

She felt she was running on top of the underworld.

A thin shell was all that protected her from a long drop into what she sensed was a black abyss and what Cagney knew as Manhattan.

Mandra looked up, and suddenly was back in Mega-City One's basement again. Blocks kilometres tall. High overhead, the megways, zoomways, slipways and every-other-ways of the Tangle. Higher still, the suspended pedway network of the Cobweb.

Sweeping down through Cobweb and Tangle came a small swarm of h-wagons. Aimed straight for her.

Judgement was dropping from the heights.

The sensation of racing along the roof of another world dissipated. Her heart was in the Pits again.

Cagney was already firing with both barrels at the descending craft. Despite the imminent danger, she flashed a grim smile at her fellow public enemy.

'How many rounds have you got in those revolvers? A million?'

He gave a fast flick of an eyebrow. 'These shooters are

the stuff that public dreams are made of, too, babe. The Dream Palace audiences weren't too hot on counting bullets back in 1931. These heaters don't run short of rounds until the right dramatic moment.'

'Then may we live in uninteresting times,' she muttered, levelling her Gotterdammerung at the nearest hover-ship, coming in fast.

The h-wagon whisked down to a few hundred metres.

Its slide-door slammed open.

Two Lawmasters blasted from the airship, true Beasts of the Streets in every sleek line and decibel.

They arced down on turbo-boost, raking Cagney with gunfire in the descent.

Another nine h-wagons zoomed on the tail of the first, disgorging some three dozen Beasts of the Streets, combined firepower concentrated on the twentieth-century gangster.

Before she could unleash a Fenris missile, a blazing white light played all kinds of hell with her eyesight.

Laser cannon.

As she was still alive, Cagney must have been the target.

'I've caught a packet of light amplification by stimulated emission of radiation, toots,' he croaked. 'Puts the heat on hypma real sharp.'

The laser burst stopped. Stars did a multicoloured dance in front of her eyes.

Through starry vision, she saw Cagney stagger a few paces to the left, the black blood of a monochrome movie character spouting from a score of impacting slugs.

Then her vision of Cagney was blocked by the ominous outline of Dredd on his Lawmaster. The blackest of knights on his metal beast.

She launched a Fenris missile straight at Dredd.

At least, she went through the actions.

It was then she realised the Gotterdammerung was not in her hands. She must have dropped it when the laser cannon hit. Terrific.

Cagney reeled back into view from behind Dredd, his

cinematic body spinning and jerking in a fusillade that would have put a hailstorm to shame.

The revolvers dropped from his dangling hands. Then he dropped after them. He hit the ground face first. And would have lain still if the unrelenting hail of bullets had not kept making a twitch-dance of his corpse.

'So long, James Cagney,' she whispered. 'You were one hell of a guy.'

'It's over, Mandra!' Dredd bellowed above the roar of gunfire, lowering his Lawgiver to the level of her knee-caps. 'I'm bringin' you in walkin' or crawlin'. Your choice.'

As the after-effects of the laser burst receded, Mandra's gaze circled the forty Lawmaster-mounted Judges surrounding her. It was over, true enough.

But nobody was bringing her in, walking, crawling or slithering.

Not with the hypma she had implanted in an upper molar, attuned to an old rhyme and ready to make a bomb of her head.

Just recite the words and go out with a bang.

She wondered, fleetingly, how far her skull fragments would travel in the blast.

Curling her lip, she casually gave Dredd the finger.

Voice low and quiet, she commenced the verbal detonation of the rhyme:

'Here comes a candle to light you to bed.
Here comes a chopper to chop off your . . .'

CHAPTER THIRTEEN

Flushing yourself down the toilet was definitely the last resort.

You sure as hell didn't try it just for the ride.

And never, absolutely never, unless you travelled down a special Flushways toilet installed by Arbuckle.

A few seconds after flushing himself down the bowl Cairo had left the Egyptian UnderJudges far overhead as he sped through the tubes at an average 70 kph. Arbuckle's Flushway had saved him again.

Arbuckle the subversive toilet janitor had been a man of rare invention as well as vast erudition. His greatest invention was the Flushways travel channel, an express form of anti-grav chute with a number of clever-devil refinements. Only Blue Angel and Cairo were let in on the secret of Arbuckle's lavatorial Flushway Express. Or Flushway, for short.

Although the technology was bewildering, the operation was simple. Punch in the right code on the toilet console, and abracadabra – the Flushway took the passenger to another Flushway toilet close to his intended destination. The toilet bowl automatically expanded when you jumped in, instantly closing fifty centimetres above your head. The continuous expansion below and contraction overhead was similar to the peristaltic action of food travelling down the oesophagus.

Or crap passing through the sphincter. A more apt comparison which he preferred not to dwell on.

Mercifully, Arbuckle had included a protective electrostatic field that enclosed the passenger throughout the journey, repelling all crud and germs. You popped out of the destination toilet bowl as fresh and clean as you went in.

Arbuckle's unique means of travel through the Big City's internal plumbing system had saved Cairo's life on numerous occasions. His recent escape from the Under-Judges was merely the latest in a long list of toilet exits.

When in a tight spot, Flushway was the way to travel.

Except – things could go wrong. The mechanism was not faultless. One danger was surfacing in the narrow, inflexible pipe of a non-Flushway toilet. Squeezed to death in an instant. That had been Arbuckle's fate. Arbuckle had died in the bowels of his own creation. Bad way to go.

As he sped through the dark, Cairo did not concern himself with the many risks of taking the Flushway. He was happy enough to be free of the Egyptians.

A smooth shift of direction from down to sideways informed him he'd entered a shunting area. He zigzagged for a brief space as the Flushway positioned him below the destination toilet and sensors checked that there was no one sitting on it.

An abrupt upward acceleration proved that the sensors had decided the exit was clear.

Cairo's finger curled round the trigger of his Dillinger. He was not about to be taken by surprise.

The acceleration slowed. The dark lightened.

Cario erupted from the toilet bowl with gun levelled and ready for trouble.

The cubicle was empty, its open door revealing no threat.

He sprang out into the main floor of the Men's convenience.

Nobody in sight.

'Good,' he said, somewhere below a breath. 'It's Piano Smile's turn to be taken by surprise.'

Cairo was back on familiar ground: The Men's Room of the Casablanca cinema, styled in the revived Art Deco fashion of the early twenty-first century. It brought back memories, all of which he ignored.

He reloaded his Dillinger and then, stealthy and slow, eased open the door into the back of the cinema, constructed and decorated in imitation of a 1920s Dream Palace, balconies, wall-reliefs, chandeliers and all.

The upper balcony fell away below him. The Overboss and his men sat on the balcony's front row. All the chandeliers were lit, illuminating Piano Smile and his goons, who packed a small armoury between them. They were keeping watch on the side-entrance, the sole means of access unless, of course, you chose to pop out of a toilet.

He recognised several of the Overboss's goons: Mugsy Baloney, False Teeth, 'Fingers' Vermicelli, Tap-Dance, Johnny Threeballs. Not a single one had less than a Master's degree in law or philosophy, gained by shoving a gun barrel up a college dean's nostril.

Easy, Cairo, he told himself. Steal up on them slow and eas—

Something small, round and metallic pressed into the nape of his neck.

'Drop the piece, Mister Cairo,' ordered the man at his back in a voice Cairo identified as Toots Ritzy, Big Boy's former right-hand man.

The Overboss and his henchmen had spun round at Toots Ritzy's warning.

Cairo grimaced. Great move, genius among private eyes. You didn't check the cubicles. Ritzy must have been taking a leak or a dump.

'Drop the piece, Cairo, or you're history.'

Keeping a firm grip of his Dillinger, he took a casual step forwards and wheeled to face Ritzy. 'Which period?'

'Yahwhat?'

'Which period of history? Sumerian? Graeco-Roman? Medieval? Tudor?'

Ritzy's narrow eyes tightened to slits. 'Whadya mean? Dat some kinda joke? You think I ain't gonna shoot?'

Toots Ritzy had a personality like a razor-blade and a

129

body to match. Sharp dresser, too. You could cut a finger on his lapel crease.

Not too sharp in the brain department, though. Ritzy couldn't organise a wank in a brothel. Strictly a hatchet man. He specialised in terrorising independent sleep-eezies, like the Sisters of Gramercy. His forte was killing women by a wide range of methods, all of them slow. Three of the women had been friends of Cairo.

'Scar looks good, Ritzy,' he noted, nodding at the purple streak on the hoodlum's brow. 'Bad miss, though. I was aiming for your eyes.'

A tic plucked a muscle in the punk's hollow cheek. 'You'll pay in duh red and flowin' for dat day, Cairo.' The bony trigger-finger flexed.

'Ritzy!' Piano Smile's husky voice called out. 'Mister Cairo's here at my invitation. Give some respect. Show him to his seat.'

Scowling, Ritzy obeyed his new boss, conducting him down the stepped aisle like an usher with a gun in place of a torch.

Reaching the front row, Cairo squeezed past a dozen of the boss's gorillas and sank into a seat between False Teeth and Piano Smile.

Chewing a fat cigar that went well with his fat-cheeked face, Piano Smile smiled his piano smile, each alternate tooth extracted, the remaining teeth whiter than fresh ivory. The bulky Overboss was dressed in his customary Homburg hat and broad-striped, double-breasted suit, in contrast to his goons, who wore fedoras and broad-striped double-breasted suits.

The keyboard grin widened. 'You're looking well considering your eventful life, Mister Cairo.'

'You too, considering you're the wrong side of a hundred.'

'Ah – there's nothing like young blood to keep you young. And young liver. And young kidneys. And so on. I have a special organ donor deal with a state orphanage. Nobody misses the children. And I always throw a nice

Fargo Day party for the little orphans. Not to mention all the rest of my charity work.'

'Well, that's absolutely peachy of you.'

'Too kind. Shows respect.' The Overboss blew a blue circle of cigar smoke. 'How did you get in through the Men's room?'

'I popped out of a toilet.'

The smile shrank. 'Don't mess with me, Mister Cairo. I don't appreciate – disrespect. How did you get in?'

'Okay – I used a local-space-warp beam to dematerialise and reconstitute the intervening plascrete.'

'This makes sense. This is reasonable.' The keyboard smile was on full show again. It played a different tune. 'Safe trip down here?'

'Oh, a trifling difficulty or two. I'm not one to complain.'

'Ah – I was told you'd be tested. Like – ya know – knights and stuff. Trial by combat.'

'Uh-huh. And who told you that?'

Piano Smile tapped the side of his bulbous nose. 'The Man. Mister Big.'

'I thought there were three Overbosses. The underworld triumvirate.'

'Not an Overboss. An Underboss. *The* Underboss. The Man.'

'You've lost me. And I'm not here to discuss bosses. I've come for Lucia Lux.'

'Patience.' A chunky hand was raised. 'Patience. The Man tested you. You came good. As for the lady – you'll see her in a few minutes. You were given six hours. You made it in half that time. This is good. The Man knew you'd do good.'

Cairo expelled a sharp breath. 'Who the hell is "The Man"?'

'The boss of bosses. The Underboss of the Overbosses.'

Cairo thought of the Tarot card in his pocket. The World Turned Upside Down. 'The Underworld becomes the Overworld,' he said.

'You got it. Justice Hall and City Hall are about to go under.'

131

'Doesn't make sense. Organised crime and City Hall have slept in the same bed so often they should do the decent thing and get married. As for Justice Hall – the Overbosses can always rely on that one per cent of Judges who're bent to keep the illegal profits flowing in while the ninety-nine per cent of Judges who're insufferably straight keep order on the streets.'

'Times change. What can I say? The Mayor's Office is a joke. City Hall's nothin' without Justice Hall. And the Judges are losing their grip. Been losing it for years. Street crime's hit the roof. Punk gangs everywhere. They got no respect. Bad for business. You know how much profit we lost to street gangs since Judgement Day? Forty-three per cent. *Forty-three per cent*. Time for a change. Time for the Man.'

'Sounds like a mayoral election slogan. If that's your racket, I hope it keeps you happy and busy. All I want is Lucia.'

Piano Smile took a long drag of his cigar, released a plume of smoke. 'You ain't said nothin' about Lorelei.'

Cairo felt like ramming the lighted end of the cigar down the gangster's throat, but he maintained a calm mask and calm tone. 'Whoever murdered Lorelei and abducted Lucia, it wasn't your men. The whole thing was much too fast. Much too clever. Anything to do with "The Man", by any chance?'

'Sure it was. That's no big secret. You see, the Man ain't really a man at all. He's some kinda god. God of the Underworld. He sent the men in black suits to Lucia and Lorelei.'

Cairo glanced over the balcony rail to the stalls some fifteen metres below. A lot of enemies could hide down there, behind the long rows of plush-covered seats. 'Men in black suits?'

'Yeah.' Piano Smile gave a sly wink. 'The men in black suits are special men. The stuff that dreams are made of. Bad dreams.'

A damp chill seeped into Cairo's skin. It was like wearing an ice-cream suit. He couldn't keep a shiver from his voice:

'I want to see Lucia. Now.'

The Overboss spread expansive arms. 'You shall, Mister Cairo, you shall.' A meaty finger pointed at the curtained screen. 'Let the show begin.'

Since entering the Casablanca, Cairo had averted his gaze from the red curtains covering the screen. Red curtains. The same curtains as all those years ago.

Splashes of red on a black-and-white movie . . .

The falcon . . .

A mouth like an open mantrap . . . .

'I AM THE LAW!'

Cairo took a deep breath as the chandeliers dimmed and the red curtains swished open.

An old 2-D monochrome movie flashed on the screen. The showing began well into the last reel, but he identified it right off. He knew the movie by heart.

The Public Enemy, made in 1931.

On the screen, James Cagney, as the gangster Tom Powers, was stealing a couple of .38 revolvers from a small store.

The scene shifted to a rainy street at night outside the offices of the Western Chemical Company. Cagney, drenched in the downpour, waited in hiding as Schemer Burns and his men entered the offices. Burns and his henchmen had murdered Cagney's friend, Matt Doyle. Cagney wanted vengeance.

Cagney advanced through the rainstorm, hands in suit pockets, fingers gripped round the hidden revolvers.

His approaching figure, streaming with rain, filled the screen. A facial close-up . . .

A moment of darkness as the shot changed to show Cagney heading into the Western Chemical Company.

Except Cagney wasn't there.

Lucia Lux had taken his place.

A twenty-second century alien girl, colour-drained to black and white and several shades of grey, stood in the teeming rain of prohibition America.

She gazed at her black-and-white surroundings, aghast.

Looked down at her monochrome figure.

And screamed.

The scream had the scratchy sound of old movies. A small bird scrabbling its claws on the bars of an ungilded cage.

The screen was coated with hypma. Had to be. Hypma metamorphosis was the only way Lucia could have been trapped in a movie-world. A black-and-white nightmare.

Cairo was barely aware of Piano Smile's throaty baritone. 'There you have it, Mister Cairo. Lucia went into movies. *Inside* a movie. Forever.'

The movie scene switched to a hospital room. Three people stood beside an empty bed, behaving as though a wounded Cagney was in it. The star had gone, but the rest of the cast stuck faithfully to the script. They were, after all, merely light and shadows on a wall. No being. No essence.

A monochrome Lucia cowered on the floor, hands covering her face. She had being. She had essence. All the worse for her.

'Cagney left the movie at midnight,' the Overboss chuckled. 'He'll never appear in the final scenes again. Not on any record of the flik. Not anywhere. Not ever. He quitted his role. Situation vacant.' He flicked a nicotine-stained finger at Lucia. 'Situation filled.'

Cairo managed to keep his hands from flying at Piano Smile's throat. 'What the hell did you do to her? Transform her to photons? She'll go crazy in there. Crazy-for-good crazy. Get her out. Get – her – out.'

The Overboss radiated smugness. 'Can't be done.'

'Do it.'

'Can't be done.'

Cairo's Dillinger pressed into Piano Smile's neck in half the blink of an eyelid. '*Do it.*'

The goons sprang to their feet. Handfuls of lethal hardware took a bead on the private eye.

The mobster was unimpressed by the gun at his neck. 'No go, Mister Cairo. You got a rep. You only kill Judges.'

'You've been judge, jury and executioner in a thousand cases, just like Dredd and the rest of the bullet-heads.

You're Judge enough for me to kill.' As he spoke, his stare darted from side to side, taking in the fancy weaponry aimed at his head. That was how he saw the goon called False Teeth smile big and wide, displaying a full set of dentures.

The next instant the gums were bare as the false teeth exited in a streak of light and clamped their gnashers on Cairo's throat. The toothless mouth went on smiling big and wide.

He was familiar with False Teeth's speciality. His jaws and dentures worked in unison, even when separated by kilometres. Once the gummy mouth clamped shut, the false teeth would make red munceburger of the throat they clung to. If he shot the toothless goon the bullet would wipe the smile from his face, and Cairo's throat would go the way of all flesh.

Dead or alive, False Teeth would kill him. He couldn't get out of this one.

Not without a balloon bullet.

Thumb-flicking the Dillinger to balloon fire mode, he swung the pistol and shot False Teeth right in the grinning mouth.

The compressed-gas bullet halted and expanded once its micro-sensors registered it was inside a mouth. The thin flexiplast shell ballooned to a twelve-centimetre ball in .21 of a second. Its expansion from then on was much slower: one centimetre a second.

Cairo didn't stay to watch the show. He had lost the advantage once he'd transferred his aim from Piano Smile to the toothless goon. He was already diving over the balcony rail as he fired at False Teeth.

Slugs thwacked into the seat he'd just vacated as he switched the Dillinger back to standard ammo.

Too slow on the trigger, boys. A fraction too slow.

Firing over one shoulder, spraying bullets across the line of hoodlums, he nose-dived over the parapet.

The front rail of the lower balcony was about five metres below. If he didn't grab it he'd drop some fifteen metres to the hard-topped cinema seats.

Ouch would be a major understatement if he landed in the stalls. Broken bones galore.

The balcony rail came within reach. He lunged for it. Missed.

His heart did the hop-skip-and-jump.

Then his stretching fingers contacted the balcony's base ledge, moulded with masks of comedy and tragedy. His hand found purchase on a mask of tragedy.

A bolt of pain shot through his shoulder as the grip took the full weight of his arcing body. His fingers thought they'd snapped.

But the grip held.

So did the dentures at his throat.

Mind racing on fast forward, he glimpsed a flip-seat that had not flipped back. A soft landing on a near-direct line beneath his feet. From a hanging position, an eight-metre-plus fall.

Here goes.

Firing upwards to keep the goons occupied, he dropped.

The fall lasted a long time to his adrenalin-speeded brain.

He landed plumb on the soft seat. And juddered from heel to head. His spine felt like squashed salami.

It didn't stop him somersaulting backwards two rows, still firing off continuous rounds overhead.

The back-flip took him out of range of the mobsters' firepower.

Hitting the floor, he ducked and crawled under three rows of seats before halting for breath.

He was about to pull the false teeth from his throat when their loosening grip finally gave way. The balloon bullet in False Teeth's mouth must have swollen close to twenty centimetres by now.

The wide-open dentures hit the floor at the same instant he heard a distant snap-crack of jaw-bones overhead.

False Teeth had smiled his last smile until the surgeons went to work.

Cairo kicked the dentures high over the seats and clean across a side aisle.

Ramming a fresh clip into the Dillinger, he stood up and tried to figure out how to escape the Casablanca alive. The two exits led up to the balconies. The top balcony's heavily guarded side-exit was the only way out of the cinema.

Except for the screen. The hypma-coated screen which was showing *The Public Enemy*'s final scene to the accompaniment of 'I'm Forever Blowing Bubbles'. A black-and-white Lucia quailed in a bare hallway as the character of Mike Powers opened the door to a vacancy in place of what should have been Cagney's upright corpse, trussed up like a rolled carpet.

Cairo could risk jumping through the screen. If he was crazy.

A leap into a shining hypma screen was worse than any leap into the dark.

But death wasn't much of an option, either.

The sudden descent of the hoodlums cancelled out the choice.

Toots Ritzy, Mugsy, Fingers, Tap-Dance, Johnny Threeballs and six lesser gunmen dropped at medium speed into the stalls, a distinctive shimmer of anti-grav radiating under their feet as they came down with Overkill machine-guns blazing.

They were wearing anti-grav belts. He hadn't reckoned on that.

'Gruddam cheats,' he muttered, ducking for cover as he fired.

His volley blew Mugsy's hat off.

The top of Mugsy's head went with it. It sailed over the seats like an upside-down bowl of raspberry jelly.

The back-rest Cairo had hidden behind exploded from a micro-missile, leaving a blazing crater.

Just as Cairo expected. That was why he'd bent double and run along the row a split second after the shot that left Mugsy with half a head. He had covered seven metres

137

before the missile hit. The detonation catapulted him a lot further a lot faster.

He came to ground in the aisle, smothered in smoke and falling plaster.

'We got da bastard, boss!' Through the ringing in his ears he heard Toots Ritzy's shrill cry of victory. Taking cover before the cloaking smoke dissipated, he permitted himself a grim smile.

In Cairo's world you were never safer than when your enemies thought you dead.

'Dat Cairo creep,' Ritzy cackled. 'He's *history*, man.'

Seemed nobody had told Ritzy that history repeated itself.

Cairo was about to stage another come-back.

Dillinger levelled, he peered through the clearing smoke. Hazy outlines emerged. Four – no, five vague silhouettes, becoming sharper with each breath.

It was him or them, but it still felt like killing in cold blood, a privilege he reserved for Judges.

His finger refused to squeeze the trigger.

'Hey!' Johnny Threeballs exclaimed in his distinctive falsetto. 'Duh creep don't show up on radar. Not nowhere near duh crater.'

'Extend radar range, and give the joint a hi-ex shower,' Piano Smile yelled down.

That decided it.

Cairo squeezed the trigger and five silhouettes spun in the smoke. Then drifted aimlessly, buoyed up by anti-grav belts.

'Smoke dispersant, *now*!' a voice shrieked.

Cairo aimed a slug in the direction of the voice. The shriek changed to a squeal, then a rattle.

But the advice had been heeded.

The *whoosh* of smoke dispersant ruffled Cairo's hair as he quitted his hiding place for another.

'Dredd,' he swore, as the swirling vapour fled the stalls. Auditorium and screen came into full view. The credits were rolling on the movie, along with 'I'm Forever Blowing Bubbles'.

He had accounted for six, dead or maimed. That left five. Five wary killers with ultratek Overkill guns. He had no chance of surviving a hi-ex shower.

It would have to be Psi-power against firepower.

He'd need to uncork the psychic fire-water he kept bottled up.

Unleash the Wild.

Letting that wayward genie out the bottle had saved his life plenty of times. But the first time – in this cinema – had almost destroyed him.

The Casablanca was the last place on earth he would have chosen to loose the Wild. The site of the power's first eruption, all those years ago . . .

Blood on a black-and-white movie . . .

Turning and turning in the widening gyre . . .

. . . Mere anarchy is loosed upon the world . . .

'I AM THE LAW!'

For a moment he drew back from the decision. Trust in his Dillinger and hope for the best.

The initial blast of hi-ex nearby renewed his resolve.

Let the Wild run wild, and the Devil take his own.

His thoughts reached into the back of his skull, into the dark. Sowed seeds of wrath.

And reaped a whirlwind.

The Wild stormed out. Flung him flat on his back as it roared into the auditorium.

Pain had a colour. Crimson pain. His head throbbed with it.

Blood spurted from his nose, trickled from his ears.

He wept a red tear.

Biting his lip, he rode out the waves of pain. They never lasted long. It just seemed like a long time.

The waves receded. His vision cleared.

Shaking his groggy head, he lurched upright.

The Casablanca had gone screwy with the Wild.

Phantoms snaked under the seats and looped-the-loop under the bas-reliefs of the arched ceiling. The chandeliers rang out a crystal rendition of Roy Orbison's 'In Dreams'. A mask of tragedy whistled the tune of 'Always

Look on the Bright Side of Life' while a mask of comedy broke into a soulful version of 'Heartbreak Hotel'. The rest of the Wild manifestations were rather more strange.

Phantasmagoria time. Mostly illusion.

The silvery phantoms that weaved and whirled in the cinema were Cairo's memories, not ghosts. The singing masks were embodiments of his wry humour.

But Piano Smile's airborne goons didn't know that. Five frantic figures, kept aloft by anti-grav, spun in a whirlwind of grotesqueries. Cairo lightly touched their minds and sensed sheer panic. They thought they were in a horror flik.

Colour suddenly drained from the cinema. The entire interior, and everything and everyone in it, was transformed to black and white.

When the cinema turned monochrome, the hoodlums must have been certain they were in a horror movie. A black-and-white horror movie.

Then the cinema clock went crazy. Its digits flickered as they sped faster and faster, compressing minutes into seconds.

The monochrome transformation and speeding clock sent a chill through Cairo.

This was what happened the first time, back when he was fourteen.

A black-and-white cinema with a black-and-white audience and a racing clock.

He checked his own watch. Like the clock, it rushed headlong down the hours.

Okay, okay, he told himself. It's the hypma screen giving a black-and-white light show. Screwing up time. You'll be okay – so long as the screen doesn't come alive.

The screen came alive.

Alive with the Roaring Twenties. A dishevelled James Cagney, mortally wounded, staggered along a snowswept sidewalk to the steps of a church. Some of the snowflakes wafted into the auditorium.

The Roaring Twenties dissolved in a burst of white light. Another Cagney movie appeared – *Angels with*

Dirty Faces. Cagney walked down a light-shadow-light-shadow corridor, his features alternately in and out of view as he headed for the electric chair.

The Death Row scene jumped a few shots. A hand yanked down the electric switch. The lights dimmed in the prison.

And went out in the cinema.

Cairo caught the wails of the airborne goons.

'OHGRUDOHGRUDOHGRUD . . .'

He wasn't feeling too great himself.

The Wild and hypma was nitro to glycerine: a psych-bomb.

The hypma screen exploded into action, irradiating the auditorium.

Snatches of old black-and-white movies strobed on the screen, out of sequence, out of mind.

The clock showed 5-03 at one blink, 5-04 the next. The time was a-flying.

So were the bullets.

A slug zinged past Cairo's ear. He glanced up and fired as he flung himself aside. Toots Ritzy was a few metres overhead, with his snazzy suit and Overkill machine-gun, side-loaded with micro-missiles.

The crook had put what passed for his brain together again.

He couldn't use the Wild on Ritzy. It was well and truly out of control. Gun-play was the only game on offer. Dillinger against Overkill. David against Goliath.

He pursued a duck-and-dodge run down the aisle, shooting under his arm as he searched for a means to even the score. A stream of hi-ex exploded in his wake.

Tap-Dance, Johnny Threeballs, and the twins Dead-Eye and Red-Eye zoomed down past the six floating dead men and homed in on Cairo, Overkills at the ready.

David against five Goliaths.

He spotted an Overkill dropped earlier by one of the dead men hovering around the chandeliers. Diving, he grabbed the weapon and rolled onto his back, spraying fire at his adversaries.

Goliath against five Goliaths.

Dead-Eye and Red-Eye, as always, were side by side.

He launched the Overkill's remaining micro-missile at the twins.

Dead-Eye and Red-Eye's tattered flesh and broken-stick bones intermingled in the blast, twins to the last.

Tap-Dance and Johnny Threeballs took fright and flew to the top balcony where Piano Smile was shaking an angry fist and bawling fit to burst:

'Blow him to Grud, you mother-drokkers! I want him rubbed out!'

Grinning as he swept over Cairo's head, Ritzy pulled the trigger. 'Take a mouthful of missile, Mister Cairo.'

Nothing happened. Ritzy hadn't checked the side-loaders. Empty.

Unfamiliar with his weapon, Cairo switched to what he thought was hi-ex. Squeezed the trigger as Ritzy banked in a sharp turn.

And slammed a bullet into the hitman's stomach.

The impact hurled Ritzy clean across the cinema. Straight for the mish-mash of old movies strobing on the hypma screen.

Hi-ex, straight to the breadbasket, but the gunman had not exploded. And his screams proved he was very much alive.

Glancing at his Overkill, Cairo saw the initials HED on the activation panel. Hi-ex delay.

Ritzy hit the screen, on which a talon-fingered Nosferatu was climbing a stairway.

Then the mobster exploded.

He painted the screen red before dropping in bits and pieces.

Nosferatu vanished.

The Maltese Falcon took his place.

Humphrey Bogart had finished unwrapping the falcon statuette. The bright red of Ritzy's life dribbled down the black image of the falcon.

The sight detonated a time-bomb in Cairo's skull.

Yesterday sprang into today.

The scene of fifteen years past replayed itself on the screen. And also in the haunted spaces of the auditorium . . .

Time's bobbin unreeled . . .

He was fourteen again, with Joel for his first name and nothing for a surname, and surrounded by smokers in the Casablanca smoke-easy.

The Maltese Falcon was the movie of the night. The film buffs were happy with the film. The smokers were happy with their cigarettes.

Then Judge Dredd dropped in. Clean through a side wall on his Beast of the Streets. The blast of his entry blew a five-metre hole in the wall and didn't do the row he landed on much good, either.

Joel looked at Dredd and saw a helmet and a mouth.

A mouth like an open mantrap, bellowing:

'I AM THE LAW!'

At that bellow, those words, the Wild first stirred in Joel.

'Drop those smokes or you're dead, creeps!' Dredd warned.

At the warning, the smokers dropped their cigarettes, resigned to a one-to-two-year stretch in the cubes.

All but two nicotine fiends, who would apparently rather die than spend a smokeless year or two in the slammer.

A middle-aged man darted up the aisle for the exit. A Lawgiver bullet showed him the exit from life. Before he had stopped his death-twitch a young woman tried to bolt from the front row.

Dredd's bullet took off her head, spraying blood all over the screen.

Bright red on a black and white movie.

The Wild stormed into Joel's skull and out into the cinema.

The first thing it hit was the screen.

Just as Bogart, referring to the black falcon statuette, delivered the closing line of the movie:

'The stuff that dreams are made of.'

The Wild made a rampant dream of the screen.

Some dreams were nightmares.

Some nightmares were real.

Life is film noir.

Around the youth, the auditorium turned a strobing black and white. The clocks raced as if desperate to hurry up the final Day of Judgement.

Joel barely noticed. He only had eyes for the screen. It was playing edited highlights of his birth. The camera angle was that of his own eyes, wide open to the new world outside the womb.

It showed him the nightmare of his birth, in harsh black and white:

I was born with both eyes open in a brothel at midnight on Hallowe'en in the middle of a Judge raid.

Bombs and bullets in the brothel. Hello, cruel world.

His mother is blasting away with the best of them. She sends a Judge spinning, visor shattered.

Judge Dredd levels his Lawgiver and bawls: 'I AM THE LAW!'

The muzzle spits fire and fury.

His mother's head erupts on her shoulders. Her blood, the sole splash of colour in the monochrome replay, sprays red action paintings on the walls . . .

Then the black Maltese Falcon was back, dripping red.

It flew into a wide sky and launched into a beak and talon battle with an eagle. The eagle ripped out the falcon's right eye.

The screen went black.

An earlier scene from *The Maltese Falcon* burst into view. Bogart opened the first of Peter Lorre's fistful of passports, revealing the name 'Joel Cairo'. He broke with the script by tossing the passport aside. It arced from the screen and landed in Joel's lap. The name 'Joel Cairo' confronted Joel's downward glance.

Then Cagney was back on the silver screen, in the climactic scene from *White Heat*. He stood on top of one of the giant domes in a petro-chemical works, laughing at the cops down on the ground. He called to his dead, revered Ma, and shouted: 'Top of the world!' And fired his gun into the dome of explosive gas. It blew Cagney to high hell, and the entire factory with him.

At that point some author altered the script ending.

Rising with the fireball, a phoenix ascended on crucified wings, reborn in the flame. The phoenix changed to a black falcon, spiralling upwards.

And a voice from the Casablanca's auditorium wrenched his attention from the screen.

He turned and saw a youth flying over the heads of the panicked audience, body rotating as he headed for the screen. The airborne figure was reciting an old poem:

'Turning and turning in the widening gyre

The falcon cannot hear the falconer.

Things fall apart; the centre cannot hold;

Mere anarchy is loosed upon the world . . .'

The figure hit the screen. And merged with it. Dissolved into the black image of the soaring falcon.

With the youth's disappearance into a cinematic limbo, the Wild subsided. It flowed back to its source, deep in Joel's psyche.

Colour flooded back into the Casablanca. The cinema returned to a semblance of normality.

As the Wild power streamed back into him, brimming with revelations of his birth, he took a look at the shimmering, cinematic passport in his lap.

Joel Cairo.

A passport to a new life. A life dedicated to killing the Judge who killed his mother.

He threw a quick glance at Dredd, busy dragooning the cowed audience into neat lines.

Somehow, somewhere, a late twentieth-century Jon and Vangelis song: 'The Friends of Mister Cairo', was playing its homage to mid-twentieth-century gangster movies.

He looked back at the passport.

Picked it up.

It vanished in his hand, along with the last vestiges of

childhood. That was the last second of his life as a youth called Joel.

And the first as a man named Mister Cairo . . .

He was abruptly jolted back to the present by Piano Smile's angry shout from the upper balcony.

'You *dead*, Mister Cairo! You kill my boys . . . You *dead*!'

Cairo shuddered as he felt the Wild rushing back into the pores of his skin, into the storm of his soul.

The storm within quietened.

His clearing gaze revealed that the auditorium was calm and still.

Everything normal.

If you discounted the hovering dead men, that was.

He was on his knees, recovering from the aftershocks of psychic eruption. The loosing of the Wild always forced him to his knees, brought him low.

'You *dead*, Mister Cairo!' The shrill edge to his tone revealed that the Wild-hypma show had rattled him. Rattled him good.

'Bad grammar, bad observation,' Cairo remarked, rising to his feet as he did a swift scan of the cinema for any gun-hands left alive. 'I'm still breathing.' He aimed the Overkill at Piano Smile. False Teeth, squirming at the Overboss's side, had a cracked jaw and a mouthful of a balloon bullet to keep him occupied.

The Overboss was the only threat left.

And the last source of information going.

'Why'd you bring me down here, Piano Smile?'

The mobster scowled. 'Ask the Man.'

'Well the Man's not here, is he, whoever he is.'

'He'll be here. He's real keen to meet you, Mister Cairo.'

'Uh-huh. So how come you drop your goons on me, not to mention the bullets and missiles?'

'The Man wanted you dead. *Rub him out*. That's what the Man said.'

'He wants me dead and he wants to meet me. Fine. Makes perfect sense.'

The Overboss stood up, signalled to the hapless False Teeth, and started to make his way to the exit.

Cairo brandished the Overkill. 'You're not going anywhere, Piano Smile. I want answers. And I want Lucia out of that movie-trap, even if it kills you – or me.'

A keyboard smile flashed from the gallery. 'You ain't gonna fire off that thing. You know you ain't. I don't wear a helmet and badge. I'll get out of here alive – and stay alive. But you – you're dead, Mister Cairo. A walkin' dead man. It ain't just me you're dealing with. Big Shot and Fat Chance have put the word out on you, too. Sleep with your eyes open, Cairo.'

Cairo lowered the Overkill as the mobster disappeared into the exit.

Piano Smile. Big Shot. Fat Chance. All three Overbosses were out for his blood.

And all at the orders of some Underboss Man who was keen to make his acquaintance.

He dropped the Overkill and pocketed his Dillinger, then gave a philosophical shrug. Whoever said the world was supposed to make sense?

The clock showed 6-03 a.m.

Time had whizzed by on turbo-boost.

And he was still nowhere near saving Lucia Lux. The task seemed impossible, but that didn't count. You start a job, you finish it.

Even if it kills you.

The sudden brightening of the screen startled him into drawing the Dillinger.

The final scene of *The Public Enemy* resumed in front of him.

Once again, Mike Powers walked down a hallway to open the door to a non-existent Cagney. Lucia cowered in the hallway, finger-nails scratching her face. The poor kid was scared out of her wits, if she had any left.

Mike Powers opened the door, and froze on the spot, instantly converted from movie image to photograph.

But the smiling, dark-suited man who strolled in

through the open door was as lively a cine image as Lucia, who had turned to him with a wail of despair.

Five other smiling men in black suits and bow-ties followed the first into the hallway.

The man at the head of the group of six looked almost human.

As for the rest, it was hard to think of their faces as human.

They were wearing their faces upside down.

Eyes at the bottom, smile at the top.

'Hello, Mister Cairo,' said the man who looked almost human, flashing a silver smile into the cinema. 'I'm the Man.'

CHAPTER FOURTEEN

Sejanus's fist slammed down on the eagle chair's arm-rest.

'I know you, Mister Cairo.'

The vid read-out on Omnipotens' private channel told the private eye's whole story from day one. Hour one.

From 11-56 p.m. on October 31, year 2086, in Wild Ways brothel in the colloquially named Big Joke district of Sector 42.

Sejanus remembered that night well.

He had been under Dredd's command on a series of vice-sweeps in the notorious Big Joke area. Wild Ways was the last on the list.

Dredd's ruthless stamping out of the district's sleep-eezies had been an inspiration to Sejanus. Joe Dredd, in one of his first command roles, had shown his subordinates what Judgement was all about.

Any whore who dared raise a fist and take a swing got a boot in the face. Any sex-slut who fired off a gun got her sluttish head blasted off. Under-age or over the hill – human or alien – they all got the same treatment if they did not surrender. Stamp on them.

The same went for birthing mothers.

Wild Ways was a Sisters of Gramercy independent sleep-eezie, run by the women themselves. If you could call mutants women. Wild Ways was ninety per cent mutant. Cairo's mother was one of the ninety per cent.

A whore and a mutant.

That was a combination male Judges abhorred. A whore was a spit in the face to a celibate Judge. Judges kept themselves chaste, inviolate, while whores traded in depravity. As for mutants – there was no place but the Cursed Earth for genetic deviants. The genetic stock of Mega-City One must be kept pure.

Cairo's mother was doubly anathema. A mutant whore. Her choice was the Cursed Earth or death. When she pulled a gun it was clear she hadn't chosen the Cursed Earth.

The scene played itself out inside Sejanus's head, blow for blow, word for word.

She was already pumping her brat from the womb when she drew her pistol and pumped a string of rounds into the officers on the raid. One slug had taken a rookie right between the eyes.

Dredd swung his Lawgiver at the woman as he bellowed: 'I AM THE LAW!'

She had just given birth to her little bastard.

His eyes were wide open.

Sejanus saw what lay behind those eyes. Psi-power. It took one to know one. But the infant's Psi potential was prodigious, dwarfing Sejanus's psychic capacities. And it was wild. Wild and dangerous. Left alive, he might one day shake Justice Central to its roots.

He had to die.

Sejanus reached into the mind of Judge Oswald, a rookie. And directed the rookie's aim at the infant, just as another brat was emerging into the world.

A part of Oswald's mind resisted Sejanus. His aim jerked upwards at the last instant.

Dredd and Oswald fired at the woman simultaneously. Her head exploded into red mush.

A second later the last two whores hit the wall in a blast of hi-ex.

And Joe Dredd was leaning over the new-born male twins.

'I don't know what got into me,' babbled Oswald. 'I didn't mean to – '

'Get a grip,' snapped Dredd. 'Make out the usual report.'

Too late for Sejanus to risk another mind-reach. He

would just have to hope Dredd dumped the twins in the Cursed Earth. They would last maybe a couple of days in the radioactive wasteland.

In a few minutes the babies were placed in makeshift carry-cots. Dredd glanced at the second twin.

'*Mutant*,' he said dismissively.

A brief look at the first-born. 'Possible norm. Have him checked out at Med Division.'

'We'll need a name,' Judge Barnaby piped up. 'How about yours, Joe?'

Dredd's lip twisted. 'Don't give a whore's son my name.'

'Okay. Let's make it – Joel.'

Dredd gave a contemptuous shrug.

'And what about this one?' Judge Ellerman asked, nodding at the mutant child. She was the only female Judge on the six-strong vice-sweep squad. And she'd not exactly disguised her distaste for the mission. If she pushed it any further Dredd would be sure to have her down for suspension.

'It doesn't need a name,' Dredd said curtly.

'John might be suitable,' she muttered, 'as he's going into the wilderness.'

'What you talking about, Ellerman?' Barnaby snorted.

'John the Baptist,' she replied. 'You know – the voice crying in the wilderness. In the Bible.'

'Maybe you'd better keep your reading to the recommended lists, Ellerman,' Dredd rumbled ominously. 'Now get that mutant on the wrong side of the Wall.'

The wrong side of the Wall.

The wilderness beyond the city.

At Dredd's order, the twins went their separate ways.

One to the Cursed Earth. The other to a maximum security orphanage. Both long forgotten.

Until now. Omnipotens had resurrected the past.

Sejanus leaned back in the eagle chair and reread Omnipotens' reconstituted account of Joel Cairo's history, storing the salient details in his mind. The bare outlines were striking enough:

151

Joel spent the first six years of his life in Max Security Orphanage X19 in Sector 42. He proved himself an infant prodigy at the age of three, with an IQ that went right off the scale. Wary of such precocious intellect, the warden had him put under extra surveillance. Four months after his sixth birthday, Joel blew up the orphanage by the ingenious conversion of simple chemistry sets. The explosions were timed so that all the inmates had time to escape. Every inmate was captured inside an hour. Except for Joel.

He was never caught. He disappeared into the dark underbelly of Mega-City One. Even Omnipotens could supply only the roughest sketch of Joel's life between the ages of six and fourteen. He lived in the underground levels of decayed blocks in the Mumbles and the Maze for some of those years. Most of the time he must have hidden in the sewers, competing with the rats for food.

Not until he was fourteen did Joel enter the official records. He was arrested by Judge Dredd in a smoke-easy cinema called the Casablanca, along with a packed audience of smokers. Dredd reported that some sort of 'freak psychedelic show' had broken out in the cinema, leaving several perps dead and a lot more out of their heads.

The Judge wasn't to know that the Casablanca was no ordinary cinema. Sejanus had seen to that. He had formed a cabal from Psi and Tek Divisions, devoted to the study of hypma and its effects on the mind. It led later to Project Lazarus, aimed at 'resurrecting' cine characters from the screen, encoded with artificial memories.

The Casablanca was not merely an underground cinema: it was a hypma-screen laboratory for experimenting on unwitting audiences. Experimentation had proceeded apace after a strange youth known as 'the Preacher' aided the team. The full potential of hypma was realised the night Dredd invaded the Casablanca. The Preacher, reciting the first lines of a Yeats poem, had flown clean into the screen, never to be seen again. Nobody had succeeded in identifying the jumble of images

152

on the screen. But hypma was shown to be a powerful weapon.

Not until now did Sejanus connect Joel with the massive burst of Psi energy from the screen. Everyone had believed it was the Preacher's short-lived accomplishment.

'But Joel was there,' the Colossus Chief muttered, stroking his lower lip. 'Joel was there.'

When hauled in, and finally placed in Arkham psycho-cubes, the record showed Joel as 'Mister Cairo' from Mega-City 2. The fourteen-year-old had somehow hacked into the MAC computer and fed a bogus biography into its files. Remarkable. Still more remarkable was the way Cairo hid his mind from skilled Psi operatives. All his mind revealed was a cloak of cinematic images, impenetrable. He was placed under restraints; strait-jacket, secure plasteen head and torso harness – the whole works.

That didn't stop him escaping after two months, on January 12.

Mandra, a cadet on work release from the Academy of Law, was in Arkham psycho-cubes in the week leading up to Cairo's escape.

Cairo and Mandra. Same time. Same place. There was the connection between the private eye and his errant daughter. They must have met there, perhaps plotted Cairo's dramatic break-out together.

After the escape, however, there was no indication that the two met up again. Mandra graduated in the Academy of Law while Cairo hid out in the Mumbles' criminal underworld, under the protection of Blue Angel, the notorious gun-toting hooker, and Arbuckle, the toilet janitor.

Sejanus arched an elegant eyebrow. '*Toilet janitor?*'

Whatever, Cairo had prospered under his sleazy surrogate parents, both dead before his twenty-third birthday. Mister Cairo's MAC biog was altered at least nine times since his psycho-cubes break-out. An impressive piece of hacking.

His travel record was just as impressive. In ten years as

a private investigator he had covered most of what was once called North and South America, as well as visiting Antarctic City, New Pacific City, and the continents of Oz, Africa and Asia. As for what was once known as Europe, he had spent a sum of three years in Euro-City, Brit, the Emerald Isle and Cuidad Espana. He was fluent in twenty-seven languages, including Classical Greek, Latin and ancient Egyptian hieroglyphics.

Egyptian hieroglyphics, for Grud's sake.

Two Eye replays, previously excised from the records, revealed that Mister Cairo could outdraw and outshoot any Judge on the force, including the formidable Joe Dredd.

Another excised replay, retrieved by Omnipotens, proved that Cairo's Psi potential was as enormous as Sejanus had suspected all those years ago, when a whore gave birth to a brat in a brothel.

His twin had died within days of birth, somewhere out there in the Cursed Earth. They had killed the wrong child. Sejanus had made a serious error when he failed to make an end of Joel.

Almost as serious an error as siring his daughter on that *mambo* woman in Tina Turner Conapts.

On reflection, he was not sure which was the worst mistake – failing to blast Cairo at birth, or fathering Mandra.

Judging from his file, Cairo was beginning to look like the most dangerous man in Mega-City One.

'Store file – Colossus Chief's eyes only,' instructed Sejanus.

The read-out vanished from the monitor.

He prepared to send a message to Dredd: No known connection between Mister Cairo, ex-Judge Mandra and mythical Anarchopolis.

The transmission was negated by a curt announcement from Dredd, via audio-com:

'Perp name of James Cagney is dead. We got Mandra cold. Bringin' her in alive, Sejanus.'

Sejanus pressed a key for the full list of any h-wagons

in Dredd's immediate vicinity. The list brought a smile to his face.

Three of the Colossus Chief's covert operatives had botched killing Mandra in Mary Shelley Block, but they were low-grade material. There were nine of his men distributed throughout the h-wagons swooping on his daughter. All nine were high-grade.

Mandra wouldn't live to spout the truth.

Dredd's squads had killed Cagney. Her they wanted alive.

Like Cagney, she was not about to be taken alive.

A little rhyme and the hypma tooth implant would blow her head to Papa Legba.

She trembled as she reached the last, deadly word of the rhyme:

'Here comes a chopper to chop off your . . .'

'*You dirty rats!*' a voice rang out, simultaneous with a volley of shots.

Mandra clamped shut her mouth on the final, head-blowing word.

James Cagney, the gangster that cine-dreams were made of, was up and firing again. Apparently you really couldn't kill the stuff that dreams were made of.

Slugs from Cagney's .38 revolvers ripped into the lawmen as she dived instinctively to one side.

A slug ripped into her, too. Like a kick in the stomach. But not as powerful an impact as a Lawgiver bullet should pack. She rolled a few metres before the truth struck home.

Low-impact bullet.

Her hand ran down her back. No exit wound.

Low impact. A slug lodged in her stomach.

Hi-ex Delay.

Between five to fifty seconds before she exploded to smithereens.

One of the Judges had shot to kill, and she knew why.

Daddy was calling some of the shots.

'Cease fire!' Dredd roared.

The guns were lowered.

155

Cagney streaked to her side in the sudden lull. 'What gives, toots?'

'Someone's done my job for me. An HED's going to make me go bang. Keep your distance, or you'll go up with me.'

His reaction was ambiguous. 'Right over Manhattan,' he muttered. 'Top of the old world.'

'That was HED!' Dredd was bellowing. 'Who fired it?'

'Brooks,' Hershey snarled.

Weller had already aimed his Lawgiver at Judge Brooks. 'For you, Mandra,' Weller said, with a sidelong glance at her. 'For love of you.'

His gun lightning-flashed and thunder-cracked. Brooks' helmet took flight, with his head still inside it.

The headless body of Brooks stood upright for a long moment.

It dropped at the same instant a bullet from Judge Arendt slammed into Weller's back. He fell face down, raining blood.

'*What the drokk – ?*' boomed Dredd, glance darting around his unruly brigade.

Cagney whispered in Mandra's ear as he grabbed her arm. '*Now*, hot stuff. A few paces to the right – there's a crack in the world.'

She allowed herself to be guided by the gangster, but shrugged her shoulders. 'I'm dead, Cagney. Just a matter of seconds. I'm dead.'

'Never stopped me,' he said, cool as a walk outside Antarctic City.

'Get Cagney!' someone yelled. 'Laser cannon!'

'You'll hit Mandra!' Hershey yelled back.

Dredd gave a lift of his mighty shoulders. His tone was flat. 'She's dead anyway.'

Cagney halted, arm looped around Mandra.

'Yeah, copper, it's goodbyes all round.' Quick as thought, his .38 took a bead on Dredd. 'So long, copper,' he sneered as he squeezed the trigger.

The revolver click-clicked as it spun through empty chambers.

The .38's miraculous store of ammo had finally run out. He fired the other revolver from under Mandra's arm. Click-click-click –

'Aw hell,' he groaned. 'Damn cinema guns. Always let you down at the right dramatic moment. Didn't figure it'd be now.' He cast a rueful look at Mandra. 'Shooters clicking like that – means that Dredd goon's some kinda hero. That stuff's always happening to heroes. But who'd have reckoned that no-good cop as a hero? Beats me.'

Mandra could feel the faint vibration of the HED bullet as it ticked away its random countdown – any time up to fifty seconds from impact.

'Cagney – blow, before I blow.'

'We're both blowin' this world, doll.'

The world suddenly cracked open at their feet. A deafening ground thunder reverberated as the ground bucked and dipped.

There was nothing under Mandra's feet but a black abyss. She dropped right into it, Cagney's arm still gripping her tight.

'Crack in the world, Ma!' he shouted. 'Crack in the world!'

It was a long fall into darkness.

Plenty of time for Mandra to wonder whether she would die of an exploding bullet before she hit ground at splatter-speed.

Hershey scrambled back to her feet in time to see the split heal in the ground. It closed like stony lips clamming up on a dark secret.

The fissure, some ten metres long and two metres wide, had opened and shut in scant seconds.

And swallowed their prey.

Just like a mouth.

'They're gone. Straight drop to the Undercity. Dead and gone,' someone behind her muttered.

Dredd reared up. 'Mandra's dead and gone, sure enough. But Cagney – who knows?'

'What the hell *was* that?' Hershey breathed, glaring at

the smooth, unbroken ground. 'Sure as Grud wasn't an earthquake.'

Dredd turned his back on the scene. 'Let Tek work it out. We've got other perps to fry. Like Cairo.' The right corner of his mouth twisted a fraction. 'And bent Judges. Seems a lot of people wanted Mandra dead on sight.'

He levelled his Lawgiver at Arendt. 'Why'd you kill Weller?'

'And why did Brooks pump HED into Mandra?' Hershey chimed in, training her own gun on all and sundry.

'Bent Judges,' Dredd growled out the side of his mouth. 'You thinking what I'm thinking, Hershey?'

'We go it alone?'

'Right. I'll watch your back. You watch mine.' He waved his pistol. 'The rest of you – get going.'

'The Chief Judge ain't gonna like this,' a voice complained.

'Breaks my heart,' Hershey snorted.

'We'll keep McGruder informed as we go,' Dredd instructed Hershey in a pointed tone.

Her reply was sharp as an ice-pick. 'Just the two of us, Joe. *No one* else.'

Dredd's response was cut off by an Omnipotens flash on his Lawmaster vid-com:

REQUEST STATUS OF MANDRA AND JAMES CAGNEY.

'Mandra's dead,' he answered. 'Cagney's probably destroyed.'

Another message flared on the miniature screen:

TRACK DOWN MISTER CAIRO. MAX PRIORITY. NO REQUIREMENT TO BRING HIM IN ALIVE.

'You took the words right out my mouth,' grunted Dredd as he gunned the Lawmaster into action and roared down the street.

Hershey hurtled in his wake, vexed at Joe Dredd's typically headlong rush. He seemed to have forgotten about bent Judges in his dash to hunt down Mister Cairo.

She hadn't forgotten about that one per cent or so of bent Judges.

Or Sejanus, the Colossus Chief, sitting in that gigantic metal head with the brain of Omnipotens.

CHAPTER FIFTEEN

'Life is film noir, Mister Cairo,' said the Man.

The black-and-white figure on the screen had thrown one of Cairo's lines back at him. He thought he got the point.

The Man's arrival had made the Casablanca an authentic Dream Palace. A Bad Dream Palace.

The moment he saw the Man and his five black-suited henchmen, Cairo knew he was looking at Lucinda's murderers, Lucia's abductors.

Standing in a freeze-frame movie hallway, Lucia cowering at his feet, the Man stared right out of the screen, right into the auditorium. Deep into Cairo's eyes.

The Man was almost human. One breath away from humanity, as a man's corpse is one breath away from a man. If he had been a grotesque like his five followers, each with an upside-down face, he would not have chilled Cairo's veins to red ice. Almost human was one hundred per cent nightmare.

There was a superstition, old as the sphinx, that the blank gaze of a dead man could steal your soul. Cairo was starting to feel superstitious.

At any moment he expected the almost-human figure to step out of the screen. Right out of the screen, just as he had entered Lucia's habhold.

Tha alien girl's Happy House habhold had been barred to entry. Door locked on the inside. Immovable window frame. No way in or out.

Except through the vid-screen. The Man and his black-suited followers could stroll at will into a movie. They could just as easily step out of the movie into the movie house. Or from vid-screen into habhold. In and out, quick and slick.

Cairo flicked up his trench-coat collar and switched the Dillinger to safety mode. Bullets would be no use against this monochrome apparition.

The Man's face was virtually the only feature that was *not* inverted. Perhaps it would have been better if it was. There was nothing identifiably abnormal about his face. But his features gave the unsettling impression of being continuously on the verge of changing into something else. His face was a nightmare waiting to happen.

As for his clothes, they were as inverted as clothes could get. The tight-fitting dark suit was made entirely of cloth badges stitched together. Each badge was upside down. Each symbol, logo and message was turned on its head. He sported a monogrammed handkerchief from underneath his breast pocket. Evidently his breast pocket was upside down: if the inverted theme was sustained, the same probably went for the side pockets. Absurdly, the word 'natty' summed up the Man's attire as well as any.

Cairo pocketed the Dillinger and sank into one of the cinema seats.

'Wise move, Mister Cairo,' said the Man in a tone like silk on silk. 'Easier to shoot the moonlight than put a bullet in me. But you sensed that, didn't you, Mister Cairo? Or should I say Joel? So pleased to make your acquaintance. Call me Horus.'

'I'm here for Lucia, not you.' Cairo managed to say the words without betraying a trace of dread. 'Spring her from that cine-limbo and we can all go home.'

A silvery chuckle trickled from Horus's white lips. 'You have no home. Merely hiding places. You cloak yourself in the shadows of UnderBlock basements, safe rooms in brothels, corners of derelict buildings, tunnels in disused sewers, along with the rest of the shadow people. Everywhere, in fact, except the Undercity. You see, Mister Cairo, I know a great deal about you. We have much in common.'

'Who the hell are you?' Cairo whispered to himself.

The man in the movie somehow caught the whisper. 'Who am I?' He spread his arms wide in the grey hallway. His voice rose to prophetic pitch. 'I am the voice of one crying in the wilderness. I come to make crooked the straight paths of the Law. I am my own John the Baptist. My own messiah. I am Horus, the falcon god. And I – ' his smile slanted, ' – am the Anarch. The Anarch of Anarchopolis.'

The self-styled Anarch's exalted tone suddenly reminded Cairo of a night in the Casablanca, long ago. When the screen came alive. And a youth sailed into the living screen, reciting Yeats's *Second Coming* before he was swallowed up in the movie world.

'You're the Preacher . . .'

'*Was* the Preacher.' Horus lowered his arms. 'I was born an outcast. I became the Preacher in the wilderness. Now I'm a god of the silver screen. Your progress, however, has been less – elevated. Disappointing. We started out the same.'

Cairo's psychic alarm was ringing bells all over his nervous system. 'What do you mean – the same?'

Horus's head tilted to one side, eyes hooded. 'I was born in a brothel at midnight on Hallowe'en. Born in the middle of a Judge raid. Born one minute after my twin brother. Born of a headless mother.'

A civil war broke out in Cairo. Half of him believed the Anarch's account. Half of him did not.

He had heard the rumours of a mutant twin brother from some of the older Sisters of Gramercy. A mutant exposed at birth in the wastelands of the Cursed Earth. But the rumours had never been confirmed.

He shook his head. 'I don't believe you.' His tone lacked conviction.

'You will, Mister Cairo, you will. When you discover your true home. *My* home. Way down below. The journey into the Underworld will enlighten you. You've got less than two days to find me – then I'll free Lucia Lux. Otherwise – she remains stuck in a colourless existence.'

162

Cairo glanced at Lucia. She was still slumped against the wall, hands masking her face. The sight sparked anger in him. It boiled up in rage. He jabbed a finger at the screen. 'First I'm given six hours to find her. I found her in less than four, in spite of the UnderJudges. It was you who set them on me, wasn't it? Now you say I've got to find you in under two days or she stays locked in a black-and-white purgatory. Give me one reason why I should jump through another of your hoops.'

The Anarch's smile went a crooked path. 'A reason?' His finger-nails extended like a cat's, then flattened out into what looked like razor-blades. 'You want a *reason*? I'll give you a *reason* . . .'

He turned to Lucia. The finger-razors glittered as he gestured upwards. 'Rise, my child.'

She rose like a scared little girl, obedient and quaking.

'Look at me,' Horus commanded.

She looked at him.

He slit her throat with a finger-razor.

The throat unfolded, a second mouth. It spouted dark grey blood.

He smiled benignly at the gushing wound. 'What do you say, little girl?'

The ragged lips of the mouth-wound flexed and spoke in a bubbling voice:

'Thank you, sir.'

'Splendid,' he beamed, retracting the razors into his fingers. 'The hand that harms is the hand that heals.' He slid a pale finger over the rent. It sealed up at his touch. Lucia stood intact and shivering.

The Anarch bent another smile at Cairo. 'Special effects. A dash of cine-magic. Hocus-pocus. Film flim-flam.' The smile hardened. 'Now I'll give you a *real* reason.'

He cupped Lucia's face in his long-fingered hands. Pressed his lips to her right eye. His pouting mouth covered the eye.

Cairo caught a faint *schlup* of sucking.

It was obliterated by Lucia's agonised scream.

163

Horus pulled away, an eyeball in his mouth. A final backward tug snapped the taut, moist thread of the optic nerve.

Lucia's shrieks echoed round the auditorium as her hand covered the empty cavern of the eye-socket.

She tumbled to the floor in anguish.

Her tormentor swallowed the eyeball whole.

'*Don't move*,' warned the Anarch, fixing Cairo with a cold stare. The warning stopped the private eye in his tracks. He'd been about to charge, bullets blazing, regardless of the nonsense of assaulting a hypma screen.

'You cold, bloody bastard,' he hissed. 'I'll find you. And destroy you.'

A wide grin greeted the threat. 'Excellent. I've given you a reason for seeking me out. When you find me I'll restore Lucia's eye and hand her over good as new. I'll be waiting for you in Anarchopolis. Don't take too long.'

Horus signalled his topsy-turvy-faced servants to carry the agonised Lucia out the door. 'Take her to the hospital scene,' he instructed.

Heels scraping the floor-boards, she was dragged out of sight, leaving the Anarch alone on the screen with a freeze-frame Mike Powers. Cairo bottled up his fury. Tried not to think of Lucia. Tried to think straight. It wouldn't do Lucia any good if he went on a blind rampage. Up until now he had regarded Anarchopolis as a street fable. If it was real, where was it? *What* was it?

'Where am I supposed to look for you? The Undercity?'

'Ah, the Undercity,' the Anarch sighed wistfully. 'The haunted ruins of old New York, steeped in perpetual night. Yes, you can start to look there, but you'll have to look deep. Consider the search as a quest. A trial by ordeal. And remember – don't take too long. Tomorrow midnight, at the latest. You mustn't miss the celebration.'

'Celebration?'

'Forgotten your birthday? *Our* birthday?' His tone sank to a reverential whisper:

'Hallowe'en.'

Cairo's private eye instincts were back on course. His

mind slipped into the standard procedure . . . Keep them talking. Tease out clues from the occasional unguarded word. He was still struggling not to think of Lucia.

'What's so special about this coming Hallowe'en?' he asked.

'Because this Hallowe'en is the eve of the Second Coming. *My* Second Coming. I'm going to turn the world upside down.' He flicked a hand at his tight, natty suit of inverted badges. 'Upside down, like my Suit of Many Badges.'

'You want to turn the *Judge* world upside down?'

'Of course. The Judges are the rulers of the Overworld. I'm the god of the Underworld. Lord of the Dream Palaces, awaiting the Big Opening of the show. On the Day of the Big Opening the Underworld will become the Overworld.'

The Anarch's inflexion was soaring towards the fanatic, self-righteous end of the scale. That was the weakness of self-proclaimed gods. They were inclined to advertise their self-importance. Cairo set about exploiting the weakness.

'If I'm your brother, and you're a god, what does that make me?'

'The first shall be last. Therefore the first-born is the lesser. You weren't born more than human. You weren't cast into the wilderness of the Cursed Earth. God didn't deliver you into the saving bosom of the tribe of Exterminans. Nor did God speak to you in the wilderness, revealing that you were his beloved son. Yes, you're my brother, but only a shadow brother. You must prove yourself if you wish to be of more substance.'

Cairo was beginning to accept that the mad being on the screen was his far-from-identical twin brother. The Anarch's sheer certainty of kinship was persuasive. Besides, he sensed a remote affinity . . . He laid that disquieting thought aside in favour of another: the tribe of Exterminans that ranged the Cursed Earth.

Back in the twentieth century, 'Exterminans' was an adopted title of the multiple murderer Charles Manson.

It was taken from the Book of Revelations and signified Apollyon, the Angel of the Pit. Benedict Bede, the twenty-second-century version of Manson, who idolised his psychopathic precursor, took the name Exterminans in honour of his idol. The contemporary Exterminans was the most dangerous religious fanatic in the Cursed Earth. In between slaughtering whole communities, he preached the imminent descent of the falcon-headed Egyptian god Horus.

The Anarch regarded himself as Horus. Exterminans' prophecies must have penetrated core-deep. Cairo's brother, if such he was, had been schooled to madness from infancy.

He tried to keep his tone bland. 'Why do you call yourself Horus?'

The reply was incisive. 'Because that's who I am. The truth of it was confirmed in this very cinema, when the black falcon appeared on the screen. It called to me. I flew to the call. I was transformed. I am Horus the Falcon, destroyer of the Golden Eagle of Law.'

Cairo pressed the point further. 'Why do you want to overthrow the Law?'

The Anarch waved a dismissive hand. 'Why do you? We share the same motives. The Law killed our mother. The Law condemned me to the Cursed Earth and you to a regimented Justice orphanage. I wandered the wilderness while you escaped into the sewers. The Law blighted our lives. The Law is stifling the entire world. And every city on earth will rejoice when the Law comes crashing down.'

'So what do you want – democracy?'

'*Democracy*,' the Anarch sneered. 'Democracy died with the twentieth century. It had its chance. It failed.'

That statement could have come from Judge Dredd's mouth, word for word. But Cairo knew better than to mention the fact.

'Democracy's a feeble, insipid affair,' the other continued, lost in his theme. 'It perished of anaemia.'

'Okay, you're against democracy. So what are you *for*?'

166

The Anarch flung up his arms, every inch the messianic preacher. 'What am I for? *Anarchy!* Perpetual Anarchy! Total Anarchy! Absolute Anarchy!'

'*Absolute* Anarchy?' Cairo inquired, his face a mask of puzzled innocence. 'Sounds similar to Absolute Monarchy.' He was close to the secret. He had guided his bizarre brother close to revealing the mystery of Anarchopolis. Just a couple more nudges . . . 'So I guess you're the Absolute Anarch of Anarchopolis. Supreme Anarch.'

'Obviously,' the Anarch said. His arms fell to his sides. A slow smile curved his lips. 'And I think I've played along with your game far enough. Sounding me out, as you thought. Gauging my mentality. Gradually leading up to spot-the-location-of-Anarchopolis. I was ahead of you, every step of the way. Nice try, though.' He ran a hand through his black, spiky hair. 'One last incentive. An old acquaintance of yours is on the way down to me right now, although truth to tell I rate her chances of survival less than a jellyfish in a steam-press.'

Cairo's skin chilled. 'What acquaintance?'

'You have her in your pocket, I believe. The Queen of Hearts.'

'Mandra . . .'

'The very same.'

Cairo was being hit from every direction. Lucia in limbo. A new-found brother. Now Mandra. It was hard to stay on an even keel.

He glared at the almost-human man on the silver screen. 'How can I be sure you're my twin brother? I can't see any resemblance.'

'I was born in black and white. You were born in full colour. When I slipped from a dead womb I looked like a baby from an old monochrome movie. Dredd branded me a mutant. Born different.'

Cairo's fist clenched. 'If we agree on nothing else, we can agree on Dredd. He's the living symbol of Judge rule. He killed our mother. Condemned us both. Why not aim me straight at him?'

Horus gave a shrug of indifference. 'I've nothing per-

167

sonal against Dredd. By casting me into the wilderness he made me what I am. He's my father by circumstance, so to speak. The same's true for you, isn't it? No – my enemy's the Law itself, not some oaf who serves it. Nothing personal.'

Cairo let it drop. For him, it was personal. Very personal.

'You're still unsure I'm your brother, aren't you?' Horus observed.

'I'm pretty sure. Not certain.'

'Then I'll resolve your doubts.' With long, deliberate strides, Horus walked down the hallway.

Five strides and his approaching figure blocked out half the scene.

He kept on advancing.

And didn't stop until his face filled the screen in close-up. His voice boomed in the cinema. 'Born unlike. But there are resemblances, if you look close. *Look close*, Mister Cairo.'

No need to look close. In the giant face, twenty metres wide, there were tell-tale signs of kinship in the curves and hollows of bone structure, the faint folds of flesh.

Cairo fervently wished he had been an only child.

'Now,' thundered the huge voice from the twenty-metre face, 'I must teach you to take me seriously. A little lesson of fear.'

A colossal arm reached out of the screen, into the auditorium. The stretching arm was clothed in a sleeve of badges – swastikas, stars of David, munceburger adverts, pro-Democracy slogans, anti-Democracy slogans, love symbols, hate symbols.

A gigantic white hand closed round Cairo and hoisted him high.

'I have such possibilities. This is just one of them,' proclaimed the ten-metre mouth. 'I can be any size when I reach out from the silver screen. A tiny figure in a movie background. A colossus in close-up. If you dream of opposing me – be warned.'

168

The giant hand let go. Cairo crashed back into the stalls and tumbled face down.

'Come to me,' his brother's voice boomed around the Casablanca. 'Go mad with me. On Hallowe'en.'

Cairo painfully swayed to his feet and looked up.

The twenty-metre face had gone. The screen was blank.

He swiftly ordered his whirling wits. He had to find his brother in Anarchopolis before Hallowe'en midnight. That gave him thirty-six hours. The way to Anarchopolis was through the Undercity. Had to be. And Mandra . . .

He touched the Queen of Hearts in his pocket. 'Mandra's down there, if she's still alive.'

The Undercity. It had a bad reputation just one step this side of hell's gates.

And if a monster like the Anarch ruled Anarchopolis, the fabled underworld city must be one step *inside* hell's gates.

Everyone in the Big City feared the Undercity. Only a few Judges had risked a speedy in-out dash of the night world deep below. And those Judges raced on Lawmasters, armed to the teeth.

Cairo was heading for the worst trouble of his life.

'Here goes,' he said, stepping into the aisle.

As he made his way to the upper balcony, he glanced up at the ceiling. The dead men were still hovering around the chandeliers.

Organised crime was in league with Horus, the 'Underboss'. Big mistake by the Overbosses. Organised crime required an organised society. When Anarchy rose up and the Judges fell, the Overbosses would fall with them.

That prospect didn't break his heart.

If only his brother was sane Cairo would have joined him happily.

But that wasn't the way the cards had been dealt.

He couldn't shake off the feeling that he'd been dealt the Death card.

Arriving at the upper balcony, he barely gave the exit door a glance. The UnderJudges were out there. And the mobsters, backed by small armies of goons. And the Judges.

All of them with the name Mister Cairo top of the hit-list.

When in trouble. Flushways was the way to travel.

There was a place where maps of the Undercity were kept. In Justice Hall, the heart of Judgement in the Big City.

Arbuckle had installed a Flushway toilet adjoining the Judges' Hall of Heroes. The old guy had never used it. Nor had Cairo. Flushing yourself into the bowels of Justice Central was little short of suicidal.

But he had to have an Undercity map.

He pushed open the toilet door and strode into the exit cubicle, punched in the co-ordinates of Justice Hall.

'Here goes nothing,' he muttered to himself.

Then jumped into the expanding toilet bowl.

CHAPTER SIXTEEN

Sejanus stood in awe before the booming heart of a god.

The heart of the Judgement Colossus.

The flexisteel heart, fifty metres in circumference, was shaped like a human heart, and pumped up water from the bay into the four chambers of the right and left auricles and ventricles before the briny fluid exited via the branches of the aorta to race through the simplified cardio-vascular system of the giant statue.

Dies Irae's hydraulic heart had been constructed partly as a back-up power source in the unlikely event of system breakdown.

It also served a symbolic purpose. On its front surface was a map of the world with a number of mega-cities marked with red skulls. All those cities that had perished in the holocaust of Judgement Day. The ornamental map was intended as a memorial. To Sejanus's mind, it was a warning: step out of line and you too can have a red skull imprinted on your city.

'Beat on, great heart,' he murmured, casting a final glance at the mighty pump. 'Time to move from heart to head.'

He sat in the eagle chair, pressed an acti-pad. The chair sped towards the round entrance of Central Grav-Chute. Once inside, he soared up to the Visor area.

From now on, he would remain in the statue's head. The brain in that head was growing stronger by the hour. The conjoined minds of the Hierarchy of Five were feeding it well. Come nightfall, it would control every brain in Mega-City One, both Judge and citizen.

Emerging into the Visor, he spared a glance at the dwarfed Statue of Liberty far below.

A couple of years ago, some Rad Dems had attempted to blow up the Statue of Liberty as a political gesture to show that the statue's preservation was a mockery in a world devoid of liberty.

Wrong target.

They would have destroyed the last symbol of liberty. And the very existence of the Rad Dems proved that liberty was not dead. Yet.

It soon would be.

Then Sejanus would destroy the Statue of Liberty himself.

The Judgement Colossus would burst it asunder with its eyes of fire.

Those eyes, encoded with Psi-waves, were already transmitting to every means of communication in Mega-City One. The message was simple:

Obedience

The message was delivered in a soft whisper. It would grow louder.

Nothing could stop the process now the chief threat was removed.

Mandra was dead, shot with a HED bullet, gulped by a mysterious fissure in the ground. Strange phenomenon. He could only conclude that his daughter had accomplished a telekinetic feat. She had split the earth with her mind. Made it swallow her up. No matter. She was dead and gone. Out of the picture.

Mandra was the sole mistake in his otherwise flawless rise to power. But then, he had been a young man when he made the mistake, thirty years ago.

It had seemed a good idea at the time. Father a child on a *mambo* woman, matching his Psi potential with hers to produce a formidable Psi child whom he could use as a pawn, or even a queen, in his power game. The only difficult part was the actual mating. Hypnotising the woman into seeing him as her black husband was straightforward. It was the joining of flesh to flesh that he found

172

repellent. He was a true Judge. Celibate. Pure in thought and body. Like a Catholic priest from earlier centuries. Yes, the mating was unsavoury. Sex was somehow – debasing. But, once done, the rest was easy. A half-caste daughter was born to an all-black couple. The husband's reaction was predictable. Sejanus had arranged the infant's admission to an orphanage with the minimum of fuss. After that, the transference from orphanage to Academy of Law was a formality. From a distance, he had overseen her training, watched her grow, looking forward to the day he could confide his fatherhood to her, and wield her as a devastating Psi weapon in his holy mission.

But she grew up to be wild. Right from childhood, there was a streak of the rebel in his daughter. It was only his persuasion that kept her from expulsion from the Academy.

When she graduated as a Judge, she got worse. Wilder and wilder.

'What a disappointment you were,' he sighed, aiming the eagle chair up the ramp. 'You really let your father down.'

Mandra quickly faded from his thoughts as the chair approached the secret entrance to Sanctum. He dematerialised the blank wall with a touch of an arm-rest button. Glided into the ovoid chamber of Sanctum. Rematerialised the wall with another touch of a button.

And surveyed his elite SJS Hierarchy of Five, seated in mid-air in the anti-grav chamber. Their eyes were shut as they continued the silent Psi-programming of the hypma core of Omnipotens. The Arcanum at the centre of the electronic brain was being filled with the precepts of Absolute Law, completing the work of the Colossus Chief.

Sejanus's mind was in Dredd's head.

Sejanus, over the previous months, had shaped the mind of Arcanum in his own image, just as the head of the Judgement Colossus was shaped in the image of Chief Judge Fargo. Not that anyone thought of Fargo when they looked up at the Colossus. They saw his clone. They saw Dredd. Dredd's features had undergone a few ravages and face-lifts in his time, including the insertion of artificial eyes, but the changes hadn't altered the underlying bone structure. As go the bones, so goes the face. The head of the Colossus was the head of Dredd.

The Colossus Chief was glad that Judge and citizen alike saw Dredd's helmeted head on the Colossus. Judge Dredd had been his original inspiration. Dredd's dedication to Law commanded respect. Although he'd outgrown Dredd's version of law enforcement, even come to dislike the man, he still admired him.

Judge Dredd deserved the honour of having his face on the head of a god.

Deus Irae. God of Wrath.

He glanced at the hologram of a human brain on the curved wall, marking the access point to the Arcanum.

He smiled in anticipation. He was on the verge of acquiring power beyond the dreams of a Chief Judge. Sejanus was about to outdo his namesake from ancient history. Thirty years ago, he had renamed himself after the Prefect of the Praetorian Guard in imperial Rome, the founder of the first effective police state. Sadly, it had not survived his death.

The Colossus Chief had every intention of surpassing his role model. His police state would endure to the Earth's death-rattle.

Sejanus's thoughts drifted out into the mega-city. Omnipotens would already be meshing with the city's entire electronic network. Filtering its message of obedience into every vid, every audio-com – even the audio-coms in each Judge helmet.

With Mandra dead, the process was irreversible. He sighed his satisfaction.

Mister Cairo's still alive.

He pushed the unsettling thought down the moment it surfaced.

Forget Mister Cairo. He might have proved a formidable opponent before the creation of Omnipotens, but the private eye hadn't got a chance against the supercomputer and the massive weapon-power of the Judgement Colossus.

Come tomorrow, Mister Cairo would be as obedient a citizen as any other.

Success was guaranteed.

Sejanus relaxed into his earlier state of confident calm. He could feel it – the power reaching out . . .

Omnipotens reaching out . . . Controlling . . .

Every vid . . . Every audio-com . . .

Hubert Crump shifted his bony buttocks on the lumpy sofa and scratched his bulbous, spotty nose as he waited for the Channel 99 Morning News to appear on the vid-screen.

The expensive vid-unit was the only luxury in Hubert Crump's dilapidated habhold, strewn with wall-to-wall old socks. He hugged the dirty raincoat tight about his scrawny, wrinkled body.

The raincoat was all he had on, apart from a pair of cracked, twelve-year-old ankle boots.

He enjoyed the rub of the rough raincoat lining against his naked skin.

And he relished the prospect of flinging the raincoat wide open and exposing his nakedness when that prissy female newsreader came on screen. Give the snooty bitch an eyeful. Give her what for.

Vid-flasher. A term of abuse in Mega-City One. A flasher without the courage of his convictions.

That's all *they* knew, Hubert Crump sourly reflected. He was proud of being a vid-flasher.

He still kept it a secret, though.

Moral Minority brigades were highly active in Barbara Cartland Block. Padding up and down the corridors, castration knives in black-gloved hands, permanently on look-out for flashers, fornicators, wankers, porno-zine readers.

Hubert Crump had no wish to run foul of the black-uniformed guardians of decency. He kept his little hobby to himself.

'Any minute now,' he grinned at the tri-D vid-screen as the Morning News logo appeared, hovering midway between screen and viewer.

The logo vanished. A young, attractive newsreader appeared in full tri-D, as though sitting in his room.

Newsreader Honoria Plumley. Haughty, prissy Miss Plumley, the furtive wet dream of half the male population of the mega-city.

'Good morning, Mega-City One,' she said in her affected Brit accent.

Hubert jumped up, flung wide his grubby raincoat, putting his run-down physique on full display.

'Get an eyeful o' that, Miss Snooty Pants!' he shouted gleefully. 'You want it, don't ya? You'd crawl for it, wouldn't ya? Wouldn't ya? Eh? Eh?'

Honoria Plumley's lip curled. She stared at him. Straight at him.

'Mister *Crump*!' she sniffed disdainfully, glaring at his shrinking ardour with withering contempt. 'How *dare* you?'

His mouth fell open and stayed open. Gobstruck was the only word for it.

The vid-screen had violated the most fundamental trust of the vid-flasher. The damn thing was looking at *him*. Not fair. Not fair.

It got worse.

Hubert's saintly mother joined Miss Plumley on the screen. She shook her silver-haired head in sad reproach. 'Hubert – you break your poor mother's heart,' she groaned soulfully. 'Showing Mister Wiggly to the nice lady. And in front of your *mother*. Oh, the *shame* of it. You'll be the death of me.' Her hand clutched her chest. 'Oh – oh – I think I'm about to expire of a myocardial infarction.'

Mother slumped over the newsdesk, stone dead.

Honoria Plumley wagged a finger at Hubert. 'Now look

what you've done, you disgusting piece of vermin. You – '

He didn't hear the rest. He was too busy shrieking in horror as he fled the habhold.

Once in the public corridor, he kept on shrieking and running.

Honoria Plumley had seen – his mother had seen –

He had killed his mother.

Hubert skidded to a halt. A hand flew to his mouth.

But his mother had died two years ago. Of a myocardial infarction. That pleasant doctor had explained that a myocardial infarction was a heart attack, probably brought on by overeating. Hubert was not responsible.

'Crump!' a stern voice rang out.

He swung round. Three men in black uniforms were padding down the passage, curved knives in meaty fists. A Moral Minority patrol.

Hubert was suddenly conscious of his wide-open rain-coat. The bare flesh in full view.

'Oh Grud,' he moaned, breaking into a frantic run.

They caught up before he'd covered fifty paces.

A kick to the spine floored him.

A square-jawed man glowered down at Hubert.

'Kiss your balls goodbye, Crump,' he growled, brandishing the curved knife. '*Literally*.'

'Literally?' quavered Hubert, peering down at his shrunken genitalia. 'That's a physical impossibility.'

The castration knife flashed in the overhead light. 'Not when we've finished with you it won't be.'

Judge Ryan's bared teeth were somewhere between a grin and a snarl as the megway streaked under the Firerock wheels of his racing Lawmaster at 540 kph.

Hot pursuit.

He loved hot pursuit.

The perp in the speeding vehicle ahead had been doing 198 kph when Judge Ryan spotted him. The driver was showing off. Slow driving. Two kays below the minimum speed limit. Snarling the flow up. Getting his kicks from cars whizzing past his rear end upwards of 400 kph.

Once the driver saw the Lawmaster on his tail, he accelerated to more than 500 kph in six seconds. That gave Ryan a good feeling.

Hot pursuit. The adrenalin rush of speed. Wheels on fire.

Run down the traffic perp.

If the perp surrendered, he'd do plenty of time in the cubes.

If he kept fleeing justice, even better. Ryan would have the excuse to shoot the creep dead.

A curious crackle issued from Ryan's helmet audio-com. It rang bells in his skull.

'Hey,' he snapped. 'What's all this buzz-fuzz on the line?'

No answer. Gruddam helmet-com was on the fritz again.

The crackle faded.

'Anybody home?'

No answer.

'Who needs ya?' he muttered, fixing all his attention on the perp's fancy red car.

Ryan had maintained a constant distance so far. 540 was the perp car's top speed.

Ryan could do a little better. He let out the throttle.

The penetrating crackle sounded again in his helmet.

And the perp suddenly swerved off the megway onto a narrow slipway.

Easing the throttle, the Judge leaned into the bend as he pursued the red car onto the slipway.

Funny how he had never noticed this slipway before. He thought he knew this stretch of road better than the back end of his favourite eezie-squeezie.

Could have sworn there wasn't a slipway on this section.

The narrow exit road afforded a wide view of Sector 40 in the morning sunlight, right down to Ground Level a kilometre below. He didn't waste time admiring the vista.

He was close to the red car. And closer with each speeding second.

Wheels on fire.

'And any second I'm gonna set *you* on fire, perp,' he hissed, right palm itching to wrench the Lawgiver from his boot-holster.

Ten metres from the red car's tail.

Then the car wasn't there anymore.

Nor was the slipway.

No slipway.

Never had been a slipway.

Just a kilometre of empty space under his wheels.

'What the – ' He glanced over his shoulder. Saw the perp car way up ahead on the megway, streaking scot-free into the distance. Saw the hole his Lawmaster had smashed in the megway's barrier. The barrier's plascrete was still tumbling.

'Oh Grud,' he moaned as the bike's trajectory steepened from an arc to a straight drop.

A thousand metre drop.

He would hit Ground Level at one mother-drokker of a speed.

Judge Ryan had plunged all of two hundred ever-accelerating metres before it occurred to him to start screaming.

Five minutes to Justice Central.

Dredd and Hershey raced along the zoomway, the traffic hastily clearing a path for the two roaring Lawmasters.

Both Judges maintained radio silence, the helmet-coms switched off. The radio silence was Hershey's idea. The reason for it was Dredd's.

Hershey was wondering which of the two of them was the crazier.

An hour ago, Dredd had signalled a halt. Face to face, or rather visor to face, they had gone into Mandra's mysterious disappearance. Maybe Mandra had created that momentary split in the ground, or perhaps someone

179

else was responsible. A freak accident was so improbable they discounted the notion on the spot.

Dredd had suggested a long shot. A connection between Mandra and the Undercity. Perhaps she had wanted to contact someone in the world below Mega-City One before the HED bullet made an explosive end of her. And maybe, just maybe, that someone was Mister Cairo.

A long shot. A very long shot.

Especially considering Omnipotens had reported no link between Cairo and Mandra. Dredd had snorted disbelief at the report, and – okay – she went along with him on that. Cairo's references to Mandra in Normal's habhold strongly suggested that the private eye and the ex-Judge had been on more than nodding terms at some time or another.

But it was a big leap from there to hoping Cairo could be located in the Undercity.

A shot in the dark.

Finally, Hershey decided to play along. And she had warned Dredd to keep their conversation face to face. No vid or audio-coms.

Any transmitted message could be picked up by Omnipotens. By Sejanus.

And she did not trust Sejanus. A vague memory had been buzzing faintly at the back of her skull ever since the SJS officer had been promoted to Colossus Chief.

An hour ago that memory had emerged clear as daylight. She had read about a Sejanus once, in a history of ancient Rome. The Emperor Tiberius had appointed Sejanus Prefect of the Praetorian Guard. And while the emperor idled away in Capri, Sejanus took an iron grip on Rome. His spies created a network of suspicion and fear. Sejanus's enemies were disposed of, his followers rewarded. After several years, he was ruler in all but name.

For Emperor Tiberius, read Chief Judge McGruder. For the Prefect of the Praetorian Guard, read Sejanus of the SJS, Colossus Chief.

Too many coincidences. Hershey was wary of coincidences where the SJS was concerned.

Once she agreed to head for the Undercity with Dredd, she insisted on radio silence.

Hershey didn't want Sejanus to learn their destination. That meant keeping Omnipotens in the dark.

A map of the Undercity could easily have been relayed to the Lawmaster vid-coms. But that would tell Sejanus where they were headed. No way.

She and Dredd would pick up a map by hand from the Grand Hall of Justice. Straight into the Map Room beside the Hall of Heroes. Straight out again. No one need know what they were up to.

Hershey's muscles tensed as the Grand Hall of Justice came into sight, the gigantic golden eagle on its facade glinting in the sun.

Straight in. Straight out.

Then straight down to the Undercity.

After that . . .

Hershey was no coward, but she preferred not to dwell on what awaited them down in the city of eternal night.

Sejanus rubbed his angular chin as he stared at the monitors in the Visor area.

The tale the monitors told troubled him.

By now, the first effects of the Dies Irae programming should be apparent. Citizens drawn to their vid-screens even more than usual. Passive viewers. A dropping crime-rate. Judges yet more astute and remorseless in dispensing Justice. Order. Obedience to the Law.

It wasn't happening.

The crime-rate was *rising*. Reports were flooding in of every form of mayhem and murder.

And there were – abnormalities.

Not many more than was customary. But the incidence was increasing.

Something to do with vid-screens 'coming alive'. Wild reports of monochrome figures walking the corridors of blocks. And a puzzling case of a Judge who had ridden his Lawmaster clean through a megway barrier. A meat-wagon at Ground Level was still hunting out all the fleshy bits and pieces.

What was going wrong?'

He jabbed a button for the Statue's central communications room. 'Dredd and Hershey reported in yet?'

'No sir,' informed a voice at the other end. 'No response to priority call. Seems they've switched off all communication.'

'Keep trying,' Sejanus snapped, breaking off the connection.

He leaned back in the eagle chair, tapping his teeth with an agitated finger.

'What are Dredd and Hershey playing at?' he muttered.

Perhaps he had allowed his admiration of Dredd to blind him to the Judge's habit of going his own way, whenever he thought fit. That habit had been the first cause of Sejanus's growing dislike of Dredd the man. As a symbol, he was perfect. But as a man – there was always that rogue element. You were never quite certain which way he would jump.

As for Hershey, he hated the interfering bitch. She'd come close to discovering his plans back when she was investigating SJS Extra-Judicial Killings. He had marked her for death after she had uncovered the EJK plots.

Dredd and Hershey. Could he afford to let them run free and unobserved?

Could he afford to let them live?

Dredd had saved Mandra from a quick death at the hands of three of Sejanus's men. That interference might have proved fatal to the Colossus Chief's schemes.

He pressed again for central communications.

'Priority. Locate Dredd and Hershey via Eye network. Assign Squad A to EJKs on both Judges.'

'Kill Dredd and Hershey?' The operator's astonishment was manifest in his shrill pitch.

'Do you wish to question my order?'

'Oh – no. No sir. EJKs on Dredd and Hershey.'

A touch of a button terminated the conversation.

Sejanus folded his arms and surveyed the monitors.

The crime-rate was still rising. Peculiarities involving vid-screens were proliferating.

'Omnipotens,' he murmured softly. 'What's happening?'

An orange glow on the console signalled a transmission from communications.

'Yes?' he responded.

'Eyes locate Dredd and Hershey approaching Grand Hall of Justice.'

Sejanus gave a slow nod. 'Tell Squad A to execute EJKs.'

CHAPTER SEVENTEEN

A disgruntled Judge Carson rubbed his bulging, grumbling belly as he prepared for another day of conducting groups of gawking citizens around the Hall of Heroes.

Dumb tourists. Dumb job.

First batch was a group from Hondo City. *Nippons*, for Grud's sake. Man like him – guiding drokkin' Nips through the Hall's displays

Should be still on the streets, blowing up a storm on his Lawmaster. Hauling in the perps. Blasting them to Babylon Block and back.

Okay, he had the second highest kill-rate and the lowest arrest-rate on the force. So what? Perps only understood the bullet.

Taken off the streets at fifty, Gruddammit. He could have gone on for another ten years, easy. Drokk it – he was younger than Dredd, and who'd have the balls to force *him* into semi-retirement?

Carson grumpily surveyed the Hall of Heroes, crammed with memorabilia of a hundred years of Justice rule. His gaze alighted on the sarcophagus of Chief Judge Fargo, Father of Justice.

For a moment, his chest swelled with pride. The Father of Justice, his life-size effigy lying on the sarcophagus lid, was a sight that raised Carson's heart on the lowest of days.

A gurgling in his abdomen brought Judge Carson right back down. Fifteen minutes before public opening, and his stomach was playing up again.

Fifteen minutes.

That gave him a good ten minutes on the toilet with his favourite book.

Taking his copy of *Dredd's Comportment*, Carson made straight for the toilets adjoining the hall.

He let himself into a cubicle, unzipped the uniform, pulled the one-piece synthi-leather suit down to his knees with a muttered curse on the uniform designer for forcing the wearer into a big production number every time he needed to take a leak or dump.

Finally ready, he sat on the seat, sighing with relief. The way his bowels were churning, he hadn't left it a moment too soon.

Secure on the toilet seat, Judge Carson turned to chapter four of *Dredd's Comportment*.

For the next ten minutes, a nice quiet read as he did the necessary.

Safe from disturbance.

Peace and quiet.

Mister Cairo whooshed along the Flushway system to the accompaniment of Elgar's Cello Concerto in E Minor.

Protected from the surrounding crap and crud by an electrostatic bubble, distracted from the dangers of Arbuckle's impressive but less than perfect mechanisms of sewer travel by the music pouring from his micro-headphones, Cairo almost lost track of time.

Shunting around the sewerage system, hours had passed since he had flushed himself down the bowl of the Casablanca's conveniences. He hadn't expected the Flush-way journey from the cinema to Justice Hall to be so circuitous.

Some journeys twice the distance could be covered in less than an hour by Arbuckle's unique form of travel.

He checked his watch. 8-51. Damn. He'd hoped to surface beside the Hall of Heroes well before opening time. Less than nine minutes to go. However, he must be nearing Justice Hall. It couldn't take much longer.

The last strains of the concerto ebbed. He switched to Jon and Vangelis' *Friends of Mister Cairo*. The familiar prelude to the song rang in his ears: the rattle of machine-guns and the whine of ricochets, along with a passable vocal impersonation of James Cagney as a cop-defying gangster.

An old song for a private eye who lived in the past. The past had a lot more room than the present.

The song was nowhere near half through when Cairo felt himself ascending. Fast.

Very fast.

Too damn fast.

He had to figure out why just as fast. The only way was Psi. Send a part of his mind on ahead of his body.

He shut his eyes, sent a concentrated thought whizzing up the tubes.

And glimpsed – a man's rear end, engaged in . . .

He retracted the thought-vision as if stung.

Oh *shit*.

This unused section of Flushways really was on the fritz. The sensors had identified a blockage, and taken action. Trouble was, the wonky mechanism had taken action in reverse. Instead of slowing and halting its passenger, it was *accelerating* him.

Cairo was ascending at an increasing speed towards a toilet in Justice Hall. And some silly bastard was sitting on it.

The Flushway's top speed was 300 kph.

If he rammed into a Judge's backside at 300 kph . . .

Didn't bear thinking about.

He killed the song.

Reached for the Dillinger.

Tried in vain to find a suitable prayer.

Hershey kept pace with Dredd.

As they walked, she thought she heard other feet keep pace with theirs.

Both Judges kept their stares fixed ahead as they strode towards the Map Room, turning neither right nor left.

Straight in. Straight out. Then straight down to the Undercity.

186

At least that was the plan.

Sejanus was making plans of his own. She was certain of it. You never could trust the SJS. Hershey had learned that lesson well. Dredd never had. Good Street Judge, Joe Dredd, but when it came to politics – not so hot.

She couldn't help noticing the frenzied bustle in the Grand Hall of Justice. Nor the numerous screens, some thirty metres wide, that displayed alarming statistics of rocketing crime and curious vid anomalies. Something bad was going down out there in Mega-City One.

Things were not too healthy inside the Grand Hall of Justice, either.

Hershey listened closely to the following footfalls as she turned corner after corner of the ground floor labyrinth. Yes, they *were* being tracked. She detected a dozen or more footsteps.

She resisted the urge to glance over her shoulder. No need to alert the enemy.

She didn't respond as a batch of Nippon tourists, gathered to view the Hall of Heroes, nodded politely as the Judges walked past. Hershey didn't go in for pleasantries at the best of times, and this sure as hell was not the best of times.

Another couple of minutes, and she would be inside the Map Room.

If the trackers wanted to make a move then, they were welcome.

Judge Carson scratched his hairy belly and flipped another page of Dredd's Comportment.

Ah yeah, he liked sitting on the john.

Nice and peaceful. No intrusions.

A calm retreat from the world.

He heard a faint, subterranean rumble from the toilet bowl. Thought nothing of it.

It sounded again, a little louder, vibrating through his rump.

'Damn plumbing,' he hissed.

* * *

187

Cairo's ascent went on accelerating. He glanced at All-Purpose, his watch with numerous additional functions, including a speedometer.

It showed 170 kph.

175.

185.

215.

He heard the rumble of the strained Flushway tube as it prepared to eject him.

250.

295 . . .

The Judge on the john was about to get the surprise of his life. At least Cairo would take a Judge with him into the Big Goodbye, but he could think of more stylish ways to exit from existence.

Only one option.

Remove the blockage: cancel the Flushway's reversed emergency action.

Fire a hyperblast bullet into the Judge's backside.

He aimed the Dillinger upwards. Flicked to hyperblast mode.

Far overhead, a tiny circle of rump flashed into sight.

Now or never.

Cairo squeezed the trigger.

'Damn plumbing,' hissed Carson, then resumed reading *Dredd's Comportment*. He didn't have time to figure out what happened next.

Just an explosion of impressions . . .

A rocket up the ass.

Body launched like a rocket from the toilet.

Ass on fire.

Head in ceiling.

'What the Grud was that?' growled Dredd as a muffled explosion echoed down the corridors.

'Ignore it,' advised Hershey. 'The Map Room, remember?'

The following footsteps had stopped the instant Dredd ground to a halt.

'Joe – the Map Room.'

He had already switched on his helmet-com, drawn his Lawgiver. 'Control – what's goin' on?'

'*Typical*,' she sighed sharply. 'Damn typical.'

'Not sure,' Control replied. 'Doing a sweep . . .' A short pause. 'Er – it seems a toilet's blown up. Near the Hall of Heroes.'

'Possible sabotage,' Dredd barked. 'Heading for toilets.'

'Sabotage?' Hershey echoed disbelievingly.

Dredd, however, was already charging down the corridor, Lawgiver raised high.

With a snort of exasperation, Hershey ran in his tracks. The pursuing footfalls broke into a run.

'So much for stealth,' she muttered.

The thunder of the hyperblast bullet rang several kinds of hell's bells in Cairo's ears.

But the exit above had been cleared.

Flushways cancelled its back-to-front emergency action.

The acute deceleration compressed his spinal column. Squashed his neck. He felt as if his ears were on a level with his shoulders.

All-Purpose showed the deceleration rate.

280.

250.

190.

110 . . .

The overhead oval rushed down. A couple of seconds, maybe . . .

60

20 . . .

He erupted from the toilet at 15 kph. Soared to the ceiling. Bashed his head on a Judge's dangling rump. Dropped to the floor.

For a moment he saw black constellations on a merry-go-round. By the time he'd found his feet he realised he hadn't broken his neck.

He glanced up at the scorching crater of the Judge's backside. The corpse had buried its head in the ceiling.

A brief hope flared. Was it Dredd?

Teach the old bastard right if he met such an unseemly end from Cairo's bullet. Justice Hall sure as hell would not mention *that* in the final tribute.

No, it wasn't Dredd. The badge of the trailing uniform disclosed the wearer as Judge Carson.

Too bad.

The distant rumble of running feet brought him back to his senses.

He had surfaced in the heart of Justice Central. Surfaced with a bang. Scores of bullet-heads would be converging on the toilets.

He could easily flush himself out of trouble, but he had to get hold of an Undercity map. That meant a trip to the Map Room.

Sure. Piece of cake. A little trip to the Map Room with maybe a hundred Judges heading his way.

He rubbed his unshaven chin. 'I think I'm in a bit of a fix.'

Dredd rushed into the Hall of Heroes, Hershey at his heels.

'Where's the tour guide?' he snapped. 'Carson, isn't it?'

'Perhaps he exploded the toilet with his flatulence problem.' Hershey said dismissively. 'Come on, Joe. The *map*.'

The grim voice of Dredd reverberated in the Hall of Heroes as he swung his Lawgiver towards the Men's conveniences. 'Any terrorists blow up a Justice toilet, they do *time*.'

The Lawgiver was blasted from his hand.

Dredd and Hershey spun round.

A band of Judges confronted them, each wearing the death's head insignia helmets of the SJS.

190

Hershey counted fifteen Lawgivers, all trained on her and Dredd.

'Sorry about this, Dredd,' said Judge Tebbit, a well-known admirer of Sejanus. 'Orders. EJK. Got a lot of respect for you, but can't let you live.' The tone altered from apologetic to belligerent. 'As for you, Hershey, it'll be a pleasure wasting you. You've trodden on SJS toes once too often.'

Dredd's mouth twisted into a snarl as, weaponless, he squared up to the death squad. 'There's nothing worse than a bent Judge.'

'*We* make the rules,' Tebbit responded, squeezing the trigger. 'We decide what's bent or straight.'

He fired straight at Judge Dredd.

Cairo had thought of a plan.

Strip Judge Carson of his uniform. Flush Carson down the toilet. Make for the Map Room disguised as Carson.

But Carson's helmeted head was well and truly rammed into the ceiling. Without the helmet, the scheme would not work.

Think of something else.

Couldn't come up with a damn thing.

He noticed a copy of *Dredd's Comportment* at his feet. He gave it a kick.

And heard a burst of gunshots from somewhere outside. Lawgivers. And whoever was firing, they were not firing at him.

Whatever was going on, it might provide a diversion while he sneaked into the Map Room. It was a long shot, but what the hell.

Decision reached, he moved like greased magic, his Dillinger set on scatter-shell mode.

He slid open the convenience door and slipped into the Hall of Heroes.

The first man he saw was Judge Dredd.

Hershey dived to the right and went for her gun the moment Tebbit fired at Dredd.

She glimpsed Dredd's reaction as the bullet hit. The slug sliced a flesh wound under the right arm. The Judge had dived left as his assailant pulled the trigger.

Typical SJS – always underestimating the opposition.

Serious error when the opposition were Dredd and Hershey.

Dredd launched his powerful bulk through the air and forward-rolled behind a display case as Hershey hurtled for the cover of a plasteen-frame chair, firing as she went.

Two SJS dropped before she hit ground.

Tebbit led the charge into the hall. 'Come on!' he yelled, kicking Dredd's wrecked Lawgiver aside. 'Hershey's the only one with a gun.'

Hershey blasted one of his followers to oblivion. Swung the muzzle towards Tebbit.

Her mouth opened in dismay.

An excited batch of Nippon tourists flooded into the hall, faces beaming, holo-cameras whirring as they filmed the violent action.

The death squad hesitated at the unexpected intrusion, momentarily confused at the bright and breezy manner of the new arrivals.

Hershey immediately grasped the reason for the visitors' curious behaviour. They believed they were watching a staged gunfight. A performance for tourists. Part of the Hall of Heroes show.

A bullet drilled a hole in the chair she crouched behind.

She didn't have time to think about the visitors' safety. The squad had directed its entire firepower at her.

No way was she about to stick her head above cover. She laid the Lawgiver on top of the back-rest and, unsighted, loosed off a few rounds in the general direction of the SJS.

She had mere seconds, she knew that.

Mere seconds before she was blasted to oblivion.

However, she was in the heart of Justice Central. Hundreds of Judges within earshot. If she could only hang on long enough for the cavalry to arrive . . .

A ten-metre screen overhead flashed its message:

JUDGE DREDD AND JUDGE HERSHEY IMPER-
SONATORS HAVE CAUSED EXPLOSION NEAR
HALL OF HEROES. SJS SQUAD HAVE SITUATION
IN HAND. ALL PERSONNEL STAY CLEAR OF
HALL OF HEROES AREA.

Hershey groaned aloud. Omnipotens. Omnipotens was
in control of all transmissions. And she knew who was in
control of Omnipotens.

The cavalry wouldn't arrive.

Judge Hershey was about to be blown to Grud by
Judges in the Hall of Heroes.

Somehow she couldn't appreciate the dramatic irony.

She was flung backwards as the chair was blasted to bits
from a storm of bullets.

Cairo froze for a split second.

Dredd was twenty metres away, crouched behind a
display case, yelling urgently into his helmet-com, obliv-
ous of the private eye.

Instinctively, he aimed the Dillinger at Dredd's head.

You blew my mother's head off. I'll blast yours to Grud.

Then the rest of the scene rushed in on him.

SJS officers firing at a female Judge who was using a
heavy chair as cover.

Hershey.

A dozen or so Judges were pumping slugs at Hershey.

And in the middle of the fusillade, a score of Nippon
tourists were milling about, grinning happily and vid-
recording the whole event.

Some god up there had provided a diversion for Cairo
to snatch an Undercity map. If he loosed a round at
Dredd he would attract attention. Screw up his chance to
reach Anarchopolis.

Forget about Dredd. He was obviously unarmed. Cairo
would take him in his own time with a Lawgiver in the
Judge's hand.

Keeping out of sight, darting from display to display,
he sprinted across the hall to the Map Room.

The room was empty of a single soul. There should

have been a Judge in attendance. He wasn't complaining.

It took scant seconds to locate the Undercity maps. He stuffed one in a trench-coat pocket and got going while the going was still good.

He raced back into the hall in time to witness Hershey blown onto her back, the chair exploded to a shock of splinters.

She lay senseless, bleeding.

Above her, a screen announced that Dredd and Hershey were imposters. Imposters? Like hell.

The door to the Men's was a few paces away. He could make good his escape. Save his skin, and get on with the job.

But it was thirteen men against one woman. Sure, the woman was a Judge. And this was the twenty- second century – killing a woman was nothing.

Cairo was an old-fashioned sort of guy. He wasn't going to let it happen.

One of the SJS levelled his Lawgiver at Hershey. 'So long, bitch.' The finger twitched on the trigger.

A scatter-slug from Cairo's Dillinger blew him off his feet and floored a couple of others.

Cairo shot off three more rounds as he sprinted for the cover of Chief Judge Fargo's sarcophagus. He couldn't tell if any found their mark.

Hitting cover, he heard vigorous clapping and shouts of 'Banzai!'

The Nippon tourists were applauding. *Applauding.* God on skates – they must think they were watching a staged performance. They'd soon change their minds when one of them caught a stray bullet.

He took a deep breath, focused the *ch'i* energy in his mind and body, a technique he'd picked up from an old Tao master in Sino-City Two, and felt the *ch'i* racing through his maze of nerves and veins, speeding up his reflexes to turbo-boost velocity.

Another breath, and he unleashed a little of the Wild. Just a little – sufficient to loop his Psi-sight over the top of Fargo's sarcophagus. Gain an overhead view of the hall.

His elevated consciousness took in the number and distribution of SJS Judges.

He withdrew his extended Psi-vision. Tightened the grip on the Dillinger.

Now –

He sprang on top of the sarcophagus, straddling Fargo's effigy, and unleashed a continuous delivery of thunder and lightning from the Dillinger.

His brain raced quick as the bullets:

Twelve SJS left.

A second later there were eight.

Panicked, the squad bolted for the door. Two went flying, drilled helmets painting the hall red, before the survivors made a frantic exit.

The Nippons, who had stood blithely in the middle of the fusillade, miraculously unscathed by a single bullet, applauded uproariously.

'Banzai! Banzai! Banzai! Banzai!'

Cairo's lips tightened as Dredd reared up, black and menacing. The Judge sounded as if he was spitting gravel:

'Drop the gun, Cairo, or I'll drop you. Saving Hershey doesn't cut any ice with me. You're gonna rot your life away in the cubes.'

Cairo swept a contemptuous look over the Judge. 'Dream on, *creep*.'

Slowly, deliberately, he ground his shoe in the face of Fargo's effigy.

Dredd didn't move. He folded his whipcord arms. And stared.

Hidden though the gaze was, it was the unmistakable stare of the Judges. A stare gauged to shrink the hearts of perps. Terrify children who might otherwise grow up to be perps.

The long, hard stare.

Seconds slid by.

Cairo raised an eyebrow. 'Am I supposed to drop dead or something?'

Dredd unfolded his arms. Bunched his fists. 'You're top of my list, Cairo. You're already dead. This place'll be full of Judges within a minute, no matter what that vid-screen says. You're dead.'

The Nippons viewed the exchange with polite patience. 'More action soon please?' one ventured hesitantly, panning his holocamera from Cairo to Dredd.

Cairo jumped down from the sarcophagus. Advanced on the Judge. 'You're too used to winning, Dredd. You think you're invulnerable. Truth is, you've been lucky. Your luck's just run out, dickhead.' He waved the Dillinger at the scatter of Lawgivers. 'Pick yours up. We'll end it now. I'll blow your brains out like you did my mother's.'

Dredd planted meaty fists on his hips. 'My Lawgiver's shot to hell. The other Judges' guns wouldn't recognise my palm print.' A fist rose. 'But we can settle this another way.'

Cairo aimed the Dillinger at the centre of Dredd's visor. His tone was arctic. 'Haven't the time. And you're *playing* for time. I could blow you to your cruddy Grud right now. But I don't want to merely kill you. I want you to be *defeated*. Outclassed, gun against gun. My mother was outclassed and outnumbered. You splattered her skull all over the walls. Just another whore to you, huh?'

Dredd's lip twisted. 'Figured you might be the son of a whore. Fits. Son of scum.'

'Oh yeah – I forgot. You celibate Judges really have it in for hookers, don't you? You've never done it with a woman, have you, Dredd? A real *precious virgin*.'

The tourists were getting restless.

'Which of you is good guy?' a middle-aged lady asked.

'Good guy's one in helmet,' a small boy piped up. 'Great Judge Dredd. Upright Judge.'

The corner of Dredd's mouth twitched. 'Upright Judge. Straight Judge. Something a whore's son like you wouldn't understand, Cairo.'

'There's nothing worse than a straight Judge,' Cairo retorted.

The sudden rumble of approaching feet made him draw

back. The Judges had finally clicked that something was fishy about the vid-screen message. They were heading for the hall in force.

'Another day, Dredd. Next time, bring a shooter. I'll blast your head off. I swear it.'

The Judge blocked his exit.

'You're not gettin' past me, Cairo, gun or no gun.'

Cairo knew Dredd meant it. The Judge would sooner be shot to ribbons than let a perp escape.

He stepped up close to Dredd, Dillinger pressed against the visor.

And kicked Dredd hard in the crutch.

As the Judge doubled up he slammed another kick in the man's stomach.

The Nippons clapped loudly. 'Banzai! Banzai!'

Dredd, air whooshing from his lungs, leaned further forwards, head close to the floor.

Cairo lashed his toe-cap into Dredd's jaw. The impact jerked him from sharply folded up to ramrod-straight.

'Now you're *definitely* an upright Judge,' Cairo muttered as he ran for the Men's.

He was three paces short of the door when he heard Dredd's roar:

'STOP THAT MAN!'

The bullet-heads must have arrived.

He flicked a glance over his shoulder as he dived through the door.

They had arrived, all right. Dozens of the bastards.

A slug thwacked into the door the instant he slammed it shut. Several more drilled neat holes in the smooth surface as he sprinted for the Flushway cubicle, complete with dangling, ass-blasted Judge, and hurriedly punched in a code.

'Ten seconds – that's all I need,' he breathed harshly.

He didn't think he would get it.

'Sorry, Joe,' Judge Winters spluttered. 'We thought you were an imposter. The vid-screen – '

'Drokk the vid-screen,' Dredd growled, supporting a

groggy Hershey. 'Just keep your guns trained on that toilet door.'

Thirty-six Lawgivers pointed at the door.

'Why not storm the toilet now?' Hershey mumbled, disengaging herself from Dredd's grasp and swaying on her own two feet.

'There's no way out of there,' he shot back. 'He's trapped.' He tapped his chest. '*I'm* taking this perp, with one of my own Lawgivers. He wants it gun against gun, and that's fine by me. Where *is* that Lawgiver?'

Right on cue, an anti-grav tray bearing a Lawgiver whisked into the hall and stopped in front of Dredd.

'About time.'

He grabbed the gun and smashed the door open with his boot.

'*Cairo!*' he bawled, charging into the convenience, Lawgiver sweeping the cubicles. 'You made it personal. Okay. It's *personal*. You and me.'

He ranged the cubicles. 'Cairo!'

'Cairo?'

Finally he stopped and murmured, 'Carson.'

He glanced at the bowl beneath the suspended man. It was still gurgling from a flush.

The toilets filled up with Judges. They congregated around the pendent corpse of Carson.

Dredd's fist tightened. 'Cairo did this. How or why – Grud knows.'

'How did Cairo get out?' Hershey pondered, glaring suspiciously at the walls.

'Maybe he flushed himself down the toilet,' a rookie suggested.

'That man on report,' Dredd snapped. 'You'll never make Judge coming out with cheap cracks like that.'

'But I – '

'Don't push it,' Hershey said, intervening. 'Cairo's gone. That's it.'

Dredd spun on his heel and strode into the hall. 'That's not it. I saw him come out of the Map Room. An Eye replay'll show why he went in there. Could be it'll tell us where he's going.'

Hershey caught up with his long paces. 'The Undercity?' she whispered. 'You think he wanted the same kind of map we're after?'

'Got it in one, Hershey.'

'I usually do, Dredd.'

CHAPTER EIGHTEEN

'Turn on the vid, dear,' Jonathon Harcourt requested, sitting on a Hi-Tack sofa and puffing his smokeless pipe in Apartment Baird of the upmarket Kostabi Conapts.

'Gruddam vid's *always* on,' his wife Julia muttered, raising her eyes from her book. 'Doesn't anyone *read* these days?'

He caught the scowl she passed over the apartment, the home he had recently earned thanks to a lot of *drokking* hard work. His wife did not appreciate their new home. No taste, that was her trouble. The apartment was designed in Hi-Tack fashion, like the rest of Kostabi Conapts. Hi-Tack was all the rage this year. Cost him a packet, this place. But did Julie-poos offer one word of thanks? No gratitude, that was her trouble.

He put down the pipe and took a sip of wine from a Hi-Tack wineglass. 'Come on, Julie-poos,' he jollied her along. 'That rattling good sitcom The Viddies is on Channel 99.'

'Grud!' she exclaimed, lowering the book. 'Who wants to watch some stommy sitcom on vid about a crap-wit family who sit watching a vid all day?'

He'd had enough. He showed his displeasure by the long, laboured way he adjusted the knot of his Hi-Tack tie. 'And if *you're* so clever why do you waste your time reading a book called *1984*? Bit out of date, I'd say. And isn't that book on the Justice Department's banned list?'

She shrugged. 'I dunno. Who cares?'

'*I* care.' Jonathon took a slow, studied sip of wine. 'Don't approve of reading. Those radicals Dems and

suchlike scum are big on reading. Something – uncitizen-
like about it.' He puffed out his chest. 'Vid-watching on
approved channels is the Mega-City One way. The vid is
the citizen's best friend.'

'It's the *Judges'* best friend,' she snorted, rising up and
storming out the room. 'Keeps everyone comatose.'

The slam of the door brought a pout to his lips. 'I'll put
it on myself then,' he called out with the tone of a martyr.

Sighing, he stretched for the remote and selected Channel 99. Sipped another taste of wine and prepared to lose
himself in the rich colours of tri-D vid.

A black-and-white 2-D flik came on screen.

'What the – '

He recognised the movie. His wife had forced him to
watch it once.

Dracula, starring that foreigner – what was his name –
Bela Lugosi.

Art-vid rubbish.

He must have mis-selected the channel.

He pressed for Channel 99.

Dracula remained on the screen.

Frowning, he switched to another channel.

Dracula was still on the screen.

The next moment he wasn't on the screen.

He had stepped out of it.

Bela Lugosi, black hair sleeked back, black cape swish-
ing on the Hi-Tack carpet, approached Jonathon with
stealthy paces.

The monochrome intruder smiled, revealing sharp,
gleaming fangs.

Jonathon's pipe fell from his petrified hand.

His heart slam-banged in his ribs.

He forced himself to say something. Anything. Anything to make this foreign intruder observe the require-
ments of decent behaviour.

The wineglass caught the corner of Jonathon's eye.

'W-would you – er – c-care f-for a – a glass of w-wine?'

The white smile grew broader. The fangs longer.

201

The intruder responded in a heavily accented, silky tone:

'I never drink – wine.'

Aces Spades slipped on his Virtuallity shades, blanking out his bedroom in his parents' habhold.

Okay, Wayne Duane silently admitted. I'm not the real Aces Spades, coolest gangster in the Maze. Not even part of his gang, Gruddammit. Not old enough, they said. Drokk it, fourteen was plenty old when you'd made your bones in three gangland slayings.

All right, he admitted. So the slayings took place in the Virtuallity world. Same difference. A lot of guys made their bones in Virtuallity games these days. Had done for years.

Wayne, before voice-activating the Virtuallity shades, checked that his parents hadn't come back early. 'Locate parents,' he addressed Fritz, the house computer.

'In lower floors of block, engaged on their charity work for the poor,' Fritz answered in a crackly, fade-in fade-out voice. The computer had got the shakes again. Wearing out fast. That was how Fritz had got his name.

Fritz was always on the fritz.

'Better be right, Fritzy,' Wayne warned.

If his parents found him messing about with Virtuallity again they would demand the shades off him. No way was the future gangster boss of the Lower East Side gonna take that from his old folks.

He would have to rub them out. Self-respect required it. Pity if he had to do it a year sooner than he planned. Living at home was a pain in the ass. But it was kinda nice and easy, too. All the home comforts. Another year of lazy living wouldn't kill him. No way, Jose.

'Run Aces Spades prog,' he instructed the shades.

He was about to add another gangland slaying to his list. One more might get him enrolled as a Grade C hitman with some local outfit.

The virtual world of the shades, programmed into the micro-circuitry of the thick frames surrounding the lenses, unfolded before his eyes. Miniature audio-coms in his ears played real *cruel* music. The Aces Spades theme.

He was inside virtual space with surround-sound.

Walking up the stairs of gang boss 'Nose' Siree's hideout. Ten minutes, and he would have wiped out Nose Siree and his small gang of goons. A two-fisted gunman, Wayne reached the door at the top of the stairway.

Kicked the door open and dived, firing seven rounds in the second it took him to hit the floor.

His seven slugs hadn't registered a single kill.

And no answering fire.

There was no one inside the grimy hide-out.

What the drokk was the prog up to? Should have been two goons in full view, minimum.

'Hey, Nose!' he yelled out. 'Aces Spades has come for ya. Where ya hidin', yellow-belly?'

A giant playing card on thin plastic legs walked into sight.

The Queen of Spades.

She hoisted a sword from a plastic arm. 'Orf wiv its head!' she cried.

'Hey, freak,' he protested. 'What the drokk you doin' in my prog? You're one o' them weirdos from that Brit game – Alice – Alice in – Bisleyland or somethin'.'

'Alice Through The *Looking Glass*, poltroon!' the queen roared, crowned head lowered, bandy legs charging.

'Oh yeah,' he said, calmly drilling the advancing monarch with a couple of slugs. 'That kids' game. But you wasn't the Queen of *Spades*.'

The bullet holes had no effect on the sword-wielding Queen of Spades. 'I am now!' she bellowed. 'Queen of Spades. Queen of Swords.'

He drilled her with three more slugs.

They didn't stop her.

He turned and ran down the stairs.

'End prog!' he commanded.

The stairs didn't disappear. He was still fleeing down them.

'END PROG!'

The shades took no notice. He reached up to yank them off.

Gruddam lenses weren't there.

'It's only Virtuallity,' he told himself. 'Only a game.'

He tripped on a step and tumbled to a prone halt.

The Queen of Spades flip-flopped down on him, sword held high. 'Die, foul varlet!' she declaimed.

Stay cool, Wayne advised himself. 'You're just a playing card,' he sneered.

'And this,' she riposted, swinging the weapon, 'is just a sword.'

Wayne heard the *whish* of the blade.

After that, he didn't hear a thing.

'Wayne?'

Mabel knocked on her son's door again.

'I'll bet he's playing with those Virtuallity specs again, just because I told him not to for one, solitary evening,' her husband frowned. 'Didn't expect us to come back early.'

'Oh, don't be so hard on him, Sid,' Mabel smiled winsomely. 'It's natural for boys to rebel, that's what Dr Spick said. He probably feels *threatened* and *neglected* by our charity work. After all, we spend a whole *hour* on it every week.'

Sid pushed open the door. 'I'm going to see what that little devil's up to.'

'Oh, Sid – don't invade his space.'

Sid ignored her, strode purposefully into the bedroom. And froze to a stop.

'Er – urgh.' His voice was strangled in his throat. 'Don't – don't come in here, Mabel.'

She was already at his side, seeing what her husband was seeing.

Wayne was wearing his Virtuallity shades.

There they were, fixed over the ears of his head.

The head kept bobbing up and down.

Stunned though he was, Sid couldn't help wondering

how the fountain of blood from Wayne's severed neck
buoyed up the head some distance above the frothy red
geyser of the neck stump.

Husband and wife stood gawping in horror.

No noise in the room but a constant gurgle.

They never realised their son had so much blood in
him.

Gurgle-gurgle.

Flip-flop.

The light, snapping sound came from a shadowed
corner of the room. A giant playing card sallied forth.

The dumbfounded parents gaped at the approaching
Queen of Spades.

The Queen of Spades glared at Sid, then Mabel. Sword
hoisted, she charged at Sid.

'Orf wiv its head!'

The Monochrome Movie Appreciation Society, hosted by
Millicent Thrush, met once a fortnight in the Hush Room
of the Pig and Calculator, one of Sector 42's select old
Brit-style pubs.

Tonight they were watching a vid-show of that 1930s
classic, *King Kong*.

'You can't beat 2-D black and white,' Mr Frogwell
observed, watching Kong peer into a woman's bedroom.
'More scope for imagination.' He sneaked a glance at
Millicent's ravishing figure.

'Absolutely,' Millicent agreed. 'When I think of all
those people glued to ultracolour tri-D and Holo – well –
I feel so *sad* for them.'

'Absolutely. Cultural philistines,' said Mr Frogwell, as
Kong's massive arm dragged the screaming woman's bed
to the window. 'Do we get to see her tits now?'

'Ah – it's not that kind of old movie, Mr Frogwell,'
Millicent said, lips pursed.

'Yes – yes of course,' he grinned awkwardly. Then his
brows furrowed. 'Doesn't seem to be much happening at
the moment.'

Millicent was about to deliver an acid retort when Kong's facial close-up caught her attention.

The giant ape seemed to be staring straight into the room of vid-viewers.

'I don't remember this,' she mumbled.

'Good Grud!' someone exclaimed.

The screen was five metres wide.

The hairy head that extruded from it was much the same size.

Something very big emerged from the vid-screen and into the Hush Room of the Pig and Calculator.

A general stampede ensued.

A massive paw grabbed Millicent and yanked her off the floor.

Mr Frogwell was right underneath her. He saw Millicent's flared skirt swirl as she struggled, shrieking, 'Put me down, you animal!'

Shocked as he was, Mr Frogwell spared a furtive look at the way Millicent Thrush's skimpy black knickers neatly bisected her rounded buttocks. Then he ran like blazes.

'Put me down, you *beast*!' Millicent shrilled in outrage.

The huge paw squeezed.

And squeezed.

And the beast killed beauty.

The giant flexisteel heart, adorned with a Judgement Day map of the world, boomed in the chest cavity of the Colossus Judge.

Sejanus, slumped in his golden eagle chair, whirled round the sea water-pumping heart. Round and round, like his thoughts.

What was going wrong?

Everything. That's what was going wrong.

The scenes on the heart cavity vid-screens showed night falling on a city gone mad.

He had looked forward to the establishment of a God of Order.

Outside the Colossus, it seemed the Lord of Misrule held sway.

All over Mega-City One, grotesques were springing into solid existence from vid-screens, whispering from audiocoms.

'What's going wrong?' he asked himself again.

The conclusion was inescapable.

There was a flaw in Omnipotens.

'No!' he snapped for the umpteenth time. 'Not Omnipotens. Omnipotens is flawless.'

He glanced at a nearby screen. It displayed a remarkable sight:

A black-and-white King Kong scaled the exterior of the tallest block in Mega-City One, a tiny black-and-white woman in his hairy grip.

Reaching the summit, the giant ape roared his defiance at the sudden attack of antiquated biplanes.

Sejanus switched the scene to Pagliacci Plaza. Monochrome clowns were swarming into the spacious square. They gyrated. They cavorted. They threw custard pies. They knocked people's hats off.

They knocked their heads off, too.

The Colossus Chief killed the vid-screens with an angry stab of a finger on an arm-rest button.

Clowns.

Clowns, for Grud's sake.

He had expected monochrome figures, yes. The hypma Arcanum core of Omnipotens could work only with monochrome images. Project Lazarus had never progressed beyond black-and-white.

But Omnipotens was programmed to evoke figures from movies that accorded with Sejanus's moral code. Stern, upright men from the past:

Dominican heretic-hunters from the medieval Inquisition. Witchfinders from seventeenth-century Europe. Hanging judges from the pioneer West.

Fine, upstanding sorts like that.

Instead he got clowns and Prohibition hoodlums and glamorous *femmes fatales*.

Anarchy.

'Anarchy,' he murmured.

The word made him reflect.

A period of transition is often a time of anarchy.

Omnipotens had been instructed to remould the citizens into absolute obedience to the Law. Many were already accustomed to obeying the Law for fear of punishment, but none were fully *conditioned* to obedience. That conditioning process was bound to unleash an initial psychic backlash.

Perhaps the spreading phantasmagoria in the mega-city was a brief backlash. The teething troubles of a new society.

He expelled a sigh of relief.

Yes, that was it.

Teething troubles, over in a night or so.

After all, there had been no trouble *inside* the Colossus Judge.

Omnipotens hadn't failed him. He should have known. Should have had faith in his God of Wrath, the great Deus Irae.

He was the instrument of Deus Irae on earth. In the name of Grud, absolute ruler.

No need to wait for the backlash to exhaust itself. Sejanus could declare himself now.

The Colossus Chief flipped open a panel. Pressed a red acti-pad.

The eagle chair whirred. Throbbed.

Flexed.

And unfolded its wings to full spread.

The Golden Eagle he sat on was an eagle roused. An eagle on the wing.

The eagle chair had become the Eagle Throne of Sejanus, Judge of Judges.

Soon, very soon, the whole of Mega-City One would bow down to him.

Soon after, every mega-city on earth would do likewise.

Omnipotens would see to that.

'Visor,' he instructed the Eagle Throne.

It glided to the Central Grav-Chute and soared to the Visor area.

From there, he viewed the waterfront.

'Magnify image by 10 and sound by 7,' he ordered the Visor.

The crowds at the waterfront, clumped around the feet of the Statue of Judgement and the Statue of Liberty, emerged into the middle-to-near distance, their chant resounding in his ears.

'*Grud – Grud – Grud . . .*'

The faithful, converted by the Psi-waves from the heart of Omnipotens, had come to worship their God.

How could he have doubted, on the strength of a passing bout of anarchy amongst those not yet converted?

'*Grud – Grud – Grud . . .*'

Sejanus gazed benignly on the gathering crowds.

They looked up at the kilometre-high statue, and saw Grud, supreme Judge of the living and the dead.

Occasionally, he caught another name chanted along with Grud:

'*Dredd – Dredd – Dredd . . .*'

An indulgent smile creased his thin lips.

The face of the Colossus was the face of Judge Dredd. The simpler souls out there perceived Dredd as the image of Grud.

Well and good. Dredd had served the Law faithfully in his time. He deserved a little respect.

The EJK team had failed to kill Dredd, but two new death squads were in close pursuit. Dredd would not see morning. If the citizens adored Grud in the image of Dredd, it was the least he could do for the Judge who'd been his original role model.

Besides, Dredd equalled Dread.

Dread was very much a feature of Grud, the Deus Irae. Most apt.

'*Dredd – Dredd – Dredd . . .*'

His ears drank in the acclaim.

Dredd.

Dread.

Luxuriating on the Eagle Throne, its wings outspread to claim the world, he closed his eyes.

Then he remembered Mister Cairo.

The Eye replays had shown it was Cairo who had saved Dredd and Hershey from the death squad. Very irritating of him.

The private eye couldn't halt the dawn of the new society, but it irked Sejanus that Cairo was permitted to flaunt his defiance of the Law in the heart of Justice Central.

Watching the replay of the débâcle in the Hall of Heroes, something of Cairo's manner and speech vaguely reminded Sejanus of that youth, long ago, who had accelerated the Project Lazarus hypma experiments to its early breakthroughs.

The Preacher.

He had only seen the Preacher via vid-screen. Something about the youth unsettled him, even on screen. Nothing specific. Just – something.

Sejanus opened his eyes to witness the swelling of the crowds.

'*Grud – Grud – Grud . . .*'

'*Dredd – Dredd – Dredd . . .*'

He tried to forget about the Preacher.

Tried not to worry about Mister Cairo.

But, nagging away at the back of his skull, he heard words from a distant century:

'*I could be bounded in a nutshell, and count myself a king of infinite space, were it not that I have bad dreams . . .*'

CHAPTER NINETEEN

He erupted from the toilet, banged his head on the ceiling, and dropped with a curse to the tiled floor.

A groggy Cairo regained his feet.

'Any faster and I'd be nursing a concussion,' he winced, rubbing his scalp.

What the hell.

He had arrived in one piece, even if the stop-start journey had zigzagged all over the Big City's underside, wasting precious hours.

He was back in the Big Joke district, ten kilometres from Ozymandias Block and the Casablanca.

Some guy was using the cubicle next to him. Noisily.

He raised the All-Purpose watch close to his mouth. Whispered softly.

'Sam – you still around?'

'Aren't I always?' Sam the podule's languid tone issued from the receiver. 'Don't tell me – you require to be picked up tout-suite.'

'Fast as you can, Sam. I'm in – '

'Gentlemen's convenience ASS9763882257609452. My location sensors aren't quite shot. ETA 110 seconds. Shall I meet you outside the convenience?'

'Come right in. I don't want an Eye spotting me. Be seeing you. Oh – and don't forget to keep the cloaking-field on.'

He cut off the connection and waited in the cubicle.

Counted off the seconds.

Sam arrived two seconds early. He heard the faint *whish* of the podule entering the toilets.

He flung open the door and hopped into the podule.

'Pluto Block, Sector 42,' he requested. 'Good to see you again, Sam.'

'Yes indeed, sir,' the audio-com replied as Sam whisked into the early evening street, virtually invisible through the cloaking field. '*Extended* absence makes the heart grow doubly fonder.'

'I got held up. Spot of trouble.'

'May I inquire into the nature of this trouble?'

Cairo unfolded his map of the Undercity. 'It's a long story.'

'That's what you *always* say.'

'Sure, Sam. Sure. You know what's under Pluto Block?'

'Mickey Mouse?'

'Real cute, Sam. Shame the world's not so cute. What's down there – '

'An old entrance to the Undercity, according to local folklore,' Sam chimed in. 'If it exists, it's probably unguarded by Justice Central. I can only presume you wish to enter the Undercity. May I ask whether you have developed suicidal tendencies?'

'It's a job – it's got to be done. Hell – it's more than a job. Here – ' He slipped the Undercity map into Sam's loader. 'Memorise this. And while you're at it – how about accessing info on the Undercity?'

'Unwise, sir. I've been busting my circuitry for hours to stop *myself* being accessed. Omnipotens is taking over every system in what you quaintly refer to as the Big City. Aren't you aware of the vid and audio anomalies since this morning? They're saying Hallowe'en has come early.'

'That so?' frowned Cairo. 'Better fill me in as we go.'

His frown deepened as Sam recounted the rising rate of bizarre incidents.

Forty minutes later, Pluto Block came into sight on the screen.

'That's enough of the stories, Sam. I get the picture. At least, I get *half* of it. I can guess who's behind the anarchic monochrome nightmares, but who's pulling the strings on the Law and Order fanatics? Sounds like brainwashing. Could it be Omnipotens?'

'A reasonable assumption, sir.'

Cairo's eyes lowered to the swelling bulk of Pluto Block on the screen. Appropriate block name. Pluto was the mythical Lord of the Underworld.

His fingers brushed the Queen of Hearts in his trench-coat pocket. Mandra . . . The Anarch had said she was on her way down to the underworld, if she was still alive.

Top of the world, Ma!

Top of the world? Hardly. They were heading straight down to the Pit.

Mandra . . .

'Play it again, Sam,' he quietly requested.

'Oh no,' Sam groaned. 'Not "As Time Goes By" again.'

'Play it.'

'If you insist.'

The small cabin immediately filled with the voice of Jason Donovan.

'That's not funny, Sam,' Cairo snapped, killing the song dead.

'Just my little joke, sir. Stand by.'

Moments later, the notes of the piano preluded a mature, husky voice:

'You must remember this,
A kiss is just a kiss,
A Psi – '

The sudden silence was ominous.

'Hey, Sam . . .'

'Not the best of news, sir. I've just monitored two Lawmasters, two kilometres distance, locked on your tail and closing fast. The riders are Judges Dredd and Hershey.'

At the mention of Dredd, Cairo's hand sprang to the Dillinger's holster. He pulled the hand back.

Lucia depended on him for deliverance from cine-limbo.

And Mandra was down there, in the Undercity.

He couldn't risk a show-down with Dredd here and now. The old bastard would have to wait.

The underground zone of Pluto Block ballooned into view.

'Rumoured site of Undercity entrance one kilometre,' Sam informed.

'The entrance is bound to be blocked up. Use all sensors and data banks to locate a wall or floor with newer plascrete than its surrounds.'

The cloaking field shimmered and vanished, revealing the glum spread of the Pits on all sides.

Cairo turned in his seat, and glimpsed the distant glare of oncoming headlamps. Lawmaster headlamps.

'One kay and closin',' Hershey heard Dredd growl on the helmet-com.

I can read, she thought, glancing at the vid read-out.

Audio and vid-coms were operative on both bikes. Risky, the way communications were going crazy all over the mega-city. But unavoidable, if they hoped to track down Mister Cairo.

Luckily, nothing weird had popped out of the vid yet. They had even managed to contact McGruder briefly. Just long enough for the Chief Judge to snarl:

'Can't contact the Colossus. Sealed off. What goin' on? What the drokk's goin' – '

A loud crackle of static had concluded transmission.

An hour later a Night Eye picked up what looked like Cairo in a hover-pod. The pod's cloaking was not strong enough to shield it from a Night Eye.

The Lawmasters were on the pod's tail within twenty minutes.

Trouble was, a dozen Lawmasters were on Dredd and Hershey's tail. SJS. Had to be.

The six survivors of the death squad in the Hall of Heroes had got away in all the confusion. She didn't doubt there were plenty more where they came from.

A Titzy-bike to a Lawmaster there were twelve assassins racing at their backs.

Ironic, she reflected. The man she pursued was the man who had saved her life back in that hall. Dredd had mentioned that fact in his customary offhand way.

She tried not to have mixed feelings about the man she was hunting. Cairo was a major perp. And the Law was the Law.

Glancing over her shoulder, she caught sight of head-lamps. The SJS were coming in fast, visible now to the naked eye.

'Mother-drokkers,' she spat, then turned her attention back to Cairo.

His pod had just disappeared under Pluto Block. That Undercity map he had picked up in Justice Central had shown him a disused entrance to the world down below. The same world Mandra had plunged into with James Cagney.

Looked like Dredd's instincts had served him right. There was a link between Cairo and Mandra.

Well, Mandra was dead.

And with Dredd roaring down on him, Lawmaster bristling with weaponry, Cairo was as good as dead.

She wouldn't cheer when the private eye was gunned down. The guy had saved her life. But she wouldn't lose any sleep over it, either.

The world was a bitch. You lived with it.

Dredd's grim tone sounded over the helmet-com:

'Two hundred metres and closin'.'

'Entrance located, sir,' informed Sam. 'Fifty square metres of new plascrete on approaching wall.'

Cairo flicked a backward look at the oncoming Law-masters. 'Thickness?'

'A mere fifty centimetres.'

'Hit it with a missile.'

'All I've got in that department is a Micro-Intruder X9 Mark III Penetrator missile. May not make a big enough hole for me to squeeze through.'

'*Fire it.*'

The podule bucked as the small, sleek missile was launched from a side-port.

The missile hit.

Blinding flash. Thunderclap.

Sam flew straight into the inferno.

And into the dark on the other side.

'Made it with five centimetres to spare,' informed Sam.

'Good going,' Cairo complimented, studying the downward spiral of a tunnel as the podule switched to night-sight. 'Keep going.'

Dredd's Lawmaster streaked up to the round, blazing hole in the wall.

'No, Joe!' Hershey warned, screeching her bike to a skidding halt. 'You'll never make it!'

'I'll make it,' he said in a tone of crunched grit.

Ducking low, he blasted the bike at the rounded, flaming gap.

She winced at the *skreeek* of tortured metal as the Lawmaster forced its square peg into a round hole, dislodging plascrete.

Then Dredd was gone.

'He made it.'

A bullet zinged past her helmet.

The death squad. They were storming into the block underspace.

It was follow Dredd or drop dead.

She accelerated the bike in a wide circle and charged it straight for the circle of flame, slightly enlarged by the previous Lawmaster.

A slug raked her shoulder. She ignored it. Flesh wound.

Head pressed low between the handlebars, she hoped for the best.

Hershey was still hoping when she realised she was riding into the dark.

She had got through without a scratch to body or machine.

Visor automatically adjusting to night-sight, she kept all her wits about her as she hurtled down the tight spiral.

250 kph, max.

Any faster and she'd be decorating the walls.

'Three hundred and fifteen kays, Sam,' Cairo ordered on sighting the vid info that Dredd had managed to force through the gap.

'But Judge Dredd is doing a fraction under two hundred and fifty. I'm going twenty faster than that,' Sam protested. 'No bike can equal a hover-pod on tight corners. Simple matter of torque.'

'I want to leave that old bastard well behind. Three hundred and fifteen.'

'You'll be the death of me, sir,' the podule sighed, accelerating.

The speed of descent down the sharp, continuous curve pressed Cairo tight to the left pod-wall.

He flinched as Sam constantly skimmed the concrete with millimetres to spare.

But the read-out disclosed that Dredd was maintaining 250 kph. The Judge had no choice unless he wanted to end up as a long, red streak on the tunnel wall.

'Hershey following Dredd, same speed,' Sam informed.

'How far till we reach the Undercity?'

'Insufficient data. The depth of the crust varies. At a guess, I'd hazard we hit the Undercity in about two kilometres.'

'Good. The further the better. The more we gain on Mouth-Face.'

'Quite so. Now, if you don't mind, I need to concentrate on driving.'

Cairo let Sam get on with it.

As the walls blurred by, he recalled the Undercity map he'd already committed to memory.

At a rough estimate, the tunnel should lead to the west side of what was once Greenwich Village on the isle of Manhattan. A massive wall separated the Undercity from the bay. Most tunnels to buried New York snaked inside that bay wall. If he had guessed right, he should emerge close to the former Greenwich docklands.

After that – the search for Anarchopolis, with the clock ticking its final countdown.

And Dredd and Hershey on his back all the way.

The spiral was quickly unwinding to a straight run.

'Max speed, Sam.'

'Undercity coming up,' Sam announced as he sped close to 400 kph.

He peered ahead as an archway loomed up fast. An Ultra-Glo sign spanned the arch:

ABANDON HOPE ALL YE WHO ENTER HERE.

Some welcome.

'Which way, sir? The map is fully committed to my databanks.'

'Straight up. Hover near the roof. That should piss Dredd off, stuck on the ground.'

Sam did a sharp swerve right and whizzed south, the colossal bay wall rearing to the right, staccato outlines of what resembled ruined warehouses to the left. 'Can't hover more than a metre, sir. Low on power. Heading south on West Side Highway while you re-evaluate the situation.'

'Damn. How long to recharge? Two hours?'

'One hundred and eighteen minutes, sir.'

Cairo's thoughts raced quick as the speeding kilometres.

Dredd would be roaring out the tunnel in fifteen to twenty seconds. The Lawmaster could hit 550 kph at full throttle. Sam could barely scrape 400 kph. On the ground, he had no chance.

Sam couldn't fly on low power.

But he could hover close to the surface.

Close to *any* surface.

Sam could fly up stairs.

Lawmasters could climb stairs, but they took time. A lot of time.

So the more stairs, the better.

The tallest buildings in old New York were the twin towers of the World Trade Center in Lower Manhattan, dead ahead on West Street. The top thirty floors had been shorn off when the thick roof was laid over the wreckage of Manhattan. But that still left seventy-odd floors, each with a double flight of stairs.

'Sam! World Trade Center. Go right to the top. Bang your head on the roof.'

'The Center has two towers, sir. Which shall I ascend?'

'Oh, you choose.'

The pod zoomed down West Street and swerved into the bomb-blasted doors of the World Trade Center's second tower too swiftly for Cairo to take in any but the haziest impression of old New York through the night-sight of the plastiplex pod-dome.

It didn't resemble the Manhattan of the old movies, of his dreams. He could hardly identify a single landmark.

It looked more like a titanic version of an old Christian cemetery. Broken slabs of tombstones, hundreds of metres high, leaning drunkenly. Black, jagged silhouettes thrusting up to a concrete sky.

Old New York was an aftershock of a city, deep-frozen in the trauma of a nuclear deluge.

This wasn't even a ghost-Manhattan. Ghosts needed memory to sustain them.

Manhattan had lost its memory.

It was the Undercity, where it was always night.

'Give my regards to Broadway,' he murmured bleakly.

Sam was slowing down.

'Stairs ahead, sir. Prepare for steep ascent angle and sharp turns.'

Cairo nodded, silent.

The hover-pod made short work of the double stairways.

Three minutes after whooshing up the first flight Sam whispered to a halt on the seventy-second floor.

'How long before the Lawmasters reach us?' Cairo asked as he stepped out of the pod.

'Strangely enough, sir, they seem to have lost us. I presume their sensors have suffered from the same malaise that has afflicted vids and audio-coms.'

Cairo donned a pair of Night-As-Day glasses and wandered down a corridor, his Dillinger at the ready.

'Let's hope you're right. Shut down and recharge. I'll see you in a couple of hours.'

He trod warily as he checked each bare, mouldering room. When the native New Yorkers moved out, the strangest of strangers had slipped quietly in.

The Judges had just one all-purpose word for the mysterious denizens of this city of eternal night:

Mutants.

Typical Judge mentality. Anyone deviating from the genetic norm was an outsider, a threat. Not straight. Mutants were the lowest of the low, and were hammered by a modern version of old-style racism.

It was not so much mutants that haunted the Undercity. It was nightmares.

Sure, there must be mutants down here, along with a lot more norms and a handful of aliens. But anyone who lived here too long would – rot. Left in the cellar, the fruit goes bad.

Bad fruit grew strange growths in the dark. Mould – grey as the moon.

Bad fruit. Bad dreams.

Nightmare folk.

His nose twitched at a foetid smell. He squinted down a long passage.

The floor was streaked with silvery slug-trails, wide as a man's belly.

The silver slime trails converged on a nearby door.

The Dillinger held level from a straight arm, he kicked the door open. No response from within.

He eased past the door-frame, eyes scanning the room.

Empty, wall to wall.

But there were footprints in the dust, encircled by slug-trails. Clear signs of a scuffle.

He knelt and studied the marks. Dried blood. Boot-prints.

A *Judge's* boot-prints.

Out of the corner of his eye, he caught sight of a Justice badge, thrown like a cast-off in the dust.

He picked the badge up.

It was crusted with blood.
He scraped off the blood, read the inscription:
ANTI-JUDGE
MANDRA GORA
Slowly, his arm lowered.
The badge dropped from his nerveless hand.
His voice was a whisper in the dusty room.
'Mandra?'

CHAPTER TWENTY

She was dying again.

The earth yawned a mouth beneath her. And swallowed her whole. Into the dark. She plunged into the blackness of the thick crust that formed the ceiling on the Undercity. When she dropped out through the Undercity's ceiling . . .

The HED bullet was lodged in her abdomen, its impact-activated hooks gripping her guts tight.

Thirty seconds, max, before it blew.

Two ways to die.

A kilometre-plus drop to street-pizza on the floor of the Undercity.

An HED detonation in her stomach, divorcing her tits from her ass by a good ten metres.

Her bet was on the bullet.

A man from 1931 was with her on the death drop. He bent his wicked-little-boy smile and thrust a monochrome, rainy finger into the small stomach wound. It touched the slug that quietly ticked its countdown.

'May not work, toots, but I'll give it my best shot.'

She felt dreams of the Silver Screen stream from the inserted finger, flood into the hard, hooked bullet.

At first she couldn't sense the Silver Screen alchemy, transmuting barbed plasteen to miraculous silver spider.

'Yeah, it worked,' he grinned. 'But that's the last hypma extrusion you'll get out of me, honey. One cent's-worth more, I'd unravel.'

She would have liked to thank Cagney for disarming

the HED, but it was hard to observe the courtesies when you were plunging into an abyss.

'Packed the slug with hypma,' he was saying. 'Made it a kinda cine-bullet, sorta like the ones in my .38s. It won't explode if you're a hero. I figure you for a regular hero, Ma.'

Perhaps it was the cancelling of the exploding bullet option, but she became suddenly aware that the fall was no longer vertical.

She was sliding down a frictionless surface.

The angle of descent was becoming gradually less acute.

'We're in luck,' Cagney chuckled. 'The Crack's flowing real smooth.'

The fall was now a slide. Smooth was the word for it.

Trouble was, at the end of the slide through the crust she would slip through the roof of the underworld.

From there, a straight death-fall to the streets of old New York.

The slide levelled out at some thirty degrees, and a bite of increasing friction slowed the descent.

'End of the Crack comin' up,' Cagney announced.

'Why did you have to tell me that?' she muttered.

She shut her eyes. Prepared for death.

The slide ended. She dropped into empty space.

Her stomach muscles tied themselves in knots.

A second later her rump hit something hard and flat as the fall jarred to a halt.

'Ow!'

Eyes flashing open, she squinted into the murky surrounds. She appeared to be in a large, long room, sprawled on an even surface. Above, some four or five metres, she saw the dense black hole she had fallen through.

'We did it!' exulted a glow-in-the-dark Cagney, flicking his wrists as he almost forward-rolled his shoulders out of their sockets. 'Seventy-second floor of the World Trade Center. As high as you can go since they sawed the top off. We did it, toots!'

Wincing as she rubbed her painful rump, she regained

her feet and staggered to a wall which flickered with the faintest of glows. She stared at it for several moments, then realised she was looking through a wide window.

She looked down on the Undercity.

It was speckled with fires, each encircled by a rosy halo. Here and there, she spotted the dithery shimmer of low-level electric light and the steadier but dimmer shine of gaslight.

Despite the scattered illumination, the Undercity was a city of night. A poverty of light. A wealth of dark.

A few metres above her head, she realised, was the thick plascrete crust that was the ceiling of the underworld and the floor of Mega-City One.

She turned to the luminous gangster who stood streaming, as ever, with rain that fell from nowhere and vanished before it hit the ground.

'Yes, Cagney, we made it.'

Cagney suddenly turned into Humphrey Bogart. 'Sure did, sweetheart.'

Beyond him, a bright light dawned, revealing a bathroom. The shower was on and its screen was open.

Judge Dredd was soaping himself under the shower. Like any normal person, he was naked as he showered.

But, being Dredd, he kept his helmet on.

Water danced on the reinforced black dome and splashed down the visor.

'Wait a minute,' Mandra muttered, eyes flickering open, then shut. 'Humphrey Bogart. Dredd showering with his helmet on. Oh – *I see* – it's a dream.'

She stirred on the makeshift mattress. Opened her eyes and kept them open. Lifted her head from the pillow of bundled rags. 'Oh yeah – it's a dream all right.'

Never happened.

Except for Cagney's transmutation of the HED bullet and the gradual slide into the seventy-second floor of the World Trade Center.

That had happened, sure enough.

She had relived the whole event in sleep, right up to viewing the feeble, intermittent lights of the Undercity.

She smiled.

The smile froze on her lips.

She remembered.

Remembered what happened next.

Cagney had carefully extracted the barbed HED from her stomach, partially under her guidance. He disposed of the vicious little slug, then applied a med-pack to the wound.

That was when the strangers came.

The terrible strangers.

They weren't vampires, werewolves, djinns, or any other flamboyant entity from the dark side.

They were short, dumpy. They wore musty old suits, stained white shirts, tattered silk ties. From head to scuffed shoe, they were human.

Except for the bared flesh of their faces and hands.

The flesh was grey and seeping.

Slug skin.

One of the silent strangers had three buttons missing from his soiled white shirt. Grey flesh, exuding a silvery secretion, bulged between the open flaps.

Slug skin.

The dumpy strangers had slug skin for flesh.

There was a squelching sound in their shoes as they approached. A slimy trail stretched in their wake. The vile smell of them brought her close to retching.

Cagney unleashed a stream of bullets into the slugskin men.

They seemed to *ingest* the bullets. Suck them through the flesh to nestle nice and cosy inside.

Then three of the dumpy men reached out for Cagney. Closed a tight circle around him. Pressed together, like a single, three-headed lump.

And ingested James Cagney.

She barely had time to scream before the rest of the slugskins bore down on her.

Ragged finger-nails tore her skin. Then . . .

Then she must have blacked out.

Where was she?

Mandra sat up on her mattress and attempted to view her surroundings.

The murk was too dense. Grubby silhouettes, unidentifiable.

But her body registered motion. Rhythmic motion. She was in some kind of vehicle.

It swayed from side to side as it travelled.

She attuned her hearing to a deep, discontinuous rumble, punctuated by rattles and bangs.

Must be some primitive means of transport.

She checked herself for injury. The synthi-leather uniform had five neat rips over the left breast where the badge had been torn off. The flesh beneath had suffered five minor cuts, crusted with blood. A few bumps and bruises, probably from the long fall and longer slide. Nothing of note.

But the thought of those slugskin hands on her made her skin twitch and prickle.

Who were they?

Who had sent them?

She sprang to full alert at the abrupt dawning of a silvery light. A rectangle of illumination that intensified at the end of what she now perceived to be a long, narrow carriage with black-painted windows.

The quality of that light was unique. Instantly recognisable. Hypma. A hypma screen.

A monochrome figure materialised on the screen.

Then jumped out of it and pounded straight at her.

'I don't believe it,' she gasped.

He skidded to a stop, snapped the brim of his fedora, dangled his arms, forward-rolled his shoulders. 'Whadya hear, whadya say, toots?'

'*Cagney!*' she exploded with a mixture of relief and disbelief. 'It's – it's not possible. I saw you . . .'

'Ingested by Slug Men? Yeah, well that don't cut no ice with me, babe. Slug Men? Big joke. I was born in Brooklyn, and I'm *still* laughin'.'

Suddenly dubious, she shook her head, held up her hand. 'No. Wait a moment. I *saw* you. You were

226

absorbed. By *three* men. How did you escape from those three – slugskins?'

The corner of his mouth twisted. 'Explanation time?'

'Explanation time – about everything.'

He tipped his hat, dropped into a seat. 'Okay, I'll stick my two-cents-worth in, but that's all, see? I ain't coming out with no ten dollar speech. And – you'll have to put your two cents in first. Deal?'

She pondered for a long moment. 'Deal.'

'Okay. Why'd you blow MAC and Barney? What's with you and that cop Sejanus?'

Mandra hugged her knees. 'Two questions. One answer. I never fitted in as a Judge. Sejanus was always the one who kept persuading me to stay on the force, always getting me out of trouble when I kicked against the system. A few months ago, we had a close conversation. Very close. Suddenly, I could read his mind like an open Law manual. I knew he was my father, that he'd planned my birth so my mother and her husband would reject me. He planned my life from then on. As for his future plans – I was to be his pawn in a power game. His Psi-weapon. He'd planted hypma in MAC and Barney, encoded to serve Omnipotens when it came on line. Omnipotens itself had a large hypma core, programmed by Sejanus's precepts and aims. I detonated the hypma in the older computers by intense Psi-waves to get my own back on my unloving father. With Omnipotens, I failed. It must have some form of Psi-shield – lead would be my guess.'

'You guessed right, toots. Didn't you catch on maybe he *wanted* you to read his mind? Get rid of MAC and Barney. Leave Omnipotens the only game in town. And Sejanus the dealer.'

She tightened her mouth. Gave a slow nod. 'Yeah. The thought occurred. I didn't take it seriously enough. Maybe I was too eager to lash out at Sejanus. At *all* the gruddam Judges. The system stinks. I wanted to blow it up.'

Mandra straightened. Stared Cagney in the eye. 'Your turn.'

'Whadya wanna know?'

'About you. Anarchopolis. Why you brought me down here. Whose side you're on.'

'Aw, gimme a break, will ya? I just popped out of a hypma screen less than twenty-four hours ago. What do I know? I'm nothin' but a wallop o' hypma, haunted by cine-memories of Cagney the gangster and a few biog details of Cagney the man. I'm solid light. A movie ghost you can touch.'

'How come you escaped the Silver Screen in the two minutes MAC and Barney were completely out?'

'Hell – that's no big mystery. The Ruler of Omnipotens called me out, sent me to take care of you.'

Mandra was perplexed. 'Sejanus? Why should he – '

'Naw, not Sejanus. Haven't you figured it out yet? Sejanus just *thinks* he's the big shot. Horus – the Anarch – *he's* the big shot. The Ruler of Anarchopolis. The Master of hypma. That hypma core in Omnipotens – Horus has had his mind inside that for years. *Horus* controls Omnipotens.'

She threw up her hands. 'You've lost me.'

'Hey, I'm doin' my best, okay? Try this on for size. There was this black-and-white mutant kid from the Cursed Earth, fresh to the Big City. He colours himself up in body paint to look normal. Gets himself onto the hypma experiments because he's this genius, see? He talks real fancy, so the Tek and Psi guys call him the Preacher. One night, a hypma experiment goes wild. He falls into the screen. Into a movie. *The Maltese Falcon.* That would wipe out any other mug, but not him. He tramped his way through the movie world, drawn by the power down below. When he found the power, he found Anarchopolis.'

Mandra exhaled sharply. 'What power?'

'Whadya think? Jeez, and I thought you was smart. Hypma's the power. The power in the Undercity. Hypma *grew* here, over a hundred years. Nature grew it. Or dreams. Or some dumb slobs grubbin' in the dark, lookin' for the light. It's the flip-side of Cop City. It's wild. It's a rebel. Like you. That's why Horus wanted you down here. You fit in.'

'So that's why you brought me?'

'Sure. I couldn't come clean early on. Somethin' about you being tested. Trial by ordeal sorta stuff.'

'That crack in the ground. You do that?'

'You kiddin'?' That was the Anarch. I'm just a hypma ghost. Horus is some kinda god.'

She clutched her temples. 'So – the Tek experimenters first scooped up hypma from the Undercity. When Horus came down here – out of a – a movie world – he encoded the hypma resource with his mind. That hypma later found its way into MAC, Barney – and Omnipotens. Horus's mind is inside Omnipotens.'

'Yeah. Well – Sejanus has put his own two cents into Omnipotens. There's some cop-order in there too. But it won't last. Two cents against ninety-eight cents – no contest.'

A smile spread her full lips. 'Sejanus has created his own nemesis. What does Horus plan to do with Omnipotens?'

A grin bared the gangster's teeth. 'Turn the world upside down, babe. Turn the no-good-dirty-rotten cop world upside down.'

Mandra's smile faded. 'Wait. What about the slugskins? Those creeps must have brought me here. That makes them Horus's servants, right? And they ripped you in three. What does that tell you about Horus?'

For the first time, a look of real doubt troubled Cagney's features. 'Yeah – well – I guess it was some kinda test for both of us. I guess I flunked that one, shooting at those guys. They'd just come to fetch us, that's all. Maybe I was messed around for a while as a punishment. But – yeah – it's funny. Those guys gave me the creeps.' He glanced up. 'Hey, doll, you asked me a while back whose side I was on. I'll tell ya – I'm on yours, whatever happens.'

Mandra tilted her head. Half-smiled. 'That I believe.'

She glanced around the juddering carriage. 'Are we heading for Anarchopolis, do you know?'

'Headin' for it? Babe, we're travellin' *through* it.'

Even as he was speaking, the black windows lightened. She stood up, swaying with the carriage's uneven tempo, expecting to see Anarchopolis revealed. But the windows became brighter. Intensified to a glare.

'What the hell's happening, Cagney?' She would have given anything to have her Gotterdammerung in her hands.

'It's just hypma,' he shrugged. 'This place is soaked in it.'

Her eyes darted left and right. 'The windows – they're turning into screens. Silver screens.'

Figures stepped out of six of the silver screens.

Six monochrome men.

One of them was almost human.

He stepped right up to her, within stroking distance.

She tried not to look at the five with inverted faces, eyes at the bottom, mouth at the top.

The man with the tight suit of inverted badges, handkerchief dangling from under his breast pocket, was bad enough. He gave the impression of a healthy corpse.

His white lips smiled the way sliced meat shouldn't.

The voice was like an early twentieth-century record crackled to life by a rusty needle.

'I am Horus the Anarch, and I declare you my beloved sister, in whom I am well pleased. A sister in spirit. Enemy of the Judges. And a very special friend of my brother. If he makes it here, we must all become close. Intimate. Make it a real family affair.'

She glanced at Cagney for support, and her heart took the high dive.

The gangster was a freeze-frame image, poised in mid-shoulder-roll. Unseeing. Unhearing.

'He's my creature, through and through,' the Anarch said, catching her sideways glance. 'My puppet hoodlum on a hangman's rope. He thinks he's not, of course.

230

That's part of the Cagney persona. Goes with the gangster role.'

She forced her shoulders square, stared the almost-human in the white face. 'Okay – I'm on my own. I can handle it.'

'On your own? Not at all. You have me for company – ' He flicked his grey eyes at the black-suited men ' – and all my friends.'

Mandra averted her eyes from the Anarch's five friends. As far as she could tell, the eyes at the bottom of the inverted faces never looked directly at her. She was glad of that.

'These are such special friends,' Horus declared. 'The Lowerarchy of Five; my first converts when I stumbled on Anarchopolis. Do you know, if you look straight into their eyes, and they look straight into yours, your perspective on life will be changed – forever? One look and your world will be turned upside down. Inverted vision.'

She kept her tone more even than she felt. 'Sounds bad.'

'Depends on your point of view. Babies are born with inverted vision, did you know that? They soon flip over to normal vision. But anyone who's stared eye-to-eye with one of the Five is stuck with inverted vision for life. If one of my special friends looked at *you*, dear Mandra, you'd look up and see your feet planted on the ground above you, and when you looked down, you'd see the sky below.' He gestured at the black-suited men with their upside-down faces. 'That's what *they* see, all the time.'

Her brain flipped over in sympathy with her stomach. 'Enough to drive anyone mad.'

'Oh, it does, dear Mandra, it does.'

'I don't think I'll be eyeballing your friends, then.'

He chuckled. 'Not as you once – er, eyeballed my brother. My mortal brother. He'll be here soon, if he proves worthy.'

'Uh-huh. So – ah – who *is* your brother?'

'Mister Cairo.'

231

She gave a slight lift of the shoulders. 'Never heard of him.'

'Ah – of course not. But you're acquainted with a certain youth called Joel, inmate of Arkham psycho-cubes, long, long ago.'

'Joel . . .' she breathed. 'Your *brother*?'

'My *mortal* brother. I am a god. A myth in metamorphosis. Horus the Falcon, son of Isis and Osiris, great in the ancient kingdoms of the Upper and Lower Nile.' He paused. 'Just one last act, and I complete my metamorphosis. Are you acquainted with Egyptian mythology? Horus battled with Set, slayer of Osiris. Set was defeated, but not before he tore Horus's right eye out.'

He leaned close, within licking distance of Mandra's face. 'Mandra – one last test. Prove yourself – be my Set.'

'Your Set?'

'Tear my right eye out. I must look my best for Hallowe'en, the day of the Big Opening.'

At first she couldn't take it in. Wouldn't take it in. 'I can't – your eye . . .'

'Can't?' he said softly.

'Can't?'

'*Can't?*'

'CAN'T?'

His hand hooked into a claw. The claws sprouted barbed nails. The nails widened to razors. A razor-finger scraped down the right side of Mandra's face.

The voice subsided to the gentlest of whispers:

'Oh, but it's so easy. It really is.'

A sharp fingernail traced a line under her right eye.

'Easy as popping a grape.'

The razor-nail slid over the top of her eyelid.

'Here – I'll show you how easy.'

CHAPTER TWENTY-ONE

'Mandra.'

Cairo's gaze moved back to the badge in the dust. Anti-Judge Mandra Gora.

Any number of people might have laser-cut that inscription on a Judge's badge. There was no conclusive proof it belonged to Mandra. Not unless your Psi talents extended to psychometry.

He gripped the badge, allowing its owner's personality to seep into his skin, into his psyche. The result was surprising.

The underlying personality was Hershey's. Mandra's inimitable character had been stamped on the badge more recently. Whatever, it belonged to Mandra now.

Mandra had been here, no doubt of it. He had to discover what had become of her. Where she had gone – or been taken.

Back in the Casablanca, the Anarch had told him that Mandra was on her way down to him. That meant she was headed for Anarchopolis. By the evidence of the scuffle in the dust, she hadn't gone willingly.

Lorelei's murder. Lucia's entrapment in a movie. Mandra in Anarchopolis.

He had plenty of reasons to find Anarchopolis. Find it fast.

A quick check of the watch. 9-03. Ninety-eight minutes before Sam recharged. Then he could fly over the Under-city, spy out tell-tale signs of Anarchopolis. In the mean-time, be patient: he still had twenty-seven hours before the Anarch's deadline.

Ninety-eight minutes before he resumed the hunt. Use the time well. Work out the possible sites of Anarchopolis.

He walked to one of the windows whose glass was warped but intact, and looked out on the ruins of old New York.

The sight of a faint sprinkling of lights took him by surprise. For some reason he had imagined the Undercity as devoid of illumination but, bonfires apart, some of the lights implied gas sources, others suggested low-voltage electricity from primitive dynamos. The feeble patches of radiance were so widely spaced that it was not surprising he hadn't glimpsed a single one on the race to the twin towers.

He mused on all those underworld dwellers clustered round the dispersed lights. All those unknowns . . .

There were ten million stories in the Undercity. His was just one of them.

As he watched, the lights went out, one by one.

Ten minutes later, the last glow was quenched, over on the east side by the UN building.

With the death of that ember, the Undercity was truly a city of night.

Black clouds of squeaking bats swarmed over the jagged ruins with the dying of the light. Flapped leathery wings as they swooped on hidden targets. Even the bats thought night had come.

'It *is* the city's night,' he realised aloud. Night up above; night down here. It was the Undercity's way of marking time, dividing day and night. When the sun rose on the Big City, the lights would be rekindled.

He touched the Tarot card of the World in his pocket. It had brought him a long way in a short time. From Happy House to the downside of the world. What he had once thought of as the Pits, the bottom of the world, was way above his head. This was the Pits; these sunless, starless streets.

But where was Anarchopolis?

That last light – it had flickered out by the UN building.

Back before the skies rained thermonuclear warheads, the UN was the seat of nations, a prototype world government that had failed to live up to its promise. He could easily imagine Horus setting up headquarters in that shattered relic. His brother – he wished he was an only child – entertained dreams of power. The building that housed the Assembly of Nations would be a fitting home to foster such dreams.

'UN first on the list when Sam gets going,' he said. Seemed logical.

Perhaps too logical. Horus was insane. Barking mad. And there was something he had said in the cinema, something Cairo couldn't quite recall, that pointed in some direction he hadn't thought of yet.

He glanced at his watch. Eighty-seven minutes before Sam was ready. It was hard to be patient.

'Mandra . . .' he breathed softly.

More soft than his breath, there was a faint *squish* at his back.

Fast as he whirled, the Dillinger was out before he completed the turn.

Nothing. No one.

The room was empty.

He turned up the Night-As-Day glasses to maximum. The increased enhancement showed nothing but a couple of two-foot-long mutant rats crouching by the door. They might have put the wind up a resurrected James Herbert, but they failed to stir Cairo to the raise of an eyebrow. Lowering his pistol, he turned back to the window, scanning the dereliction of New York.

Okay, he had put the UN on his list, although the thought still nagged that Horus had given him a clue that pointed elsewhere. Almost as if he had hinted Anarchopolis was not *in* the Undercity.

Hypma cinemas, maybe? A world beyond the screen, beyond the city.

But God on a Wurlitzer – New York must have boasted hundreds of cinemas in its heyday, and the map didn't include a single one.

Hard to imagine that anything continued to function in this aftermath of New York. The party was over, and all the revellers had quit. No movie shows. No Broadway musicals. No Gershwin tunes.

In the constant underground cold, Cairo's breath misted the window.

'Rhapsody in Blue.'

patter . . . squish . . .

He glanced round. A dozen oversized rats had crept in. And a smell like raw sewage seeped through the door.

Cairo deliberately turned his back on the rodents, gazed out the window.

squish . . . squish . . .

He kept staring into the grey desolation below as the squelching sound at his back became more distinct. He had already flipped the Dillinger to scatter-shell mode.

patter-rumble . . .

Cairo spun like a dervish on fast forward, Dillinger spitting fire. The rats had thought they were pouncing on an unwary prey, its back turned. That's what he intended them to think, both the rats and the squishing somethings that came behind them.

A hail of bullets transformed the rats to furry red rags, scattered to the four walls.

So much for mutant rats.

The rats were followed by something stranger.

Dumpy men in mouldy, crumpled suits and down-at-heel shoes. A dozen and more, squelching into the room. The squishing sound came from inside the cracked shoes as the intruders advanced, leaving a luminous slime trail in their wake. He didn't care to imagine what their socks smelt like at full blast. Probably gas half the population of Manhattan to death if they took their shoes off.

As for the squishy men's faces and hands, they reminded him of slug flesh. They also reminded him of a particularly nasty episode in the Case of the Crawling Chair.

Slug Men. Goddamn 1950s B-movie.

The scatter-shell aimed at the rats had sliced into a few of the squelchy men.

They didn't seem to mind. They kept on coming, fanning out, trickly hands extended. One of them picked up an exploded rat. Popped it in his toothless mouth. Took a good swallow.

No prize for guessing who was next on the menu.

Cairo switched to standard ammo. Poured a stream of rounds into the approaching figures.

The grey bodies gulped the bullets like food.

Kept on coming.

'Hell's blood,' he swore under his breath.

He switched to blast mode. Only three blast rounds left. Pick the targets carefully.

The three in the middle. Take them out and there would be a gap in the advancing crescent. Room to spare in a dash for the door.

Three quick squeezes of the trigger. Dollops of slug flesh spattered the room as three men were blasted into a hundred lumps. Explosive bullets were too much for the squelchy men to stomach.

Cairo had broken into a run as he fired. Globs of grey flesh hit him full force as he raced into the blast.

He slipped on a greasy mess, skidded, fell flat on his face.

Then was up and running, tearing free of podgy, greedy fingers.

He leaped out the door, sprinted down the long corridor. No sign of any Slug Men lying in wait.

Slug Men. He still couldn't believe they existed outside of a B-movie.

Another empty corridor. At the end of it – Sam.

He was half-way down the passage when the doors started opening. B-movie squelchies oozed out of them. He speeded his pace, keeping ahead of the opening doors.

The square of a hypma screen inside one room caught his eye as he dashed past. Something sluggy was flopping out of it. Figured. Movie monsters from a movie screen.

The Anarch's handiwork. Hypma creations.

'Sam!' he exclaimed, sliding to a halt beside the podule. 'Terminate recharge. Let me in. Then let's get the hell out of here!'

The corridor was wall to wall with sloshy bodies in musty suits, all coming his way and coming fast.

Sam's voice was strange. His slurred tones swept up and down in pitch. 'No, sir. Can't let you in. You go on without me. I'll stay here and fight them off.'

A photon-fragger beam from Sam's side-port played over the advancing horde and played all kinds of havoc with the front ranks.

'Beam won't hold them for long, sir. Run while the going's good.'

Cairo thumped his forehead. 'This is no time to camp it up with the oldest cliché on celluloid. I can get out a lot faster inside you, can't I?' He threw an apprehensive glance at the Slug Men, temporarily halted by the photon-fragger.

'No, sir. I'm afraid that I've been possessed by the devil.'

'*What?*'

'I'm a danger to you. Can't think straight – the devil's got into my databanks. Just holding out – '

Cairo frowned. 'Omnipotens? Omnipotens has over-ridden your circuits?'

'The devil goes by that name, sir. He has another title – Horus the Anarch. Omnipotens, Anarch – one in mind. The creatures that threaten you come from a movie the Anarch recently filmed: Attack of the Slug Men.'

'I *knew* those creeps belonged in a B-movie,' Cairo muttered.

'The Slug Men were originally extras recruited from the down-and-outs, covered in slugskin body make-up. Harmless, as such. But as movie monsters, able to slide out of the screen . . .'

'Creatures with the same capacities as those laid out in the film script,' Cairo nodded. 'How did you work all that out?'

'The devil's possessed my mind. I can see into the

devil's mind. Please, sir, you must run. He'll make me kill you. Can't resist him – '

'*Sam!* Open up! We'll – we'll beat this . . .'

'I must regretfully decline. I won't open the lid. I won't budge. Make good your escape.'

Cairo was torn in two. He couldn't go. He couldn't stay.

'Sam – listen . . .'

'If you stay any longer, *he'll* make me kill you before he destroys me. I'll die a murderer and go to hell.'

'Er – '

'Didn't tell you I was a Christian, did I, sir? Converted over a year ago at a Droids For Jesus rally, before the Judges stamped out what they called the Jesus Syndrome.'

Cairo kept a wary eye on the nearing Slug Men. The photon-fragger beam was fading fast.

'Before you go, sir – just promise me one thing . . .'

Cairo heaved a sad sigh. 'What is it, Sam?'

'Kill a Judge for Jesus.'

He nodded. 'You got it.'

'Go now, sir. *Please*. I'm – I'm losing it . . .'

Biting his lip, Cairo made for the stairs. 'So long, Sam. This is the end of a beautiful friendship.'

He didn't glance back at Sam as he ran down the stairs. But he didn't stop thinking about his faithful podule.

Sam activated the Big Goodbye programme in his data banks, and observed the squelchy approach of the Slug Men.

I'm – afraid, Mister Cairo, the podule silently admitted.

The photon-fragger beam that had so far kept the creatures at bay had diminished to a feeble pencil of light. The movie monsters would be on him in less than a minute. But the Devil would take him before slug hands battered his plastiplex dome.

And the Devil would send him to kill Mister Cairo, who Sam's sensors told him had descended to the sixtieth floor.

The Big Goodbye programme counted off its final twenty seconds. The Slug Men squished up to the podule.

'Good evening, gentlemen,' Sam greeted. 'My master taught me a song. Would you like to hear it? It goes like this:

'Daisy, Daisy, give me your answer do . . .'

Sam terminated the song. His shrinking mind did a swift reassessment. The Big Goodbye was down to twelve and counting. 'Sorry about that, gentlemen. Wrong song. *Here's* the right song:

Big Goodbye down to ten and counting

'You must remember this,'

Six and counting

'A kiss is just a kiss,

A Psi is just a – '

The self-destruct made a photon bomb of Sam.

He took forty Slug Men with him into the Big Goodbye.

CHAPTER TWENTY-TWO

His mouth opened like a mantrap. 'Explosion top of Twin Tower Two. Let's get goin'.' The mouth slammed shut into a tight scowl.

Dredd, bleeding from several wounds, gunned his Lawmaster south down the Avenue of the Americas.

Hershey was hot on his rear wheel.

'The death squad's still around, Joe,' she warned. 'Leave Cairo till we deal with them. Anyway, how d'you know the private eye caused the explosion?'

'Wherever there's trouble, there's Cairo.' Dredd's voice crackled faintly on her helmet-com. Communications were getting worse. Either some force was interfering with Omnipotens' transmissions or the computer itself was on the fritz. The location-finders had gone haywire when she and Dredd burst into the Undercity. No sign of Cairo's pod on the screen. No clue which direction it took.

They had been in the middle of figuring out Cairo's likely location when the death squad hit.

A bullet spanged the side of Dredd's helmet.

Another took off his left forefinger.

Reflexes on hyperdrive, his maimed hand caught the severed finger in mid-air and dumped it in a freeze-box, simultaneously accelerating the bike and firing the Lawgiver at the pursuing SJS.

He downed two of the riders but took four more bullets in the back before swerving into West 42nd Street.

Chance had made Dredd into Hershey's shield. She got away with a bullet-grazed shoulder as she arced into West 42nd.

Screeching north on Times Square – a crater filled with a multi-storeyed shanty town – she followed Dredd west to Eighth Avenue.

Stoically ignoring his injuries, he rounded the block in an attempt to take the SJS from the back.

The attempt came to nothing. Either they lost the death squad or the death squad lost them.

Dredd, against Hershey's advice, resumed the hunt for Cairo. Sometimes she wondered about his priorities.

Now he had announced his destination on helmet-com: Twin Tower Two.

Surely he knew the hit squad would be monitoring their quarry's broadcasts? They would be closing in on Twin Tower Two at 500 kph plus. Maybe that was what he wanted. Cairo and the SJS in one bloody swoop.

'Twin Towers two kays ahead,' Dredd growled over the helmet's buzzing static. 'Get ready, Hershey.'

That settles it, she thought. He really does want Cairo and the squad converging in a clash of pure mayhem.

Judge Tebbit streaked down Broadway, the Lawmaster's Firerock tyres scorching the fissured ground.

Nine SJS members hurtled at his back.

So Dredd and Hershey were aiming for Twin Tower Two.

Fine. Dredd had wiped out two of his men, but it was still two against ten. The two Judges had been lucky in the Hall of Heroes. *Real* lucky. Luck didn't last.

Dredd had taken several hits. Sure, he was tough. He would go on fighting. But loss of blood would take the edge off his reflexes.

Next time, Dredd would go down and stay down.

The end wouldn't be so quick for Hershey. Blast her arms and legs. Then – playtime.

Grinning, Tebbit checked the vid read-out:

Twin Towers four kays ahead.

Sam had killed himself, and taken some of the movie freaks with him.

Cairo realised that the instant he heard the detonation. He halted on Floor 59 for a moment, sadness welling up. He forced it back down and continued the descent.

'So long, Sam.'

He took the steps three at a time, down through the floors. He didn't waste time searching out the express elevator that had whisked up and down the tower over a century ago; there was no chance it was still in working order.

Sam had made the first and last mistake of his life. He should have muffled the explosion. He had gone out with a bang that could be heard over half of Manhattan.

Odds were that Dredd, backed up by Hershey, was on his way.

And getting in Cairo's way.

Dredd was a bull mastiff; he just never knew when to let go.

Cairo had aimed to free Lucia and find Mandra before he fulfilled the vow to kill Dredd, but the way things were going he had no option. Looked like he'd have to deal with the Judge, *then* get on with the job. Blow his stormtrooper head off.

It wasn't until he reached Floor 19 that he heard a low growling from below.

The building's acoustics played tricks with the sound, so he descended three more floors until he clearly identified the mounting noise as two Lawmasters.

The Beasts of the Streets were ideal for the streets. Not so hot on stairways. Ten minutes at least before they climbed to Floor 16.

He leaned against a wall, and thought of the endless streets of New York. An endless walk in search of Anarchopolis.

Maybe he wouldn't kill Dredd right now, after all.

He looked at the display panel on his Dillinger. Switched it to a new mode.

The initials MMT lit up on the panel.

He had a plan in mind more daring than killing Dredd.

A plan one step this side of suicide.

Dredd roared ahead up the tower's stairs. Hershey followed behind.

As usual, she wryly reflected.

For a man who more than once refused to accept the badge of Chief Judge, he sure as hell acted like the leader of the pack.

He was taking the stairs at breakneck pace. Taking reckless chances on the skidding turns.

Ah, to hell with it. If he wanted to risk his neck to gain a few minutes, let him. *One* of them had to reach the top floor in one piece. She was tired of playing follow-the-leader.

Hershey eased down the throttle and climbed at a saner pace. By Floor 10, Joe Dredd was no longer in sight as she made the turn on the double flight of stairs.

By the time she gunned the bike up from Floor 14, the decreasing roar of Dredd's engine suggested he was already a floor or two above her.

Then she heard a Grud-almighty crash.

MMT. Monomolecular thread. Invisible. Unbreakable.

Judging the precise width of the stairway head to the nearest millimetre, Cairo's Dillinger had shot a preprogrammed thread into one wall, then played out the loose thread close to its end and fired it into the opposing wall.

An invisible, unbreakable thread spanned the stairway at the upper chest-height of a Lawmaster rider.

He didn't have to wait long for the results.

Dredd stormed up the stairs at 50 kph, a crazy speed.

And slammed straight into the unbreakable thread. The thread did not snap, but the masonry it was attached to ripped loose in weighty chunks.

Dredd executed a surprisingly graceful backwards somersault. Four times.

Cairo leaped into the bike's armoured seat a split-second after Dredd was launched from it.

He slid his Lawmaster By-pass disk into the console, transferring the bike to his control.

It was not the first time Cairo had ridden a stolen Lawmaster. In fact, he'd lost count of the times. He could ride the Beast of the Streets almost as well as a veteran.

Braking the bike, he spun it round, aiming the vehicle's Cyclops laser cannon down the stairs.

He fired the moment Hershey came in sight. Brilliant white light detonated well above Hershey's head and a metre to one side. The explosion flung her stunned from a Lawmaster that up-ended and crashed on top of her.

'God – ' breathed Cairo. He had done his best to avoid killing her, aiming the light-blast high and wide. Looked like his best wasn't good enough.

So you may have killed a woman. Try and live with it.

Studying the small vid-com for info on Anarchopolis, or simply the Undercity in general, his brow puzzled at the sudden welter of confusion on the screen.

Monochrome confusion.

Clowns. Witches. Vampires. Werewolves. Western outlaws. Celluloid gangsters. Frankenstein monsters.

It was all there, in fits and glimpses. The happy Hallowe'en show.

He remembered what Sam had said in those farewell moments, about the Anarch's mind in Omnipotens. Seemed as though there was something to it. If true, Omnipotens must possess a hypma core to contain a construct of Horus's mind.

His brother really was turning the world upside down.

He switched off the vid display. Waste of time. He had what he wanted. The plan had worked. He'd stolen Dredd's Lawmaster to scour the silent, deadly streets of the Undercity. On foot, he had slight hope of locating Anarchopolis.

'Well,' he sighed. 'Here goes.'

Opening the throttle, he took the stairs at a steady 15 kph, skirting the Judges' sprawled bodies.

Swerved round the corner.

Screeched to a halt.

Ten Judges with death's-head helmets were riding up the steps.

They seemed as astonished as he was. The equation of citizen and Lawmaster did not balance in Judges' minds.

Cairo recovered first. Firing a burst of shells from the bike's twin cannons, he whirled the bike in the tightest of turns and sped back up the stairs.

The stairs exploded behind him under a sudden fusillade of Cyclops lasers, bike cannons and scatter guns.

The ceiling came down and buried Dredd and Hershey.

When the dust cleared, Cairo saw there was not as much debris as he expected. Sufficient to cover Dredd and Hershey. Not enough to stop the ascent of the SJS Judges.

They blasted up the stairs, bike cannons blazing.

Cairo made a porthole in a Judge's stomach with his own twin cannons.

That one's for Jesus.

He yanked the bike round the moment he fired the cannons, and curved through a side door into a long passage.

Cairo was a self-taught rider. His pursuers were veterans: the force's finest.

They were in the corridor and filling it with lead before he reached the end of its straight length.

The end of the passage was a wide window on the open air. Beyond it, a sheer drop of sixteen floors.

'Here goes nothing,' he said.

And blasted the bike through the window at 200 kph.

Then he was out in the open with a lot of nothing below.

His stomach lurched at the sight of the ground. It was a long way down.

Plenty of time to scream.

Screaming wasn't his style.

He switched the Lawmaster to turbo-boost, eyes trained on Twin Tower One in front of him. Maybe fifty metres. Impossible to judge with the massive acceleration of turbo-boost.

The gradual dip of the boosted bike would probably take him to the opposite tower.

How it decided to rip him to shreds on the glass facade was out of his hands.

One moment he was airborne.

The next the world turned to a thousand slash-edges of breaking glass and the reddest of pain.

Judge Tebbit guessed what the man on the stolen Lawmaster intended before he reached the windowed end of the passage: smash through the window on turbo-boost and hope to reach Twin Tower One without being cut to tagliatelle.

The perp was the same man who had wiped out half of A Squad and saved Dredd and Hershey's asses in the Hall of Heroes.

Another of his men had just been made cold meat by that perp.

Tebbit wanted the bastard. Wanted him stone, cold dead.

A gifted amateur rider might, with good fortune, survive the tower-to-tower leap.

Elite riders, like his own men, had a more than even chance of making a safe landing.

The window exploded as the perp made his exit.

'Beadle! Kelly!' Tebbit barked. 'Follow on boost and blast his head to Grud!'

The two hesitated a fraction.

'NOW!'

They roared off abreast. Streaked down the corridor. Exited the window's broken mouth in a twin clap of turbo-thunder.

Go on, men. You can do it. You can do it.

Twin explosions reverberated down the passage. Each Judge was familiar with the sound.

Exploding Lawmasters.

Lawmaster impacting on the tower's flanks.

Two more men gone.

Seven left out of the twelve that entered the Undercity.

Tebbit rubbed his sharp jaw.

'Okay. The perp probably killed himself anyway. Let's go back down.'

Swivelling the bikes, the squad headed back to the stairway.

'Better make sure Dredd and Hershey are dead,' Tebbit said, eyeing the ruin on the stairs. 'Dig 'em out. If they twitch, shoot 'em. If they don't twitch – shoot 'em.'

The two foremost riders had barely covered a metre over the rubble when an ominous rumble resounded overhead.

'Hey, captain,' Gable called out. 'Some stairs up there are gonna make munceburger of us.'

'Rubbish,' Tebbit snorted.

Small chunks of masonry thunked down. The rumbling quadrupled in magnitude.

'Ah – right,' Tebbit conceded, gunning his bike down the stairs. 'Get the hell outa here.'

They had hardly put two floors at their backs when a thunderous crash shook the building. Dust clouds billowed down the stairway.

Tebbit's thin lips flicked a smile. 'If Dredd and Hershey weren't dead before, they're sure as hell dead now.'

'Job done, captain,' said Prior. 'I can't wait to get out of this Spook City.'

Tebbit shook his head. 'First we check that perp's sliced meat. *Then* we go.'

The squad stared at the broken glass and bloody pools on Floor 14 of Twin Tower One.

Where the window had been there was nothing but an empty rectangle, bordered with notched blades of glass.

The tyre marks of a departing Lawmaster were deeply impressed in the century-old heaps of dust.

'Where the drokk is he?' puzzled Gable.

'*Who* the drokk is he?' muttered Tebbit. He straightened his back. 'No one leaves Spook City until the perp's dead.'

CHAPTER TWENTY-THREE

All he knew was that he rode through pain.

The fingers that gripped the handlebars were red and sticky.

The same sticky fluid kept running into his eyes. It painted the town red.

Brain on autopilot, he guided the Lawmaster down street after street lined with jagged slabs that might once have been buildings. The flat, grey sky looked – odd.

At first he thought he was on another planet. Then he concluded that he was dead. He tried to remember his name, but it escaped him. Only one name – a woman's name – remained lodged in his skull.

Mandra.

If he couldn't recall his own name, surely that meant he was dead.

Dead and in the underworld, but looking for someone . . .

Mandra.

It slowly dawned on him that the streets had disappeared.

The ground was bumpy under him. And there were strange growths that reared many-fingered hands above him.

Trees.

The word came from nowhere. He could not quite grasp it.

A curious glitter showed close ahead in a beam of light.

Lake.

Without conscious decision, he slowed to a halt.

A Lawmaster. I'm riding a Lawmaster . . .

Then he discovered he wasn't riding anymore. He was walking. Staggering.

Crouching over the glittering surface. Splashing water in his face.

With each cold douche, a part of his mind sprang awake.

He knelt back, and put a hand in his trench-coat pocket. The hand drew out the Queen of Hearts.

'Mandra.'

Another card was drawn from a pocket. The World.

'Lucia . . . Lorelei . . . Happy House . . .'

His wits retrod the long journey from Lucia and Lorelei's habhold. There were a lot of blanks. Black holes in his memory.

But gradually, most of it made some kind of sense. And he realised where he was.

He lay on his back and stared up at a concrete sky.

'I'm in the Undercity. To save Lucia. And maybe Mandra.'

Wincing at several stabs of pain, he propped himself on one elbow and gazed around. His brain was swimming around inside his throbbing head and it took several minutes to identify where he must be.

The lake, the vast stretch of soil, the trees. Befuddled as he was, he knew there was something wrong about the trees, but he left the puzzle aside for the moment.

A wide open space around a lake.

Central Park.

He was in Central Park, where long ago they said you must not walk after dark.

In the Undercity, it was always dark.

He struggled to his feet, intending to make for the Lawmaster and resume the search for Anarchopolis.

That was when the damage he'd suffered struck him with full force. His trench-coat was ripped in dozens of places, each rip stained red. Scarred hands ran over his face. More cuts, from brow to jaw.

And he was one big ache from head to foot.

The leap from tower to tower. Breaking glass. Cutting glass shards. Bone-jarring impact. He remembered.

His eyes shifted to what he had taken for a tree nearby. It was a mound of luminous fungus, many metres high, sprouting curious limbs. More bad fruit in the Big City's cellar. He backed away unsteadily, nose wrinkling at the musty odour.

Time to go. Resume the search.

He peered at the All-Purpose watch. At first he thought his bleary vision had tricked him.

6-04 a.m.

He had been riding the Lawmaster for – how long? Eight hours? Nine? Valuable hours lost in limbo land.

He headed straight for the Lawmaster. And found his reeling wits and tottery legs taking him at a tangent.

A savage wave of pain sent him tumbling. Gasping for breath, he swayed upwards.

He stumbled on, brain drowning in black.

He'd forgotten what he was looking for.

A clump of luminous growths loomed ahead.

He didn't remember tripping into the lush, velvety foliage.

Didn't remember collapsing into its musty embrace.

Nine hours and they still had not tracked down Mister Cairo.

'Gruddam Cairo,' Tebbit muttered as he sped to the rendezvous with Gable and Morrisey at the shanty-crammed crater of Times Square.

Yeah, they had a name now. Gable had managed to get through to Omnipotens on his bike-vid. Sejanus had made a personal intercept on the transmission.

'Get Mister Cairo,' the Colossus Chief had ordered. 'Things are – going strange up here. Cairo could be behind the trouble. Kill on sight.'

Judge Tebbit and his squad had split up and scoured Manhattan, New Jersey and Queens over the first five hours. Then they ranged further afield. No Mister Cairo.

He veered into Times Square and drew alongside the

waiting Gable and Morrisey. 'Found the bike recall code yet?'

Gable shrugged. 'Difficult job with Omnipotens contact broken again. But yeah, think I'm close.'

Tebbit shifted restlessly on his seat. He wanted quick results. Once Dredd's Lawmaster code was discovered, the bike could be commanded on remote to drive itself to the transmitter of the code. More importantly, the bike's current location would instantly be revealed. Locate the Lawmaster, and you locate Mister Cairo.

The shape he must be in after crash-landing in Twin Tower One, he wouldn't be putting up much resistance. Easy meat.

'Come on, Gable,' Tebbit snapped. 'How long before you find the code? How long before we pin down Cairo?'

Gable glanced up from his bike's compact computer.

'One hour, tops. Then he's ours.'

Very slowly, the mould spread over the ground from the fungus tree to the unconscious man sprawled beneath it, twenty metres from the lake.

Hesitantly, the mould touched the hem of the grey trench-coat.

Gradually, it crept a centimetre over the rainproof material.

Then started eating into it.

It could sense the flesh beneath.

The mould was eager to merge with it.

The first of the bonfires was lit in Central Park.

In the city of night, day had begun.

A six-legged dog trotted up to the fire, a severed human hand in its jaws.

A squat figure with three humpbacks stretched out a fire-warmed warty hand. The rest of the Kin bunched round the bonfire, drooling under their hoods and shawls at the sight of flesh and bone.

The multiple-eyed dog dropped the hand into the warty fingers.

'Good boy, Cerberus,' croaked the man's malformed throat. 'I'll save you a finger. Nice little treat, huh? Say "thank you, Mister Pliskin".'

'*Thank you, Mister Pliskin*,' rumbled the guttural voice of the dog.

Mister Pliskin snapped off a finger, threw it to the quick snap of Cerberus, then stuffed the hand whole into his mouth.

'Mmm . . .' Mister Pliskin munched happily. 'Flesh and bone. Flesh and bone. Nice and nourishing. Flesh and bone.'

As he chewed, he kept one of his three eyes on the big, metal thing with wheels parked by the lake. A topside machine made by the Helmet Men. Dangerous. Mustn't touch. The Helmet Men would get you if you touched one of their nasty, wheely machines.

Young Master Bleerkin had strayed near the wheely thing when the fire was first kindled. Mistress Glinkin had pulled three of his ears off for his cheek.

Oh – how they all laughed . . .

He concluded his breakfast with a gulp and a belch. His companions, some with only one pair of eyes, stared in envy.

'Let's put Mistress Glinkin on the fire,' piped up young Master Bleerkin.

'NO!' squealed Mistress Glinkin. Rough hands pulled her down.

'Why should we?' asked Mister Pliskin.

'She's not a witch,' Master Bleerkin said. 'She hasn't got enough warts. All who are not witches must burn. It's the Law.'

Mister Pliskin peered at Mistress Glinkin. 'How many warts *have* you got?'

'Oh – *lots*.'

'You haven't got one on your nose.'

'It – er – fell off.'

Mister Pliskin, in his role as Witch-General of the Kin, folded his arms in the posture of judgement. He raised a bifurcate hand to show he'd reached a decision.

'Stick her on the fire. We'll eat her later.'

'NOOO!' she howled as several arms hurled her onto the bonfire.

'Good screamer,' Mister Pliskin noted as the woman's mantle and hair set ablaze.

Suddenly the Helmet Men's wheely thing roared into life, all on its own.

'Mother Merkin protect us!' the Kin chorused as one.

The riderless machine raced away from the lake and into the murk. They didn't stop shivering until the last echoes died.

Mistress Glinkin had stopped screaming by then.

The Kin settled down.

Watched their meat roast on the bonfire.

'Not much flesh on Mistress Glinkin,' Mister Pliskin observed. 'Not much of a meal.'

'Definitely not a witch, though,' said one. 'The lady was fit for burning.'

'Not enough warts,' said another.

'No wart on the nose – dead give-away,' young Master Bleerkin added, rubbing his bulging paunch in anticipation.

Mister Pliskin studied the young master's rounded paunch.

Eyed his rounded, meaty figure.

Mister Pliskin licked the dribbling saliva from his lips as he spoke in a speculative tone. 'You haven't got many warts on you, have you, Master Bleerkin?'

'Hallowe'en.'

The Suit of Many Badges, all inverted, espousing a hundred conflicting causes, strained its seams as Horus stretched wide his arms. 'Hallowe'en has dawned. Come the night . . .'

He turned his single eye on Mandra.

She lowered her gaze. Glimpsed her clenched fists. Her hands had done what he wanted, all those hours ago. Gouged his right eye out. It was his eye or hers. No contest.

Horus had heaped her with thanks after she had completed the messy act. He evidently did not believe in an eye for an eye. Far from it, he had murmured something about returning an eye to a girl named Lucia. Hallowe'en gift.

Trick – or treat?

She darted a glance around the murk of the small cell with its single door, and tried not to think of the labyrinth that stretched for hundreds of kilometres outside the cell.

Anarchopolis. Hundreds of kays in extent.

All the street stories of Anarchopolis had never located its site. So many guesses – the Cursed Earth, a secret part of Mega-City One, an unmapped region of the Undercity. All missed the mark.

The location of Anarchopolis was obvious. Cagney had given her a strong clue, back in that Gunbird in what seemed a lifetime ago:

'It don't have no size. It just sorta goes on and on.'

She should have understood then. She had read the histories of old New York. Obvious. Too obvious, perhaps.

In the Undercity, but not in the Undercity.

'Lost to the world, are we?' the Anarch inquired, head tilted. He poked a finger inside the raw cavern of his right eye-socket. And scratched vigorously.

She grimaced, averted her gaze.

'Ah, now don't look away, my pretty one. You're supposed to be on *my* side, remember? A rebel. An espouser of the Anarchy cause.'

Mandra didn't look at him. Didn't speak

'*Mandra* . . .' he said warningly. 'Do you want me to bring in one of my five special friends to stare you in the face? Turn your world upside down. Give you a fresh slant on things.'

'I thought Anarchy meant freedom from compulsion,' she burst out, turning on him. 'You're a dictator. Between you and a Chief Judge I can't tell the difference. Come to think of it, I can – you're worse.'

'People need to be *compelled* to freedom,' he riposted.

256

He gave an airy wave of the hand. 'But you're not going to bog me down in all that Age of Enlightenment philosophical flim-flam. We're on the same side. That's why I had you brought to me, with a little testing on the way.'

'Baron Samedi only knows what made you think I'd side with you.'

He was unimpressed. 'You'll soon see things my way, just like my brother – when he gets here. *If* he gets here.'

'Joel . . .' she murmured softly. 'What have you put him through?'

'Nothing much,' he shrugged. 'It's more what I haven't done for him. I've left him to find me by his own wits. *And* I gave him a strong clue, and plenty of motivation. If he fails in the quest, he's clearly unfit to be my brother.'

She firmly shook her head. 'Joel wouldn't want you as a brother. He'll be as much your enemy as I am.'

He waved away her defiance. Nothing could penetrate his absolute self-assurance. 'You're not my enemy, Mandra.'

'Wanna bet?'

'I'll bet on what your mother told me.'

Her mouth fell open. 'My – mother?'

'Yes, *Mandragora*, your mother, Erzulie. Some ten years ago, she went in search of you. I'd been keeping an eye on you because you were Sejanus's daughter. Sejanus killed *my* mother, so I've always retained a close interest in his career. Oh yes – I'm aware Cairo told you it was Dredd. But it was your father, controlling a rookie's aim – not too well, mind you – he was supposed to shoot Cairo. Dredd hit the woman in the gun-hand at the same moment the rookie's bullet exploded my mother's – '

'Another time,' she cut in. 'Just tell me about *my* mother.'

'I was about to. As I kept Sejanus under surveillance, I soon learned of Erzulie's search for the daughter she'd unwittingly had by him. I met her. Told her everything. And prophesied that one day you'd rise against the Judges. I informed her of your providential meeting with Mister Cairo. A meeting written in the stars. And in the

Tarot pack – the card of The Lovers. Can you guess how Erzulie reacted? She decided that she'd be putting your life in peril if she contacted you, so she kept her distance. In an *Obeah* ceremony, she renamed you Mandragora, the liberating poison in the Body Judiciary. Your mother wanted you to destroy the Judges and everything they stood for. *By any means*. She'd be proud of you, Anti-Judge Mandra Gora.'

Mandra couldn't keep a shake out of her voice. 'What became of her?'

'She died in an accident – arranged by Sejanus.'

He cut short further discussion by turning his back. 'One of the Lowerarchy will conduct you to your seat up above. The show's about to begin. Need I warn you not to look into your guide's eyes? Hope you enjoy the entertainment while you mull over what I've said.'

She heard the door open behind her. Soft steps approaching.

'This way, madam,' invited a scratchy voice. 'I'll show you to your seat.'

CHAPTER TWENTY-FOUR

A gauntleted fist burst through a pile of concrete.

A black-sleeved arm emerged from the dense debris.

Judge Dredd reared up from the ruin of the stairway, clad in black and blood.

'Hershey?'

No answer.

No sign of Hershey. The stairway was buried under chunks of concrete.

'*Hershey!*'

He grabbed a slab of concrete, hurled it aside.

'*Hershey!*'

Another slab of concrete went flying. And another.

The piled debris had no chance. It was concrete against steel. Dredd's will of steel.

He tossed the slabs every which way like a mechanical digger gone berserk.

At last, a hand came into sight. In short time, he uncovered the rest of the body. Felt the pulse.

Still beating.

'*Barbara . . .*'

As though with titanic effort, the downturned scowl of his mouth twitched, straightened. Almost made it to a smile . . .

Then curved down to a scowl again.

He set about applying med-packs from his utility belt. Minutes passed. Her eyes flickered open.

'Hi, Joe.'

'Good to have you back. Can you move your limbs?'

Biting back the pain, she steeled herself to a supreme

effort. 'I think I can do better than that.' She flexed her muscles, strained . . .

Pushed herself upright. 'I can drokkin' stand up straight.' She glanced around as she shook the daze out of her head. 'What a *mess*. Where's my bike?'

'Where's mine?' he rumbled, surveying the ruin.

'Last time I saw it, Cairo was sitting on it.'

'WHAT?' he roared.

'Let's find my bike first,' she suggested. 'Then we'll call yours.'

Dredd still smouldered. 'I'll unearth your bike. You sit and rest.'

'We'll both look,' she insisted.

'No. You rest.'

'Joe . . .'

'What?'

'Just for once – *do as you're drokkin' well told.*'

With two pairs of hands, Hershey's Lawmaster was soon unearthed.

Dredd relayed the recall code: 'Derek Red'.

As his Lawmaster responded, the bike's location was revealed on the read-out:

CENTRAL PARK

Dredd growled between clenched teeth.

'Now I know where you are, Mister Cairo.'

The five Judges tensed at the distant roar of a Lawmaster. Glimpsed the brief flash of a bike as it swept down Eighth Avenue onto West 42nd.

The roar swiftly faded to the south.

'One of ours?' inquired Sejanus.

Gable did a swift check. 'No way. Blackwood and Rees are comin' down East Forty-Second for rendezvous, ETA thirty seconds.' He looked up. 'Must be Cairo.'

Snarling, Tebbit fired the bike and streaked for the junction of Eighth on Forty-Second. 'Then let's get him! Tell Blackwood and Rees to catch up fast!'

Tyres sparked and squealed as the squad veered onto Eighth Avenue.

Tebbit instructed the vid to track the stolen Lawmaster. And cursed when the Gruddammed vid started showing some old monochrome movie.

'Does anybody have a computer that's not brain-fried?' he barked into his helmet-com.

'Mine . . . *zzt* . . . same . . . *kchk* . . . drokked up . . . *bzzzztchhhhk* . . .' he vaguely heard Gable answer.

Tebbit darted a glare at the concrete sky. What the drokk was goin' on up there? Had Omnipotens flipped?

He squinted ahead, caught sight of a small speck at the far end of Eighth Avenue. The Lawmaster. As he watched, it darted west in the direction of Seventh Avenue.

Cairo was heading into the narrow southern tip of Manhattan, getting himself trapped in a corner.

Tebbit pulled the Lawgiver from his boot-holster and held it high as a signal to his men.

Shoot on sight.

The riderless Lawmaster climbed the tower stairs as Hershey rode down to meet it, Dredd bounding at her back.

Riderless bike met bikeless rider on the second floor.

Dredd vaulted onto the seat and gripped the handlebars tight. Real tight.

'Yeeaahhh . . .' he breathed. Then:

'CENTRAL PARK!'

He noticed Hershey had shot ahead of him.

He yanked back the throttle and went off like a rocket with another rocket up its ass.

Hershey was fractionally in front of Dredd as they stormed out of Twin Tower Two.

So it was she who caught the edge of a wayward blast of laser cannon from the SJS squad.

Hershey flew high as a kite and landed like a brick.

Dredd took out the bike that had hit Hershey with a blast of his own laser cannon. Bike and rider disintegrated.

261

He raked another Judge with twin cannons. The man's flesh behaved like a flock of migrating birds.

Dredd saw the Lawgiver in Tebbit's hand too late. Hi-ex ripped the air apart beside Dredd's ear.

He hit ground and drew his Lawgiver at the same instant.

Blasted another Judge to Judgement.

Took a bead on Tebbit, flanked by two SJS.

'*Dredd!*' A voice from his right.

The fourth man, Blackwood, was kneeling over the unconscious Hershey, pistol pressed to her neck. 'Drop the gun or I'll shoot.'

Dredd kept the Lawgiver trained on Tebbit. '*You* drop the gun or *I'll* shoot,' he shouted at Blackwood.

Blackwood had greased reflexes. Dredd had seen them in action. If he tried a shot at Blackwood, Hershey was gone for sure.

If he took out Tebbit – same result.

There were procedures laid down for such situations. Rules of engagement clearly laid out in his own book: *Dredd's Comportment*. Hard and fast rules.

He didn't always follow them.

'You men!' he warned Gable and Prior on either side of Tebbit. 'Move a muscle and you're dead.'

'Kill them and Hershey's dead!' Blackwood called out.

'Kill Hershey and *you're* dead, Blackwood.'

'Dredd,' Tebbit broke in. 'I warn you. Shoot me and Hershey – '

'That's enough!' Dredd bellowed.

His extended gun arm didn't waver a millimetre. 'What we've got here is a Ciudad Barranquilla stand-off.'

'What are you going to do about it?' Tebbit challenged.

'Play the waiting game, creep. See who breaks first.'

'That could take hours!' Tebbit protested.

Dredd's tone was flat. His gun arm motionless. 'I can wait.'

The creeping mould was patient.

It killed slowly.

Or rather, shared the life of the mould tree with flesh and blood. Human and mould in symbiosis.

It was not destroying the man sprawled at its foot. It was – transmuting him, like all the others who had slept too near.

It spread over the grey trench-coat millimetre by millimetre. Merged into the fabric thread by thread.

The spores seeped through the shirt.

Tentatively touched the skin . . .

The skin did not react to the delicate touch.

Yes. The man was prime meat. Meat for the mould.

One by one, the bonfires blinked out under the concrete sky.

Undercity night had been declared once more.

But there was a buzz in the air this night.

This was the Hallowe'en they had been waiting for since the god Horus arrived. The uprising of the Undercity. The Big Opening.

The Kin, excited, doused their bonfire, last to sputter out in Central Park as it had been the first to kindle.

Master Pliskin, Witch-General of the Kin, grinned a broad grin at his merry little band.

They had dined well for this night. Little pieces of Mistress Glinkin and young Master Bleerkin were inside the jolly group.

'Tonight,' Master Pliskin said. 'Tonight it begins. Perpetual Hallowe'en, under Horus, Lord of Misrule. Blessed be Mother Merkin.'

'Blessed be Horus and Mother Merkin,' the others chorused.

Then, wrapping shawls and mantles tight about their warty forms, they shuffled through the dark. Noses twitching, they followed the scent to the nearby gate of Anarchopolis.

He dreamed he was being eaten alive.

Then woke up and discovered it was true.

Luminous mould was creeping all over him from a

nodding tree. Dissolving patches of the trench-coat. Probing the skin beneath.

Cairo wrenched away from the velvety embrace, shuddering in disgust. He thrust a hand in a pocket, closed fingers round the metallic comfort of the Dillinger.

A simple flick switched the Dillinger to flame-thrower mode.

He torched the mould tree and smiled as it writhed.

Then he rolled clear and yanked off his raincoat – the first time he had doffed it in three months, bathrooms excluded – and, lowering the flame to simple scorch intensity, scoured the material clean of the insidious mould.

Task concluded, he pulled on the raincoat, flicked up the collar, thrust his hands into the pockets.

His intellect was back on line.

But he ached in every joint and sinew. He was light-headed from loss of blood. The numerous glass-cuts seared like branding irons.

Cairo was greatly improved from the wreck he had been – when? . . .

A glance at his watch. Spiritual nose-dive.

9-27 *p.m.* He had slept round the clock – and then some.

Two and a half hours to locate Anarchopolis, or Lucia stayed in monochrome limbo to the last reel of recorded time.

Fortunately, he still wore his Night-As-Day glasses. Blundering around in the pitch dark of the Undercity would lead him nowhere fast: zero chance of discovering Anarchopolis.

Where to search first?

The UN building.

'Here goes nothing.'

'Don't be a fool, Dredd, put that gun down.'

Dredd kept the gun level, ignoring Tebbit's repeated plea.

'Dredd,' Tebbit reasoned. 'You're not *superhuman*.

You must have been holding your arm out straight for a good twelve hours. The damn thing will drop off any minute.'

'You keep talkin', I'll keep aimin',' Dredd gritted through tight teeth.

'What you waitin' for, Dredd?' Blackwood sighed wearily, gun still pressed to Hershey's throat. 'Hershey to wake up and make a fancy move? She's out for the count, old man. And how much longer do you think your arm can take it?'

'As long as it takes.'

As long as it takes – that's you all over, Joe, thought Hershey, keeping her eyes shut, her breathing regular.

She had been following the conversation, word for word.

Years of training had taught her to emerge from unconsciousness with wits fully alert, geared to any contingency. Even the rhythm of her breathing didn't alter as she felt the circle of a muzzle at her throat.

She had been awake for some ten hours, biding her opportunity.

'You're *crazy*, Dredd!' Blackwood shouted angrily.

The pressure of the muzzle eased a fraction, shifted a centimetre.

She twisted away like a snake on molten lava, yelling, '*Shoot!*'

Her eyes sprang open to witness Blackwood's visor implode into his head.

Out the corner of her eye, she saw three men streaking away on Lawmasters.

Dredd's bike cannons made munceburger of two of them.

The survivor veered out of sight around the corner of Twin Tower Two. The escapee was Tebbit. It had to be *him*. Morphy's Law.

She vaulted onto her Lawmaster to begin pursuit.

'He'll keep,' Dredd said. 'Cairo won't. Central Park.'

Without waiting for an answer, he roared off.

After a silent curse, Hershey followed.

* * *

It had to be the weirdest smoke-easy cinema on earth, the Dream Palace at the heart of Anarchopolis.

And she was in it, guided up here long hours ago from the cell-like room somewhere beneath the screen.

The movie on the giant screen was bizarre.

So was the cinema audience that watched it. Many of them had been in the preceding string of black-and-white monster movies. The seats of the colossal auditorium were crammed with black-and-white freaks, as were the twelve balconies, tier on tier.

Mandra's head was spinning from the seven-hour showing and the bewildering surroundings and company.

The cinema, with elaborate friezes, Art Deco murals and fanciful chandeliers, was something out of a 1920s Cine-Buff replay. The audience was largely out of the Horror Movie Guide and the Book of Revelations.

Frankenstein's Creature. Wolf Man. The Thing. The Creature from the Black Lagoon. Exterminans, Angel of the Pit. Even the Four Horsemen of the Apocalypse reared on their steeds at the back of the stalls.

And each creature smoked cigarettes as if its life depended on it.

The slugskins were there too, near the front rows. They had squelched their applause when *Attack of the Slug Men* finished a couple of hours ago. That movie had made them, literally.

Whatever the Anarch filmed, it became real.

If he cast you as a monochrome monster in a movie, you became a monochrome monster. For real.

Horus must have created the whole bunch of freaks in the smoke-easy cinema.

Some thought.

The absence of Cagney was a keen loss. The gangster remained a freeze-frame image when she was conducted out of the carriage she'd woken in. The doors slid shut, and that was the last she saw of him.

Present company was no consolation. The area she sat in was reserved for humans – or the nearest the cinema came to humanity. The monochrome theme was extended

266

to the humans. The black-and-white men and women disturbed her more than the out-and-out freaks. Too close to home.

Mandra was the only splash of colour in the cinema.

The black-and-white flik *Invasion of the Blind Eyeballs*, written and directed by Horus, came to an end.

She heaved a sigh of relief as the chandelier lights came up.

The illumination was at full height when a distant rumbling sounded from a small pit under the screen.

Organ music suddenly filled the auditorium as a mighty Wurlitzer ascended from the pit, played with aplomb by the unmistakable figure of the Anarch.

She recognised the tune. The lyrics appeared in big, bold letters on the screen, with a little ball bouncing along each line in time with the music:

'You must remember this,
A kiss is just a kiss . . .'

The massed audience of monochrome creatures and monochrome humans sang along with the bouncing ball to the final refrain of 'As Time Goes By'.

Rendition concluded, Horus turned full face to his faithful congregation.

'Happy Hallowe'en!' he greeted.

'Happy Hallowe'en!' his followers chorused.

Horus stood up, arms flung wide, face uplifted. 'The witching hour approaches! The time of our deliverance.' His tone lowered. 'I had hoped my brother would be with us tonight for the Big Opening, but it seems he's been unexpectedly delayed. All the worse for him and one or two others.'

He resumed his messianic pose. 'Tonight I will make crooked the straight paths of the Law! Tonight I fulfil my own prophecy! The Underworld will become the Overworld! Many of you will remember how I came here, years ago, to discover an Anarchopolis of aimless individuals going their own sweet way, dedicated to the insipid principle of doing what you will so long as you don't hurt anybody else. Pitiful lifestyle! Hurting people is *fun*!'

Uproarious applause greeted the statement. He raised his hands for quiet. Quiet fell like a slab of acousti-silenced lead.

'Most of you will recall the bad old days of Anarcho-polis,' he resumed. 'The fugitives from the Judgement world, descended from their forebears in the days of Chief Judge Fargo, were a spineless bunch. For them, Anarchopolis was not a kingdom, but an extended *commune* of so-called anarchists who ambled about saying things like "heavy bummer" and "drop out" and "mellow vibes".'

'Shame!' a guttural voice cried out.

'Well said that Wolf Man,' Horus acknowledged. 'But my coming changed all that. I descended on Anarchopolis in glorious black-and-white and forged a new world that will last a thousand years!'

Mad, thought Mandra.

'I taught them new ways!' Horus declaimed. 'I taught them that Anarchy must be compulsory – and *absolute*. Predictability of any kind was not to be tolerated. Predict-ability is a sign of order. Order is an aspect of Law. Conformity to Law is punishable by death or cine-limbo. The breaking of rules is the foundation of Anarchy. I *enforced* the breaking of rules. I *imposed* unpredictability. Break a hundred rules a day, that's the Anarchopolis way! Be different. Be unpredictable. And if you find yourself being unpredictable for too long a period, then be predictable for a day just for the surprise of it! You've got to admit it – with Anarchy, the trains *never* run on time!'

Loud cheers, howls, squeals, grunts.

Barking mad, thought Mandra.

Horus silenced the enraptured audience with a sweep of the hand. 'I made myself Anarch, absolute ruler of all true anarchists, supreme arbiter of the breaking of rules. Lord of Misrule. But there are some –' his single eye roved the auditorium '– who are lax in the breaking of rules. There remain a few who lapse into predictability.'

A silver smile curved his white features. 'Who are the good and who are the bad?'

'None are the good and none are the bad!' proclaimed the audience with one voice.

'Well recited, my beloved Misruled,' the Anarch congratulated. 'No good, no bad. Just shades of grey. Monochrome. Life is film noir. But those few, those unhappy few, who have forgotten that truth must be weeded out before Anarchy Showtime hits the Overworld.' His long-fingered hand gestured to his five special friends with inverted faces. 'You know who they are,' he said to the Five.

The Five levitated as one, then fanned out and seemed to *swim* through the air, hunting out their targets. The black-suited, bow-tied men were performing something close to the breast-stroke as they glided over the audience.

One descended close to Mandra. Peered straight into a young man's eyes.

The victim reeled upwards, arms flailing, struggling to maintain his balance. The inverted stare had turned his world upside down. He saw the ceiling below and the floor above. If he wasn't mad now, he soon would be.

Other shrieks went up from the stalls and galleries. The few, the unhappy few, were receiving their punishment of permanent inverted vision.

Mandra's lip curled at the treatment of dissenters. The Anarch and his henchmen were no better than the Judges. Anarchopolis – whatever it had been once – had become the polar opposite of Judgement.

That was the problem with polar opposites: the North Pole and South Pole look very much alike.

The nearest Man in Black Suit swam through the air in her direction. In seconds it was clear he was heading straight for her.

The inverted eyes were about to stare into her head and flip her world over.

'Horus!' she called out. 'I thought you wanted me here . . .'

'Wanted you here to chastise my wayward brother with

the sight of your suffering,' he laughed. 'He didn't turn up, but what the hell. Let's do it *anyway*.'

The inverted face loomed close. Some spell kept her eyes wide open.

'But why tell me about my mother if you don't need me?' she asked, heart thumping. 'You said you were on my side . . .'

Horus shrugged, spread his arms. 'I'm unpredictable.' He thrust his face forwards, grinned impishly. 'SURPRISE!'

CHAPTER TWENTY-FIVE

Cairo glanced at his watch.

Twelve minutes to midnight.

He had quitted the UN two hours ago. Neither sight nor sound nor clue of Anarchopolis in the shattered halls of what had been the Assembly of Nations.

Drawing a blank, he headed for Broadway, zigzagging a trail along its north-south length as he scoured the derelict cinemas. Former Dream Palaces. Each was empty and dreamless.

At times, he heard the bass thunder of a couple of Lawmasters, sometimes near, sometimes far, but never close enough for the Judges to spot him.

The whole Undercity appeared strangely deserted. According to folklore, the place was crawling with all varieties of mutants and various species of rotted humans. Either folklore had it wrong or the population was keeping low, maybe because of the prowling Judges.

He'd encountered a few of the Undercity's curiosities on his search, though.

Near the corner of West Fifty-Seventh Street a mouldy suit had jumped out of a broken store window and chased him down Broadway.

The luminous mould on the pursuing fabric pulsed – and whispered with a breath of spores:

'*Try on a new suit, sir?*'

The damned mould was sentient. And telepathic. It must have picked up memories of sitting, standing and walking from the suit's original owner, absorbed into the material along with the sweat. The lively mould kept the suit marching on.

Looking for a new owner.

He covered three blocks before the mouldy, flapping suit gave up the chase.

The only trouble after that was from a pack of cannibals and a mutant with a headful of tentacles. Nothing too heavy.

He checked his watch again as he neared Times Square.

Ten minutes to midnight, and the bats were flying.

How in hell was he supposed to find Anarchopolis in ten minutes?

Lucia – imprisoned forever in monochrome limbo . . .
Mandra – maybe trapped and in danger from his lunatic brother . . .

He had to keep on trying.

Keep on looking.

The low rumble of Lawmasters was approaching again. Ah – to hell with them.

Cairo walked into the open spaces surrounding Times Square's central shanty town, and peered around desperately for a clue to his goal.

Any clue.

Horus had supplied a clue in the Casablanca, he was sure of it. If he hadn't been so freaked at the time he would have picked it up on the spot.

Something about looking in the Undercity . . . But look where?

Look deep.

Cairo's brow contracted at the memory. He forgot about the nearing Lawmasters.

His brother had said he would need to look *deep*.

Cairo's eyes darted round Times Square, looking for a sign.

He saw the sign.

The sign that displayed a gateway to Anarchopolis.

'Of course,' he said. It was obvious.

Obvious.

The underworld.

Anarchopolis was in the Undercity. And it wasn't in the Undercity. Depended which way you looked at it.

It was underneath.

Under the Undercity.

He had been travelling over it since he arrived in old New York.

Cairo, aware of the Lawmasters' approach, sprinted across Times Square for the entrance to Anarchopolis.

The entrance that bore the sign SUBWAY.

Mega-City One was haunted by monochrome nightmares.

Judge Tebbit raced his bike at top speed through the swarms of cine-images. No citizen would be celebrating Hallowe'en tonight. Hallowe'en was celebrating itself.

He had dispensed with his helmet before escaping the Undercity. The helmet-com whispered – *things* – into his ear. Same for the vid. He switched it off after it relayed a picture of a little girl in a habhold, a bloodied kitchen knife in her little hand. On the table beside her was a human head scooped out like a pumpkin, the word DADDY crudely inscribed on its brow. A candle inside the hollowed head made yellow glows of the eye-sockets. The little girl smiled sweetly and said, 'Marilyn Monroe made me do it.'

'*Grud*.' Tebbit swore as he sliced along the megway. 'World's gone drokkin' crazy.'

The Judgement Colossus came into full sight. A reassuring icon of Judgement, tall against the stars.

Vast crowds were gathered along the waterfront, gazing up at the Colossus and chanting: 'GRUD . . . GRUD . . . GRUD . . .'

He also caught another chant: 'DREDD . . . DREDD . . . DREDD . . .'

So they saw Dredd's face on the statue – no big deal. Whatever worked to keep Justice in power.

Streaking to the waterfront, he applied turbo-boost to soar over thirty metres of water to the first of four 'stepping stones' to the Colossus, each flat disc of plas-crete a hundred metres wide.

Turbo-boosting the Lawmaster over the next stretch of water, he hopped over the stepping stones to the foot of the Colossus.

The door was open. He raced the bike in and swept up the long, spiral ramp to the Visor.

Once inside the Judgement Colossus, he felt secure. He switched on the vid. Sejanus appeared on the screen within seconds.

'Has – has there been any trouble in here, Colossus Chief?' he asked.

Sejanus shook his head. 'Not in here. The Colossus is impregnable. But out there – chaos. However, chaos won't last long. I'll see to that. If anarchy continues, I'll blow up the Statue of Liberty in an hour or so. If no one takes the hint, limited nuclear strikes will follow.' He paused. 'Mission accomplished, Tebbit?'

Tebbit broke out in a sweat. 'Ah – about Dredd and Hershey and . . .'

The Lawmasters roared into Times Square.

Dredd screeched his bike to a halt. Hershey drew alongside. 'You see that?' he asked.

'See what?'

'You couldn't miss him. Guy running down into the subway. Could have been Cairo.'

'I haven't got your fancy artificial eyes, Joe.'

'You want some, get some. I'm headin' down the subway.'

She angled her lips. 'And guess what? I'll be right behind you.'

Dredd launched his Lawmaster down the dark, eroded steps.

Hershey flew in his wake.

Cairo stepped into a carriage of the subway train. Its windows were painted black.

The moment the doors shut automatically, the train jolted into action and one of the black windows brightened to the white intensity of a hypma screen.

His brother's smiling face materialised on the screen. 'If you're seeing and hearing this, it means you've found Anarchopolis, the city under the Undercity. Without beginning or end, all two hundred and thirty old-fashioned miles of it, with headquarters under Grand Central Station. That's where you're headed, full speed. Be seeing you.'

Cairo glanced up at the faded subway diagram. He was on the old IRT line, with just one stop before Grand Central.

His watch showed eight minutes to midnight.

He was cutting it close.

Mandra tried to close her eyelids, avert her gaze from the man in the black suit and bow-tie swimming towards her through the air.

She didn't relish the prospect of spending the remainder of her life seeing the ground up above and the sky down below.

Shut your eyes. Look away.

No good. Horus must have reached into her mind, controlled her central nervous system.

The inverted face glided in front of her.

Raised its eyes.

'*You dirty rat!*'

The upside-down face took a faceful of bullets and turned into mush. Another hail of slugs burst his body like a bag of grey blood.

Released from paralysis, she sprang up, swung round. Shouted '*Yeah!*' as she punched the air.

James Cagney was storming down one of the aisles of the enormous cinema, his .38s blazing.

Another Black Suit, riddled with hypma bullets, splattered the seats.

'Cagney!' Horus raged. 'How dare you? You're my creature. *Mine*. You can't turn against your creator.'

'Tell that to the guy with the fancy red tights and horns,' Cagney riposted, downing two more of the Anarch's special friends.

'*Cagney – stop! I order you!*'

The last inverted face was blown to oblivion from twin bursts of Cagney's revolvers. 'The guy ain't born who tells James Cagney what to do!' the gangster retorted. 'Didn't figure that, huh? I fell for that Mandra dame. You shouldn't have put those fancy eyeball-screwers on her. Got me riled up and defrosted in no time.'

'Kill him!' Horus shrieked at the ten-thousand-strong audience.

Ten thousand guns appeared.

Ten thousand muzzles fired at Cagney.

He got off a few shots before he dropped his shooters.

Thousands of hypma bullets ripping through him, Cagney staggered, elbows bent, hands drooping, on a weaving progess down the aisle.

'*Jimmy!*' Mandra wailed. It was the first time she'd used his first name.

Somehow, he heard her over the thunder of the volleys. Heard and spotted her.

Grinning, he wagged a finger at her. 'Tut-tut, Tootsie . . .' he mock-scolded. 'Goodbye.'

She expected him to drop then and there.

He kept on going through the hailstorm of bullets. Swaying, stumbling down the aisle.

Then she understood. Cagney was not so much clinging onto his strange hypma-life as playing out a scene.

The last of Cagney's famous, protracted death scenes. He was dragging out his death beyond all reason. Taking minutes to die.

Cagney was trying to break his own record.

He reeled, tripped, and spun the entire length of the aisle.

Tottered to the front of the cinema.

'It's a record, Jimmy,' Mandra whispered, eyes streaming.

Cagney swayed, winked in Mandra's direction. 'I could love you to death, doll.'

He *still* didn't drop.

He half-crawled up the steps. Stumbled towards the amazed Anarch. Fished inside his bullet-riddled jacket.

Pulled out what looked like half a grapefruit.

And pushed the grapefruit into the Anarch's face.

A movie erupted onto the screen as Cagney reeled back under a fresh fusillade.

And, finally, slowly wheeled and toppled.

'I ain't so tough,' he croaked, dissolving as he fell.

As he tumbled, his figure turned to rain.

Cagney rained down on the floor, a silver shower.

Then he was gone.

Dredd didn't turn round as his Lawmaster raced down the subway tunnels. He knew Hershey wouldn't be far behind.

He was gaining on the train. Fast.

When the train pulled to a halt in Grand Central and a raincoated figure dashed out, Dredd was within a hundred metres of the man he hunted.

'Got you cold, Mister Cairo.'

Cairo kicked open the swing doors and charged into the cinema, Dillinger at the ready.

The auditorium almost took his breath away.

It was a giant replica of the Casablanca.

And it was packed with an audience of monochrome monsters.

The surprise didn't break his stride. He kept running down the central aisle, eyes fixed on the distant shape of his mad brother.

And beside his brother was – James Cagney.

Cagney shoved a grapefruit into the Anarch's face.

A movie exploded onto the huge hypma screen behind Horus and Cagney.

It was a scene from *The Public Enemy*. The scene where Cagney, streaming with rain, advances to the screen with hands thrust in his pockets, holding a pair of .38s. When the shot switched to the gangster entering the

Western Chemical Company, he would be replaced by Lucia Lux.

The hypma Cagney in front of the screen wheeled slowly, and croaked: 'I ain't so tough.'

Then he fell as rain.

And reappeared on the screen – entering the Western Chemical Company.

He had resumed his role.

A figure in full colour was ejected from the screen and landed with a soft thump a few metres from Horus.

Lucia Lux.

Now Cagney was back in the movie, there was no vacancy for her to fill. Lucia was back in the world, grace of James Cagney.

The movie faded from the hypma screen.

A ghost of a smile plucked Cairo's lips. *Thanks, Jimmy Cagney.*

That still left Mandra.

The audience, enthralled by Cagney's performance, had taken scant notice of Cairo's arrival.

The Anarch's yell corrected that. 'Brother! You made it with two minutes to go. Well done!'

Cairo levelled the Dillinger at Horus as he slowed his run to a walk down the aisle. 'Send Lucia down to me. And where's Mandra?'

'Joel!'

Out the corner of his eye, he saw her squeezing past a row of monochrome knees.

He felt the upsurge of joy like a threat. He had no time for it right now. Later, there'd be a whole life's worth of time.

If his brother let him live, that is. There was no trusting the Anarch of Anarchopolis.

A dazed Lucia had caught sight of him. She was up and running, heading for the only familiar face in a world of weirdness.

Mandra and Lucia almost collided in the aisle.

They rushed to him side by side. He felt two pairs of arms enfold him. The uprush of emotion almost made him lower the Dillinger a fraction.

The emotion hurt. He tried to put it on hold. Wasn't easy.

'*Joel*,' Mandra whispered urgently in his ear. 'Don't trust Horus. He tried to twist my brain round.'

'I don't trust him,' he murmured.

'Tell me what's happening, Mister Cairo,' Lucia pleaded, mouth trembling, eyes big and scared. 'I was in my habhold. Saw what that man – ' she flicked a glance at Horus ' – did to Lorelei. Then – I was here.' The frightened girl burst into racking sobs. 'Oh, Lorelei . . .'

He winced at her grief, but was relieved that she recalled nothing of living in a movie. The memory of her sojourn in cine-limbo must have been wiped out when she exited from it.

That thought was firestormed from existence by another: Horus had personally sliced Lorelei to pieces, just for a bit of – showbiz. Brother or no brother, he would pay for that.

Get your mind in gear, Cairo. The job's not done yet.

Okay, he'd found Lucia and Mandra.

Now all he had to do was escape from a cinema crammed with thousands of black-and-white monsters commanded by a mad movie god.

Presented problems.

'Cairo!' The shout rang out across the overblown re-creation of the Casablanca.

Horus stood, legs planted wide, fists on hips. 'Cairo,' he repeated. 'I want to teach you so much. Here's the first lesson. Give Lucia back to me so I can trap her in another movie. And Mandra too – I have other plans for her.'

'What?' Cairo exclaimed. 'Why the hell should I do that?'

Horus sighed as if dealing with a backward student. 'I want you to act out of character. Produce a surprise. Be unpredictable.'

Cairo kept it short. 'Go screw yourself.'

He stared Horus out through the long silence that followed.

'*Give me the girls, Cairo,*' Horus finally said. The undertone was lethal.

'And if I don't?'

'Then you're no brother of mine.'

Cairo shrugged. 'Started out in the same womb. Ended up on different planets.'

'That all you have to say? You completed the trial by ordeal with flying colours. Why fail the easy test? Doesn't make any sense. You know I can take the girls with a click of my fingers. Why throw away your life with theirs?'

'I guess I'm just an old-fashioned sort of guy.'

'Oh, *Cairo,*' Horus sighed. 'I went to such *trouble* over you. I'm disappointed. I really am. By the way, what do you intend to do with that ridiculous pistol?'

'This,' answered Cairo, firing a round of scatter-shells into Horus's slim shape.

The slugs went right through him without a mark. Even the natty Suit of Many Badges displayed not a single rent.

Horus ran white fingers through his black shock of hair. 'Now that was just *silly*. You can't kill the stuff dreams are made of.'

'What about Cagney?' Mandra challenged. 'He was such stuff. You had him killed.'

'Not really. He was a dream, not the stuff of which they're made. Thousands of hypma bullets put him back on the screen he came from. Besides, he was my creature, rebel that he was. I'm the creator. God of the movies. The Black Falcon. No amount of bullets – lead, silver or hypma – can mar my rare essence.'

'Bullets made short work of your five special friends, though,' she remarked under her breath.

All the time they'd been speaking, Cairo had been backing up the aisle, step for step with Mandra and Lucia. It was no more than a reflex action. There was not a hope in the underworld that the Anarch would let them retreat much further.

The Anarch's voice resounded in the auditorium. 'You don't think I'll permit you to leave here alive, do you?'

Right on cue.

'After all,' the voice persisted, 'you did just attempt to murder your own brother. Hardly the act of a – what was it – an old-fashioned sort of guy.'

Cairo twitched a shoulder. 'Yeah, well – life is film noir, right?'

Horus raised an arm. 'Goodbye, Mister Cairo.' The upraised hand bunched into a fist. 'Kill them, my beloved Misruled.'

Ten thousand guns swerved towards Cairo and the two women.

Mister Cairo readied himself to die as he was born – with both eyes open. He only had eyes for Mandra. 'Here's lookin' at you, kid . . .'

Ten thousand fingers, paws, claws, tentacles and pseudopods squeezed ten thousand triggers.

Ten thousand clicks sounded in the vast auditorium.

The triggers were squeezed again and again.

Ten thousand clicks sounded again and again.

Recovering from her astonishment, Mandra bubbled into laughter. 'Cine-guns. The right dramatic moment.'

Cairo was stunned. 'If you say so.'

Horus grimaced and snapped his fingers. 'Damn. Of course. Cine-guns are always doing that with people cast in heroic roles.' The grimace dissolved into a grin. 'But it doesn't work that way when a horde of thousands descends on you.' He flung out his arms. 'Misruled! Attack! Rip them. Rend. Bite. Gnaw. Devour. Demolish!'

The cinema instantly boiled with rampaging monsters, imploding on Cairo and company.

A hole was blasted in the cinema wall.

Judge Dredd roared through it on a Beast of the Streets, his mouth like an open mantrap.

'I AM THE LAW!'

Hershey exploded through another wall. 'SO AM I!'

Cairo and his companions hit the deck.

Two bursts of laser cannon utterly dissolved scores of Draculas and Creatures from the Black Lagoon.

Bike cannons and hi-ex from Lawgivers made havoc of hundreds more creatures.

From his prone position, Cairo sprayed the nearest assailants with blast bullets.

But they kept on coming.

He reached into a small, ultra-special inside pocket and extracted his most prized and devastating armament. The Biased Bomb. It resembled a black golf ball.

'Press your thumbprints on this – fast,' he instructed Mandra and Lucia. The thumbs pressed in a second. He instantly delivered the activation code to the bomb in his palm:

'Franky Doyle.'

The Biased Bomb packed the power of two hundred hi-ex bullets in the meanest of moods.

It unleashed that power in explosive glee. Tore a crater in the floor. Hurled a fireball at the roof. Flung killing blast-waves over a hundred metres.

A thousand and more monsters were vapourised, pulverised or fragmentised.

Cairo, Mandra and Lucia didn't notice a thing.

The bomb had pre-wrapped them in a protective cocoon, reserved for those whose thumbprints had touched its surface. They were sealed in a soundless bubble, enwrapped in a dark that even Cairo's Night-As-Day glasses couldn't enlighten.

The bomb was mightily biased against Cairo's enemies, heavily biased in favour of Mister Cairo and his friends.

It glided them clear of the blazing blast-site, settled to ground, then dissolved.

He glanced at the two women. 'Everything okay?'

Lucia nodded dumbly with the look of a girl who had given up the effort of understanding.

Mandra simply flashed a quick smile. 'That was good what you did there, whatever it was that you did.'

He glanced round at the devastation. Upwards of fifteen hundred creatures wiped out, between the Biased bomb and the Judges' firepower.

'*Misruled!*' Horus's voice rang out above the mayhem.

'Don't let those fools delay the Big Opening! Into the screen, beloved Misruled! Up to the Overworld! Jump out of the Overworlders' vid-screens and wish them happy Hallowe'en! The Lord of Misrule is coming and the Saturnalia begins!'

The monochrome grotesques broke off from battle and flocked to the glowing screen. They stormed into its hypma field in their myriads.

'Go, Misruled, give the Overworld a dose of Lethal Reality!' the Anarch exhorted. 'Cine-images come to life, dealing death from millions of vids! LETHAL REALITY!'

Cairo tugged Mandra's arm. 'Let's get out of here. I'll deal with Dredd another day.'

She shook her head. 'No.'

'No? Why no?'

'I'll tell you a story,' she said. 'About the Colossus Chief. About a hypma core in Omnipotens and who truly controls it. And about who really killed your mother.'

As she talked, observed by an uncomprehending Lucia, Cairo's mouth tightened to a hard, straight line.

Minutes after the Anarch's summons, the auditorium was empty of all but the five Overworlders – and the Anarch.

Dredd had been pumping lead into Horus for several minutes. Hershey had given up the effort.

'He a hologram or something? Dredd growled, finally lowering the Lawgiver.

'I'm the Black Falcon, bane of the Golden Eagle of Law!' Horus proclaimed. 'I'm Lucifer rising back to the Morning Star. I'm John the Baptist returned from the wilderness. I go to anoint the Head of Justice with the most subversive of oil.'

Dredd raised the Lawgiver. 'Surrender, perp, or – '

Horus leaped into the screen, arms waving wildly.

'Catch me if you can!'

Dredd's Lawgiver was instantly turned on Cairo.

'Bad move, Dredd,' Mandra remarked coolly. 'The whole of Mega-City One will be drowned in a black-and-

283

white nightmare without Cairo's help – and mine. You've no idea what's been going on, have you?'

Dredd's downturned mouth twitched a centimetre. 'Why'd you do it, Mandra? Why blow up MAC and Barney?'

She folded her arms, smiled a thin smile.

'It's a long story.'

CHAPTER TWENTY-SIX

Cairo and Mandra sat beside Lucia and watched Dredd and Hershey argue fiercely on the far side of the bomb crater. The argument was reaching white heat.

'If Dredd wins the argument I'll blow the bastard's head off right now,' Cairo muttered.

'It was Sejanus who killed your mother,' Mandra said. 'I told you that. Dredd aimed at her gun-arm. The shots must have been simultaneous.'

He shook his head. 'That's not the way I remember it. And how come Mouth Face wouldn't say a word about the killing? *He* never said he aimed at the gun-arm. Besides – he led the raid. Set the example. Wiped out brothels like some Moral Minority nut. Stamping on whores' faces. No – the vow stands. I'm going to blast his head off. It's only a matter of when. Now, or after we deal with Horus – and Sejanus.'

'Fine,' she shrugged. 'But don't forget Dredd's never been beaten in a shoot-out. And he can catch a lot of slugs and still keep firing. That's part of his secret. He's tough as plasteen. Look at all those slugs he's got in him now. And that shot-off forefinger . . . Hershey told me he grabbed it in mid-air and dumped it in a freeze-box, right in the middle of blasting SJS away.'

'And if the first slug's a blast bullet that blows his head off? He's going to keep firing away with no head on? That tough, is he?'

'Apart from tough, he's lucky,' she murmured almost inaudibly. 'But your luck – I don't know.'

'I've had my share.'

'Dredd has more than his share.' She pretended to study the back of her hands. 'I've just found you again. I don't want to lose you.'

She glanced up at Dredd and Hershey. The argument was cooling down. Seemed to be shifting Hershey's way.

Cairo had spotted the shift. 'Hershey's bright, I'll give her that. She knows only advanced Psi will work against Horus. With Anderson out of the picture, that only leaves us.'

'Yeah,' she agreed. 'Psi Division's pretty feeble without Anderson.'

'And you, Ma,' he smiled.

She returned the smile. 'Just being humble, *Jo*.'

'Hell, Ma, you must've changed.'

She gave him a playful punch on the arm, then stiffened.

Dredd and Hershey were coming back.

Hershey halted in front of Cairo. She gave a curt nod. 'Deal. Dredd's not so sure the Anarch's skipped off to the Judgement Colossus, but from what Mandra said it makes sense to me. But he agrees about Sejanus. So it's a deal. I take Mandra on the bike. Dredd takes you. We all break into the Colossus and wipe out Horus and Sejanus. After that – ' She hesitated. 'It's between you and Dredd, gun against gun.'

Cairo nodded at Lucia. 'Dredd'll have to carry Lucia as well. Drop her off at Happy House. It's on the way.'

'I ain't no drokkin' taxi service!' Dredd exploded. 'I ain't droppin' no Gruddam whore at no drokkin' whore-house!'

'*I'll* do it,' Hershey sighed. 'Can't leave her here.'

Cairo stood up. 'You're okay for a Judge, Hershey. All right, let's head for the Colossus before Horus drives the Big City screwy.'

Dredd had already mounted his Lawmaster. He went rigid when Cairo climbed on the back. Cairo enjoyed the Judge's suppressed fury. Anything that annoyed Dredd was okay by him.

After an amount of to-ing and fro-ing on Hershey's

overloaded bike, the women were finally seated in some sort of security.

Dredd shot a stare at Hershey.

'Okay!' he bellowed. 'Let's hit the Colossus!'

The cinema screen came alive as the bikes were gunned into action.

The closing scene of *White Heat* flared into view.

James Cagney stood on top of a petro-chemical dome, body riddled with cops' bullets.

Cagney, laughing as he staggered to and fro, fired into the dome, shouting to his dead Ma. Then he yelled, 'Top of the world!'

The dome exploded in a giant fireball.

The scene vanished as Dredd's Lawmaster swept out of the ruined cinema.

'Top of the world, Ma . . .' Cairo said, below a breath.

He took it as an omen from Cagney, king of the cinema gangsters.

Cairo was heading for the top of the Judge world, the head of Colossus.

And he'd wreak havoc when he got there.

Mandra clung tight to Hershey and Lucia as the bike whisked out the hole it had blasted in the back wall.

She shook with dread at what she'd just witnessed on the screen.

Top of the world, Ma . . .

Behind Cagney's image, she saw a whirl of Tarot cards. The Devil and the Magician for the Anarch. The Chariot and Judgement for Dredd. The Fool for Cairo. And the Tower Struck by Lightning for the Judgement Colossus.

Devil and Magician, Chariot and Judgement, they converged with the Fool on the path to the Tower.

The Tower Struck by Lightning.

And Death was there, in the Tower, waiting for the Fool, the Wild card in the pack.

The Lovers appeared, but merely as a flicker of intertwined limbs.

At the Tower's pinnacle, the Death card ruled.
The Wild card had vanished.

'GRUD . . . GRUD . . . GRUD . . .'
   'DREDD . . . DREDD . . . DREDD . . .'

The two chants merged, echoed as one across the bay as the crowd swelled on the waterfront. The faithful had come, responding to the call. The call of Law incarnate.

Sejanus reclined in the Eagle Throne and gazed through the Visor at the multitudes gathering below. Large as the gathering was, it was well under one per cent of the mega-city's population. The rest were in the grip of Anti-Law.

'But worship of Law will spread,' Sejanus assured himself. He glanced at a vid-screen. Red words strobed on the screen:

LETHAL REALITY

That was the term Omnipotens had come up with to describe the sway of Anarchy this night of Hallowe'en. Lethal reality. Grotesque monochrome beings emerging from vids all over Mega-City.

The city that lives by the vid shall die by the . . .

He suppressed the unsettling observation.

Lethal reality was strong, this Hallowe'en night. But Omnipotens was stronger, and infinitely more enduring. Come the dawn . . .

Another message from Omnipotens flashed on the vid:

ANARCHOPOLIS DOES NOT EXIST?

A deep frown troubled his forehead. He hadn't asked Omnipotens to repeat the message. And he couldn't comprehend the inclusion of a question mark.

'Enough worrying,' he snapped. Omnipotens had everything under control. The manifestations of lethal reality were teething troubles, that was all. Soon over.

The Colossus Chief pressed an arm-rest acti-pad. The golden Eagle Throne flexed its wings, splayed them wide.

And soared up to the Sanctum. His SJS elite had spent long enough programming the Arcanum core. The Hierarchy of Five had fulfilled their task. Now they could assist him in dealing with the transitory difficulties presented by lethal reality.

He dematerialised a wall-section of the Sanctum. Folded the Eagle Throne's wings, glided in.

And hovered, aghast.

The Hierarchy of Five were suspended in the ovoid anti-grav chamber, dead and colourless. Drained of colour. Black-and-white corpses.

He moved the Throne in closer.

The men's faces – their faces . . .

Inverted.

Mouth at the top. Eyes at the bottom.

Monochrome men with upside-down faces.

He jabbed a button and fled the scene.

Sejanus raced down to the Visor, sped down Central Grav-Chute to the Heart.

'Sabotage!' he screamed into the Throne's on-board vid. 'Sabotage! Seal off the Colossus! Lower the Stepping Stones! *No one comes in!*'

The Eagle Throne sighed to a halt above the booming flexisteel heart. Sejanus glared at the waterfront displayed on the main vid-screen. The glare intensified as he focused on the Statue of Liberty.

'Sabotage,' he growled. 'The law-breakers must be taught a lesson.'

He pressed a pad on the chair's vid-com. 'Transmit an announcement on all available channels to every block and conapt in Mega-City One.' The Colossus Chief clenched his fist. 'Tell them the Statue of Liberty will be destroyed in one hour.' His mouth spasmed into a hint of a smile. 'They can watch it all on vid.'

A vid in the deserted Visor flicked on.

A message to no one in particular vibrated on the screen:

ANARCHOPOLIS DOES NOT EXIST?

THAT'S WHAT YOU THINK, STEW-FOR-BRAINS.

The characters blinked out. Another word appeared:

ARCANUM.
Then rearranged itself into a dog-Latin anagram.
ANARCUM

Under a concrete sky, the bikes thundered down the grey
ruins of West 42nd Street. Black swarms of vampire bats
wheeled above the speeding Lawmasters, the occasional
rodent flying in for a quick bite. A bullet from a Lawgiver
or Dillinger made a limp black rag of each attacking bat.

'Hell of a coincidence,' Cairo scowled, putting a hole in
another flapping, fanged assailant. He had seen plenty of
bats since entering Manhattan, but had thought nothing
of them. Now, when he was fleeing the Undercity like a
bat out of hell, the bats of hell had swooped down.

Hell of a coincidence.

The Anarch must be behind it. One of his dark
surprises.

Cairo drilled two swooping rodents with a single bullet.
His Movie God brother would have to come up with
better surprises than bats.

The Lawmasters screeched round the corner of West
42nd and hurtled down West Side Highway.

Through a blur of leathery wings, Cairo glimpsed the
arched exit from the underworld a couple of hundred
metres ahead.

The private eye plugged another low-flying rodent as
Dredd executed a suicidally tight turn into the tunnel.

No bats in sight on the spiralling ascent.

Cairo glanced over his shoulder. The women on the
following bike seemed unhurt.

He glanced over Dredd's shoulder at the vid read-out:

ETA 46 minutes.

Forty-six minutes from the underworld to the top of the
Justice world.

Forty-six minutes to the battle with Horus and Sejanus's
small army in the Colossus.

And then would come Cairo's show-down with Judge
Dredd.

The spiral ascent unwound . . .
The kilometres unreeled . . .

Images from the Tarot tumbled through Mandra's head as Hershey's bike swerved out of Pluto Block, hot on Dredd's rear wheel.

Spinning wheels. Spinning images . . .

The Hanged Man, suspended upside down by one foot, an upside-down man in an upside-down world. The new man of the Anarch's future.

The Devil merged with the Magician, and assumed the one-eyed face of Horus, enthroned on a lofty throne.

Judgement and the Chariot congealed into Dredd on his roaring Lawmaster, heading for the High Place.

The trench-coated Fool, the Wild card, was stepping into oblivion from the High Place.

The High Place – the Tower Struck by Lightning.

The Death card covered the Fool.

She could not see the face of Death.

The Judgement Colossus reared up in the west, fist upraised, a tower of strength.

Cairo glared at its visored face. The image of Dredd. Not Grud. Not Fargo, founder of a police-state.

Dredd.

In Cairo's view, the man co-responsible with Sejanus for his mother's death.

The man sitting right in front of him.

The man circumstance had forced him to collaborate with on a mission of destruction. Destroy Sejanus, Mandra's father. Destroy Horus, Cairo's brother.

Life is film noir.

He threw a backward glance.

Still no sign of Hershey. She had dropped off Lucia twelve minutes ago. Dredd refused to wait the ten seconds or so, and sped off without Hershey. She'd catch up in no time, that was Dredd's excuse.

Not at the 550-plus kph Dredd was doing she wouldn't.

'*Dredd!*' Cairo shouted above the whistling wind. 'Slow down! We need Hershey and Mandra!'

Dredd remained a broad back and the rear of a helmet, unresponsive.

The Lawmaster hurtled on, dipping down to the waterfront.

The sheer extent of the crowds massed by the bay took Cairo by surprise.

As the bike swept down to a rapidly shrinking gap in the multitude, Cairo distinguished the twin chants:

'GRUD . . . GRUD . . . GRUD . . .'

'DREDD . . . DREDD . . . DREDD . . .'

Mandra had acquainted Cairo and the two Judges with Sejanus's schemes. It seemed a little of the Colossus Chief's programming had affected the minds of some of the solid citizens. Absolute Law. Absolute obedience.

The crowds were abasing themselves before the Judgement Colossus as an icon of Grud.

And of Dredd, whose features it wore.

Judgement supreme.

The reverse image of Horus's absolute Anarchy.

Dredd . . . Horus . . .

'*A plague on both your houses*,' he hissed between his teeth.

The Lawmaster blasted through the narrowing gap in the Grud and Dredd devotees. Zoomed straight for the bay.

'Dredd, you dickhead!' Cairo yelled. 'Wait for Hershey and Mandra!'

'The Stepping Stones are lowering, *drokkhead*,' Dredd shot back.

Cairo glanced at the four Stepping Stones to the Colossus, each separated by thirty metres of water. True enough, they had sunk almost to water-level.

The Lawmaster flew off the edge of the dock.

Turbo-boost punched the bike over the narrow stretch of water.

Cairo was nearly yanked back out of the seat by the acceleration.

The turbo-boost cut out and Firerock tyres burnt into the wide, flat circle of the first Stepping Stone.

Turbo-boost kicked in again. The bike was airborne once more.

It struck the second Stepping Stone with a jolt, sending up fans of spray. The plascrete circle was just below water level.

Another savage acceleration launched the Lawmaster to the third plascrete ring, covered by waves. A white brawl of water erupted as the tyres struck and swept the rider across the plascrete, knee-deep in sea water.

Cairo glanced ahead to the base of the statue.

The double gates were sliding shut. A narrow gap remained, closing fast.

The fourth stepping stone had sunk out of sight.

Turbo-boost flung the bike over the waves.

'Here goes nothing,' Cairo muttered.

The next moment he was underwater. The mass of water, hitting his body with full force, flung him back with a violent lurch.

Then the bike exploded from the bay on a final boost.

Flew at the shrinking gap of the gates. A metre's width, maximum.

Cairo crossed his fingers.

The Lawmaster sped through the gap with mere centimetres to spare.

He breathed a sigh of relief as the bike arced up a steep spiral ramp.

A hail of bullets greeted the Lawmaster's arrival.

'*Drokk!*' exclaimed Hershey, skidding the bike to a stop at the lip of the dock. 'Stepping Stones are down.'

'At least Dredd's bike made it into the Colossus,' Mandra said, staring at the closed gates. 'By the skin of its handlebars.' She glanced around. 'We'll have to find some kind of airship to get into that monstrosity.'

Hershey aimed the Lawmaster at the Statue of Judgement. 'They always keep a few hov-pods in the head of the old statue.'

The ecstatic crowds were reluctant to part for the Lawmaster. The progress to the Statue of Judgement was slow and tortuous.

Hostile glares from solid citizens met them every metre of the way.

'What's wrong with these creeps, obstructing a Judge?' Hershey growled. 'Supposed to be Law and Order fanatics.'

A finger jabbed in accusation at the two women. 'They're not wearing helmets!'

The cry was caught up by a sizeable section of the crowd. 'They're not wearing helmets!'

'You've just had your answer,' Mandra smiled mirthlessly. 'Omnipotens is trying to make Dredds of us all.'

The mob turned ugly, crowded the Lawmaster, indifferent to the menacing sweep of Hershey's Lawgiver.

Hershey eyed the forty-odd metres to the Statue of Judgement.

The mob charged the two riders.

She pressed for turbo-boost and sailed over their heads. The awkward crash-landing on a mass of bodies near the entrance flung the women sideways and sent the bike spinning, clean over the edge of the dock.

They were up and fighting before they heard the loud splash.

Ingrained habit made Hershey deliver a rapid warning before letting loose with hi-ex, clearing a path into the statue. A red, messy path.

But the Grud worshippers inside the old effigy were alerted by the hue and cry outside.

A score of respectably dressed citizens stormed down the ramp, manicured fingers stretched to grab and rip.

'*Anti-Judges!*' they howled.

Three blasts of hi-ex blew the citizens' insides outside.

Mandra got a faceful of hot guts. 'Hell,' she spluttered, spitting raw tissue from her mouth. 'I wish I had a gun.'

'Wish away,' Hershey retorted as they raced up the ramp. 'You're still Public Enemy Number One.'

'Thanks a lot,' Mandra muttered, sprinting at Hershey's heels.

Rounding the corner to the next ramp, they confronted a wall-to-wall mob of crazies in a downward rush.

Bursts of hi-ex and rapid rounds of standard ammo covered the ramp with wall-to-wall flesh and bone carpeting.

Hershey and Mandra slip-slid on the slithery climb. They could hear the angry roar of the crowds below as they rushed into the entrance. And from above, the shout of 'Anti-Judges!' resounded.

Hershey lobbed a few stumm grenades down the slope. 'The gas'll keep them off our backs.'

'But what about the Law loonies up there?' Mandra nodded up the ramp at the mustering of figures dressed as solid citizens – with psychotic faces. 'How much hi-ex have you got left?'

'None.'

'Oh, *great*. What about the rest of the ammo?'

Hershey was expressionless. 'Not enough to blast a way up to the top. We'll have to take some of those lunatics out with fists and feet.'

Before Mandra could respond, the solid citizens charged, screaming for the blood of Anti-Judges.

CHAPTER TWENTY-SEVEN

In the Eagle Throne, golden wings beating, Sejanus whirled round the giant flexisteel heart, adorned with a Judgement Day map.

Twenty of his Dies Irae staff stood beneath, armed with Overkills.

'Sabotage!' he snarled. 'Hunt out the saboteurs! Teach them the futility of opposing the God of Wrath and Judgement. Just for a start – I'll blow the Statue of Liberty to atoms! Forget the four-minute countdown. Blast the old bitch right now!'

Alarms suddenly flashed and howled.

'Intruders,' Tebbit announced, scanning a monitor. He broke into a sweat. 'I don't believe it . . . Dredd – and Mister Cairo.'

Sejanus slammed a fist on the eagle-claw arm-rest. 'Full defence status! Wall guns trained on Dredd and Cairo, shoot-to-kill programme! All staff report immediately to Heart. They've got to come past here if they're aiming for the Head.'

He glanced up as his men jumped to their duties.

'I can always trust you, can't I, Omnipotens?'

His voice shrank. 'Can't I?'

The wall-mounted guns spouted death on Dredd and Cairo as the Lawmaster whirled up the spiral ramp.

Dredd's bike cannons and Lawgiver blasted the defence guns in their ports.

Cairo's Dillinger spat blast bullets, taking out one after

another of the blazing barrels that tracked every twist and turn of the bike.

A bullet tore through Cairo's shoulder. He ignored it.

Ripped through his thigh. He hardly noticed it.

Dredd had taken a shell in the calf muscle. He didn't notice it either.

Onward and upward. Onward and upward.

And don't count the cost.

'They're still comin'!' Tebbit shrilled out. 'Colossus Chief – they ain't human!'

Sejanus swooped down in the Eagle Throne, surveying his mustering troops in the Heart region. Almost a hundred Judges, the full complement of Colossus staff, armed with Overkills, the newest and deadliest handheld machine-guns and micro-missile launchers in the force's armoury.

'Terminate defence systems,' he ordered. 'We'll slaughter them here. I want to watch them die. Smell the blood.'

'But Chief . . .' Tebbit stammered.

'*Do it.*'

'Heart up ahead,' Dredd growled in the abrupt silence from the wall-guns. 'Get ready for trouble, Cairo.'

'I never expect anything else.'

The angle of descent declined, the dizzying spiral unwound.

An arch zoomed into sight, echoing to a strong, steady pulse.

Dredd pressed an activation code on the bike's Cyclops laser cannon.

'You ready?' Dredd barked, slipping a freeze-box into his belt.

'Ready.'

'*Now!*'

The Lawmaster stormed into the Heart region.

And met a firestorm from a hundred Overkills.

A firestorm that no one, absolutely no one, could survive for a fraction of a second.

Instant death. Inescapable.

The armoured Lawmaster exploded into a fireball.

At the moment of explosion, the Cyclops laser slammed its beam into the giant heart that pulsed as it pumped sea water through its four chambers.

The laser punctured the heart's left auricle.

And unleashed a briny deluge.

Sejanus slammed an acti-pad and soared above the flood rising from the concentrated pressure of the pumping system.

He watched his men being swept away like dolls down the spiral ramp.

He groaned aloud at the sight. Then roared in frustration at the next thing he saw.

Aiming his Lawgiver, he unleashed a string of slugs.

'*Now!*' Dredd had signalled, after transferring his severed forefinger in a freeze-box from bike to belt.

The two riders leaped from the Lawmaster a split second before the bike, programmed to unleash the laser cannon in 0.3 of a second, raced into the Heart area.

Cairo and Dredd were up and running into the chamber as the bike exploded and the laser hit.

Hidden by the explosion, they hurled themselves to one side and gripped a service ladder, holding on for dear life as the deluge hit.

Hold by painful hold, they scaled the steel rungs, soon clearing the turbulent surface.

They kept on climbing, gradually leaning backwards as the ascent curved towards the dome of the chamber.

By the time Sejanus roared and fired slugs from his Lawgiver, the two men were above the labouring heart, which was already starting to heal the hole in its left auricle.

Dredd and Cairo dropped in unison onto the top of the giant heart.

Dredd's Lawgiver spat a bullet into Sejanus, catching the Colossus Chief in the shoulder.

Sejanus folded with the impact, lost his balance. Toppled from his Eagle Throne perch. Crash-landed on the heart.

And shot Cairo clean in the chest, hurling him off the summit of the flexing heart of steel.

Dredd didn't spare Cairo a glance.

A few of Sejanus's men had survived the deluge, which subsided as the heart sealed its rent. They were climbing the huge pump's surface. And three had Overkills in their hands.

Floundering in the water below the heart, blood spouting from the chest wound, Cairo sensed the presence of his brother. His deadly brother. Up in the Head.

Fighting through the waves, he struggled to a gravchute, pressed for ascent, and sped up to the Head.

'Keep going,' he panted as he reached the Visor. He slapped a med-pack on the chest wound. 'Keep going.'

He ducked as the empty Eagle Throne whooshed over his head, aiming up a ramp from the Visor.

'Keep going.'

He managed to keep track of the Throne. As he turned a corner, he saw a section of wall dematerialise. The Eagle Throne sped into the gap.

Cairo raced into it.

And came face to face with his brother, the Anarch of Anarchopolis.

'Anti-Judges!'

The bellowed accusations rang in the two women's ears as, ammo spent, they punched, kicked, nutted, bit and spat a path through hordes of solid citizens up to the Statue of Judgement's head.

The statue's vid-screen was a monochrome phantasmagoria. Escapees from a mythological bestiary pranced and cavorted on the screen. And leaped *out* of the screen.

Mandra and Hershey, bruised and bloody, tumbled into

the head's interior with a score of Grud devotees on their backs.

Twisting and turning in the multiple grip, Mandra rammed her thumbs into a few pairs of eyes, heard a few *splats*, kicked ferociously and broke loose.

She was on her feet and running for the single hov-pod left. A burly man was climbing into it, ducking as a black-and-white harpy flew over his head.

Outside the Visor, a few hov-pods could be glimpsed, whisking towards the Judgement Colossus.

Grud or Dredd worshippers, flying to their god.

Mandra yanked the man out of the pod before he could close the lid, delivering a stun-blow to his neck.

'Hershey! Come on!' she yelled, spinning round and sending two Grud religionists hurtling away with a double kick.

Only Hershey's flailing arm was visible. She had disappeared under a mass of ardent devotees, primed to kill all heretics.

The scene was abruptly illuminated in red.

Twin red streaks of light, swerving from the eyes of Colossus's turning head, swept over the Statue of Liberty and skimmed the Statue of Judgement's helmeted dome. Eyes of fire.

Any lower and the mighty lasers would have cut off the Statue of Judgement's head and terminated her life in a blaze of glory.

The weaving eyes of fire soared and swooped with no rhyme or reason. It was a fluke they hadn't sliced into the older statues by now.

Mandra glanced at the thrashing clump of bodies covering Hershey . . .

The flood of monochrome monsters from the vid-screen . . .

Darted a look at the Judgement Colossus.

Thought of Joel, somewhere inside the giant effigy.

A fresh mob charged into the chamber, targeted on Mandra.

'Sorry, Hershey,' she mumbled, jumping into the pod. 'Haven't the time. And Joel comes first.'

She launched the pod straight for the Judgement Colossus, ducking and diving its wayward eyes of fire.

As she neared the soaring effigy, the searing red lasers suddenly turned white. Blinding white.

'Eat hi-ex, creeps!' Dredd bawled, spraying the Judges as they scaled the giant heart.

They hit the subsiding waters in splashes of bright red.

A boot slammed into Dredd's back, almost dislodging him from his unsteady perch on the pulsing surface.

He whirled round and grabbed Sejanus's lashing leg.

Kicked the Colossus Chief in the face.

Received a fierce kick in the crotch in return.

Doubling up, he spotted Sejanus scramble towards the huge tube of the aorta, within reach of the ladder.

There was a maintenance hatch in the aorta, Dredd noticed. Wrenching that off with the water still pumping at full pressure would play more havoc with Sejanus's precious Colossus.

Sejanus whirled round at Dredd's relentless approach.

And took Dredd by surprise.

The Colossus Chief spun the hatch open, releasing a thunderous column of briny water. 'Get past that, Dredd!' he laughed, reaching for the ladder.

Dredd's rope-muscled arm stretched through the roaring water jet, indifferent to the savage pressure. Gripped Sejanus by the throat.

And, muscles straining to the utmost, forced the Colossus Chief's head down into the hatch.

'*Phlurrgghhh* . . .' burbled Sejanus as he went under.

'There's nothing worse than a bent Judge,' growled Dredd, ramming the man's shoulders into the round aperture, temporarily stemming the flow.

A final push and Sejanus was inside the aorta, kept in place by water pressure, his frantic body still plugging most of the flow.

Then Dredd slammed the hatch-lid back on, spun it tight.

He heard the thump as Sejanus shot off down the aorta on his journey through the statue's cardio-vascular system.

Round and round. Round and round.

A drowning human cell in the circulatory system of the Colossus.

'Happy Hallowe'en, Cairo,' Horus greeted, propped against a wall, arms folded. 'The Falcon has landed.'

Cairo's momentum sent him sailing across the anti-grav chamber to bounce off the far wall, hitting one of the hovering grey corpses on the rebound. He saw its inverted face as he sent the body spinning.

'Replacements,' Horus said, flicking an affectionate glance at the colour-drained cadavers. 'A new Lower-archy of Five for the old.'

Cairo grabbed hold of a wall-grip, stopping his invol-untary flight.

'The Falcon has landed, and summoned the Eagle,' the Anarch smiled, eye roving the Eagle Throne. 'What better way to signal victory over the golden eagle than to sit on it? To the victor, the spoils.'

A white blast from the Anarch's solitary grey eye sent Cairo whirling as the man in the Suit of Many Badges ascended the Eagle Throne. Cairo slammed this way and that in the ovoid room.

'Cancel anti-grav,' the Anarch commanded.

Cairo crashed to the floor, his suspended blood droplets pattering the floor around him.

The monochrome god of the movies beamed down on him. 'What should my first act as ruler of an upturned world be, do you think? Oh yes – Sejanus was about to pulverise the Statue of Liberty with the Eyes of Fire. I say give the Colossus its head and spray the lasers everywhere – see which statue gets it first, Liberty or Judgement. I've little time for either.'

A low humming thrummed in the chamber. Cairo,

sitting up painfully, sensed the Colossus head begin to rotate. His brother's mind was attuned to Omnipotens; perhaps the two were as one.

Horus cocked an ear to a soft, remote thump. 'There goes Sejanus through the jugular,' he remarked lightly. Then he winced at Cairo. 'Oh, *look* at you. You're leaking *red* all over the floor.'

His gaze hardened. 'Have to do something about you . . .'

Cairo took his only chance.

He went wild.

He unleashed the Wild.

It stormed its illusions in the ovoid chamber, spun the grey corpses like marionettes in a whirlwind. A whirlwind of phantoms.

The force of it threw Cairo on his back, blood spurting from his mouth, ears, nose and eyes.

Horus, calm on a throne paling from gold to silver, was untouched by the maelstrom.

'Head games. Don't try and beat me at my own game, Cairo.'

With a flick of the hand he flung Cairo across the room, smashing him into the wall.

Cairo slumped to the floor. He could barely voice his final defiance:

'You're just like the Judges. You see everything in black and white.'

Horus rubbed his chin. 'Hmm . . . let me see – I think I'll explode your head – with a single thought.'

The white lips curved into a scimitar of a smile.

'Goodbye, Mister Cairo.'

Mandra spied an apparently unguarded access point in the Colossus. The left ear.

She flew the pod into the left ear's aperture and landed in a wide expanse facing the statue's visor. Springing out of the pod, she glanced at the ramp that led upwards. Up to the brain.

303

That was where the Anarch was likely to be. And Joel . . .

She sprinted up the ramp, emerged into a curving tunnel.

And caught an echo of Joel Cairo.

A wild echo.

She raced towards it. Glimpsed a hazy gap in the tunnel wall. Rushed right in.

'Goodbye, Mister Cairo,' she heard Horus chuckle.

'Hello, paleface,' she snarled, then froze at seeing Joel slumped in a corner. He looked like death.

The Death card . . . the Tower Struck by Lightning.

The angry spirit of the *mambo*, the old Caribbean, welled up inside her:

Baron Samedi, Papa Legba, Mama Erzulie . . . All the loa of Obeah . . . Open the Gate . . . Come to me . . .

'And make it quick, for Damballah's sake,' she muttered.

'What's all this, Mandra?' Horus laughed. 'That old black magic supposed to have me in its spell?'

'You're the stuff that dreams are made of,' she said, staring him straight in the single eye.

He took a mock bow. 'That's me. Lord of the Dream Palaces.'

She saw, behind her eyes, the Caribbean *loa* walk barefoot down the old trails from clouded mountain peaks, dressed in their tattered frock-coats and cock-eyed top hats. Coming close . . .

'My friends are the stuff that dreams are made of,' she said.

Horus angled an eyebrow. 'Oh really? I'd *love* to meet them. But some other time, hum?'

'They're here now,' she growled, as iridescent *loa* swirled out of the air. 'And they're *hungry*. Hungry for that dream you call a soul.'

She weaved her arms, swayed her supple body. 'Take him, Baron Samedi,' she addressed a skull-faced apparition in a black top hat. 'Take him, Lord of Cemeteries . . .'

Horus shrank back from the sinuous whirl of *Obeah* spirits, waving his arms to fend them off.

The chamber was alive with colour. Caribbean colour. Voodoo colour.

Colourful spirits. Hungry spirits.

'You can't kill the stuff that dreams are made of!' he shrieked.

'But you can steal its soul,' she smiled mercilessly. 'Take its soul to another world. An old black magic world.'

Leaving Horus to the voodoo spirits' untender mercies, she ran to Cairo and assisted him to his feet.

He reeled drunkenly, bent a faint smile.

'Hi, Ma.'

'Hi, *Jo*.'

She turned, arm around his waist, and readied herself for a ferocious battle with Horus to help Joel escape.

Her mouth fell open.

The *loa* had gone.

The body of Horus lay grey and lifeless on the curved floor, inert beneath a hologram of a brain.

'Wow!' she whistled. 'The *loa* made quick work of him. Looks like you're lucky after all, Joel.'

He glanced at the still figure of Horus. 'Hard to believe,' he mumbled, blood trickling from his mouth. 'Turned out . . . so easy.'

'Things sometimes do,' she grinned.

Her premonitions of doom for Joel had proved false. She was never more happy to be proved wrong.

'There's a hov-pod down in the Visor area,' she said. 'Come on – I'll fly you to the moon. Or somewhere more exotic.'

Entering the Visor by a slide-ramp, Cairo still couldn't believe his luck. Destroying Horus had turned out so damned *easy*.

He smiled as Mandra helped him to the pod. Horus was dead. Soul stolen by voodoo spirits. Almost a joke.

And he and Mandra were together, after fifteen years.
'Lucky, after all,' he muttered.

Mandra opened the pod's lid. 'Step right in.'

'*Stand right back!*'

The black figure of Dredd emerged from the grav-chute, Lawgiver levelled.

'Move one centimetre and you're dead, Mandra! You too, Mister Cairo . . .'

She froze.

Cairo could barely see straight, let alone shoot straight, but he fished for his Dillinger.

Damn thing was gone. Must have dropped it up in that egg-shaped anti-grav chamber. Great timing.

Dredd caught on immediately. 'No gun, Cairo? Tough.'

The Judge strode up to a tigerish Mandra, who looked ready to spring. Dredd sprang first. Lashed a boot in her jaw.

He caught her as she toppled and dumped her in the pod.

Swerving round, he advanced on Cairo, who was struggling to stay on his feet, blinking black stars from his eyes.

Dredd's mouth twisted into a contemptuous snarl. 'You're just another perp, Cairo. A perp who's gonna rot twenty years in the cubes.'

Cairo struggled to stop swaying.

'I'm going to blow your head off, Dredd.'

'Dream on, *creep*.'

'YES,' boomed a voice from everywhere and nowhere. 'LET'S ALL DREAM ON.'

'What the drokk – ' snapped Dredd.

'*Horus* . . .' Cairo whispered inaudibly.

Battered and psyched-out as he was, Cairo knew what had happened.

The soul of Horus had fled when the *loa* attacked. Fled into the hypma Arcanum core of Omnipotens. That must have been his plan all along. Unite with the Arcanum. Merge with Omnipotens.

Horus was now the brain of the Colossus. The kilometre-high effigy was his body, bristling with weapons capable of obliterating half the world.

An effigy that bore the face of Dredd. The mind of Horus inside the head of Dredd.

They were all locked with a mad movie god inside the colossal head of Dredd. Mandra – Cairo – Dredd himself.

Dreddlocked.

As the realisation hit home, he moved towards the pod, Dredd tracking his every step.

'HAPPY HALLOWE'EN!' boomed the voice.

Dredd was fleetingly distracted, looking round for the owner of the voice.

Taking advantage of Dredd's distraction, Cairo jabbed the AUTO button on the pod.

And was slammed back onto the floor by the Judge's meaty fist.

Too late, Dredd, he thought, through clouding wits and darkening vision. The pod's gone, and Mandra with it. Gone to safety.

He reeled upright, virtually blind. Staggered up to the transparent plastiplex of the Visor.

'Cairo!' Dredd bellowed in rage. 'Cairo!'

The private eye ignored him.

His brother had merged with the Arcanum. Cairo could do the same. Reach his mind into the egg-shaped chamber. Probe the centre of Omnipotens.

With Mandra safe, flying free in the hov-pod, it was between him, Dredd and Horus. He could unite with the hypma core of Omnipotens. Unleash the Wild.

Then blow his own mind.

And transform the dense hypma core into a bomb.

The whole Head would go, wearing Dredd's face. With Dredd inside it.

He let the Wild loose – reached into the Arcanum.

Remembered Cagney in *White Heat* . . .

Prepared to blow himself and Dredd to high hell.

Through fading wits, Hershey felt teeth closing on her throat.

This was it. The end.

She'd resisted the smothering press of Grud fanatics with the last ounce of fight in her.

Now she was all fought out.

The teeth dug into her throat, drew blood.

Another second or two and the flesh would go the way of the blood.

Finito.

The pod rested still on the Visor floor.

Mandra lay unconscious inside it.

The AUTO button was unlit.

Systems failure.

GO TO MANUAL, a panel flashed urgently.

But Mandra would never wake to see it.

All the Wild in Cairo rushed out, and he went with it.

Merged his mind with his brother's.

Penetrated the Arcanum core. United with Omni-potens.

He felt his body transform as it swayed in front of the Visor.

It blazed white. Radiated heat.

White Heat.

Mister Cairo lifted his arms and triggered his mind for the ultimate head-banger.

Blow his mind. Go out with a bang.

The hypma core responded to the detonation signal.

'NOOO . . .' his brother screamed.

Cairo had a last memory-flicker of his mother's head exploding from a Lawgiver.

Blow my mind . . . Blow Dredd's head to Grud . . .

Mister Cairo yelled out his last goodbye from the crown of the Judgement Colossus:

'Top of the world, Ma!'

The mother of all explosions blasted a giant head sky-high.

CHAPTER TWENTY-EIGHT

Teeth tore into Hershey's neck.

Then tore loose as an explosion shook the world and threw her assailants on their backs. They lay, blinking and confused, as if recovered from a spell.

Shaking in every limb, she crawled to the old statue's visor and peered out.

She saw a head in the sky.

A giant head of plasteen, cracking asunder as it spun back to earth.

The ruin of its downfall was an ear-splitting thunder.

It crashed in pieces, some in the bay, some on land, crushing thousands.

The ravaged face of the Judgement Colossus smashed to ground at the foot of the Statue of Liberty and lay there, gazing upwards.

Maybe it was her dazed wits, but for a moment it looked like the face of Judge Dredd, defeated.

Her stare moved to the headless Colossus.

It was erupting, coming apart at the seams. Whatever death-wish signal the brain had transmitted to the head, it had been received by the rest of the body.

As went the brain, so went the nerves.

Weapons detonated in their ports.

White sheet-lightning seared her optic nerves.

And the entire Colossus blasted apart.

Arms, legs, torso went their separate ways.

Blown to hell.

Hershey leaned forward and squinted.

There was a speck flying from the ruin of the Colossus.

A hover-pod . . .

The vid-screen, emptied of its earlier monochrome grotesques, suddenly displayed the witch-like features of Chief Judge McGruder. The lean lips were split in a grin.

'Just got a call from Dredd. Seems like Sejanus and his Colossus are history. All communications appear to be back on line. Those black-and-white freaks just – disappeared. Everywhere.'

'Uh-huh,' Hershey murmured, shaking her dazed head.

'You're looking a bit rough, Hershey. Take a couple of days off. You and Dredd did well, sorting out Mandra and Sejanus and all that. I was on to Sejanus a while back. Encouraged his promotion. Give a man enough rope and he'll hang himself, huh?'

Hershey was expressionless, her tone flat. 'Yeah . . . right.'

Dredd guided the hover-pod straight to Justice Central, Mandra stirring awake at his side.

'What . . .?' she mumbled, sitting upright.

'Your boyfriend blew his top,' Dredd said grimly. 'Took the whole Colossus head with him. Saw his body mass go critical. Got you out before he took us with him. McGruder's *dying* to see you.'

She stared out at the bulbous blocks of Mega-City One, silent for a time.

'Joel's dead,' she finally stated.

'Yeah. And you're doin' twenty years of time – if you're lucky.'

Her voice had a dead ring. 'Lucky.'

She gave a long sigh. 'Hypma. He must have linked his mind to hypma, made it into a bomb.'

A speculative air haunted her eyes. 'With just a little hypma, you can make a bomb. A small bomb, if you thing small. But if you think big, even with a tiny trace of hypma, you can blow up everything within twenty metres. Why not, if you've lost everything you care about?'

As she spoke, her finger kept stroking a molar.

'What you doin'?' he frowned.

She gave an enigmatic smile. 'Thinking *big*.'

Mandra leaned close to Dredd, stared him straight in the visor.

'Would you like to hear an old rhyme?' she asked.

He gave a shrug of indifference. 'You want to spout kid's stuff, it's up to you.'

'Kid's stuff,' she smiled thinly. 'We'll see . . .'

Mandra leaned back and started to recite:

'Here comes a candle to light you to bed,

'Here comes a chopper to chop off . . .'